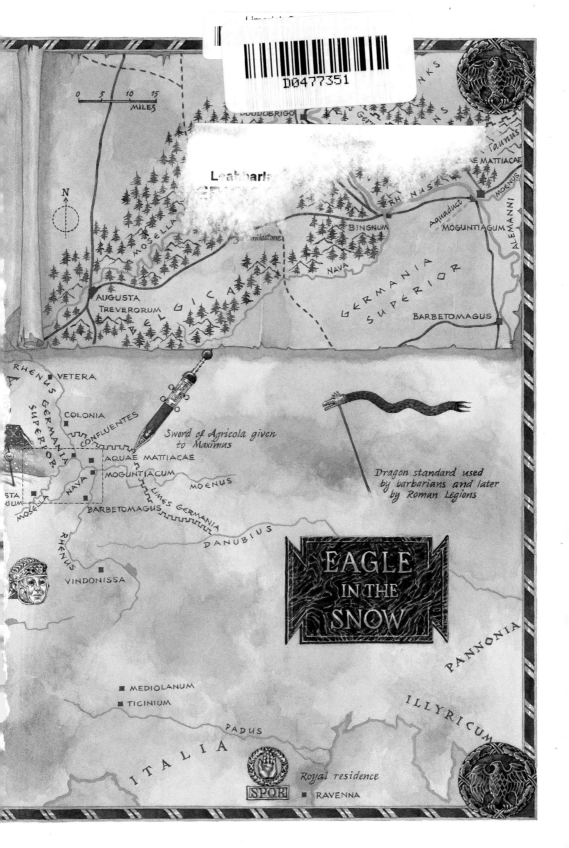

EAGLE
IN THE
SNOW

Also by Wallace Breem

The Leopard and the Cliff
The Legate's Daughter

EAGLE
IN THE
SNOW

GENERAL MAXIMUS AND
ROME'S LAST STAND

WALLACE BREEM

Introduction by Steven Pressfield

Weidenfeld & Nicolson
LONDON

First published in Great Britain in 1970 by
Victor Gollancz Ltd

This edition published in 2003 by
Weidenfeld & Nicolson

A CIP catalogue record for this book is
available from the British Library.

ISBN 0 297 64561 7

Printed in Great Britain by
Clays Ltd, St Ives plc

Weidenfeld & Nicolson
The Orion Publishing Group Ltd
Orion House
5 Upper Saint Martin's Lane
London WC2H 9EA

TO RIKKI,

FOR WHOM IT WAS WRITTEN

CONTENTS

INTRODUCTION

Historical fiction has always been a literary stepchild. It's thought of as a genre, like the Western or the detective story, and not a particularly lofty genre at that. It rarely wins prizes. It takes a Robert Graves or a Mary Renault or a Patrick O'Brian to endow it with stature. It shouldn't be this way.

Consider the difficulties the writer faces when he ventures into the past. Before he even sits down to think, he has to master the historical material—to learn who's who, what's what, where's where. That's hard enough. Beyond that, he must reconstitute this world for the reader with such vivid authenticity as to transport him to another time and place and make him believe it. That's even harder.

Next, he must craft credible, multidimensional characters and bring them to life in a story that's compelling, involving and true to its era (in other words, to do the same thing a contemporary novelist does, only, like Ginger Rogers dancing with Fred Astaire, in high heels and backwards.) By the time a writer is operating at this level, he's really cooking.

Beyond that, comes the next plateau: to found the story upon a genuine moral, ethical or spiritual theme, to make it truly "about" something—something that is not only true to the historical epoch in which the work is set, but something relevant and vital to our contemporary era. That's the Holy Grail of historical fiction.

When a writer pulls off this four-part hat trick, as Wallace Breem does in *Eagle in the Snow,* I want to say his work transcends the genre, but it's better than that; it employs the genre in the highest way it was intended. It doesn't hark back to the past for the fun or color of the trip; it uses the past, a very specific past, to illuminate a very specific present.

Wallace Breem is a master of this, as he shows brilliantly and (seemingly) effortlessly in *Eagle in the Snow.* Breem's story feels as if it were written then, not now; the reader experiences it then, not now. Yet when it's over, the reader knows it is about now, not then, and that it could not have been set in any other place or time. Wallace Breem belongs on that very short list of writers whose work elevates historical fiction beyond the genre and sets it alongside the best writing of any kind, in any period.

STEVEN PRESSFIELD

PROLOGUE

In the deep valleys between the black rain-lashed mountains of the western coast there is little to do of a winter's night if you belong to a beaten people. Defeated, sick at heart, and afraid, you sit huddled in a tattered cloak round the great spluttering fires and dream of a tomorrow. that will never come. The women nurse their wailing children and long for warm huts and a world in which milk is always plentiful; the young warriors sharpen their dulled spears and pray for just one victory against the men from the sea, while the old remember a time when no fires betrayed a burning village to the night sky, and there was peace in the lands from which they are now exiled forever.

The talk of tomorrow dies away with the sparks blown from the hot ash, and tales of the past are recounted by the elders of the tribe. Despair and fear recede a little into the darkness and curiosity and hope take their place as the well-loved stories are told again for the hundredth time. Perhaps a fresh tale is told by an old man whom no one knows, and the defeated listen in silence. They hear of the great conspiracy beyond the Wall and of a man with no hair who had the misfortune to become a god. They hear of the soldier who carried an Emperor's message across half Europe in his severed hand; and, for the first time, they hear too of how the last of the Eagles was destroyed by a river of ice.

CHAPTER I

You think I am lucky because I am old, because I knew a world that was not turned upside down. Perhaps you are right. As you, too, might have been lucky if the ice had only cracked. You don't really know what I am talking about, do you? Well then, listen to me and I, Paulinus Gaius Maximus, will tell you.

I was born and brought up in Gaul, though my ancestors came from Rome herself. As a young child I lived on the outskirts of military camps, and from the very first my life was regulated by the trumpets that roused the soldiers in the morning and told them when to sleep at night. Then, when I was six, my father was asked to give up command of the Second Flavia at Moguntiacum, and retired to his villa near Arelate.

We were a large household as I remember it. I had a cousin, Julian, who was brought up with me. His father, Martinus, had been head of a province, but later he became Vicarius of his native Britannia. He was a just man, and was liked by everyone, but he fell foul of a usurping Emperor and found himself proscribed. My aunt was with Martinus when he heard the news that he was to be arrested. She took the knife and stabbed herself first. And then she held it out to him, all bloody in her hands. "See," she said. "It does not hurt, Martinus." My father told Julian this when he was old enough to understand. He wanted Julian to be proud of his parents and to know what fine people they had been. But it was a mistake; it did not make Julian proud; it only taught him to hate. But that came later. At lessons or at play we were inseparable, and like all children we planned to do great things to help Rome when we were grown men. We were like brothers.

When I was thirteen my father was appointed Legate of the Twentieth Valeria, stationed in Brittania. He owed this to the young Caesar, Julian, who, like us, worshiped the old gods.

The day we left Gaul there was an eclipse of the sun. It was uncanny the way the brightness vanished and the day turned into night. It was like the end of the world. Julian shivered, I remember, and said that to sail on such a day would bring bad luck. But my father sacrificed a cock and decided the omens were good. So we went on with our journey.

When old enough, we went into my father's legion as equestrian tribunes. We were initiated into the mysteries of our faith in the same temple and on the same day. Together we took the sacred oath: "In the name of the God who has divided the earth from the heavens, the light from the darkness, the day from the night, the world from chaos, and life from death. . . ." And together we came out into the sunlight, carrying the words of our God upon our shoulders. Those were the good times, for we did everything together. We learned to be soldiers at Deva and I learned, too, something that was fast dying out, to take a pride in the legion of which I was a member. In my great-grandfather's day the legions had been the shock troops of Rome, the best disciplined and the best fighters. But under Diocletian things had changed. A new field army began to grow up, consisting of auxiliary regiments made up from provincials and even Barbarians willing to accept Rome's service. Cavalry became all the fashion and the legions dwindled into becoming mere frontier troops. But here in Britannia the three legions still mattered, and I was glad. I was sorry when the time came for me to leave because it meant parting with Julian, who was to remain on my father's staff. It was three years before I saw him again.

I did a tour of duty with the Second Augusta at Isca Silurium and then was sent to our army headquarters at Eburacum. There I spent my time doing administrative work, worrying over accounts, pensions, and burial funds. It was dull work.

One day Fullofaudes sent for me. He was the new Dux Britanniarum, an Aleman from the banks of the Rhenus.

"A part of the legion at Deva has tried to mutiny," he said. "The rebellion has been put down and the ringleaders arrested. You will go to Deva at once with reinforcements and take charge until I have appointed a new commander."

I looked at him in astonishment.

"The Legate is dead," he said, harshly. "I am sorry."

He picked up a roll of documents from the table. "Three days ago we caught a slave carrying these. They contain details about this plot—and others as well. It is full of names. Much too full of names."

"Dead," I said. I could scarcely hear him.

"The disaffection is widespread. Too many are involved. Too many think that the province should break with Rome."

"They can be arrested and executed."

"No. To go further into this affair would do no good. I should have few officers and no men left." He looked at me hard. "No one will be executed," he said. "Do you understand?"

He gave me a roll of sealed script. "Here are your orders and your authority. As for these—" He bent to the table, picked up the documents and flung them into the fire. "I do not believe that this province should separate from Rome. I want no martyrs whose memories can inflame the dissatisfied. But I do need time to build up loyalty. Do you understand now?"

"Yes," I said. But I didn't really. I only understood that my father was dead.

I reached Deva a week later. I paraded the legion and they stood for two hours in the rain before I came to them. Decimation was the punishment they expected and they were gray-faced and full of fear. Only at the end when they were wet with suspense did I say that there would be no executions. In their relief they cheered me and I dismissed them. I was hoarse with speaking. I went into the Legate's quarters—my father's quarters—and there the eight ringleaders were brought to me in chains. Five were tribunes and three were centurions. The anger of the parade ground had gone. I felt nothing now except a great coldness.

"You will not be executed," I said. "But you are convicted of treason and deprived of Roman citizenship by order of the Vicarius. Your status is now that of slaves and as slaves you will be treated. Those of centurion rank will go to the lead mines at Isca Silurium, where you will work for Rome till you die. As for the rest—since you have a taste for fighting your own kind, you will have a chance to gratify it further. You will go to the gladiatorial school at Calleva and afterward be matched against each other in the ring. You may, if you are lucky, survive five years."

Before they were taken away I spoke to their leader.

"Why did you do it, Julian?" I said. "In the name of Mithras, why?"

"Your Emperor killed my father," he said, in an empty voice.

"But you—? A Roman officer."

"I was," he said, and he tried to smile.

"But why? Why?"

"If you do not understand," he said, "then I cannot tell you."

They took him away and I was left alone in that empty room with its memories of my father and my boyhood memories of Julian. I remembered the quarrels we had had and the fights; I remembered the things that we had enjoyed together, days in the hot sun, learning to drive a chariot, other days spent in hunting and fishing, and the long evenings in Gaul spent in talking and playing draughts, and the fine plans we had made and the dreams that we had dreamed together. I remembered it all with a pain that was indescribable, and a sense of anguish that could not be extinguished. And I wept.

I went back to Eburacum and I returned to my accounts. I worked hard so that I never had time to think except in the long, lonely nights when I could not sleep. But I never went to the Games and those who did never spoke about them in my presence.

Three months later I was sent on leave and went to Corinium, which I did not know. I went to the officers' club, and I drank, and I hunted a little, for they were much troubled by wolves that autumn. Then I met a girl with dark hair, whose name was Aelia, and I married her. For a wedding gift I gave her some gold earrings that had belonged to my mother, and she gave me a signet ring with the likeness of Mercury stamped on it. She was a Christian, though more tolerant than most.

It was there I received news that I had been posted to the Wall, to a place called Borcovicum of which I had never heard. It was at the end of the world, or so it seemed to us. A harsh country of heather and rock, bleak and terrible in winter, yet austerely beautiful in summer; a vast lonely land that was pitiless in its climate to both men and animals. Step out of earshot of the camp and you would hear nothing save the forlorn cry of the curlew and feel nothing but the bite of the everlasting wind.

My fort had some importance. It stood at the junction of several roads and guarded the track that led north into tribal territory. My auxiliaries were the First Cohort of Tungrians, originally from northeast Gaul, a mixed crowd of Iberians, Parthians, Brigantes, and Goths, divided by centuries into tribal classes. Only a single century were Tungrians now, but I found their inscriptions all over the camp. There was one, I remember, on the wall of my quarters. It said, "May I do the right thing," and I used to look at it every day and wonder what that first commandant had been like and what particular need had driven him to carve just those particular words in that particular place.

My adjutant, Vitalius, was a man of about thirty, anxious-faced and solemn. Gaius, my second-in-command, was older. He was a Sarmatian from beyond the Danubius, and from his bitter manner, I think, had hoped for the command for himself. My Chief Centurion, Saturninus, formerly of the Second Augusta, was a man of great calm, few words, and immense experience. It was a long while before I gained his respect.

The mile castles and signal towers along the frontier were manned by militia—the Arcani, we called them—who were recruited from local tribesmen from either side of the Wall. The frontier then was very quiet, and there was little to do except work, but I was happy enough. Aelia did not like the place, for there were few women and she was lonely, but she never complained. She saw little of me during the day except at meals, but at night we were happy, and we would lie awake and listen to the drunks singing in the wine shop in the settlement outside, and smell the goats that grazed under the walls by the west gate if the wind was in the wrong direction.

Sometimes I used to ride over to a neighboring fort, Vindolanda, and play draughts with Quintus Veronius, its praefectus, though he got angry when I called him that. "I am a tribune," he would say haughtily, "even though I do command a rabble of auxiliaries." He was my own age, always rode a black horse with white feet, and was the best cavalry officer I ever met. He had been posted here from the Tenth Gemina in Pannonia following a scandal over some girl, and when he was drunk he would talk excitedly of a troop of Dacian horse he had once commanded and who, he would swear, were the best cavalry in the world. But he never spoke of the girl. His family came from Hispania and he missed the sun and was always hoping for a transfer there. But though he wrote numerous letters to influential relatives nothing ever came of it, and I was selfishly glad.

Quintus took a great interest in our catapults, which surprised me, for cavalrymen usually thought of little but swords and charges.

"I was on the Saxon Shore under my countryman Nectaridus," he explained. "He is a great fighter."

"Did you enjoy it?"

He shrugged. "It was so cold standing there on those great flat-roofed towers at Lemanis. The wind howled in your face and your eyes ached as you stared out into the darkness. The Saxons used to slip in quietly if they could, sails lowered, on the midnight tide. If you spotted them you hit them with the ballistae until their ships broke up. Then you killed the survivors with arrows while they struggled in the surf."

"Good shooting," I said. I was impressed.

"That was Nectaridus. He insisted that we must never fight dry Saxons: we must always kill them while they are still wet."

"Why did you leave?"

He said, casually, "I wanted command of the Ala Petriana, but I was turned down. Then, oh—I got drunk and did something stupid." He looked at me with a smile. "So I was sent here."

I said, "It is a good place if you like fighting."

"It is also a good place in which to be forgotten. I was always cold on the Saxon shore, but I would return tomorrow if they would let me."

I said, "We must go hunting together sometime."

He cheered up then and said, "That would be good. It is lonely here, and I am somewhat tired of the company of slave girls who speak bad Latin."

I laughed. "Come to Borcovicum and meet Aelia. She is a great talker."

He said, "I met her once when I was out riding, I think. You—you are very lucky."

"Yes, I think I am."

He said, suddenly, "Maximus, why are you here?"

For a moment I did not answer. Then I said, quietly, "One posting is much like another. I hope I shall not be here always."

It was then that he changed the subject.

When Aelia came back from the birth of Saturninus' firstborn she was very quiet, after the initial joy women show on these occasions. I took her hand and said, gently, "You are not to worry. There is plenty of time yet. We shall have a son. You pray to your god and I will pray to mine. That way we shall have two chances of favor instead of one."

She laughed, momentarily, and then her face changed. "Perhaps it is a punishment for my sins." She was very serious now, and I was worried.

I said, lightly, "There is not much opportunity for committing wrongs at Borcovicum."

She said, in a low voice, "With us they can be in thoughts as well as deeds."

I returned to my letter. Presently she looked up from the fire. She said, "Do you remember the time that sentry slept at his watch and Saturninus asked you to overlook his offense?"

"I remember."

"I came in when you were discussing what to do with him. And he said—do you remember?—he said, 'You never had pity, sir, on the other one either.' What did he mean?"

My hand shook. I said, "He thought I was being too strict."

She said, "You are a good soldier. Even I can see that. But I think Saturninus is right. You can be very hard."

"I try to be just."

"It is sometimes better to be kind."

She was silent then and went on staring into the fire. I stopped writing and looked at her. I loved her so much, but I did not know what she was thinking.

We had been there two winters when, on a warm spring day, I rode out to the second-mile castle east of the camp, where some of our men were repairing the road. After my inspection was over I sat on a boulder, not far from the gate, and chatted with the post commander. A I did so I could see a man walking up the track toward us. I finished my conversation and mounted my horse. There was something in his walk that disturbed me, so I sat still and waited till he came up. I knew that kind of walk well, and when he stopped ten paces away and stared at me with that terrible tight look they always have, and the eyes that watch every flicker of a shadow and yet have no feel in them, no warmth of any kind, I knew who it was.

"Julian," I said. "It is Julian." And I waited.

"The noble commander knows everything," he replied.

"What are you doing here?"

"I am a free man." The words were spoken tonelessly. He fumbled inside his cloak and produced a square of parchment. "If the commander does not believe me I have this for proof."

"So they gave you your wooden foil."

"Yes. They gave me my wooden foil. We killed each other as you predicted, though some died more quickly than others. They were the lucky ones."

I watched him in silence. Then I said, quietly, "But you lived."

"Yes. I lived, if you can call it living."

"And so?"

"In the end there were two of us left, myself and—but you would have forgotten his name, no doubt."

I shook my head. "No," I said. "I would not have forgotten his name. I remember them all to this day."

"As I remember yours, noble commander. They matched us to fight at Eburacum. We were the spectacle for which everyone waited, and the commander of the Sixth Legion sat in the seat of honor. It was a holiday, and his daughter newly married, and he wished to celebrate by showing his—mercy. He gave me my freedom while the blood of my companion dried on my sword."

"I see. Where do you go now?"

"Beyond the Wall to where Rome does not rule."

I leaned forward then. "Are you mad? What will you do up there, even supposing they don't kill you first? What kind of a life will you live?"

"That is my concern."

I said, harshly, "Julian, I have a villa and land in Gaul which I have never seen since we—since I was a boy. You can go to it; you can live on it; you can own it if you wish. I offer that much for the sake of a dead friendship. But don't, I beg of you, go north of the Wall."

He looked at me then, and there was still nothing in the eyes of any warmth or human feeling. "I go north," he said. "And no one shall stop me." The spear, that I had thought at first to be a staff, was balanced lightly in his hand, but he was standing carefully on the balls of his feet, and I knew then that he would kill me if I moved. Any other man I could have run down with a fair chance of success. But he was different. He had been a gladiator. They were trained to move with a speed that no soldier could emulate. They could pick flies off the wall with their bare hands. I knew. I had watched them do it.

I turned my horse to let him pass. "You are a freedman under the law, as you said, and you may go where you will."

"I shall indeed."

"A word of warning, Julian."

He turned at that, and for a moment I thought I detected something in his eyes that was almost human. "Well?"

"Go north by all means. But, if you do, then never come south again within spear range of my wall."

He said, tonelessly, "I will remember that. When I do come you may be certain I shall not come alone."

I watched him go up the track, saw him show his papers to the sentry and disappear from sight into the heather beyond. He had changed out of all recognition and perhaps I had too. I wondered what the Piots would make of him—a man with no hair.

CHAPTER II

Sometime in the middle of winter, on a stormy night, two men and a woman, mounted on ponies and riding for their lives, came in out of the heather and clamored for shelter. They were allowed through and in the morning I interviewed them. By their dress and by the way they did their hair Saturninus thought they might be Vacomagi from the great mountains in central Caledonia—a tribe untouched by Rome since the days of Agricola. But we did not ask them. All were young. The woman was dark, with long black hair and skin the color of warm milk. She was very beautiful. The two men were her brothers. I heard a confused tale of a tyrannical uncle, of the young lover slain in jealousy by this man, of the brothers killing him in his turn, and of a blood feud that had split the tribe.

"There was a meeting of the elders, excellency," said the younger brother in a tired voice. "We were proscribed and fled to avoid our deaths."

"Very well," I said. "You may stay under the protection of Rome, provided that you are obedient to our laws. But what will you do now?"

The elder brother said, nervously, "We can shift for ourselves. But our sister is another matter. Does your excellency, perhaps, need a woman to manage his house? She is a good cook and obedient and would give no trouble."

It did not seem to me an accurate description of her at all, but I understood what he was trying to say. "Thank you, no," I said. "I have a wife and my household is full. I have no need of any servants." The woman stiffened at that and put up her chin. There was, for a moment, an expression in her eyes that I could not read, and then she dropped her head and stared sullenly at the floor.

They stayed in the civilian settlement for a while, and then the woman was taken up by my second-in-command and he asked my permission to marry her. The brothers were agreeable and the woman too, and I said yes without hesitation. She was a woman to turn men's heads and already there had been fights in the settlement over her. Married she would cause less trouble.

I could not have been more wrong.

Quintus became a regular visitor to our fort, and did much to cheer up Aelia during the cold months of rain and snow. Spring came early that year, and then summer burst upon us in a blaze of heat. Aelia was very pale at this time and a little unhappy, I think, but I put it down to her remorse at having lost one of the earrings I had given her, though I had told her a dozen times that it did not matter. To give her a change I arranged for her to spend some months in Eburacum, and after much argument she agreed to go. At the last moment she changed her mind and wanted to stay, but Quintus, who had ridden over to try our new wine and who was lounging on the steps, agreed with me, so she gave in to our persuasion. I missed her badly but I was soon to be glad that she had gone.

The trouble began in July on the night of the full moon. I was in the office, working late, when my adjutant, Vitalius, came in. There were beads of sweat on his face and he had the look of a man who has talked with demons.

"What is it?" I said. "What's the matter, man?"

"We have been betrayed, sir."

"Sit down. You look ill. Tell me about it."

He licked his lips. "It's that woman, the wife of Gaius. She knew I was married. She's been on at me for weeks, pestering me, asking me—she wouldn't leave me alone."

"And so?"

"I love my wife." He stared at me defiantly. "I do. But—but she is very beautiful and—and in the end I forgot myself." He buried his face in his hands and his shoulders shook at the memory of the betrayal.

"Is that all? Does Gaius know?"

"No. At least I don't think so. Afterward, she threatened to tell him unless I helped her. She said I could have her always if I helped her."

"What help does she want?"

"There is a great conspiracy. The tribes of the far north have promised to join with the men between the walls. She is a spy. She came with her brothers for that purpose. Their story was false."

"What else?"

"They have been bribing and suborning the auxiliaries. All the brigantes among the garrison will mutiny when the time comes. The province is to be freed forever from Roman rule."

"Boudicca had the same idea."

"It is true. I swear it. The tribes have taken the blood oath. And they have allied themselves with the Scotti."

"How many men in this garrison will stand by us?"

"Less than half."

Now I, too, was afraid.

"When is the rising timed for?"

"Tomorrow night."

"We have twenty-four hours, then, in which to save something from the wreckage." I spoke lightly and he said, incredulously, "You don't believe me, do you?"

"I believe you—though not about the Scotti. When have the Picts and they ever been friends?"

He shrugged his shoulders.

"Never mind. On whose side is Gaius? Don't tell me. I can make a good guess."

"What shall we do?"

"Get your sword," I said, as I buckled on my own. "I am going down to the house of Gaius and you are coming with me."

We went out silently, through the gate and across the hard-packed turf to the settlement. Most of the huts were in darkness, but through the open door of a wine shop I glimpsed a girl with lank hair, dejectedly sweeping up oyster shells that lay scattered on the floor. Moving quietly, we went round the back of a timber-framed house, along the colonnade, and up the stairs to a room where a torch burned in a bracket high on the wall. They were both there, sitting together on a couch, and they had the look of people who have just been making love. Gaius rose as I entered and his face went white as he saw my sword. But the woman beside him did not move.

"Gaius," I said, "I have proof that your wife is a spy and a traitor. She is also a liar and an adulteress. Now prove to me that you are not a traitor also."

He stared at me, licking his dry lips. "How?" he said at length, and the one word told me that Vitalius had not lied.

I held out a knife to him. "Kill her," I said. "Now. With this." He took the knife, stared at it blindly for a moment, and then let it drop to the floor. "I cannot," he said. "If you kill me for it, I cannot."

He looked at me, anger and despair on his face. "I should have had your command," he said. "It was my right. I had looked forward to it all those years. And you took it from me—a man half my age."

"Kill her," I said. "And I will forget the rest."

He shook his head. In his own way he was a brave man.

"I love her too much," he said.

I nodded to Vitalius and he moved and struck awkwardly so that the point went in against the breastbone, slid off with a terrible grating noise, and then broke. Gaius screamed and went down onto his knees like a praying Christian, the blade clutched in his hands. Vitalius pushed the sword home then, and Gaius fell sideways to the floor.

I turned to the woman. "He sent you," I said. "I might have known it. He knew I cared for women like you, women with dark hair and a white skin. And if I had not already been married it would have been me and not Gaius you would have worked upon. Is it not so?"

She stood up and smiled. "Yes," she said. "He came to my people, and I took him into my house, and we planned it together. He is a warrior among warriors. He has the power. It is a great gift to make others see what you wish them to see, to make others believe what you wish them to believe. I know, I can feel his power flowing into me when I touch his hands. My people know that he is descended from the Old Ones. That is why they believe him to be a god."

I stared at her. I did not understand.

"He is only a man," I said.

"You are wrong. He is not like other men. Who but he could have done what he has done? He has united the three peoples and together they will destroy this Rome of yours. He will become the God-King and I, who have served him with my body, shall be his Queen."

"What three peoples?"

"The Picts and the Scotti and the Saxons are at one in this thing. Though you know all now, it is still too late to stop him. You of the Roman kind are all doomed. The Eagles will die. He has said so."

I hesitated. She was so very beautiful. She had spirit and courage and she had great intelligence. I hesitated again and she saw me hesitate, and laughed. "I shall wait for him," she said. "If need be I shall wait for him until he joins me. We are of the same web, he and I."

I remembered Julian. He had loved this woman and had hated Rome. I did not hate Rome. I was a soldier and I loved Rome—that city I had never seen. So I killed her.

Though it was against the law we buried them secretly beneath the house and told no one. I hoped that the mystery of their disappearance would puzzle the disaffected and perhaps make them hesitate. Whether I succeeded or not, I do not know. It made no difference in the end.

Just before sunrise I issued my orders to those I could trust. Quintus, who had ridden over at my request, was in attendance.

"They won't attack the Wall itself," I said. "The north face is too steep, too rocky. They'll infiltrate by the Burn Gate and the two flanking mile castles. The Arcani will let them through."

Saturninus said, "The settlement is the danger. Its buildings provide cover up the southern slope and all the way to the fort."

"Evacuate it at dusk and then burn it."

He said, "We are very short of missiles. The mule train is late as usual."

"The drivers are probably sleeping it off in a ditch," said Quintus, dryly.

"Use the stones we quarried to build that new granary. They only need breaking up a little. Quintus, I must leave it to you to warn Eburacum. Say a prayer to Epona that your horsemen get through."

Saturninus said, "I have a married sister at Aesica. We must warn the other forts, sir."

"Not until dark. We cannot spare the men."

He nodded in silence. "And the pay chests, sir?"

"Oh, block up the strong room, of course. If anything goes wrong the money will still be there for our successors. They won't want to use their own burial fund on us."

Quintus looked at the sky. "It will be a fine day. We shall not have to shiver for long."

Later that morning I altered the dispositions of my troops and sent the suspected ones out of camp upon patrols. In the afternoon I began to block up the south portal of the east gate, and all the while the air was thick with a great rasping buzz as the centuries sharpened their swords on the iron rim of the stone tank by the north gate. Then, as night fell, I paraded my few men and we stood to arms along the Wall. I lit the signal fires and they flared up into the night, but no answering flare came from the mile castles to our right and left. Then a glowworm shone faintly in the west, and I knew that Vindolanda had caught our message, but from the east came no answering signal. The Arcani, faithful in their treachery, waited in silence for their friends.

"At ease," I said softly, and the men leaned against the parapet and rubbed their hands gently against the hafts of their spears. We had done all that we could. There was nothing left to do now except wait, and the waiting was not for long.

They came at dawn, and the scarlet disc of the rising sun was an omen that foretold the deaths of those who stood against them. The savage violence of their first silent rush carried the defenses at many points. Mile castle after mile castle opened its gates and they streamed through to burn huts, destroy the young and old, and make slaves of the women who did not die beneath the violence of their lust. Then they moved on to crush the few forts and towers that dared to stand against them. Their ships came in from the sea like hungry wolves, Scotti on the east coast and Saxons on the west. They outflanked the forts who resisted and their men poured ashore like a spring tide and overwhelmed them. The wounded and the dying, the living and the dead, all were flung contemptuously from the walls. Their bodies choked every ditch and every well, and there was blood and smoke and fire through the whole land.

We held our fort for two long days of continual fighting, till we were cut off and surrounded by the very men who had once called themselves my soldiers, men whom I had liked and trusted and helped, men whose grief I had shared and whose happiness had meant the world to me. The fort was a shambles, and somewhere beneath the floor of a gutted hut in the settlement outside lay a woman who had smiled even as I killed her.

Twice I heard his voice outside the walls, crying hoarsely to his men, though I never saw him—this man who had become a god. He cried for our destruction but I was too exhausted to feel hate, too angry to feel pity. Vitalius was gone and Saturninus wounded. The tribesmen were even now burning brushwood against the oak doors of the fort, the granaries had been set on fire, and the north wall had been abandoned to the enemy and our crumpled dead. Suddenly I could stand it no longer. I had no stomach to fight for a lost cause, a general who was dead (they showed us his head upon a pole), and a wall that had been betrayed. With the remnants of my men, Saturninus and I cut our way out through the smoke and set off for Eburacum.

The road to the south told its own story. It was lined with bodies, little groups of men who had held on, as we had, and then retreated stubbornly, still fighting until they were overwhelmed. At Bravoniacum we found the supply fort gutted and the remnants of the Ala Petriana, our finest cavalry, among the blackened bodies. It was there that Quintus joined us, riding a tired horse. He was quite alone. At Maglona we made contact with the Second Ala of Astures. They had suffered few casualties and so we marched the rest of the way to Eburacum under their protection.

There we learned that a Saxon fleet had landed in the southeast; the great sea forts that Quintus knew so well had been silenced; betrayed by treachery from within, overcome by violence from without. And somewhere among the broken catapults, Nectaridus, Count of the Saxon Shore, lay silent in the company of his men. In answer to Fullofaudes' summons the Second Augusta, at Isca, was already marching across Britannia, but harassed by raids and ambushes their progress was slow. A gray-faced decurion who had pushed on ahead alone told us bluntly that they would never reach us in time. His worst news he kept to the last. The Attacotti, a confederacy of tribes from Hibernia, had landed at Mona, and they were even now pouring through the mountain passes into the undefended center of the island. The Twentieth, cut to pieces, had fallen back on Viroconium, and behind them Deva, unguarded save for a handful of veterans, was already a wrecked and smoking ruin.

Fullofaudes said, "If they destroy us, then they will destroy the Second also. We stand or fall alone. Go back to your Legate and tell him to hold Ratae and to keep contact with the Twentieth until he hears my news. If it is good I will send fresh instructions. If it is bad he must make his own."

We went out against them the next day, and the enemy so outnumbered us that we could not count the odds. All day we fought and twice I saw a painted man on a white pony whom I knew, but I never had the chance to find out if indeed he had become a god. By nightfall we were beaten, Fullofaudes was dead with all his staff, and the Barbarians were in the streets of Eburacum. Our officers were dead too, so I took command and withdrew the Sixth down the road to Londinium, while Quintus screened us with the remnants of the cavalry. There we stayed, penned in like sheep behind the walls, and hoped that Rome would remember us.

All that autumn they ravaged the land. The Second fell back and held fast to Corinium, while the villas were sacked and the harvest rotted in the fields for lack of men to gather it. They took the grain from the barns and all the food that people had stored against the bad days. They took the cattle and the ponies as plunder and drove them north. Houses were stripped of their valuables and they killed all who protested at the theft. The roads were empty of traffic, there was no trade, and the towns, shut in upon themselves, began quietly to starve. And as always it was the women who suffered most. In the spring we had news that the Barbarians were splitting up, that the war bands were getting smaller and that many were beginning to move north again. The Picts began to quarrel with the Scotti and both, in turn, began to quarrel with the Saxons. When I heard that news I began, as out of a long darkness, to see a faint pinprick of light that was the dawn of hope. They had made him a god but he had failed after all in his great purpose. The Barbarian conspiracy was near its end.

And then, on a cold wet day when our food was nearly gone, we heard the news. The Count Theodosius had arrived. He had sailed with a fleet and an army all the way from Augusta Treverorum in Gaul. All the way down the Rhenus and across that cold sea they had rowed upon an Emperor's orders and made landfall at Rutupiae. We knew then that we were saved.

CHAPTER III

I had thought Aelia dead, but I wished to make certain. In the end I found her in a mean village outside Eburacum. She was very ill and they told me that she had been so for months. Her hair was streaked with gray and she looked thin and wasted. Her eyes reminded me of another's. They were without hope. She would not speak to me; she turned her face to the wall and she cried. For three days it was like that, and then they told me what had been done to her, and I—I understood at last. When I came to her next and she turned away, I pulled her to me and I said those things that a man says to a woman whom he loves.

She wept. "I am ashamed," she said. "I am so ashamed." And then she added, wildly, "It is a punishment for all my sins."

I did not feel like laughing. I said, "You are my wife, Aelia, and there is only shame if you do not live to keep me company."

From that moment she began to get better. Later, because I was so thankful to have her back, I made an offering to my God, and I sent for a vase of colored glass from Colonia, where they specialized in such things. It cost me a great deal of money, but she liked pretty things and was pleased with it when it came.

After Theodosius had settled the north and made terms with the Picts I went back to Borcovicum. Now there were great changes made. The administration was impoverished and our auxiliaries could not be paid. So Theodosius gave them land instead. Each man had his own patch and became a farmer, and lived with his family inside the camp, and the civilian settlements along the Vallum were abandoned. The Arcani were disbanded, and the long work of restoring our broken defenses began. Quintus Veronius was made Praefectus of the Ala Petriana. He deserved the command (it had once been the post for the

senior officer on the Wall) and it was his ambition to have a regiment of cavalry. But we both missed him, for there were few enough people to talk to in our small world. Yet we had peace in the heather, and so the years went by.

One evening a lone horseman from Corstopitum rode up the track. It was Quintus Veronius. I was glad to see him, but Aelia, whose face had shone like a candle when I cried his name, stopped smiling when she saw his face. He looked tired, strained, and angry. "I have come from Eburacum," he said. "I am no longer in command of the Ala Petriana. I dared to complain to Magnus Maximus, our beloved Chief of Staff, about the corruption of Quartermasters and illegal profiteering in high places. So here I am, back at Vindolanda in disgrace."

"And what else?" I asked.

He said, bleakly, "Our iron soldiers are made of iron no longer."

When he had finished talking everyone was silent, for there was nothing to say. There had been a great battle between the Army of the East and those of the Goths who had settled on the west bank of the Danubius. It had been fought at a place called Adrianopolis, of which I had never heard, and the whole of the Roman army had been engaged—and beaten. The Barbarian hordes on their ponies had cut the legions into pieces, and the most disciplined and best equipped army in the world had been destroyed by a rabble of horsemen from the Steppes. The Emperor Valens, his generals, Trajan and Sebastianus, together with thirty-five tribunes, the prefects of a dozen regiments, the Master of Horse, the High Steward, and the entire staff—all lay dead on the field of battle, and with them two-thirds of the entire army.

Forty thousand men had been killed in an afternoon.

I could not believe it. It was so horrible, so unimaginable that for days I could not take it in. I accepted the facts, but I dared not interpret them, for to do so would have meant acknowledging what would be unbearable—

that the civilized world could be destroyed.

I stayed on the Wall in my overcrowded fort, an aging tribune in charge of a rabble of men who scarcely deserved the name of regiment now. They were quiet years disturbed only by the news that Magnus Maximus had got himself proclaimed Emperor. This made little difference to us, but when the troops in Gaul denounced the Emperor Gratianus, Magnus Maximus saw that his chance had come—to try for two provinces instead of one. He raised troops wherever he could lay hands on them and stripped the Wall of its best men. In a week he undid the work of ten years and we were left naked to defend the frontier with our bare hands. When I, in my turn, received orders to send half my men, I would not do it. Together with Quintus I rode down to Eburacum, where I knew Maximus was, and asked to see him.

"I have heard of you," he said. "You bear my name. You served Fullofaudes and Theodosius well, but you do not wish to serve me. Give me a reason why I do not have you executed or broken?"

"Because you cannot afford it," I said. "Not one man can you afford to waste. I serve Rome as well as this island, and the safety of both depends on her frontiers."

"I am the Emperor."

"That is disputed by one Emperor in Rome and by another in the east. I will believe it when they are dead."

"I shall not fail."

"Of course not. To you, Caesar, the throne; to us the war."

He tried hard to smile. "In my service you could have had a regiment, or perhaps a legion. You could have gone far."

"To my death in a Gaulish mist?"

"You may do that yet when I return."

"When you return, Caesar, I shall be with my cohort on the Wall. Or dead under it."

He looked anxious then. "The Wall must be held," he said.

"It has never yet been taken by direct assault." I looked at him and added, slowly, "Only by betrayal."

We returned to our forts. We had kept our men, but we were lucky to be alive.

He failed, of course. He destroyed Gratianus, but the son of the man who had helped him to power proved another matter. And so, Theodosius, I became the last sole Emperor of the Roman world, while we shivered in the rain and prayed that the Picts might leave us alone.

Then one day a strange tribesman came to the north gate and said he wished to see me.

"Well?" I asked. I was curious, for he wore the marks of the Epidoni, of whom I had heard much but seen nothing.

"I bear a message for the tribune of the Tungri."

"You may give it to me then," I said.

"I have a friend who wishes to see you."

"Who is this friend without a name?"

"I was to say that you would know him when you saw him."

"So."

"He is two days' march to the north and waits upon the coast."

"And is that all you have to say?"

"It is all I was told to say."

"It is a clumsy trap," said Quintus. "Do not go."

I turned back to the dark man before me. "And if I do not go?"

He looked disconcerted. "My friend told me to say—come for the sake of an old friendship."

I felt very cold. "I will come," I said. "But not alone."

"My friend expected that. But you must carry a green branch or not come at all."

"It is agreed."

I took Quintus and twenty men from the fort. Quintus was quietly curious but he asked no questions. For two days we rode north along the old military road, built by Agricola, and then, with the wind in our faces we made toward the sea. It was very cold, but we came at last to a long beach of silver sand. The wind blew in the sharp grass and the seabirds walked among the wet flats, for it was low tide and the sea was calm. On the beach, among the tufted dunes, stood a small tent, and a wood fire burned smokily in front of it. Away to the right with its prow over the sand lay a long narrow boat with a dragon head, the sails furled below the single mast. I left Quintus, and rode down to the sand with the guide trotting beside me. He had heard us coming for he came out of the tent and stood motionless, waiting for me as I rode forward, the green branch in my sword hand. I dismounted and walked toward him, and he to me. Both of us stopped when we were ten paces apart. Neither of us smiled or raised a hand in greeting. But I knew him still and I had a pain inside me for all that was past.

"I have come as I promised."

"I knew you would."

He had not changed all that much. He wore the clothes of his adopted people, but there were no tattoo marks on his body that I could see. He was very thin and he was nervous, I think, because he could not keep his hands still, and his fingers played ceaselessly with the hilt of his dagger. There were lines upon his face and on his forehead, and there was a scar across his neck that had not been there before. But his eyes were no longer dead. He had the appearance of a man who was at the end of his strength.

"What do you want of me?"

He flinched at my tone. "I want only to ask you a question."

"You could have come to the Wall."

He half smiled. "I did that—once before. But you were not in a receiving mood on that occasion."

"Nor you in a forgiving one."

"That is in the past. If we talk of the past we shall only quarrel."

"I have no wish to quarrel. I would have killed you at Eburacum once, but there is peace here now." I looked at him steadily. "The past is dead."

"You are well and happy?" he asked.

"I am content. Few who serve Rome in these times can be happy."

"You are fortunate."

"If I am, then I work hard for my fortune."

"Yet you risked all when you spoke to Magnus Maximus thus."

I said, "How did you know that?"

"If a rat squeaks on your Wall we hear it in those mountains." He glanced behind him as he spoke. "For example, I can give you news from Mediolanum that you will find hard to bear. Your fanatical Emperor has passed laws against those who do not worship his god. Sacrifices are not permitted and the temples are to be closed. Not even in the privacy of your home may you pray to the Immortal One."

I stared at him, speechless with shock.

"It is true," he said. "I would not joke on such a matter—not to any man. For those who do not profess his faith the road to high office in the empire is now barred forever." He paused. He said, coldly, "Were I still a Roman I swear I would not serve a man who passes such unjust laws."

I remained silent.

He looked at my face, half stretched out his hand, and then let it fall to his side. "Oh, Maximus, do not look like that. Though you walk through the seven gates of our faith, still you will not know which way the wind may blow you."

I said nothing and he stared at the ground with blank eyes. Then he looked up and tried to smile. "Will you drink with me? Just once, for the sake of forgotten things."

"Of course. Willingly and with all my heart."

He went into the tent and came out with an amphora and two drinking cups. "This came from a wrecked ship," he said. "I kept it until now, thinking to drink it on some great occasion. I have not tasted your wine in years."

I poured the libation and said alone the words that we had been used to saying together in another life, while he watched without comment. It was like a dream, this meeting, and I wondered how it would end. I raised my cup and said to him, "May you be happy."

He half smiled. He said, "You have a wife and a home and a people: all the things you wanted except one. Is the dream good now that it has become reality?"

"I like to think so."

"I had a dream, too, but it was conceived in hate."

"I know that."

"Is that why it failed, do you think?"

"Perhaps. Yet it nearly succeeded. How did you do it?"

He poured the dregs from his cup onto the sand and shaded his eyes. "By hard work."

I thought of all that it must have taken. The endless talks by smoky fires in rock-bound valleys that we had never seen; the ruthless patience required to smooth over jealousies and blood feuds that were old when Agricola built his forts; the sheer, hard, grinding work of welding tribes, clans, and sects into an organized whole, equipped, prepared, and willing to follow a single plan, to obey a single order, and to strike the aimed blow in the right place at the right time.

"No Roman could have done it." I did not realize that I had spoken aloud.

"But I share their blood."

"I had forgotten."

"Even that was not enough. Village after village would not have me. I was a stranger, an outcast, a man with no shadow. But one night I came to a secret place where the priests of the tribe celebrated their mystery. It was a night of storm and lightning, a night of great violence that would make even a Roman believe that the gods he had forsaken were angry with him. They saw the brand that you know upon my forehead, they saw my head with no hair, and they saw that I had the look of a man who has gazed into a great darkness. Their priests gave me food and shelter without a word, and in the morning they sent me the high priest's daughter to be my servant. From her I learned that they believed I was a god."

He paused and looked up. "After that the work began that I had made my purpose."

I shivered.

He said, "It is I who shiver now. I knew that we had failed even before we began. In that night of waiting, while I lay in the heather and looked at the walls of your fort, I had a great feeling of coldness inside me. For the first time since I had met the high priest's daughter the warmth left me and I was cold again. I felt colder still when I stood triumphant inside your shattered walls. She was so far away. I knew then that I did not care whether I lived or died, whether I won or lost. I went on with my purpose but it had no meaning now, and when the tribes broke up to plunder and to quarrel I no longer cared."

He threw his cup onto the ground and tried to smile.

I said, "And what do you do now?"

"I have been waiting for that ship," he said. "For five days I have been waiting." He smiled with his teeth. "A man who fails is not popular. After it was over I crossed to Hibernia and lived there. But it was always damp and I was always so cold—here." He touched his belt briefly. "In the end I returned to Caledonia. But I could not bear to go back to those mountains again and live alone, inside myself. So, I set sail in a Saxon ship for a Saxon land. They are still my friends." He spoke with a defiant pride. "Perhaps I shall find another purpose somewhere, someday, that will not break in my hands."

Above us a gull wheeled in the sky and cried shrilly; the guide sat motionless, cross-legged by the tent, and the sea rolled upon the beach. He put his hand to the mark on his forehead and said, "We both carry a burden upon our backs, but mine is heavy with things undone."

I could have cried out to him then and repeated the old offer of the villa in Gaul, but I knew that he would refuse. He had too much pride, too much bitterness, too much hate. There was so much between us that lay in a golden past and that we could not remember without intolerable pain. So I kept silent.

He spoke to my guide, who answered him and nodded, pointing briefly at the tent. Then he turned to me, his face suddenly like stone.

"When the tide turns I shall sail. But you must go now."

"You have not asked your question."

"I kept it till the last, hoping that I would not need to ask it."

"Do you need to?"

"No. But I must ask it all the same."

I waited.

He said, "What happened to her. What happened to my high priest's daughter?"

"She died."

"You killed her."

"Yes."

He said, "And for that I could kill you, even now, though you hold a green branch in your hand. But I will not. Instead I will give you a warning. Stay here where it is safe. Stay on this island which is now your home."

"Why?"

"I cannot answer that, Maximus. But on the day that you become the father of your brother, and the sun stands in the sign of Capricorn, you will wish that you had stayed upon the Wall."

I shivered, not understanding what lay beneath the words I knew so well—I who had been present at his pain and his rebirth, as he had been at mine.

"Shall I see you again, Julian?"

"Do you want to?"

I was silent.

He said, "That is a question I should not have asked. Yes, I think we shall meet again."

He raised his hand in a salute of farewell and I acknowledged it before turning away.

My men were sitting huddled round a fire when I came to them and Quintus, wrapped in his white cloak, was walking his horse up and down.

"Well," he said, "what did he want?"

"I was just saying goodbye to an old friend."

CHAPTER IV

Aelia coughed and said, huskily, "Shall we ever leave Borcovicum, do you think?"

Quintus rattled the dice again and smiled bitterly. "The Wall is a place only for forgotten and disgraced men. But at least the frontier is quiet and we may live in peace."

I said nothing. My unfulfilled dreams hurt no longer; the seasons passed, one like another, and I was content that it should be so.

Then an imperial courier rode up from the south with the news that Theodosius had died at last. I paraded my men, as in the old style, and with the snow falling upon our battered armor and our dulled swords I told them that the child, Honorius, was now Emperor and bade them take the oath of allegiance. They did so, four or five hundred shabby men in worn cloaks, whose hands, toughened only by farming now, had not held a sword in years; while the bored sentries on the guard walk turned their backs upon the white dumbness of the heather and leaned upon their shields to watch a ceremony that once—performed by the legions—might have made or broken an Emperor.

We had other news later. A horse trader on his way to Petriana told me that a Vandal general in the service of the empire had been named guardian to Honorius, and that this General—Stilicho—was looked upon as the one man who might yet be the saving of Rome. He had driven the Franks and the Alemanni back into Germania and had secured the Rhenus frontier once more.

That winter it was bitterly cold and we had difficulty over fuel. By the shortest day the stock of black stones that we kept in the old guardroom by the blocked-up eastern gate had run low, and it was hard to chip out a fresh supply from the icebound outcrop we had worked for years. Aelia developed a bad cough that grew worse instead of better. Even when packed in blankets by the meager fire in our quarters she did not cease shivering, and the sight of her face, with its sunken eyes, made us all afraid. I would have sent her south but the roads were impassable and in any case, as Saturninus said afterward, she would not have left us. Quintus was a good friend at that time. He would ride over and sit beside her on those occasions when my duties took me from the fort, and he did much to cheer her up. I kept on saying to myself that when the spring comes she will be well again. Each night and each morning I prayed to Mithras, and I prayed to her god as well. He at least should have heard me. Her god cared for the weak and the sick, she used to say, but he did not help her now, and when the spring came at last, she died.

That summer I went down to Eburacum and asked for a transfer. Constantinus was Chief of Staff now; an ambitious middle-aged man who had shared a hut with me in my legionary days with the Twentieth. He had a son, Constans, in command of an ala. Him, I did not like. He was contemptuous, cruel, and conceited, and had too much of a following among the younger officers.

I spent my time either waiting in the empty anterooms of the repaired headquarters of the Sixth, or walking through the neglected streets. Sometimes I would sit in the empty amphitheater and try not to think of my wife.... He had come out of that gate there, leading the rear of the procession, while the Legate of the Sixth had smiled at his daughter and the sun beat down on the sweating crowds. Down there in that smooth circle of sand the two tiny figures had swayed and darted, until one was dead and the other stood motionless, while the packed seats roared, awaiting the hollow gift of a freedom he could do nothing with. The Legate could make him free, but he was a prisoner of his thoughts forever.

Then in a wine shop one evening, I heard through the smoke, the chatter, and the click of dice, the bored voice of the young Constans.

"Someone should tell the old fool he's wasting his time. It's more than my father's job is worth to give promotion to a pagan." I got to my feet and crossed to the counter where a girl was taking dirty wine cups off a tray. "Give me that," I said. I picked up the tray, rubbed it with my sleeve, and held it up to the light. In the reflection I could just see my face. I looked at the polished bronze in silence, then I turned and went out. The next morning I collected my horse from the cavalry stables and returned to Borcovicum. I had accomplished nothing.

Later we heard that the Guardian of Rome had landed at Dubris. He was paying a visit, so it was said, to reorganize our defenses. When we heard that he was coming north to Eburacum, Quintus, whom I had not seen for weeks, rode in to tell me that he was going down to see Stilicho.

"You are wasting your time." I looked at his tired face impatiently. "He needs young men, not their ghosts."

"Perhaps. But he may need soldiers of experience who did their training in a proper legion. Maximus, we have rotted here long enough." His voice sounded desperate.

"Enjoy yourself," I said. "And bring back some wine. Try his staff for Mosella. I am sick of drinking vinegar."

A week later he returned, but he was not alone. A cavalry detachment was behind him and in front a group of horsemen surrounding a scarlet cloak, gilded armor, and a great horsehair plume that overtopped them all.

I ordered the trumpeter to sound the "alert" and my men fell in outside the south wall. Stilicho, the Military Master of the Western Empire, was a big man, with broad shoulders, blond hair, and restless blue eyes. He inspected everything. He saw the record room that had become an armory, the adjutant's office, now used for making arrowheads, and the accounts room in which the paymaster slept as well as worked. He visited the quarry where we dug the stones to repair the walls, and always he asked questions. He never stopped asking questions.

"How old are you? And how long have you been on the Wall?" he asked. I told him and he paused a moment and then said, abruptly, "I have heard how you defied your namesake and lived. I have heard also how you commanded the Sixth Legion in retreat. What would you say if I told you I may have to withdraw a legion to help me in Italia?"

"If the General needs the legion, then that legion is indeed needed," I replied, carefully.

He said, "We cannot any longer fight the Barbarians in the old way. In the days of the legion it was possible. Your armored soldier was the finest in the world. But not after Adrianopolis. Valens died, but if he had lived he would never have known why he was beaten. But I know." He smiled. "I am a Barbarian myself. Can you tell me why they were beaten?"

I was silent.

"Come. It was not a question of numbers or bad leadership, though both played their part."

"The legionaries had beaten cavalry before," I said slowly. I was thinking of what I had read about Maharbal, Hannibal's great cavalry commander.

"Yes," he said. "But they had never fought cavalry who used stirrups."

I thought for a moment. "You mean the stirrups gave them some kind of extra stability to make better use of their weapons," I said, hesitantly.

"That's right," he said. "Your friend Veronius said you could still think like a soldier and he was right."

"But the Sarmatians used stirrups too," I said.

"They did, but they used their horses for skirmishes, raids, and ambushes. They never charged, shoulder to shoulder, in a mass. No man on foot can stand up against that."

I was silent. I was interested but I could not see where this was leading.

He said, "The Sixth must stay at Eburacum as a mobile force in case your heather catches fire again. The Second must stay at Rutupiae to guard the Saxon Shore. That leaves the Twentieth. They are below strength, badly led, and underpaid. They have little discipline and no fighting skill. You will take over as their General. Call yourself Legate in the old style if you wish. Keep the name of legion and keep the Eagle too, if it is of help. Organize them how you will. Appoint your own officers. But forget the battle drill they taught you in the old legion. You will need bows, not javelins now. What I want is a field force of six thousand men, part horse, part infantry, trained and disciplined to fight masses of cavalry in the open, one moment, or build and man a line of forts the next."

His eyes were on me and I could not look away. "How long will you give me?" I asked. I could hardly take in what he was saying.

"Be ready in a year and expect my summons after that." He handed me a parchment. "Here is a commission, signed by the Emperor. The name has not been filled in, but I will do that before we eat."

I said, "Does the Emperor know that I am not a Christian?"

"Oh, yes. Why else do you think a man of your ability has stayed up here all these years?"

"But did he not mind, sir?"

Stilicho smiled. "I persuaded him to bend his own laws a little."

He stayed for the midday meal, talking all the while, and then left. His last words were typical. "I will order two cloaks for you in Eburacum. It is well to assume the dignity with the power. The one always helps the other."

I stood outside the gate and watched him go. He was the last Roman general ever to see the Wall under arms.

"We must drink to the occasion," said Quintus. "The world is at your feet. From Legate to Emperor is only a step." He gave a mock salute, but there was an anxious look in his eyes.

"Don't be a fool," I said, irritably, for I was nervous with excitement. "What lies did you tell him to make him do such a thing?"

"I told him the truth: that we were the only two honest men upon the Wall. He believed me. You do not lie to a man like that."

"No," I said.

"When will you leave?" His face was beaded with sweat.

"In two or three days." I turned and walked slowly toward my house.

He followed, even more slowly. "I see." His voice was expressionless.

"I want you to come with me to command the cavalry."

I could hear his footsteps quicken. "Good," he said, and there was joy and relief in his voice. "I always knew I could be a second Maharbal if I had the opportunity."

Saturninus, when I told him the news, stood very still. "Will you take troops from the Wall, sir?" he said. I shook my head. "No, you are Praefectus here now. But I will take your youngest son, Fabianus, if you will let me."

We said our farewells inside my residence and then, alone, I stood and looked at the shrine that had meant so much to Aelia and wondered, for a moment, if what she had said had been true, and that I would see her again, and that this long, intolerable ache was, indeed, only the symptom of a temporary parting. Then I went out into the sun and inspected my men for the last time.

Outside the south gate Quintus was waiting with a group of horsemen. He and Saturninus gave each other a long look. They had never been friends. There had been a curious constraint between them for years that I had never attempted to probe or understand. We, who spent our lives in small communities, had long ago learned that it was wise not to ask too many questions.

Saturninus said, calmly, "You keep your promise then, Praefectus?"

Quintus nodded. "I do," he said, and I wondered to what god or person he had made a promise and what it was. But I noticed that neither wished the other good fortune.

Saturninus had dug a hole in the earth by the gate, and inside it I put carefully the surviving earring that I had given Aelia, together with the signet ring she had given me. Saturninus produced a coin from his belt. "I found this years ago beneath the floor in number two granary; a sestertius of Commodus. I kept it for good luck. May I add it as my gift, sir?"

I nodded and he put it in. I had thought Quintus might join us, but he did not do so. When the earth had been stamped hard and the libation poured, I held out my hand.

"It has been a long time," I said.

"Over thirty years," he replied.

"Hold the fort."

"As long as I can."

I mounted my horse and rode off down the road to Corstopitum. I did not look at the deserted bathhouse, the crumbling vallum, or the abandoned mile castles. I looked only to my front the whole way.

The first thing I did when I reached Eburacum was to visit the baths where I sweated off the dirt of weeks and had a massage, a shave, and a haircut. Then I looked in the mirror. I was gray now and troops did not care overmuch for gray-haired commanders, so I had my hair dyed, leaving a little gray tactfully at the sides. I told Quintus to do the same. Then we collected our new scarlet cloaks and went to headquarters.

Constantinus smiled as we entered. "I have heard of your good fortune," he said. "And I congratulate you, of course. How may I help you? Not with men, I fear."

I said, "I want the treasure chest that Stilicho left me to pay my men with. I shall recruit my own men, but I do need equipment and supplies."

He smiled. "I am sorry but I cannot help you there. You will have to make returns in the usual way to the government factories in Gaul and Italia."

"That will take months," I said.

Constantinus shrugged. "You know the regulations," he said.

Quintus said, icily, "You have supplies. You have more equipment than men. I know how these things are arranged."

"You have been misinformed." Constantinus' smile vanished. "It will be an ill service to this island if you take more troops out of it."

"You are lying," said Quintus, coldly.

Looking up suddenly I saw that the door had opened and the young Constans was there, leaning against the wall. He was wearing the overburnished armor that he always affected, and smelling strongly of perfume. "I have heard of the miracle," he said, languidly. "I came to offer my felicitations."

Constantinus said, softly, "And what if I don't let you take the Twentieth out of Britannia? We are short of everything, I tell you. What point in helping Rome if we cannot help ourselves?"

"Oh, if he cares for the Barbarians so much, let him go to them," said Constans with a yawn.

"We are Rome," I said. "We are all Rome whether we wish it or not. The Barbarians are pressing in along the Rhenus frontier. If that frontier goes we shall be cut off from Rome. What help will the central government give us then if we don't help them now?"

Constantinus said, in exasperation, "How can we help?" He spread his hands wide in the gesture of a moneylender. "There is no money. How can there be when the tax returns are so negligible. Our administration is at its wit's end to meet the demands of the central government."

Quintus said, "Is the province to be endangered by the corrupt indolence of a few fat, idle old men? When the Saxons come again perfume will be a poor substitute for a leather shield."

Constans laughed. "You are not suggesting corruption, surely?"

I turned on him. "I only suggest. You, of course, know." To his father, I said, "All that I need now, since I can get no help, is the gold that was left me."

Constantinus smiled blandly. "But we need that gold for our own defense."

"No," I said.

He rose to his feet. "I beg your pardon," he said, softly. "Did I hear you aright?"

"Yes. I am not under your orders."

"Perhaps he aspires to be another Magnus Maximus," said Constans, viciously.

I crossed the room and slapped him hard across the face. "No. If you were a man you would understand."

Constantinus, white with anger, said, "It is not you who gives the orders here." He smiled with an effort. "You can have half the money or none at all."

"And if I refuse and take it all?" I touched my sword hilt lightly.

"My legions may be below strength, but—by the gods—you will find it easier to defy an Emperor than two thousand of my men."

I said, "I have the orders of Stilicho to obey. Not yours."

"Then obey them," said Constantinus.

"He might come back," said Quintus softly.

"Our Barbarian General has married his daughter to the Emperor. He has considerable power," I added gently.

Constans said, "Oh, he might come back, but he is a busy man. And if he has need of troops out of this island, then it might seem that he would be hard put to send them in again."

I looked at the pair of them, and I hated them. On the Wall I had commanded loyalty, but here I commanded nothing. Without men I was helpless, and they knew it.

"Very well," I said. "Half then. But if I do not get my half, then I swear by the Great Bull that I will come back here and I will take the whole on the point of my sword."

We went out into the bright sunlight and neither of us spoke for some time.

"It is a conspiracy," I said. "With half the money he can re-equip his own men at the same rate as I equip mine. If I had it all I should have the strongest single command in the island. What is he afraid of? That I aspire to be Dux Britanniarum?"

"Of course." Quintus grinned. "But he, at least, aspires to wear the purple."

"Will he give us even half?"

"He must. He is a greedy man, but practical too. To keep all he must murder you first. But that would mean a break with Honorius. That he cannot afford, so he gets rid of you best by letting you go. He expects us to die in a forest in Germania." He added slowly, "And we probably shall. Oh, Maximus, my friend, we probably shall."

Two days later I rode southwest in the spring sunshine. Behind me I left my youth, my middle age, my wife, and my happiness. I was a general now and I had only defeat or victory to look forward to. There was no middle way any longer, and I did not care.

CHAPTER V

I rode through Deva, a ghost town of crumbling walls, burned-out houses, and empty streets whose few inhabitants, their memories scarred by the raids of the Attacotti and their ghastly customs, hid from me as I passed by. At length, after endless, twisting miles through the mountains, I felt the wind blow fresh and clean on my face and I could smell the sea. Segontium reminded me of Eburacum, and the Twentieth, when I had seen its sentries and met its officers, reminded me of the Sixth. There was the same slow smell of decay and indolence that made me long for my farmer-soldiers of faraway Borcovicum. Within an hour of my arrival I held a meeting of the senior officers and centurions. At the end I said, "There are going to be many changes, I warn you. I want no officer who is not prepared to do everything that his men have to do. Not only that—he must be able to do it better."

I dismissed them and the next day we got down to work. I needed two key men for the cornerstones of my command, and after a week of careful watching I sent for Aquila and Julius Optatus, two of the younger officers who seemed to have something that the other century commanders lacked.

Aquila was a native of the region, a man of medium height, with a hooked nose and a quiet expression. Julius Optatus was short, square, and stocky, and he had a craftsman's hands and a voice like a bull. But he had a good memory and a talent for organization.

"You two," I said, "are going to be promoted. You, Aquila, to be Chief Centurion. You have only had five years' service and you will go over the heads of men your senior. This is an unusual step to take, but then this is an unusual legion. You will have jealousy and envy to contend with. You won't be able to beat that with a vine staff, so don't try. Remember three things: you have got to be more efficient than anyone else except myself; never give an order that cannot reasonably be carried out; and never hesitate over making a decision. Lastly, if the legion is inefficient, remember, I shall blame you and not the men."

He smiled. He said, quietly, "I will do my best, General."

To Julius Optatus, I said, "You are now the quartermaster. You will get more money and seven times as much work. In addition, you are going to be a most unusual quartermaster: one who does not take bribes or sell stores for personal profit. If you do, then I will break you. Is that clear?"

He nodded, speechless.

At the end of the week Quintus arrived with the bullock wagons and the men were paid. Selected centurions were sent out on recruiting campaigns and, while we waited for the young unmarried men to come in to us, our hard core of two thousand began to learn, for the first time in their lives, what it meant to be soldiers. But stores were also a problem. We needed so much equipment and it took so long to obtain through official channels that I despaired of our ever being ready in time for Stilicho's summons. I had to send my requirements through the Chief of Staff to the Praefectus Praetorio in Gaul, who in turn would forward them to the appropriate factories, all of which were widely scattered. Those for woolen clothing, for ballistae, shield works, and officers' armor were at Treverorum; but—and this was typical of our administration—breastplates for the men were made in Mantua, while cavalry armor had to be requisitioned from Augustodunum. I could order arrows from Concordia, but the bows to fire them were made in Mantua; and the swords, of course, came from Remi. In addition, craftsmen had to be found or trained who could repair what we received, or make what we could not afford to buy. A special area of the camp, under the supervision of Julius Optatus, was set aside for these men to work in. It was a noisy, smoky area and the sound of iron beating upon iron went on all day long.

By the end of three months the legion had doubled its original size and the men were getting fit. At the end of a twenty-mile march in the pouring rain, their clothes sodden and their feet sore, they could erect a camp complete with defenses in the space of forty minutes and then fight a sixty-minute action afterward. "It is no good," I would tell them, "learning to march fifteen miles if you are so out of breath at the end of it that you cannot kill a man the first try when he is stabbing at you. He will kill you first instead, and your long walk will have been a waste of time."

In the evenings, in camp and out of it, I gave special training to my officers and my centurions. "There are four things you must learn if you wish to be a good officer," I would say to them. "You must learn self-discipline, initiative, patience, and independence."

"What about loyalty?" asked a centurion whose men had been grumbling at his too frequent use of the stick.

"You cannot buy loyalty," I said. "You can only earn it."

There was difficulty over horses. We needed close to two thousand, and Quintus had the utmost difficulty in getting even four hundred. By the end of five months I had my full complement of men but still not enough horses. It was agreed between us that Quintus should cross to Gaul, base himself on Gesoriacum, and look for the remainder of the animals there.

"It will be a big job transporting the animals I have got," he said. "We shall need a lot of equipment."

I looked at Julius Optatus. "Well?" I asked.

He grinned. "It will be an expensive business, sir."

"I will give you the money. Just get on with it."

To Quintus, I said, "A good deal of the stores we need have been sent to Gesoriacum to await our coming. I will write to the Dux Belgicae to see that he gives you every assistance."

He laughed. "You mean you don't want him taking our supplies. I will see that he accounts for them all."

The cavalry left on a wet morning at the beginning of the new year and the camp seemed empty without them—empty, certainly, without Quintus.

When summer came I had a surprise visit from the young Constans, who rode in one day with some brother officers. "I came to learn when you would be ready to leave," he said carelessly.

I was not surprised. They were growing anxious at Eburacum, wondering, perhaps, what my intentions might be now that my legion was raised and partly trained.

"You may see how ready we are," I said. "You can watch my men to-morrow at exercise. Perhaps now you would care for refreshment and then look over the camp."

"Of course," he said insolently. "It is my duty, on behalf of the Dux Britanniarum, to see that the funds of Rome have not been wasted."

I was tempted to slap him again but restrained myself with an effort. What was Constans to me?

Yet, for all his swagger and his rudeness he seemed to know what he was about, and I could not have made a better or more thorough inspection myself. The next morning he saw the men parade and go through their drill. In the afternoon he watched a field exercise, saw the ballistae fired, saw the cohorts make an attack on a prepared position, and frowned as a signal tower was erected, a defensive ditch dug, and a light bridge thrown across a river by the legion's engineers. He said little and I wondered what he was thinking. I was soon to know. He came into my office at sundown and leaned idly against a wall while I dictated a letter to my clerk. "Next, to the tribune of the factory at Treverorum. I am returning the armor you have delivered. I need it for use as well as smartness, and this consignment has been so highly burnished that it has lost weight and is, as a result, dangerously thin. A spear will go through it easily, as you will see from the tests we have carried out. Please keep in future to the specifications I laid down in my original orders."

"I did not realize you were a soldier," he said, softly. "With a sword like that in his hands a man could aspire to the purple."

"I gather you approve," I said.

"My father was wrong. He did not believe you could do it."

"Neither did you."

He flushed and rubbed his cheek. "I do not bear malice," he said, with a flash of his teeth. "I have a good ala. And you need as much cavalry as you can get. I've half a mind to join you. I'm sick of Eburacum and those endless patrols along the signal forts, looking for Saxons. When they do come they arrive so half drowned that they don't even give us a good fight."

"You forget," I said, "I might not take you."

He grinned. "You would," he said. "You would take anyone who was a soldier. I know you now. Why don't you try for the purple? The men would elect you." He spoke as though it were a game of some kind.

"And what would you be?"

"Oh, your deputy, of course."

"I see. Yes, of course."

"Why not? The province is yours. You could take it like a ripe plum. With a strong army to keep out the Saxons and the rest, it could become a rich land again. Yours and mine."

"But it's not mine. It's a part of Rome."

"Oh, well, if you want more you could have that too. Gaul, Hispania, and then the empire. But why bother? They're too much trouble to hold down. Magnus Maximus, your namesake, found that out. Why not stick to this island. It would be so easy. Why bother about the rest?"

I stared at him. "I don't want the purple," I said. "Neither here nor in Ravenna. As for the rest, everything that this island is, is Rome. Cut yourself off and you will be nothing, a rotting carcass without a head. We can't manage without Rome. We are Rome."

"You're wrong," he said. "We need a strong man here who can establish a strong government and run things properly. Not one of them at Eburacum can do that. Not even my father, though he often thinks—" He checked himself and said, lightly, "Oh, well, it was worth trying. It is not often that I think of anyone except myself. A pity that. Rather a waste of good intentions."

I did not trust him. "I shall bring the legion back when Stilicho lets me. Meanwhile you have the other legions and the auxiliaries. If you need activity, why not work on them? The Wall will not stay quiet forever."

He said, pettishly, "But it's such a bore working on one's own."

Before he left for the return journey to the north, he said to me from the saddle, "I will make a good report, General."

I smiled.

He leaned down toward me and said, urgently, "Don't go, sir. Maximus went and the men he took never came back. It will be the same with you whatever your intentions may be. None of you will come back and all this will have been wasted."

I walked back to my office in silence. He had not smiled when he spoke. He had meant every word he said.

A fortnight later we left Segontium for the south, and two months later we were in Gesoriacum. As I came in sight of the camp, the measured tread of the cohorts behind me, I gasped. The road leading to it was, for the last half mile, lined with men, rank upon rank of armored men on horseback, each holding spear or sword, while Quintus, mounted on a black horse with two white feet, his red cloak spread behind him, the scarlet horse-tail plume of his helmet moving in the breeze, stood motionless by the gates with his hand raised in salutation.

I rode alongside him and he greeted me as though I were an Emperor.

"You found your horses?"

"Yes, I found my horses. Oh, it is good to see you, Maximus. Come and meet the General of Belgica."

Late that night, when the camp was sleeping, we sat over a jug of wine in Quintus' tent and he told me the news.

"Stilicho arrives tomorrow," he said. "He is collecting all the troops he can lay his hands on. Apparently Italia is about to be invaded and our beloved Emperor, Honorius, has retired discreetly to Ravenna. Rumor has it that he spends his time worrying about the health of his pet chickens and wondering if the marsh air will kill them off. So much for the Emperor. Now, what of our friends at Eburacum?"

I told him, and when I came to the visit of Constans he looked puzzled. "I don't understand," he said at length. "Something must be going to happen that the young man doesn't like or he would never have applied to you."

"Yes," I said. "I think we are both well out of the island. It is not likely to be a safe place for a general."

He said, somberly, "Nowhere is safe when you are a general."

We sat in the sun outside my tent and, while Stilicho gave his orders, I watched him closely. This was the man who had helped Theodosius to defeat Maximus, my namesake, and who had married a niece of his Emperor afterward. This was the man who had warred against the Goths of the Eastern Empire, who had checked Alaric once already at Larissa and who had destroyed the power of the Moorish prince, Gildo. This was Stilicho, the last General of the West, this man who sat so still in his chair and who gave his orders with such confidence and rapidity.

"I am stripping the frontier of its troops," he said. "I am pulling out the Thirtieth Ulpia and the First Minerva from Germania Superior, as well as the Eighth Augusta from the lower province. It's a gamble, but one I must take. I need every trained man who can bear arms if I am to win against Alaric—thirty regiments at least."

"Will the frontier hold?" I asked, thinking of Maximus who had not cared.

"Long enough, perhaps." He smiled. "The Teutons beyond the Rhenus are feeling the pressure of the Huns from the east upon their backs, and they are moving west. In time they will crowd out those already settled along the banks of the river your father once guarded. But things will hold for a while. I have made treaties of peace with the more influential chiefs along the Rhenus. Gold is a good cement for a temporary friendship."

"What of the east?" asked Quintus quietly.

Stilicho frowned. "The Vandals this side of the Danubius—my people—are restless. They wish to migrate also. I have been forced to grant them fresh lands. They are, in theory, under our rule." He shrugged. "You see, I live from one expedient to the next. I have to."

"And Alaric?" I asked.

His face darkened. "Alaric is a prince of the Visigoths, a member of the family of the Balti. He failed to win a kingdom for himself in Graecia and now marches in search of another."

"What are our orders, sir?"

"You will march to Divodurum, where you will find the Army of Gaul. I will join you there."

"We are going into Italia?"

"Yes." He smiled. "I understand that it has been an ambition of yours to see Rome. Well, pray that we don't see it. Because if you do it will only be in defeat."

A week later, on a hot July day, the Twentieth Legion, six thousand strong, set out on its long march south, toward that country in the sun, whose capital I had never seen.

CHAPTER VI

Our fifth winter in Italia was a wet one, the wettest they had known in ten years. But it was also our last. In the spring of 405 Stilicho, whom I had not seen for eighteen months, came to our camp in the valley of the river Padus. It was a day of high wind and rain. The wind came from the east and it was very cold, and the wind blew in our faces and shook the tents so that even their poles seemed to vibrate like the skin of a beaten drum. He inspected my troops, drank wine with my officers, and then, late that night, held a conference with Quintus and myself inside the large leather tent that was my home.

He carried two flat parcels, wrapped in goatskin, which he put upon a spare stool very gently. He said nothing about them, however, and I did not like to ask. His beard was now quite white and there were shadows under his eyes. He moved restlessly up and down and I realized then that the frictions and jealousies of that insane court at Ravenna were bearing upon him hard. I had been there once. Honorius, I had not seen, but I had met his chancellor, and the court reeked of a eunuch's rule. I had met his sister, too. Galla Placidia was young and beautiful and she behaved like the cats that she kept in her private apartments. She purred one moment and spat the next. The gods alone knew what secret ambitions she concealed behind a wanton's smile. I did not like her.

Stilicho spoke. "I need you on the Rhenus," he said.

I was startled. I looked first at Quintus and then at him. The wind had risen and the oil lamps spluttered as their flames were touched by the icy fingers of air that streamed in through the string holes of the tent.

"The men that Magnus Maximus took into Gaul never went back. It damaged the defenses of our island for years," I said desperately. "We have been away five years."

"And have done good work. Without your aid we should not have held Alaric and forced him to withdraw to Illyricum."

"Our return was promised."

"Matters have changed."

I said to him, "I have never questioned your orders before—"

"So?"

"I must do so now."

He said, in a tired voice, "The pressure is growing along the Rhenus. I knew it would. I have had reports. The treaties I had made were only a temporary expedient. I didn't expect them to hold forever."

"But you stripped the Rhenus of its troops to defend Italia."

"It was necessary."

"And now?"

"Alaric, for the moment, is quiet. I have been making preparations to move into Illyricum and deal with him properly. I hope to move this year. But now—" He clenched and unclenched his hands. "Now, I have news that the Ostrogoths, the Vandals, and the Quadi have formed an alliance under Radagaisus and are preparing to invade Italia on their own account."

"You will need us here then."

"No. Someone with a trained force must hold the Rhenus and keep the peace, while I deal first with Radagaisus and then with Alaric."

"The peace?"

"Yes. The Alemanni are restless. I have had reports—how true, I don't know—that they are planning to migrate."

"I see. But why the Twentieth?"

"Because it is the Twentieth—your legion—and you command it."

Quintus said, curtly, "It took eighty thousand men to hold the Rhenus in the old days. Do you expect us to hold it now with only six?"

There was silence, and the wind drummed on the tent walls so that they curved inward as though pushed by a giant's hand. It was very cold and I put on my cloak. I felt chilled inside.

Stilicho said, patiently, "They held it on the east bank along the defenses they called the Limes. These were abandoned long ago. Later, it was a matter of raids and skirmishes, war bands and looting. It was easy for them to cross the river in boats and make night raids upon a bored garrison. But now it is not a question simply of war; it is a question of a migration. You cannot move a whole people across that river unless there are bridges."

"But—"

"Listen to me, please. In summer the Lower Rhenus floods its banks for miles and the whole countryside is waterlogged. That provides a natural barrier. The high Rhenus is in the mountains and the passes are few and easily defended. That only leaves the middle Rhenus, in Germania Superior, to be guarded: a distance of fifty miles or so, and there are only a handful of places along that fifty miles where a crossing can be made. A tribe migrating needs a road, and roads are few. I do not say that one legion is enough, but skillfully handled it could be."

He looked at me then and I saw the appeal in his eyes. "It must be enough, Maximus, my friend. I cannot spare any more men."

I held the center pole of the tent and felt it shake under the strain. The wind was howling through the camp and I could hear men shouting outside to each other to check the ropes and the pegs. The rain crashed upon the roof like a flight of arrows striking a shield and a spattering of drops came through a worn patch in the leather above my head. I moved away.

I looked at Quintus and he looked at me. I knew that we shared the same thoughts. We were neither of us young and we had had our share of the fighting. The exhilaration of the big command had almost gone. In its place was worry and work and sleepless nights. In five years we had had no regular camp. We were sick of living in tents, sick of hardship, sick of the dust and flies in summer, and of slush and rain in winter. We needed a rest. We had deserved one.

"For how long?" I asked. I could not refuse him.

"Give me eighteen months," he said. "That is all I ask. Hold the Rhenus for eighteen months. By then the danger will be past and I shall be able to send reinforcements. When that day comes, and I promise you it will, you may take your legion back across the water."

I said, "Are you quite sure, General, that you do not wish for a new Legate."

He smiled faintly. "Neither a new Legate nor a new Maharbal."

Quintus said, "You have told us how to defend the Rhenus in summer. But what about the winter?"

"In a very bad winter, which does not happen often, there is a chance that the Rhenus may freeze. But if it does not, the heavy rain and the melting of the snows raises the level. There will be a fast current too. In winter it is an impossible river to cross. No war chief would take such a risk."

Quintus said, steadily, "It last froze thirty-nine years ago."

Stilicho said, "Then the odds are in your favor. There is a risk, indeed, but it is a very small one."

"I will hold it," I said, and I added quietly, "If I can."

"You must hold it," he replied. "We cannot afford any more disasters. One major disaster and the Western Empire, like a cracked dam, will crumble slowly into pieces."

I said, "If that happens, my General, then be sure of one thing: neither I nor Quintus will be alive to watch it happen."

He did not say anything. He turned to the stool and picked up the wrapped parcels that he had put there. He handed one to each of us.

"They are gifts," he said. "From one friend to another. There is also a cavalry standard which I have given into the safekeeping of the camp praefectus." He smiled at Quintus. "Your present one has suffered much in my service."

Quintus undid the wrappings on his parcel first. Inside was a most beautifully curved Sarmatian sword such as are worn by their horsemen. It had a wonderfully decorated hilt and the edge was as sharp as a razor. I could see from the expression on Quintus' face that he was pleased.

"I would have given you the sword of Maharbal himself had I been able to find it," said Stilicho with a smile. "You would have deserved it."

I picked up my present in its turn. It was a short officer's sword of a style that dated it from the great days of the legions.

"I found it by chance in Rome," said Stilicho, quietly. "If you look on the blade below the hilt you will see from the inscription the name of its owner."

I looked as he had told me. Very faintly I could see the marks cut by the swordsmith at the owner's request:

J. AGRIC.LEG.XX.VAL.

He said, "I thought it fitting that one Legate of the Twentieth should carry the sword of another."

CHAPTER VII

Three months later, on a day of alternating rain and sunshine, I rode with Quintus at the head of my bodyguard into Augusta Treverorum. It was the oldest city in the Roman world, once the capital of the Praefectus Praetorio of Gaul, the seat of the Caesars of the West, and sometime residence of the imperial court. Since the reorganization of the provinces, however, it had dwindled to being only the capital of Belgica, though it was still a great center of industry and commerce. But it was not Rome, that city I had never seen.

The journey had been a depressing one. The countryside was bare and neglected. Here and there I passed a farm on ploughed land or saw in the distance a villa surrounded by vines that were still shaped and tended. More often, though, the farm was a disintegrating huddle of broken huts, and the land round it so full of weeds that you could tell at once it had not sown a crop in years. The surfaces of the roads were pitted with holes, their once carefully built edges crumbling away, and the ditches on either side so filled with dirt that, at the least shower of rain, the whole surface flooded over and made marching difficult. The towns I passed through had few people in them, and those listless and with unsmiling faces. The streets stank of refuse, and the aqueducts that should have brought water to the public baths had fallen into ruin. The peasants we passed looked gaunt and thin, their hair greasy, their clothes in tatters, and their children covered in sores. At the posting houses the horses looked out of condition and the carriages stood in need of repair. It was obvious at a glance why the imperial messenger service was often bad and unreliable; some of the animals were so out of condition that they could barely make the journey between one posting station and the next at a walk, let alone a canter. I was told by a sullen ostler that the crops had failed and that hay and oats were in short supply.

The men sang as they marched and made jokes. They were pleased to be over the mountains and out of the flat plains of Italia. Gaul was next door to the island from which many of them had come, and to be in Gaul, any part of it, was to be near home. But for me it was the land I had to defend, and upon the help of whose inhabitants I must rely if I was to fulfill the orders of a gray-faced man, now in Ticinium, collecting troops for his war against Radagaisus.

Once, I stopped a man to ask him a question about the distance to the next village, for even the milestones had been allowed to collapse onto the ground; the local officials were apparently too incompetent or lazy to attend to their duties. This man had blue eyes and fair hair and spoke Latin vilely. I learned that he was a Frank whose family had been allowed to settle west of the Rhenus and who had come south seeking work. I asked him, being curious, why he had not stayed in his own land.

He shrugged his shoulders. "We are a restless people, highborn. We like to move and to see new places."

"But why come to our lands?" I asked in exasperation.

He shrugged again. "You are Rome," he said, simply. "We all know that the Romani are rich." He wrinkled his nose. "That is what we thought," he said, gutturally. "But we come and we find we must work as before. I do not see that you can be rich if you have to work."

"You could go home," I suggested.

"I should have to work there. It would be the same." He looked at me expectantly. "Perhaps if I go on far enough I shall find those Romani who are so rich that they do not have to work."

"Perhaps," I said, and rode on.

Further on I met a great column of men marching purposefully toward us. They carried staves but no other weapons and had the look of servants, not free men. When my cavalry surrounded them they did not seem put out, but stood their ground and waited quietly till I came to them.

"And where are you going?" I asked. "You are slaves, aren't you? Look at that man, Decurion. He has the brand mark on his heel."

One of them bowed and held out a roll of parchment. "If you please, excellency, your excellency is correct. But this order will explain."

"Explain what, man?"

"We come from Remi, excellency. We were told by the Curator of the city that the noble Emperor, Honorius, has need of men for the army. If we go to Italia to take up arms we shall receive money and, when the war is over, our freedom."

I read the paper and passed it to Quintus, who did not say a word. Now I understood Stilicho's agitation that last night in my tent. Things must be desperate indeed for Honorius to make an offer that had never been made before by any Emperor of Rome in all its history, save only Marcus Aurelius.

I smiled, and my cavalry sheathed their swords as though at a command.

"And what will you do when you have gained your freedom?"

"I shall buy a small farm, excellency, and if it prospers then I shall be able to afford slaves to work it instead of my family."

I turned to watch them pass. As I did so I wondered how many of them would survive to enjoy the freedom of which they dreamed and which they, who had never known it, believed to be so wonderful.

A fortnight later we reached our destination and, leaving my legion to make camp outside the walls, I rode through the south gate into a city that was bigger and grander than any I had ever seen. I have often wondered since how it compared with Rome. The south and north gates, known familiarly to all legionaries as Romulus and Remus, were staggering in their size, over a hundred feet high as near as I could judge, their twin arches containing gates that three men, standing on each other's shoulders, could not have seen over. Built of massive white sandstone blocks they were monuments that would endure forever to the patience, industry, and technical skill of the military engineers who had made them. Each had three upper floors around a square with a courtyard between the gates, and could house a cohort without difficulty. But they were more than gates: they were fortresses in which garrisons could still hold out even should the city itself falling.

The city was crowded and we trotted down the broad street with its shops, its fountains, and its red sandstone buildings, across the forum, forcing a way through the crowds, the cattle, the oxcarts, and the traders' stalls, while the people stood back to gape at us as we passed. They looked clean and well fed and smiling and I was glad at last to be in a town whose citizens had some heart in them. But I noticed a number of young men whose right hands were covered in bloody bandages, and this struck me as curious. I wondered if there had been rioting in the city when they heard of our coming. The army was never popular when it came to a city or a town. The people bitterly resented having troops billeted on them, but we were used to that. On down the road past abandoned temples, some half pulled down, children and dogs all over the arcaded pavements, and then right, toward the basilica where the Curator and two officials of the Governor's staff were awaiting us. With them were the members of the council: the civic magistrates, the quaestors responsible for finance, one or two senators (but that was only a term now for a man of wealth and dignity), and the minor officials in charge of docks, public buildings, and the granaries, the factories and the aqueducts. In a group, to one side, formidable in their appearance, stood the Christian Bishop and his priests.

The Curator was a sharp-faced man named Artorius, about half my age, and with a nervous manner that concealed the efficiency with which he managed his own affairs. He apologized for the absence of the Praetor—the Governor—who was on a visit to the Dux Belgicae in the north. He regretted, too, the absence of the Praefectus Praetorio of Gaul who must have been detained by pressure of work at Arelate, for he had promised to be here if he could. He himself had not, however, been warned of my coming, save by the arrival of my own advance party.

I was so tired that I scarcely heard him and, when the formalities had been concluded, moved on to the north gate, Romulus, which was to be my headquarters.

"Well?" said Quintus, unlacing his helmet in the large room on the second floor that I had decided would suit me best. "We are here. When do we start?"

"Tomorrow."

"I did not like that Bishop."

"Nor I. We shall have to be careful or we may offend him."

"Pagans."

"Of course."

We both laughed.

"Must we start so soon?"

"Yes. The sooner the troops are split into their camps and at work, the better. If everything remains quiet they can be sent back to Treverorum on leave in groups."

"Don't you trust them any longer?" He glanced at me with a guarded expression on his face.

I hesitated. "They have not been paid in months and it will take time to get money out of this overtaxed province."

"We have had no trouble so far. They were glad to leave Italia."

"Yes. There, they were part of an army. Here, they are the army. Their sense of their own importance may swell if they have too much leisure."

I leaned out of the window and watched the sentries of the auxilia leaning on their spears while the customs officials checked, with unusual thoroughness, a wagon train of supplies waiting to enter the city. The merchant owner was expostulating bitterly, both at the delay and at the charges he was expected to pay.

I turned my head. "It is odd that so many were absent whom I expected to meet here."

"But their reasons were good."

"Oh, yes, excellent. Our young curator forgot to mention only what had kept the General of Gaul away."

Quintus said reprovingly, "You mean the Magister Equitum per Gallias. He will be offended if you call him less."

"They change the titles so often I find it hard to keep up with them."

"He will have a good excuse, no doubt. Perhaps he was hurt boar hunting. It is a sport I believe he is keen on."

"Perhaps."

Quintus said anxiously, "Don't look for trouble, Maximus. Except for the Governor, they are all appointments of Stilicho. We shall get all the help we need. I am certain of it."

I frowned. I said, "I hope you are right."

Later, we stood in the Cardo Maximus behind Romulus, watching the cavalry groom their horses while the stall holders watched us with resentful curiosity.

"We shall have to move them tomorrow or the good citizens of this city will never forgive us."

"Naturally."

I turned and looked at Romulus. Through these gates, like a steel sword, slipped the great military road that ran to Moguntiacum, once the supply town for the abandoned Limes on the east bank of that river I now had to defend. There at Moguntiacum the road ended on a broken bridge. And beyond were the green woods, thick and impenetrable, wet with rain in winter and heavy with scent in summer, in whose shelter lived those peoples whom we of Rome had never conquered. This was the road down which Quinotilius Varus had gone to lead three legions to defeat and death in the Teutoburg forest. It was along this road that countless

Legates had marched at the head of their men on their way to the east and the barbarian darkness beyond. It was a road to nowhere.

The next day we rode round the city on a tour of inspection. As befitting the capital of a province that once had sheltered the Emperors of Rome, it still bore the signs of great luxury and great wealth. But, even here, one could see and feel the marks of that decay which, like the rot holes in a piece of wood, were eating the heart out of city life.

The town stood on the east bank of the Mosella, a wide, lazy river that crept indolently, like a snake in the summer sunlight, between steep banks and sheer cliffs until it joined the Rhenus. Outside the west gate, which was another Romulus in size, stood the bridge, and the road beyond coiled and shifted its way to Colonia, a small garrison town on the west bank of the Rhenus. Below the bridge there were docks and warehouses where, in the old days, the Rhenus fleet that escorted the troop transports on their long voyage to Britannia would put in for repairs or lie up during the winter months when the loose ice that swept down the main river made navigation too dangerous for safety. Now, only a few merchant ships were tied up, loading their cargoes of wine, while the slim hulks of the warships rotted upon the hard till they were stripped bare by the poor in search of free timber for their fires.

"We could do with a fleet to patrol the river," I said.

"They couldn't build them in time."

"No. But we might do something with the boats belonging to our fat merchant friends down there. One of the tribunes in the third cohort was on the Saxon Shore for a time. I forget his name—Gallus, yes that's it. Get hold of him and put him in charge."

I looked at the skyline. The city was hemmed in by hills on every side. Like a rabbit in a bear pit, I thought.

"Is it all like this?"

"Yes, sir," said the decurion who had arrived the week before with the advance party. "The whole district is a mass of hills and tiny valleys. Most of them are only connected by straggling paths. Each valley has its own village. And that usually means only a cluster of timbered huts and a handful of goats."

The hills were formidable, their lower slopes lined with vine orchards. Above the vines were outcrops of rock and thick scrub and above them, higher still, the hills were thick with trees, while forests of pine covered their rounded crests like the dark caps worn by Jewish traders.

"At least we shall not die thirsty," said Quintus, carefully. He was thinking of the wine that was sold in fat barrels in the forum market and then sent by oxcart to all the distant parts of Gaul.

"I shall want the legion to parade tomorrow in the Circus Maximus for their orders. It will impress the city. We shall need more horses. Some of ours are only fit as remounts."

Quintus said, "Don't worry about that. The Treveri are famous horse breeders. I met one this morning and he asked if I needed animals. I told him I had eighteen hundred and he grinned and said, 'You have brought owls to Athens.'"

The decurion asked, "When will you see the officers?"

"At the third hour. I will give my orders then."

The city walls stood nearly twenty-five feet high and were ten feet thick. Not even our Wall—the Wall of Hadrian—had been so great. I never heard of a city in my life that had walls like this. The limestone wall, supported at intervals by guard towers (there were forty-seven of them), had been badly damaged in the great disaster of 278 and the scars still showed. Great gaps that had been torn in the original stone were now filled in with crude messes of rubble taken from damaged buildings and then hastily cemented together.

We rode round on our tour of inspection and it was obvious at once that, massive as these fortifications were, the city was too large to defend without a larger force than I could afford to leave behind. I had no intention of being trapped within its walls. On the east side was the amphitheater, sited between the walls, and capable of holding twenty thousand people at a popular show. It was regularly cursed by the Christian priests as a place of abomination but, in this respect, so I was told, their views had little effect upon the passions of the populace. In addition to the amphitheater entrance there was yet a fifth gate to the southeast, of the same size as the others and equally impressive in appearance.

On our return to Romulus we rode through the district where the majority of the temples had once stood, temples to Jupiter, to Victory, to Epona, to Diana, and to other gods, many of them local deities of whom I had never heard. Some had been pulled down and Christian churches erected in their place. Others had been abandoned and were slowly being stripped of their stone for the building of dwelling houses, while the Bishop and the priests looked on and approved. Quintus and I looked at each other but said nothing. What was there to say? The great statue of Victory in Rome itself, which had been for six hundred years the very spirit of my people, had now been cast out and it was forbidden by imperial edict to worship in the old way, each man according to his own desires, each man following his own path to the heart of his existence. But I—I was too old to change. I, who had prayed to her god that she might live. I was a part of the old Rome, and I should be dead myself if I proved a bad general. Meanwhile the new Rome still had a use for me.

I had made a map in sand upon the floor and the officers of my legion, my tribunes, and my centurions, stood round it in a half circle while I pointed with a long stick and told them what must be done.

"It is a triangle," I said. "At the apex is this city which will be our supply base and my official headquarters, though I shall use it very little. The garrison will consist of two cohorts and a cavalry squadron. You, Flavius, will be in command and the auxiliaries, too, will take their orders from you. You will provide guards for all gates and flank towers, as well as the dockyards and public buildings. Gallus, I want you to take over the dockyard. You will be in charge of our fleet. I will discuss the details with you later. I intend to establish a river patrol which can check infiltration by boats or rafts and which can land patrols on the east bank of the Rhenus if need be."

"How many ships, sir?" asked Gallus.

"Six. One for each fort."

I went on to explain what I wanted and I was conscious, all the while that they listened intently, that they were waiting for something to happen. I looked at Quintus and I knew that he knew, too. I might guess at it but Quintus was in the dark.

At the end when they had asked their questions and I had answered them, the Chief Centurion stepped forward.

"May I speak, sir?"

"Yes, Aquila. You intend to anyway."

"The men have not been paid—"

"I explained all that. Within two months at most they will have all their arrears."

"It has been a long march from Italia, sir, and now they are to go straight into camp fortification work without leave."

"They had six months, drinking themselves silly outside Ravenna and Ticinium."

"They thought they were going home, sir."

"Have they homes?" I asked. "They left wives and families in Britannia and they left wives and families in Italia. Which particular home do they want to go to now?"

He said, "Sir, you are their general. Gaul has no troops. It is a rich country. The men—we—we want you to take this province and—" He hesitated and glanced at Quintus.

Quintus said, quickly, "Well?"

The Chief Centurion looked at me and raised his arm in the beginning of the salute that is only made to an Emperor.

I threw my stick onto the floor. "No," I said. "I will not. I am too old. I have an Emperor in Ravenna, and thirty years ago I took an oath to be faithful unto death to the Senate and the people of Rome. Proclaim an Emperor now and you will have war with Honorius. How will you defend your province then with a single legion, while you have the legions of Stilicho to fight on the one hand and the Barbarians across the river on the other? You will be buried by both and will never see the gold you hope I shall bring you."

A young tribune, Marius, said angrily, "We could kill you and elect another." His eyes flickered toward Quintus, who stood as still as stone.

With a great rasping sound I drew the sword of Agricola and held it out so that the sun, through the windows behind my back, glinted on the polished steel.

"You can try," I said.

There was a long silence. I threw the sword to the Chief Centurion, who caught it awkwardly.

"Kill me," I said. "I am old enough."

They looked at each other.

I said, "But for me you would have been starving still, most of you, in your miserable villages and your foodless towns. I made soldiers of you and turned you into a legion. I did not bring you here to indulge in a crazy mutiny. Is that what you want? To die, butchered on another legion's swords. It would be easier to invite the Alemanni over the Rhenus and let them do it for you. What happened to the soldiers of Maximus? Shall I tell you? They died, too, for having just such an idea as you have now. But keep me as your general and you may be sure I shall not let one man die without necessity. I led you for five years in Italia and we were never beaten. All I ask is that you trust me. Hold this frontier till it is safe and we are sent reinforcements and I will see that you have all the gold you want. It will be gold with honor. I promise you."

They murmured their assent. They saluted me and then they left. I was their general still.

I wiped the sweat from my face then and turned to Quintus, who stood there motionless, watching me with eyes that were full of pain. Slowly the pain vanished and he smiled, though with an effort.

"And what did you want?" I asked.

He said, "I wanted what they wanted. You are a fool, Maximus. Stilicho would have let you hold the province for him. He knows you. He would trust you with his life."

I said, "He has. That is why I refused."

The next day the legion marched to the city and paraded inside the Circus Maximus, watched by a huge crowd who were duly impressed by the soldiers' smartness and efficiency. This was what I intended. The city would know now that my men were not a rabble but a body in whom they might have confidence. They needed my aid, though they might not realize it, but I also needed theirs. After the parade the legion withdrew to a new camp just outside the walls and a select number of troops only were allowed to go into the city, though strictly on military business.

But the real work of the day was still to come. That evening I held a meeting with the city council in their chamber at the basilica. They were not accustomed to working after sunset and the light of the oil lamps shone on their startled faces. The Curator gave what for him was a warm smile and said that he hoped I would continue the tradition of making Treverorum my personal headquarters. A good relationship had always existed between the officials of Belgica and Germania, and he hoped that it would continue. He paused then, smiled again, and said smoothly, "The Dux Belgicae pays us frequent visits, so you will not be lacking in military company, should you get tired of ours." There was a murmur of laughter at this, but I noticed that the faces round the table were watching me anxiously.

A magistrate with a bald head said, "We can offer you, I think, amenities quite as fine as you have enjoyed in the south. There is good sport here, if you wish it, as well as good wine."

Another said, "When you have seen your troops settled into their forts you must come to stay at my villa. I understand"—he nodded pleasantly at Quintus—"that you have an interest in horses. I breed them on a large scale. You must inspect my herds and tell me what you think of them. I should value your opinion highly."

I said, "Your offers of hospitality are kind but I shall have little time for recreation."

"I don't understand," said a voice to my right.

"It is quite simple," I said. "I am here only to re-fortify our defenses against the Alemanni; and there is a great deal to be done." I paused and turned to the Curator. I said, "I wrote to the Praefectus Praetorio before leaving Italia, informing him of my needs. So what I say should not be new to you." There was a sudden stir and Artorius frowned, his eyes never leaving my face. "I need corn for my men: five hundred bushels a week." There was an exclamation at this. "Yes," I said. "My men eat too, just like yourselves. They need two pounds of bread, a pound of meat, a pint of wine, and a tenth of a pint of oil a day. In addition, there is the question of my cavalry. I have over eighteen hundred horses to feed and they eat, between them, roughly forty-five thousand pounds of food a day. Besides this, I shall want timber to build my fortifications, wagons and ships to transport my supplies, and men who can dig ditches and be paid for it. Finally, there is the matter of remuneration for my troops."

I went on and gave details, supplied to me by Julius Optatus, of exactly how much of each I required.

There was a long silence and then the bald magistrate said politely, "I understand that you are now also Governor of Germania?"

"That is correct."

"And your responsibility is to the frontier?"

"Yes."

"Surely then, your administrative problems are ones that can be settled within your own province? They are nothing to do with us."

"Quite right," muttered a red-nosed man whom I could not identify.

I said, "You know very well that Germania is a military zone; and a province in name only. It is, I believe, a poor area."

He shrugged. "There is trade across the river with the Alemanni. The customs revenue is in your hands." He smiled slyly.

The tribune in charge of the granaries gave him a curious look and said hurriedly, "It is true there is trade but it is variable."

I said, "I cannot rely on that. I am a soldier, not a merchant. Besides, the trade, such as it is, will cease when I close the frontier." There was a sudden click and a clerk blushed and bent to pick up his stylus. It had snapped in his hands. I heard the heavy breathing around me. It was very warm, and there were beads of sweat on Artorius' face.

One of the senators said, incredulously, "You are going to close the frontier?"

"Yes. I have information that the tribes across the river are on the move. That is what I am here to prevent. There is to be no repetition of their last invasion of Gaul."

The Bishop leaned forward, his long face yellow in the light. "Can you be certain of this?"

"Quite certain, my lord Bishop. That is why I need the utmost cooperation."

The Curator looked at me and then at his colleagues.

He said, nervously, "You ask what I cannot give. Besides, the Praefectus Praetorio of Gaul is responsible for the granaries, not I."

"They can be opened," I said.

The tribune in charge said, plaintively, "I cannot release grain without a warrant bearing the Praefectus' signature."

I said, patiently, "Here is a commission, signed by the Emperor, appointing me Dux Moguntiacensis. That should be sufficient."

Artorius said icily, "General, the grain is already allocated. It will mean raising the taxes. Only the Praefectus can do that. Besides, this province has paid the state its share for this year. The burden would be unjust. We are not as wealthy as we appear."

I said, "You are, pardon me, more wealthy than you appear. Your merchants do great business. If you are rich it is because you have taxed even the sweat from the bodies of your slaves. If you feel poor it is because the peasants have been taxed of their blood and have run away rather than work your farms and your land."

The Bishop said, "The people are poor, as you say, but is it not better to live at peace in poverty than grow rich in war?"

I said, "You may count yourself lucky that this city was sacked by the Barbarians before you came here. Most of its inhabitants had to flee—those who were not killed—and they saved nothing but their lives. I need money and help so that it may not happen again."

The Bishop said smoothly, "Exile is no evil for him who believes the whole world to be but a single house."

"Go then to the east bank of the Rhenus and you will soon find out what your relatives are like."

"They are Barbarians, perhaps, in that they do not enjoy the benefits that Rome confers." The Bishop spoke as though to a congregation in one of his churches. "But still they are Christians, many of them, even though, alas, their views are tainted by the Arian creed. Still, I console myself with the thought that their hearts are in the right place even if their heads are wrong."

Pushing my hair back off my forehead in exasperation I saw the Bishop's eyes narrow suddenly.

I said, "I doubt if it is much consolation for one Christian to be killed by another."

The Bishop raised his voice as though appealing to a multitude. "They at least are not pagans," he cried. "They do not worship false gods."

Artorius said anxiously, "Is the situation really so dangerous? We have had no trouble these last few years."

"Yes, it is," I said. "This frontier has always given trouble. The great Constantine—your Constantine, Bishop—who built this palace in which we sit, fought a campaign to defend this city and Gaul against these tribes. And when I was a child these same tribes broke through again and there were thirteen years of bloodshed, pillage, and rape before order was restored by Julian and Valentinian. When we had troops we had peace."

Artorius said, "But I had no word of your coming from the Praetor. Is not that—unusual?"

I said, startled, "I know nothing of the Governor but I wrote to the Praefectus Praetorio before I left Italia. I know that communications in Gaul can be slow, but they cannot be that bad."

He said stubbornly, "I received no official letter of any kind. Surely if the matter were as urgent as you make out—"

The insolence in his voice died with the words, upon the look I gave him. I said in a loud voice, "The Praefectus Praetorio of Gaul is happy in that his government sits at Arelate. It would seem that those who sleep in the sun seldom worry about those who shiver in colder climates."

A senator with a brown, narrow face said sharply, "If I understand you aright, you propose to commandeer our ships. It is disgraceful."

Artorius said hastily, "Of course, I and my department are at your service. But as for money—really!"

I hit the table with my clenched fist. "Enough of this. It is for you to arrange matters with the praefectus—not I. Though I will do it over your head if you prefer it." The Curator gasped at this. "Time is short and I cannot wrangle all night. If you cannot raise the money, and I do not advise that you tax your wretched peasants further, then sell the ornaments, the gold, and the silver in your eight churches and in your fine cathedral, for a start."

The Bishop glared at me. "That would be sacrilege. Only a pagan would suggest such a thing."

"I am a pagan, as you term me."

"I know."

I said, "If I do not get what I ask I shall take over this city and rule it under martial law in the name of Honorius and Stilicho, his general."

I picked up a silver cup that stood on the table between us. "I think it better to save lives," I said, "than the lifeless."

"Thief!"

I swung round on the Bishop in a rage. "I would not advise you to hold what you cannot defend."

"It is robbery," he spluttered.

"It is your god who approves of poverty and abhors wealth—not mine."

I left the room with his cries of sacrilege echoing about me. I had not expected their cooperation, but their bitter, blind stubbornness and obstinacy in the face of danger made me feel sick. Their indifference and their fatalism had about it a hint of madness. I had met it in Britannia and in Italia—this blind refusal to face facts and to accept the need for change in a time of change. It was not new to me. If the empire were to die it would be because the people in it who held posts of responsibility no longer cared. They could not govern themselves and they had lost the confidence to govern others.

I found myself in the great hall that was the throne room. I called out and a servant came and lit the oil lamps. It was immense, the walls plastered and painted with faded designs which I found difficult to make out by the flicker of the yellow lamps. Galleries of wood ran round the walls, beneath windows whose outlines I could only just see in the half darkness. The floor on which my nailed sandals rasped was of marble, intricately patterned in black and white, and with glass mosaics that gave off a wonderful golden color in the throne hall at the end.

I walked toward it, saw the raised dais and the great chair upon it that not even the Bishop had dared to take for the adornment of his faith. In this chair, in turn, they had sat, those Emperors of Rome who had eaten and slept and worked in this city, and who had shouldered the burden that now lay upon my shoulders. Their ghosts came crowding in upon me out of the dark: the great Constantine, who had created the new Rome; Julian, the ambitious Caesar of the West; Valentinian, the soldier-Emperor, who never in his life conceded a foot of Roman soil to Barbarian rule; Constantius Chlorus, who defeated Allectus the usurper of my island.... They had fought the Barbarians all their lives and strengthened Rome's frontiers, protecting always those who could build from the insensate fury of those who could only steal and destroy.

I mounted the dais and touched the arms of that golden throne hoping, perhaps, that it might transmit to me something of the power and the personality of those friendly ghosts whose faces, in my imagination, I could almost see. The vastness of the hall seemed overwhelming and I was conscious of a strange stillness and a quietness and peace such as I had never known. All these years the memory of Julian had haunted the jagged edges of my thoughts and he had stood, pale and reproachful, behind the faces of everyone to whom I spoke. The pain was always there. . . .

The flames from the oil lamps stood upright and still and the darkness lifted a little and I could see a young man with a helmet upon his head and a sword in his hand. And behind was the black shadow of a bull. The man's face I could not see for it was in the shadows, but we looked at each other for a long time and I knew then that I was in the presence of my mystery.

"In the name of the Great Bull give me strength," I cried, and my voice crashed in echoes round the walls and the high vault of the roof until it died.

In spite of the hypocaust it was very cold now, and the oil lamps spluttered as drafts of air played about the walls. The hall no longer seemed as light and down at the far end I could see two figures, standing motionless among the shadows. They moved forward and I saw then that they were the Bishop and Quintus.

The Bishop said, "Do you aspire to the throne also, like Victorinus?"

I walked down the hall and passed him in silence. To him I would not speak. Quintus turned and followed me in puzzled silence.

Out in the street, on our return to Romulus, with the torches flaring in the summer night and the reassuring tramp of my guard about me, we looked at each other.

He said, "You went into that room of ghosts to ask a question. I see from your face that something happened. What, I will not ask. But this I do ask—did you receive an answer?"

"Yes," I said. "It was not the answer I wanted, but that in itself is of no importance."

"What will you do?" he said.

"I shall do what Stilicho asked. Afterward, if the spirits are kind, I shall take over the province in the name of Honorius, not for myself, but for Rome."

"Which province?" he asked.

"I will tell you that when the time comes."

The duty centurion showed the Curator into my office, and he sat down cautiously upon a stool facing the table at which I sat.

"Will you drink with me?" I said. He nodded and I poured him a cup. He watched curiously while I poured the libation. He said, "I have never seen a man do that before." He looked at me steadily. "You know it is against the law?"

"Yes. Of course, this is a great center of your religion. Do I offend you? I hope not."

"It is wrong."

"Is it? That is a matter we might debate all night. Come, if I can tolerate your faith I am sure that you can learn to tolerate mine."

He did not smile. He said, "Do you really mean to close the frontier?"

"I do."

"There is a silver mine at Aquae Mattiacae opposite Moguntiacum. It used to be worked by the government. But that was before I was born. Now the Alemanni use it. They set a high value on silver and they exchange it for goods that we are willing to sell them. Many of our merchants do a considerable trade across the river in pottery and glass and clothes and—other things." He paused and then said pleadingly, "Many people will be upset if this trade is stopped."

"I cannot help that."

"You will not change your mind?"

"No."

He said enviously, "You must be a very wealthy man."

"I am not. But what has that to do with it?"

"Forgive me, but—if you are not—then I do not understand...." He trailed off awkwardly into silence.

"I am sorry, I do not follow you."

He said hesitantly, "Few imperial posts pay well. It has always been accepted custom that—well, there are ways in which one can add to one's salary. There are certain perquisites, of course. This matter of closing the frontier is, surely, properly a matter for disputation before an appointed commission. You, as Governor, have judicial powers. Those with vested interests would appear before you to plead their case. Such a matter would—would provide suitable—opportunities—for—for a settlement of some kind."

I remained silent.

He said, "I—I thought that, perhaps, was what you had in mind." He looked at me hopefully.

I said, "I understand quite clearly what you are saying. I would not presume to suggest that you are dropping hints on behalf of others. That would be ungenerous." I paused. I said, "It is kind of you to take such a close interest in my welfare but it is quite unnecessary."

"Then you really meant what you said?"

I nodded. "In administrative circles, I believe, there is a saying that good Governors die poor. I shall do my best, I promise you, to live up to it."

He said coldly, "Then if you really intend to close the frontier I shall have to report the matter to the Praefectus. It is my duty."

"I shall not stop you. Tell me, Artorius, is that why the council was upset when we had that meeting? They have interests themselves, perhaps."

He said stiffly, "A civic council is naturally concerned about trade. It is a part of their responsibility."

"Naturally."

He drank his wine and made a face as he did so.

I smiled. I said, "I am sorry if the wine is not up to your standard. As for myself—I have drunk tavern wine all my life."

He said, "What did you wish to see me about then, if not the frontier?"

"A number of matters. I shall need a great deal in the way of supplies from the government factories here. My quartermaster will give your department the details. I shall need them quickly. The work must be speeded up. Five years ago when I needed helmets for my men I was told that each worker could only make four in a month. I want six."

"It is too many."

"In Antiochia they can make six each in thirty days, and decorate them too. We must do the same."

He made a note on a wax tablet. "I will see what I can do."

"Then there is the matter of recruits. A good number of my men are due to retire shortly. I need more troops. I must have them. I want an order out conscripting all sons of soldiers and veterans who are fit. They are to report to the garrison commander here who will train them." He looked startled at this. He said, "I will write to the Praefectus Praetorio for authority. Is that all?"

"No, there is the question of pay for my troops."

He said, "It is customary for field troops to be paid in kind. They get bounty payments from time to time but, normally, they rely on their rations."

"Thank you for telling me. But my men are not part of the field army now. They are frontier troops and these are paid only in money. They are owed half a year's pay as it is. I imagine the provincial treasury can arrange matters."

He frowned. "I shall need a warrant from the Praefectus."

"Of course." I paused and then raised my voice. "I need the money urgently."

"But surely your men will have little to spend their money on in a frontier fort?"

"That is not the point. It is a matter of morale and confidence."

"I will inform the Praefectus."

"There is a treasury here."

"Yes, but it is not mine to touch. It belongs to the provincial government and even the Governor would need—"

"I know—permission from the Praefectus." I looked at him and sighed. He was the kind of man who would always do his duty by the book. He had no initiative, no imagination, no understanding. It was hard to blame him. He was, after all, only a civil servant.

CHAPTER VIII

The rising sun was just touching the twin towers of Romulus when the legion left the city and marched toward Moguntiacum at the regulation pace that would carry us twenty miles in five hours in good weather. On our second day, thirty miles out, in the midst of a plain of thick grass, with the men sweating under the hot sun, we reached the point where the road forked into two. The left hand led to Confluentes, the furthest fort downriver that I intended to hold. To this I assigned a cohort and an ala. This road also led to Salisio and Boudobrigo, higher upriver, and to these I had ordered a mixed garrison of two centuries of infantry and a squadron of cavalry. Then, with the column of the legion shrunk in length, we pushed on to Bingium, which we reached on the third day. Here we halted for twenty-four hours while I inspected the camp and made a short reconnaissance down the road that led to Boudobrigo. At Bingium the river Nava joined the Rhenus, and the fort was protected on two sides by water with hills to the back of it. From the camp as you looked downriver great cliffs of rock towered high on the left bank, making an impregnable barrier against those who might wish to cross from the east. The cliffs continued along the south bank of the stream and it was at the foot of these that the road ran till it joined the bridge leading to the camp. If Bingium were captured, those at Moguntiacum would find their retreat cut off, it being an easy matter then for the enemy to break the bridge while at the same time commanding the road to Augusta Treverorum. From there the way into Gaul would lie open. Here I left another mixed cohort under the charge of a senior tribune while the diminished legion continued its march to its headquarters at Moguntiacum, which was reached on the fifth day.

Moguntiacum had once been the capital of Germania Superior but that was in the great days of our power when the province had possessed a civil as well as a military administration, and the legions held the east bank in strength. On the rising ground behind the town was the old camp. It had been built to hold two legions, but that was in the time of Domitian. It was abandoned later when the town was fortified, and the garrison now lived in huts on the city side of the river wall. The town had grown up along the river and had once been a place of some splendor. It boasted a number of wide streets, still lined with open-fronted shops, and there was a forum, a Christian church, a ruined theater, innumerable abandoned temples, and a carved column to Jupiter, now covered with grime. Outside the town walls, along the riverbank, there was a string of wooden huts, some of which hung over the water on stilts and which were occupied by the very poor. A market fair was held occasionally but trade was lethargic, for the town had so often been sacked by raiders from the east that it was no longer a place in which the energetic and the ambitious wished to stay if they could move elsewhere. Those who remained were a mixed population of Franks, Burgundians, and Alemanni whose blood was inextricably mixed by the confusion of marriage with the descendants of legionary veterans who had come from Hispania, Pannonia, Illyricum, and all the parts of the empire. The harbor lay a little way downriver outside the protection of the town walls, and around it was a small settlement, occupied mainly by veterans and their families.

The Twentieth had been stationed at Novaesium in the time of Claudius. It was from there that they had been sent to Britannia, so their return to the Rhenus was, in a sense, a homecoming; though the only part of the legion that had ever before seen this river was the bronze Eagle that had been given us by the first Emperor of Rome.

I ordered Aquila to pitch camp in the ruins of the old fort for the night and rode with a handful of officers on an inspection of the town. Barbatio, the Praefectus of the Auxiliaries, was expecting me. He was a heavy young man of about thirty, already running to fat and as obviously out of condition mentally as he was physically. He looked frightened when he spoke to me, and he had cause. His cohort was a rabble of unshaven, scruffy-looking individuals who appeared never to have done any drill in their lives. Their quarters were crammed with their wives, their children, and their cattle, and the remaining contents of their huts seemed to suggest that the majority spent the greater portion of their time in mercantile activities.

In answer to my questions he told me, hesitantly, that there was little traffic across the river in boats because the current was difficult (this at least was true) and the Alemanni hostile, but traders on their way to Borbetomagus, the last and highest of the forts to which I was to send a cohort, would pass through the town from time to time.

It all reminded me strongly of Corstopitum as I had last seen it. It was very depressing.

"The old camp is too far back," I said to Quintus. "I want another built, here on the bank to the left of the bridge. My men are going to have to kill wet Barbarians, not dry ones."

He said cautiously, "That will mean taking over a part of the town. We shall be popular."

"They will get used to it. I want the ground cleared north of the road between the present camp and the river. We shall need, approximately, six acres. The cavalry—the majority of them anyway—will have to be housed on the old camp site."

The river at this point was about seven hundred and fifty yards across and it flowed more swiftly than any river I had ever seen. In the middle there were two long narrow islands, as flat as sword blades, and the lower end of the northern one was submerged in summer. They were thickly wooded and uninhabited, providing only a refuge for occasional outlaws from the communities on both banks. A third island, also long and thin, passed close to the west bank and sheltered the harbor from the force of the main channel. From the town walls we could see the broken bridge that jutted out forlornly over the water as far as the third pile. "What about that?" said Quintus. "Do we get it mended?"

I shook my head. "No."

Across the river lay the ruins of the bridge-head camp that had once protected the settlement and the villas that had sprung up round the baths at Aquae Mattiacae. My father, I remembered, had always sworn that it was the hot springs there that had cured the injury done to his leg by an Aleman spear when he was a young man. And even in his later years he always insisted that its waters would have been better for his rheumatism than the baths at Aquae Sulis. The camp had been abandoned, finally, when the Alemanni sacked Moguntiacum in the year that my Theodosius came to our aid. It was unlikely that anything was left of the baths or the settlement now.

Quintus said stubbornly, "We could repair it. A useful thing, I would suggest, to have a toehold on the east side."

I screwed up my eyes against the glare. "I'll think about that one," I said. "The important thing is to get ourselves established here first."

That first evening I walked out through the river gate and down the bank to where the bridge stood. I walked out onto the broken planks and stared at the remaining piles, stretched out to the further shore, stepping-stones for some giant in a child's story. Patches of mist drifted above the swirling water. I threw a stick into the current and was amazed at the speed with which it was taken away. Barbatio explained to me that a little way upstream from the bridge the river Moenus flowed into the Rhenus. "That's the division, sir, between the Alemanni and the Burgundians. The Burgundians' western frontier lies between here and Confluentes, where the Franks take over."

"Are their frontiers firm ones?"

"No, not really, sir. It depends who is on top at the moment."

"Well, what's the position now?"

"You see those escarpments, sir, downriver on the east bank. Well, all the country behind that, extending from this town to Bingium, is disputed. At the moment it's held by a Frankish clan who guard the right bank for us in return for subsidies."

"You mean Roman silver; and they stay loyal just so long as the bribe is sufficiently heavy?"

He looked startled. "Yes, sir."

It was getting cold now and I shivered, staring hard at the east bank. That bank there—on that my father had once walked in civilian dress and bearing no arms. But I, if I walked on it, would risk death as an enemy. In my father's time we had owned it with as much certainty and as little doubt as we had the crumbling city of which I was now Governor.

Quintus twisted the bracelet on his wrist and said, "This place is like the end of the world." It was as though he were thinking my thoughts.

"Yes," I said. "It is—the end of our world."

He said, moodily, "I still think it would be a good thing to repair this bridge and take back that camp on the further bank. It would give us a fine start if we should need to take the offensive."

Barbatio said diffidently, "The Alemanni, sir, would see that as an act of war. General Stilicho, by his terms, gave them absolute rights over the east bank."

"In that case there's no point in provoking them without cause."

Quintus turned to the Praefectus. "Have you seen the old camp? Can it be repaired easily?"

Barbatio said hastily, "Yes, sir, though half the walls have been pulled down and the huts destroyed. They did the same to the villas."

"Who burned the bridge?"

"That was done many years ago, sir, after Rando sacked the town. It was he who destroyed the cathedral."

"Who is Rando?"

"He was a prince of the Alemanni then. He is now their king." There was a note of enthusiasm in his voice that had been lacking before. I turned to him and said, "Have you had dealings with him?"

He licked his lips and the sweat rolled down the sides of the leather chin straps of his helmet. "Come on, man, tell me."

"Yes, sir," he muttered.

"Slaves, I suppose."

He nodded.

I said to Quintus, "There isn't a tribune of frontier troops anywhere in the Empire who doesn't trade in slaves. They're more interested in that than in their military duties."

Barbatio flushed. He said, defensively, "We get paid so little. They give it to us in food and supplies instead, but half the time the rations are short. We get cheated by everyone."

"You should receive money," I said sharply.

"That's what I mean, sir."

"I know all about that. I have been on a frontier too. Tell me, have you heard of the new law which allows you seven days' rations a year from your men which you can commute for silver?"

"Yes, sir."

"And have taken advantage of it, no doubt."

He nodded again, his eyes shifting from face to face.

"Stick to the law, then." I stared at him hard. "You will have little time for being a slave dealer from now on. You will be too busy being a soldier. Your unit is in a disgusting state. Mend it quickly or I will have a new commander appointed."

He saluted and started to back away.

"Don't go yet. There is another matter I want explained. I thought your cohort's strength was five hundred, but you've only two hundred, in fact. Why?"

He said, "We had sickness, sir. Some died, others have gone on pension recently and—and there are a number on leave." He spoke confidently.

I said, "I saw your ration statements at the imperial granary. You have been drawing food for five hundred with regularity for the last four years."

"Well, sir, I—my quartermaster always asks for the rations of—of the men on leave. It is customary." He sounded aggrieved now, as though I did not understand something that was obviously a matter of simple common sense both to him and to his quartermaster.

"Stop lying. You haven't had three hundred men on leave, now or at any time. You've been indenting for food for men who are dead or who were pensioned off years ago. Is that not so?"

He did not say anything. He opened and shut his mouth like a fish.

"Answer me," I said. "What was the cohort's strength when you took over. I want the truth."

He rolled his eyes as though in prayer. Then he licked his lips. "One hundred and eighty," he whispered.

I prodded him in the chest with my stick. "I could have you broken for this. You've recruited twenty men in four years. That must have been hard work."

"Everyone does it," he muttered.

I said, "I am not everyone. Remember that from now on."

When he had gone, Quintus said, "You were a little hard on him, Maximus. The poor devil's been rotting here or in places like this for years."

I said, "How many years were we on the Wall? And we never rotted."

"Didn't we?" he said. "I am not so sure."

I looked at him. His face had gone pale and he looked sick and unhappy.

"Quintus." I touched him on the arm. "Don't look like that. Are you all right?"

He nodded silently and I wondered if he was thinking of his home in Hispania, which he had not seen in thirty years.

"Don't worry about Barbatio," I said. "He'll prove a good soldier from now on. I'll give you twenty denarii if he hasn't shown an improvement by the end of a month."

Quintus smiled. "Done," he said.

I won my bet and it was Barbatio who acted as a guide whenever I wished to explore the countryside. In the plain around Moguntiacum the Franks and Burgundians who had settled in the district made some effort to develop the land they had been allowed to annex by agreement. In places the woods had been cut back and clearings made where straggling villages of smoky huts sprang up, strongly fortified by stockades of heavy pine. Strips of land outside were cultivated and each village had its cattle, its goats, its dogs, and its few horses. The people were large, cheerful, and good-looking with their flaxen hair and blue eyes. They drank a great deal of beer and fights between them were frequent, though seldom over women.

These people I liked though I had difficulty in understanding their speech, and their guttural Latin was atrocious; but I did not trust them and the sentries on the town gates had instructions to admit no one bearing arms.

It was nearly midsummer now and I thought that the dangerous time would be in the early autumn when the harvest was gathered. It was then that the tribes would be restless and eager to look for plunder if their own food supplies for the winter seemed to be insufficient. Barbatio discounted Stilicho's suggestion that the Alemanni had thoughts of a migration, and I was inclined to agree with him. Those whom I met were friendly enough and my spies brought back little information that was of value. But still I had to be careful and before the autumn came there remained a great deal to be done.

At all the garrison centers the troops were kept busy, repairing and fortifying their camps. I gave instructions that all were to be protected by palisades of earth and timber, with square towers at the corners, each strong enough to mount a ballista. Around each camp protecting ditches were dug while traps were prepared in the ground outside each gate. Signal towers, large enough to hold a section of ten men, were erected on the roads linking each camp with the next, each guarded also by a palisade and a ditch. Another line of towers was built along the road between Bingium and Treverorum. In time I hoped to have these manned by auxiliaries so as to relieve the legionaries for more important work.

It was within the area of Moguntiacum, however, that the most important work was done. Between the river wall and the north wall a huge area was cleared, large enough to hold two cohorts and an ala of cavalry, and walled off again from the rest of the town, which was too large to defend with the few men at my command. The huts were cleared from the waterfront and a triple row of ditches dug along the front of the east wall. Each ditch was V-shaped, the outer face being at an angle of forty-five degrees. The outer face was lined with timber to prevent filling in, while the bottom of the ditches, fifteen feet deep, were planted with pointed stakes. Between the two outer ditches was a flat space, forty feet wide, and between the middle and inner ditch a space of ten feet. The distance from the fighting platform on the fort wall was ninety feet to the outer edge of the furthest ditch: the length to which our soldiers could throw a spear with lethal accuracy. The main killing area, however, was the forty feet between the two outer ditches. These ditches would break up any attack while there were still men to stand on the walls and hurl missiles.

To the left of the town and just to the east of the Bingium road, at a point opposite the northern end of the southern island, I had three small camps built, each to hold a century. The walls were of turf and timber and the whole was protected again by the usual ditches. The old camp, too, behind the town, was put into repair as a barracks for the horses.

While this work was going on, cavalry patrols quartered the countryside and the first ship of our fleet, a converted merchant vessel, made a hesitant appearance on the river, armed with ballistae and manned by archers.

I went aboard at Bingium and found an anxious Gallus on the poop, having a heated argument with the Master.

He saluted and said gloomily, "The rowers aren't up to much. None of them have ever been on the water before."

The Master said something under his breath.

"We made very slow time coming up. She answers sluggishly to the river."

The Master tightened his mouth and said nothing.

He took the ship up the Rhenus, hugging the right bank, and it was as Gallus said. We found the greatest difficulty in altering course in midstream. She would only turn in an arc that took her nearly from one bank to the other, and ran into trouble the moment she hit the heavy water. Broadside on to the full force of the current she lost way dangerously and drifted badly, so that it was all the rowers could do to get control over her again.

"She is too big for the work you want from her," said the Master wearily. "I could have told you this at the start but the tribune would not have it so."

Gallus said, "I am afraid he is right."

"What is her length?"

"Two hundred and seventy feet."

"What length should she be for this kind of work?"

The Master hesitated. "One hundred and twenty feet at the outside, but much narrower in the beam. The ballistae you have mounted have upset her balance and the oar banks are not distributed right. Besides, she takes too large a crew. At this rate we shall not find enough oarsmen for the remaining ships."

Gallus said bitterly, "If we built a smaller boat we should only get one catapult in the bows."

"That is better than nothing. I must have a ship that can turn in the space of a denarius."

We went downstream again toward Bingium and found that the only effective way we could turn quickly was to throw out the anchor and, when she had gripped hard, let the current swing her round. The force of the river was tremendous and I was glad to be rowed ashore and to stand on firm ground again.

"Do what you can," I said. "I shall need ships by the time the harvest is cut."

News came from the outer world infrequently. There was an early letter from Gallus, telling me that he was not happy about the plans for the new warships submitted by the Master and that there was a shortage of carpenters owing to an outbreak of fever in the city; that the Curator had complained to his superiors at Arelate about the taxes; and that the Bishop had written to the Emperor complaining about me. He added, in a postscript, however, that the money had been made available and that we need not worry about a shortage of unskilled labor, the peasants being quite willing to work for the price of a meal a day for themselves and their families.

Another letter came, this time from Arelate, but it was full of polite evasions, veiled threats, meaningless assurances, and hollow sincerities, the whole so wrapped in the stilted language of the civil administration as to rob the contents of any value whatsoever. I took no notice of it.

Messages came in from the various forts. Confluentes reported a willingness from the Frankish settlers to serve as auxiliaries and that their defenses were completed, their quota of signal towers finished. Boudobrigo reported hostility among the tribesmen in the district and said that planned accidents had wrecked a half-completed tower, while a three-man patrol had been killed in the woods, but by whom no one knew. At Bingium all was quiet, but there was considerable movement on the east bank and everything that they did was spied upon. Their commandant added, naively, that he trusted no one save his own troops, though the new auxiliaries were behaving well. From Borbetomagus the cohort tribune wrote that tribesmen were infiltrating across the river in small boats, and that two attacks had been made on the supply trains that we had sent him. Patrols, landed on the east bank, however, had found the countryside apparently deserted and had returned safely with unsheathed swords.

Walking through the streets one morning my eye was caught by a half-naked man sitting dejectedly in a pen by the slave market. He was dark skinned and wore round his neck a leather thong with a disc on it. His wrists were chained in front of him, which was unusual except in newly made slaves, and he was making patterns in the dust with his fingers. He was about my own age.

"Just a moment," I said to Barbatio. "I want a word with this man. Find the dealer and have him brought out to me."

The man was filthy; his one garment stank and I could see the movement of things in his hair. I put my stick under his chin and forced him to look at me. "What is your name?"

"Fredbal," he muttered sullenly.

"Where did you get that disc on your neck?"

"It is mine."

"Is it? Give it to me."

Barbatio cut the thong and I took it between my fingers. It was a lead identity disc such as our soldiers always wore.

"Are you a Frank?"

"Yes."

"Where did you get this? In a fight with our people, I suppose."

He shook his head violently. "No. It's mine."

"You're lying."

He stared at me and the sudden anger vanished, to be replaced by a look of incredible misery. The change was astonishing.

"Wait a minute. Barbatio, look at his ankle."

The tribune did so.

"Is he branded?"

"Yes, sir."

I said, "Then you were in our army. A deserter, I suppose?"

He looked at me gloomily, and said in bad Latin, "No—sir. I was—an optio in the auxiliaries here at Moguntiacum. I was taken prisoner when the Alemanni raided the town." He dropped his eyes. "I was only a boy at the time." He added, in a low voice, "I have been a slave ever since. That was a long time ago."

I turned to Barbatio. "Thirty years," I said. "In the name of the gods! Thirty years."

Barbatio, his face flushed, said, "All the men in this pen have been sold, sir. To a merchant from Treverorum."

"Did you tell the dealer you were a Roman citizen?"

Fredbal shrugged his shoulders. "It never makes any difference. They sell you just the same."

"How do you know that?"

He said, "I used to listen to—to my master talking. He was an Aleman. People never care what they say in front of slaves. It's a common thing. They all do it. There's a big trade in the likes of us across the river."

Barbatio said, "Yes, that's true, sir."

I said savagely, "You, certainly, should know that. Have him brought up to the camp. Get the records looked up and check his story. If it's true then we can find a use for him—as a free man."

Barbatio said in a shocked voice, "There will be complaints. This is a common practice."

"You mean it was. If the merchant complains, arrest him. It is an offense to sell a free citizen in his own land. And get the magistrates and have the market closed at once."

"But, sir, he's one of a lot already bought and sold." The tribune added desperately, "They've been purchased for work on one of the new churches in Treverorum. The merchant told me."

"You heard my orders."

"But, sir, the Bishop—the Praefectus—"

"I am the governor here."

"Yes, sir." He saluted and hurried off.

I turned and walked back toward the camp, the man following me like a dog.

Thirty years, I thought He kept that disc for thirty years in hope. And then he was bought and sold by his own people to work for the church. O, Mithras, you would not ask that of any man.

At last came the news for which I had been waiting; first a rumor only of a great victory in Italia, brought by a wine merchant returning from Mediolanum; and then a letter, containing the facts and the details: a letter from Stilicho himself.

Radagaisus had been beaten. He had tried to besiege Florentia, had been besieged in his turn by Stilicho, had tried to fight his way out, and had been captured and executed. More than a third of his men, Suevi, Vandals, Alans, and Burgundians, had died beneath the walls of the city. The remainder had retreated north into the country of the Alemanni.

At the end Stilicho wrote: "We took so many prisoners that we glutted the market and, at the end, we were selling them at only one solidus a head, which was absurd. Many chose to enlist in our forces, however, and because of this I had hoped to return a part of my army to help you gather grapes in Gaul; but the news from Illyricum forbids this, unhappily, for the moment. From the complaints I have received about you from those close to the Emperor I judge that you are fulfilling my expectations to the uttermost. Alaric is, as before, the problem that I have to solve. To quiet his ambitions we have been compelled to appoint him to a high office in the imperial service, but the fact remains that those who follow him represent too large a lump for the stomach of the empire to digest in comfort. I intend to move into Illyricum next spring with all the forces I can muster, but I must not alarm Alaric as to the nature of my intentions toward him. This time a final settlement cannot be avoided. And I have affairs to smooth over in Dacia and Macedonia that can no longer be delayed. I must, as they used to say, hasten slowly.

"This means, my dear friend, that I must ask you to hold Germania Superior for another twelve months. Give me this time, I pray you, and all will yet be well. I have ruled this empire, who am no Emperor, for ten years now, and I shall continue to rule it until I die. You may believe in my judgment as I believe in yours. Serena sends her greetings as I do to you both."

I showed this to Quintus and he said, "Shall we ever get relief? I think they will only send more troops when we ourselves are in trouble. And then it will be too late."

"That is what I am afraid of," I said.

CHAPTER IX

Two days later I received a visit from Guntiarus, the Burgundian King, who crossed the river to meet me at Bingium by arrangement. He was short and swarthy and he reminded me strongly of a kestrel about to fly. But he was an old kestrel and I judged that he was fiercer in looks than in performance. Like all his people he greased his hair, which he wore down to the nape of his neck, and, it being a hot day, I could smell him before he came. Most of our auxiliaries were Burgundians and there had long been a standing feud between them and the Alemanni on account of a dispute over some salt springs which both tribes claimed as their own. I prayed to Mithras, unworthy though my prayer was, that the dispute might continue.

I showed him round the camp and, though he said little, he was properly impressed.

"This is only my advance guard," I said. "Soon I shall have a great army. Rome does not forget its provinces when they need help."

"Do you need help?" he asked shrewdly.

"No," I lied. "But I can allow no more of your people across this river. That is what I wish to tell you."

He looked troubled. He said, "Things have changed since Stilicho and I held hands over the salt. My people have increased in number and we have had bad harvests. The land is too poor to support so many."

"Then you must spend more time in growing crops, less time in breeding horses."

"It is not the same."

"Rome can help with silver, if you are not too proud to accept the gift." I paused and he blinked at me. "We would not wish your children to starve."

He hesitated. "I am still a king in my own land," he muttered.

"That is understood. And as a king in your own land you would hold it against all who tried to take it from you." I paused again and looked at a squad of marching men. "My soldiers defend the allies of Rome as well as the citizens of Gaul."

He put his knuckles to his mouth. "The Alemanni—"

"Are not as strong as they would have others believe," I said.

Still he hesitated.

"Silver," I said. "But no land."

He said grudgingly, "My people are content with what they have."

I did not smile.

That night we feasted him and he became very drunk. "I have fine daughters," he said. "They are young and strong and pleasing. I will send you one and she shall be your wife as a sign that we are friends."

"You do me great honor," I said.

He left next morning, dripping with water that his servants had flung over him to get rid of his headache. I hoped that he would forget his promise. I did not want another wife.

Later I crossed the river at Bingium with a large escort and rode into the dark green hills that lay between the Burgundians and the desolate plain that belonged to the Alemanni. In a thick glade, full of dark shadows and shifting sunlight, we suddenly found ourselves surrounded by armed men. I raised my hands to warn my men to keep theirs low on their saddles. Then I rode toward their leader, who sat barebacked on a roan mare as still as himself.

"Prince Marcomir," I said.

"Yes." He saluted me in the Frankish fashion.

"You know me?"

"Yes." He was taller than Guntiarus and young enough to have been my own son. Suddenly he smiled. "My people have talked of little else since your soldiers lined the river." He added grimly, "It was not before time."

I said, "Do you wish to cross the Rhenus also?"

He grinned. "I have a small territory which I hold with difficulty. My problems would not be less if I enlarged it."

"Can I count on your support?"

"Why not?" He added softly, "We all need help."

"There was a time——" I began.

"But it is not now," he cut in quickly. "Do not worry, your excellency," he went on. "I made a pact with Stilicho. He is a man. I am in friendship with Guntiarus, and the Alemanni tolerate me because I am between them and the Burgundians."

He laughed quietly but without amusement. "My strength lies, you see, in not being strong."

I looked at him, sitting there half naked on his horse, the sweat trickling across a pattern of scars on his chest and arms. He was young and strong and had a sense of humor. I liked him and felt that he was a man I could trust.

"I spent some time in Gaul," he said. "I was a hostage for my father's good behavior. Treverorum is a fine city—very rich. Too rich," he added gloomily.

"Do you know the Alemanni well?"

"I know their swords," he said grimly.

"Tell me what you know. It will be of great use to me."

We dismounted from our horses and walked toward a fallen tree trunk.

Quintus said, "We need more men. We want twice the auxiliaries we have at the moment."

"Perhaps we can raise them in Gaul."

"Do you really believe that?" He snorted his contempt.

"Where else then? I agree with you about the men. I have had a stone in my stomach ever since the letter came from Stilicho."

He said, "There is supposed to be an army of thirty thousand in Gaul."

"Yes, on files, in the archives at Mediolanum. And not enough money in the provincial treasury to pay a third of that number."

"Well, what then, my General?"

"I think I had better go back to Treverorum and talk to the Curator. If we have taken all the veterans' and soldiers' sons we can get hold of, and there are no more volunteers, then we must use other means. I can see Gallus too. He will have time enough now in which to build his ships. In any event something must be done to smooth our relations with the officials there. They will have to endure us another year whether they like it or not."

He frowned. "Perhaps longer. Shall I come?"

"Of course. Lucillius can take command. He is reliable and the experience will be good for him."

There was a knock and the Chief Centurion came in. "About the bathhouse, sir. I am having great difficulty in getting the men to use it."

"Why, Aquila? Don't they like washing?"

He smiled. "Yes, sir, but they prefer to use the river."

"When I was young they used the bathhouse as a club. They played dice in it and gambled away their pay."

He said patiently, "They prefer to do that in the town, sir."

"Habits change, is that it? Yes, of course. The thing is, I don't want trouble with the local women. These people have very strict ideas, and if our men get their girls into the family way there will be some fighting. I had to buy off a village last month when some young fool in the second cohort got too friendly with their chief's daughter. I need gold for more important things than that."

"I know, sir."

"Very well, Aquila. See what you can do. Find some other way of amusing them in their spare time."

He said, "Are you going to Treverorum, sir?"

"Yes. Why? Do you want me to bring you back a present?"

He smiled. "No, sir. But there's that business of the legionary who killed himself last week."

"I remember. He was in the headquarters cohort. Flavius Betto was his name, wasn't it?"

Aquila nodded. "He was a Brigante, sir. Worried about his family. Wanted his discharge papers."

I said, "We all want our discharge. I refused him, didn't I?"

"Yes, sir."

"What's the problem?"

"It's about his property, sir. His father owned a big estate near Eburacum, sir. He bought it out of his profits as a silversmith."

"Yes. Land was cheap enough then. I remember."

"The father died a month ago and left him everything."

"Any next of kin?"

"One sister, but she may be dead."

"Did our chap make a will?"

Aquila looked straight ahead of him. "We haven't found one yet, sir."

I knew what he was thinking. If there were no will and no next of kin his property belonged to the legion. We were short of funds. Even a patched-up estate in Britannia might bring in some revenue.

I shook my head. "You had better see if you can find it. Give me his documents and I'll put the matter in the hands of the magistrate. He can sort the thing out."

"You won't forget the boots, sir?"

"No. I won't forget the boots."

We made a slow journey to Treverorum, stopping to inspect the signal posts on the way and taking pains to establish contact with the new auxiliaries who now manned them. Twice we met detachments of men returning from leave, for I would not let them travel alone, and once a cavalry patrol appeared suddenly out of the scrub, their commander, young Marcus Severus, explaining apologetically that he had used us as a target for a practice ambush. Quintus said brusquely, "Very well done, but don't spread out so much. And get those horses' manes plaited. I've told you about that before."

Back in the city we established ourselves in Romulus and sent for the Curator and his staff. Briefly I told him the news. He went white when he learned that our stay was to be extended indefinitely.

"What can we do for you?" he asked cautiously.

"Firstly, there's the matter of trading dishonesty. My quartermaster made a contract with a number of leather smiths here for the supply of boots. They were to be made in standard sizes and each was to contain four thicknesses of leather in the sole. When they were delivered and issued it was found that they had only two thicknesses of leather. Here is a pair in proof of the matter."

Artorius turned the boot over in his hand. "This is a matter for the courts."

"I have not the time to go to the courts to sue the man for fraud. I need the boots now, not in four months' time."

He said nervously, "How can I help?"

"I am not going to pay again for a fresh supply. Quintus Veronius has the details. A word from you, and a little pressure, and the matter is attended to. You had better tell your guilds that my legion has an unusual quartermaster—one who is honest. He neither makes money for himself nor allows others to make a profit out of him. Value for value is all we ask."

He nodded, speechless. He owned two big estates to the south of the city and kept herds of cattle and goats that supplied much of the leather for the entire district. And he knew that I knew this thing.

"One other matter. The grain supply we received last week, and for which we paid, was two pounds underweight in each sack. I know, because I weighed them myself. This also, Quintus Veronius will deal with."

I paused and looked at the silent, hostile faces around me.

"And now," I said gently. "I want men for the army."

The Curator stiffened and I saw his knuckles whiten. But he kept himself admirably in check.

He said apologetically, "I don't really think—"

"Just a moment," I said. I took from my tunic a rolled letter that even Quintus had not seen. "I had this a week ago. It is from an old friend, a man named Saturninus, who succeeded me in command of Borcovicum, a fort on the Great Wall where I used to serve. Would you like to hear what he says?"

I had their interest now, and Quintus was looking at me with something of the old expression that I had not seen since the early days with Stilicho.

"The Wall has been abandoned, the whole seventy miles of it. Do you know what that means? The garrisons have gone and the local people use the stones to build their houses with. The great gates lie open and rattle in the wind until they drop to the ground from their rusted hinges. Nothing moves along the sentry walks except the wild cats, while the kestrels fly above the empty towers and leave their droppings on the roofs where our sentries once kept watch. The forts crumble in the rain and the slates drop from the roof of the house in which I once lived." At my side, Quintus started violently and I saw, out of the corner of my eye, his knuckles whiten as he clenched his hands. He, too, had his memories then . . . "Only the inscriptions remain to commemorate the men who served there. . . ."

I broke off and turned away and looked out at the road that led north to where my legion stood at arms. What had happened to her stone? Did it stand upright still or was it lying on the damp ground, covered with weeds? What did it matter anyway?

I thought of the words I had carved on the stone. "She died but not altogether." Saturninus had suggested them. It was what she believed and perhaps she was right. But I found it hard sometimes, to think that it could be so.

I turned and said, "Even Corstopitum is an empty husk. And Eburacum, where the Sixth Legion once proclaimed an Emperor of Rome, is deserted too. The troops have moved south and the great headquarters is an abandoned barrack, occupied only by mice."

"Is that what you want to happen here? Do you want your city to sink into the ground and have the wild birds build their nests in the scrub which hides its ruins? Because if it is I will take my legion and go, and let the Alemanni do their worst."

A senator, who owned half the vineyards in the area, said, in exasperation, "What exactly do you want?"

"What do you want, Statitius?" I said politely. "Shall I tell you—peace. You were born here, and your family before you. Your ancestors never knew peace or security till Rome came. Peace means soldiers; soldiers mean pay; pay means taxes."

Statitius yawned. "Oh, if it's more money then—"

"No."

The Curator, his face pale, said hoarsely, "How can we help more than you have had us help already?"

"I want men—young men—who are willing to become soldiers. And I need educated young men who can be trained to become their future officers. Is it too much to ask that the people of Gaul learn to defend themselves?"

"That is—that is the business of the Magister Equitum per Gallias."

"I am not concerned about the paper army of a paper general."

"Oh! How many then?"

"As many as we can get. I want troops *I* command. I need at least twelve hundred for my fleet alone. I want fifteen thousand men on the Rhenus."

"We cannot force them to take up arms," Artorius said. "The conscription is done annually by different districts each year. It is not the city's turn this year."

"This is an emergency and, if necessary, I will conscript, if I have to. But with your help it may not be necessary."

"Conscription cannot be imposed without the sanction of the Praefectus Praetorio," he said doggedly.

"When I rode through the forum this morning there were great queues of the poor, lining up to receive their free distribution of bread and bacon that the city gives them each day." I glanced sideways as the door opened and Mauritius, Bishop of Treverorum, entered the room. "That is charitable work indeed. But not all of those poor were either young children or old men. They could earn that food, and, by earning it, be more useful than they are. They are free men."

The Bishop said, "It is sinful for Christians to take up arms against each other."

"You," I said. "You live in a world where you make sins. You would not be happy without them. Would you?"

"I shall forbid it from the pulpit."

I said, "Just what do you want from our Empire?"

He said, "Rome is the house of Christianity and by our works shall you know us. I pray as do we all that, for the miracle vouchsafed to the blessed Constantine, we shall see eternal Rome ascend to heaven in a ball of fire!"

"If you are not careful you will see Augusta Treverorum ascend in the same manner. But sooner than you think." I paused. I said, "Who has influence in this city beside our Bishop here? Who is interested in life rather than death?"

Artorius said, nervously, "Julianus Septimus."

"Who is he?"

"He used to hold my office in the days of Valentinian. He is an old man now but he is rich, and he lives across the river, six miles up the road. He has two sons and a fine house."

"Would he help me?"

"He is a pagan," said the Bishop.

"Then he probably will."

I left Quintus to read my proclamation in the forum while I set out along the twisting hill road to visit the man who had once known Valentinian. It was a hot day; the wooded hills soaked up the heat and I could feel the sweat from my horse through the saddlecloth against my thighs. I rode through a gorge shadowed by the sun, turned right to ford a pebbled stream of bubbling water, and entered a track that led between vineyards on the left and furrowed land on the right to a large, low rectangular villa whose yellow tiled roof seemed to shimmer in the heat. I dismounted, my horse was taken by servants, and as in a dream I followed a barefoot slave through a courtyard where a fountain played and two girls laughed as they threw a ball to each other in the leaf-mottled sunlight. My host was in the large reception room in the north wing and I stood there admiring the elaborately patterned mosaic on the floor and the plastered walls against which, on pedestals, stood the busts of long dead ancestors. He did not seem surprised to see me and, while we drank wine and talked politely of nothing and everything, I thought of my bleak quarters in Moguntiacum and of how I, too, had once thought to own such a house.

I said, politely, "I seem to have made a bad beginning with the Council. They don't like soldiers."

A faint smile creased his face. "So I have heard. Taxes and soldiers go together," he added cryptically.

"What of this young man who is now Curator? I find it hard to talk to him. Do you know him well?"

"Artorius. Hardly. He is young and ambitious and keen. His grandfather was a freedman, I believe."

"Then he has done well for himself."

"I suppose so. His father certainly managed to establish himself in the curial class. But that might well happen in a city like Mediolanum." He spoke with a tinge of contempt.

"Is that where he comes from? I thought—"

"Oh yes. I would have thought the accent was obvious. He trained as an advocate, I believe; held one or two minor civic posts and then secured an office in the imperial service—something to do with finance. Then he came here. His appointment was unusual to say the least of it—even irregular. For, as you know, the Curator is normally appointed from out of the local council." He paused to drink his wine delicately. "But then, you know how it is. Influence was brought to bear. I was against the appointment myself." He shrugged. "One cannot argue with a Praefectus Praetorio." He added grudgingly, "Still, he is efficient, so my old friends tell me."

"I don't understand why he wished to come here," I said, puzzled.

"Oh, that is easy to explain." The thin lips curled a little. "He wished to escape his own past. This is still an important city and under the eye of the Praefectus he may yet go far. He will do well for himself by his own modest standards."

I smiled. "He takes a keen interest in trade."

"Oh yes, and in land too. He has made money, that young man. And invested it wisely, too. A modest villa for his family, so I understand. Not that I have seen it, of course."

"Of course not."

"Everyone wants land. They think it means security. Perhaps it did once." He paused and took another sip of his wine. "Of course, things are very different now—difficult too. My peasants, as is customary, pay a tenth of their crop but they are lazy and I find it difficult in getting my rents from them. They don't work as hard as they used to. They run away when they cannot pay and it is hard to find others to work the land in their place. Food is scarce too." He nibbled a grape. "We used to get grain from Britannia, but the deliveries are now so uncertain. In season, of course, we get roast swam and wild duck. That is something."

"You had harder times when you held office in the city."

His pale eyes brightened. "The central government was strong then. We had a Valentinian and not a Honorius. It was dreadful for a time, but we drove them back and prosperity slowly returned."

"It could again."

"These Franks aren't bad fellows. It was the best thing that foreigner Stilicho ever did, to settle them on this side of the river. With all the slaves running away we need young men to work on the farms."

"Do they?"

He did not answer me. He said, "And is that what you want? Men for your army?"

"Yes."

"Well, if they won't join, you can only conscript them."

"Yes, I may have to do that. But I would like volunteers also. I was hoping that you might persuade—use your influence—you are much respected—the situation is dangerous."

"Oh, they always say that. But nothing happens. A few raids, perhaps, but little harm done."

"What happens when they raid you?"

"Oh, I give them some silver and they go away. Curious that. They have no use for gold. Just as well. I should be ruined if they had."

I said, "We are all in very great danger. You remember that other time. Then an army, armed war bands, plundered the country. This time it will be worse. They won't merely steal and murder and then go away. They will steal and murder—yes—and they will stay."

"We can go to Italia," he said. "If it is really as bad as you say. I have estates there in the south. I have cousins in Africa too. A rich land that. They tell me many people are going there now. The climate is so much better."

"The rich," I said.

"But naturally. The artisans and the peasants could not afford the journey."

"I need men, desperately. I hoped that your sons——"

"My sons are middle-aged." He smiled. "I am an old man. I have grandsons, of course."

"They would do. They would do well. I need an example set. I want auxiliary alae with young men like your grandsons to lead them."

"I am not sure——"

"Would you ask them?" I insisted. "Military service is honorable. Young men like adventure."

"But not death," he said dryly.

"It is better than dishonor," I said lightly.

He seemed to shrink inside his chair.

I said, "Would you ask them."

He hesitated.

"Let me ask them then? I must."

He said, "Your determination—you remind me of Theodosius—the Emperor, of course."

"Did you know him?"

"Yes. He was my friend." He spoke with a flash of pride.

"I am glad," I said. "You see, I know his father."

His hands began to tremble. He said, "I think you had better go. I am very tired."

"You said I could see your grandsons."

"They are not here. I remember—they are out riding. I had forgotten."

"I can wait."

"They may not come back for——" He broke off as voices sounded on the terrace outside and his hands dropped helplessly to his lap. There was the sound of laughter and scuffling and a dark young man entered, to be followed by a boy in his third year of the toga. They were fine boys all right. I would have been proud if they had been my sons.

They fell silent as they saw me and stood awkwardly in the doorway. They looked at my riding dress and at my helmet in the crook of my arm, and their faces wore a curious expression, compounded—I could have sworn it—of fear and hatred. I waited stiffly for Julianus Septimus to introduce me. He said nothing but I heard a gasp and the wine cup fell to the floor with a crash.

The dark boy moved forward, crying, "Grandfather."

Instinctively he stretched out his right hand, the fingers splayed outward, as though he would have caught the falling cup had he been in time. It was then that I noticed that his right thumb was missing. The puckered skin was pink and newly healed. It was a great shame. It was a horrible accident to have suffered. He was such a good-looking boy.

He saw my look and dropped his hand sharply.

The grandfather said faintly, "It is all right. No harm has been done. Metellus can clear up the mess in a minute. I have a guest. Run along and come back when I am free."

The boys bowed to me stiffly and turned to go. As they did so I saw the hands of the fair one quite clearly. He, too, had suffered an accident, just like his brother. I remembered the day that I had entered Treverorum and the young men I had noticed in the crowds with injured hands.

It was then that I understood.

I swung round sharply and put my hand to my mouth. I felt physically sick and the swallowed wine was sour in my throat. The skin on the backs of my hands prickled with sweat and my forehead felt cold. I knew then the shame, the horror, and the degradation of it all.

I said in a whisper, "Who put them up to it? Was it you? You, the friend of my Theodosius' son, the friend of Valentinian who labored to rebuild this province after its years of disaster and misery."

He did not answer. He turned his head away, but I saw from the angle of his jaw that his face trembled.

"Do you want to lie skewered in the sun like a condemned criminal while your villa roasts your servants behind your back? See your sons killed for your gold, your grandsons as slaves, serving their barbarian masters on bended knee? See your granddaughters tremble as they are stripped naked for the pleasure of their stinking conquerors? Will you die content in the knowledge that you have brought such things about?"

He did not answer.

I said, "Your family bears a great name. You are the owner of fertile lands, rich treasures, and a beautiful house. You have all that most men would welcome, nothing that they would refuse."

"Stop it," he cried. "How dare you?"

"Dare," I said. "I am only a poor man. I am rich in nothing except courage and even that I must earn. Each day I have to win it afresh as a peasant sweats to earn his food. It is not easy to earn what I need that I may do what I have to do. I am only a soldier. But you—you have everything, save only one thing." I turned my back on him and walked to the open door. "You lack only the Huns as your guests."

I rode back to the city and all the while I shivered as though with a fever. It was as though the heat had gone out of the sun and the golden brightness of the day was but an illusion.

Outside Romulus a sweating horse stood tethered in the courtyard between the double gates, and a messenger awaited me in my room with a sealed scroll, penned two days before at Moguntiacum. Quintus' eyebrows were raised, framing an unspoken question.

"The family of Septimus have joined the thumbless ones," I said.

He said scornfully, "Thus avoiding military service like all the others. You should fine them as Augustus did."

I broke the seals and read the message through twice to make certain that I understood it properly. "The Alemanni have sent an ambassador across the river. Their King, Rando, wishes a meeting to discuss certain matters."

"On the east bank, I suppose, preceded by a feast and with girls of his tribe to entertain us," said Quintus, sardonically.

"I wonder what he wants. It is curious, that. The Alemanni must have moved north."

"You are not going to see him, surely? It may be a trap."

"I must. I want to know his intentions."

"Those. I thought they were obvious enough."

"Too obvious, perhaps. I shall arrange a meeting on one of the islands off Moguntiacum."

"That should be interesting. My cavalry will then be of great help to you if we are attacked."

"I am glad you said we."

He laughed and began to unlace his riding boots. "I have never seen a King of the Germans. I am curious to know what he will be like."

That afternoon I went down to the dockyard to see Gallus. Our converted ship was out in midstream and, judging by the oar splashes, was being used for training new rowers. Quintus remarked, sadly, that they were only good for frightening swans, and I was inclined to agree with him. On the hard, men were at work building the new warships. The keels of three ships had been laid and carpenters were busy fitting the stern posts onto one, the ribs onto another, and the planking onto a third. The fourth ship was near completion. The air reeked as the craftsmen caulked its planks with tarred rope, while a group of half-naked men, who only a month before had been jobless, wrestled to fit the two rudders into position. One group were sawing poles into oar lengths while another planed the surface of the blades, after which they were carefully oiled by a boy and an old man and then leaned against a shed to dry in the sun.

Gallus said cheerfully, "I think it will be all right this time, sir. We are working to the original plans of the old Rhenus fleet. I sent a man down to Colonia and the Curator there found them for me in the naval records section."

"What's this?" Quintus asked, pointing at a huge block of oak that was being rubbed down by two boys.

"That's to set the mast in, sir. It's a good thing we were able to get plenty of seasoned timber. We're short of decent rope though, but they've promised to send some up from Colonia. It should arrive by the end of the week."

"What about armaments?" I asked.

"She'll have one light ballista in the bows that will fire up to three hundred yards, and one small carroballista in the stern. But oarsmen are the real trouble."

"What crew do you need? I told the Curator twelve hundred. Was that correct?"

"Nearly, sir, Two hundred and twenty, including archers, to each ship. Of those a hundred and fifty will be oarsmen, arranged for seating in twenty-five banks of threes. That makes a total of thirteen hundred without reserves. We shall have to allow for sickness, injury, and other things."

"And you've had no more recruits?"

Gallus rubbed his nose irritably. "Those are my recruits, the crew out there, splashing away unhappily. Most of them wish they had never joined."

"A pity we can't use slaves, isn't it?"

He looked shocked. "Slaves, sir. We couldn't do that."

"I know. I suppose not."

Quintus said, "But why not? It's been done before."

"In the fleet, sir? Only free men are allowed in the imperial navy."

Quintus picked up a lantern and began to play with it. "Yes, precisely—free men or freedmen." He put the lantern down onto a pile of planks. "If my memory serves me, I seem to remember reading in one of these tedious books of Appian that Augustus Caesar—but he was Octavius then—enlisted twenty thousand slaves for his campaigns against Pompey's son."

I frowned. "Are you sure?"

"Oh, yes. He freed them first and then asked for volunteers."

"Well, that's the answer then."

He smiled. "It's a good thing someone reads your books."

Gallus said, "But could we get enough slaves without running into trouble with their owners. The ones you see in the Treverorum market are poor quality as a rule."

Quintus said, dryly, "We shall need an edict, signed by the Praefectus, of course."

"I doubt it," I said to Gallus. "But we could get convicts. Yes, Quintus, the Praefectus Praetorio will have to authorize it. I'll write to him. They'll have to be paid though, and fed and clothed."

"Up go the taxes, sir," said Gallus with a grin.

"How soon will the ships be ready?"

"In thirty days, sir."

I swore.

"You wanted them to impress the Alemanni," said Quintus.

"It would have helped."

"We can manage without them." Quintus smiled at Gallus. "They can be a surprise for later. Tell me, have you tried out your liquid fire yet?"

I sent a message to the Bishop's house but he was not there, and I learned he was on the site of a church in the temple district. I rode out to find him and I noticed that the women, fetching water from the public fountains, paused in their work and drew back as I passed by. It was quiet away from the shops, and grass grew between the cracks in the paving stones that made the road. Everything was shabby, neglected, and desolate. When I arrived Mauritius was watching a group of masons at work, fitting chips of colored glass into a corner of a vast mosaic pattern which had been outlined on the floor in the center of the nave. As usual he was talking, giving instructions as to the way the patterns must flow one into the other. I had never heard him be so eloquent or so sensible. But then I did not attend his sermons.

He nodded to me as I walked out of the sunlight into the dust. "Have you come to be converted?" There was no sting in his voice and I wondered if he had thought it wise to declare a truce. He had his church and the Emperor behind him; but I had Stilicho.

"May I speak to you here or outside?" I asked.

"Why not here? He will hear us just as well as in the open."

"I have seen Septimus."

"And?"

"You have a saying, I believe, my lord Bishop, which is of great comfort to those who wish to avoid trouble."

His eyes narrowed. "To what do you refer?"

I said, "'If they persecute you in one city, then flee to another.' "

He said, "It is easy to twist words, to distort meanings."

"It is," I said. "But more important than that. Is that what you believe?"

"It would depend on the circumstances," he said cautiously.

"You know very well the circumstances. This city is in no small danger. I need men for the army to avert that danger. If I do not get volunteers then I must use the law to conscript them. Even so, I need some volunteers."

"And you expect me to help you in this task?"

"Why not? Or do you prefer that those who believe in a heresy should rule your land and celebrate their heresy in your church?"

"I do not say that. You are trying to trap me," he said in anger.

"If you refuse to help then I may trap you. The bishops in council might not see your refusal to assist as true zeal for the defense of your faith."

He flushed. He said, "You would pit your influence against mine. How dare you suggest that I do not know my duty."

I said, "It is not I who will do the suggesting, my lord Bishop. Honorius is a true son of your faith: would he wish to see such heresy spread further? He is also an Emperor: would he wish to lose a whole province?"

"Your problems are not mine." He spoke coldly but there was a note of anxiety in his voice.

"You are quite wrong. In this matter, my lord Bishop, whether we like it or not, we stand or fall together."

He blinked.

I said, "I need your help and if I do not get it then I shall write to Ravenna and I shall say, in short sentences, exactly what I think."

"You would not dare."

"Honorius is a ruler first and a Christian second. I think you will find that he prefers a pagan who does his duty to a Christian who fails in his."

He said icily, "You know the laws concerning conscription. Apply those laws if you must. Do not expect me to help. It is not my province."

"I do not want all conscripts, as I said before."

"Of course not. You want a willing sacrifice, is that it?"

I nodded. "Yes. Is not that what you want also?"

We measured glances for a moment.

"Are they then so afraid of me?"

"Yes," he said. "They are, and of what you stand for."

I said in exasperation, "In the name of—any god you choose, use your influence—tell them not to—it is all too horrible."

"Horrible—of course. Fear is always horrible."

"It is also contemptible."

"To a soldier, perhaps."

I said, stung by the tone of his voice, "I have enough to bear without that also."

"Why should you care?" He looked at me keenly and—it was absurd, of course—for a moment it was as though he were reaching into my mind, trying to take hold of the thing I had discussed with no one in all the years that I had lived with it—that fox under my tunic.

I said, "Some of them had done this thing before ever I arrived." I added harshly, "Not all the wounds were new."

"No, not all."

While we were talking we had walked slowly, almost without realizing it, to the open space where the doors of the church would be. I looked across the litter of building material to a roofless temple beyond. No one would dare to enter it now, except alone and by night.

I said, "It was people who worshiped in temples like that who made the Rome of which you are now so proud."

"It was a godless state, profane and barbarous and cruel. Not until the coming of the blessed Constantine—"

"Do not go on," I said. "I am in no mood for a sermon."

"Then it is your loss, not mine."

I swung round on him angrily. "You are so certain that you are right. That, I do not mind. But I do mind that you insist on forcing your certainty upon others, forcing it upon them whether they wish it or not."

"The truth must prevail," he said placidly. "You do not care to be persecuted, as you term it, but it was we who suffered once, the threats of fire, of torture, and of death."

"But you were not persecuted for your faith, only for putting yourselves above the state."

"There is a higher power."

"Do I deny it?"

"Your so-called worship is a blasphemy in the eyes of my church. You imitate, and by imitating make a mockery of our sacred rituals."

"My lord Bishop, the certainty of the Christian is only equaled by the certainty of the Jewish people. You teach humility, I believe. You would do well to remember that to the Jews—those I have met anyway—your faith is equally—unusual."

He smiled suddenly. "That is a point of view. Tell me, in how many gods do you believe?"

"In fewer than yourself. My god is not divided into three."

He said, "Your wife was a Christian, I think."

"Yes."

He nodded. "I thought so." He hesitated as though he would say more and then fell silent.

"If your church were still persecuted," I said, "would your people have the courage to face martyrdom for their faith?"

"I do not know. I like to think so. But—I must be honest with you—I doubt it."

"Why?"

He said dryly, "Courage, as you should know, is something all men think they have, though few in fact possess it at all. They have other qualities which they delude themselves into thinking are the attributes of courage. Do you really expect to find courage in a slave who may be branded for striking a thoughtless master? Or in a peasant who will be turned out to starve if he cannot pay his taxes? Why should you expect to find it more in a rich man's sons who have been pampered all their lives, who live for pleasure and who are ignorant of duty?"

I said, "But your church—"

"You are thinking of our martyrs, perhaps. Of course, we had some. Though not as many, I fear, as we sometimes say. In men's enthusiasms numbers often run away with them. You must remember that of the first Twelve, eleven deserted Him in the moment of crisis, while the other turned traitor."

"You do not hold out much comfort."

"Neither do you." He smiled slightly. "You have taken our wealth to pay your men, and now you will take our young citizens also."

"Yes. You may tell your congregation, for good measure, that I will put a special tax on those families who have men in them without thumbs."

He said, "You are a hard man."

"No, only a desperate one."

"I shall not flee," he said. "But I will bear your words in mind. Only the foolish oppose those they cannot overrule."

"You are a wise man."

"No, only a bishop."

We looked at each other.

He said, ironically, "Do you wish me to add my prayers, also? They at least are free."

"Do not pray for me," I said. "Pray only that we have a mild winter and that the snow does not come and the river does not turn to ice."

CHAPTER X

It was a fine October day when I went to my meeting with the chiefs from across the river. I did not think that there was likely to be treachery for there was little to be gained by it, but I thought it wise to take no chances. The camp guard stood to arms and the gates of Moguntiacum were closed to traffic. Two cohorts lined the banks and the cavalry ala waited on horseback by the broken bridge. It was a time to demonstrate my strength. The converted merchant ship moved out of harbor a little after dawn and patrolled the river clumsily while two centuries went ashore on the island to clear the ground, erect tents, and take up positions suitable to the needs of honor and defense.

A little before midday I was rowed across in company with Quintus and Lucillius, while Barbatio, with the aquilifer and the cohort standards, followed in another boat. In a third boat were ten centurions whose armor and helmets, upon my instructions, had been carefully gilded. At the same time a boat pushed off from the other shore. The further bank was lined with a vast horde of bareheaded men, roughly dressed and carrying a motley of weapons: swords, javelins, and throwing axes. Many had shields but none wore armor of any kind, it being their custom to fight naked as the saying goes. The boats landed and the two groups approached each other, each with an escort of armed men. A hundred paces apart the guard halted as I raised my hand, and I and Quintus, together with two senior tribunes, walked forward unarmed to meet the two kings who would talk with me.

Rando, King of the Alemanni, was a tall, broad-shouldered man with a red beard and only one eye, but the other made up for both in fierceness. He was the hardest-looking man I had ever seen. He had a scar along the right arm and another below the left eye. Yet he had great dignity and I thought that here was a man one could talk to, a man one might fight and still respect. He was a king among eagles.

Gunderic, King of the Vandals, was blond-haired and young. He smiled a lot and had beautiful teeth, but the smile was empty of emotion like the eyes above it. He had a finger missing on his sword hand and walked with the grace of a Greek athlete. He was a man any girl would have run after, but I would as soon have trusted the African leopard I saw once at the games at Arelate when I was a child.

I said formally, "I am Maximus, General of the West, and this is Quintus Veronius, my lieutenant and master general of my horse."

I heard a quick intake of breath, saw Rando blink suddenly with his one eye, while the Vandal King frowned, the smile slipping from his face like a salmon from the net. "Shall we sit down," I said. "At this table we can talk and I will listen to what you wish to say."

Rando unbuckled his sword and laid it across his knees.

I said mildly, "I have come with no sword, as you can see. Do you always bear arms at the council table?"

"It is our custom," said Gunderic. He glanced at my soldiers in the distance and smiled ironically.

The Aleman said, "I have not heard your name before." He spoke carelessly as though to imply that I had been—that I was a man of no importance.

I said, "You have heard of me now. I was in Britannia during the years when your people made war on Gaul. We, too, had a great war with the Picts and the Scotti and the Saxons who invaded my island. I lived and they died."

Rando raised his hand and signaled to one of his servants, who came forward carrying something wrapped in cloth. "I make you a present," he said. "I hope that you will honor me by accepting it."

The servant unwrapped the gift and held it out. It was a belt of solid silver, decorated in the Celtic fashion. It was very beautiful.

"Thank you," I said. "It is, indeed, a belt fit for a king."

Rando smiled. "It was made for one, though he never wore it."

"I, too, have gifts for my guests and brothers: two white colts from the old royal herd of the Treveri, whose ancestors have carried kings." I nodded to Quintus, who called out, at which a groom came to us, leading the animals on a bearing rein.

Rando looked at them and said, "Ah," very softly. Gunderic grunted and, for one fleeting moment, gave a smile of sheer pleasure.

"If they are to your liking," I said, "then it is General Veronius whom you must thank. It was he who chose them."

Rando said thoughtfully, "It takes a warrior to choose such beasts."

"And now, what can I do for you?"

The Aleman touched the belt that lay under my hand. "This was made from the silver out of a mine not far from here."

"Aquae Mattiacae," I said.

"So—that is how you call it. Yes, it came from there." Rando paused and then looked at me directly. "Before you came there was much trade across the river, trade in silver, in slaves, and in goods of all kinds. Your merchants wanted our slaves and our silver, and we wished to buy their goods in exchange. This you have stopped. Why?"

I said, "I have heard a rumor that your people are restless and wish to move to new lands. Perhaps the rumor is false. If it is then you will tell me."

He ignored what I had said. "We made a treaty with your General—him they call Stilicho—and this treaty we have kept."

I said, "That is so, but the treaty depended, in part, upon my government sending you subsidies—corn among other things. Last year there was a famine in Gaul and there was no corn to spare. When it was not sent you crossed the river at Borbetomagus and raided the land with armed men."

"Our people were starving. They needed the food you promised and did not send."

"We could not send what we had not got."

Gunderic said, indifferently, "That is your concern, not my brother's here."

"It is certainly not yours," I said, sharply. "King Rando, you were told the delivery would be late because the corn fleet from Britannia was delayed by storms. You should have known we would keep our word."

Gunderic laughed.

Rando said, "In the treaty it was agreed that the corn should be delivered on certain dates. It was not we who broke the treaty but yourselves."

Quintus said, "A king who was a king in more than name would have had better control over his own people."

Rando said, quietly, "Then you do not understand my people. I do not rule them in all matters, only in some."

I said, "Rome is not a feeble woman to be threatened and made a mock of in this way, as you will learn."

Gunderic yawned.

Rando said, softly, "I hope the tribute will not be late this year."

Quintus leaned forward. "Rome does not pay tribute to any race. It is the Alemanni, as we know, who make excellent slaves."

Gunderic smashed his fist upon the table. "Are we to be insulted?"

Quintus said, "It is not possible. You are a Vandal."

Rando did not move. He looked at us with quiet curiosity. He said, "I thought to ask for terms, not to listen to them."

"I will tell you my terms," I said. "Keep to your side of the river and we will keep to ours. It is as simple as that. There will be no more trade—not even in Roman slaves—until you have paid a fine in cattle for the damage done to Borbetomagus."

"Is that all?" asked Gunderic.

"That is all."

The Aleman said, "My brother needs land for his people. They wish to cross the river and settle in Gaul."

I said, "My brother in arms, Stilicho, has made terms with you on this matter already." I smiled at Rando. "Many of the Burgundians of Guntiarus, as well as those of your own people who wished to cross the river, have been allowed to do so up to the numbers that were agreed." I looked from him to Gunderic and smiled again. "Are you people not happy under their own kings?"

The Vandal flushed but said nothing.

The Aleman King said harshly, "That is not in question."

"What is?"

Gunderic said, "You have a great empire and vast lands containing many people. And you are rich and prosperous. We, too, are a numerous people but our land is not prosperous and—"

"You have no lands," I said. "You came out of the east and abandoned your own lands. Why should you expect others to give you theirs?"

"We did not abandon our lands. We were forced to leave—"

Pride, perhaps, forbade him to mention the truth, that they had been driven out by the Huns. But perhaps he was speaking the truth: he did not know. The story had been twisted in the handing down, as fathers, determined to retain the respect of their sons, tried hard to turn stories of defeat into those of victory. Even we in Rome had done the same thing.

I said, "Italia was not your land but you tried to take it from us. Now you cross the white mountains. Why should we help you? Let the Alemanni do that, who are now your hosts and brothers."

Rando said quickly, "It is our desire that those who wish be allowed to cross the river peacefully." He glanced significantly at my sentries. "Without war," he added softly.

I looked at them in silence. They had fought us in turn for years now, yet there were Alemanni serving with Stilicho, Burgundians married to citizens of Treverorum, and Vandals without number in the army of the east. They envied us, they feared us, and they hated us. They had never known a time when Rome did not patrol their frontiers and punish their raids with a strength they could never overcome. The enmity between us was an unhealed scar that reached down to the bone.

"Were you so peaceful when you visited Moguntiacum as a young man?" I asked. Rando did not answer me.

I said, "Let who wishes speak for himself. Do you, King of the Alemanni, wish to move your people into our lands and accept the protection of Rome?"

He hesitated. "I?" he said. "My people and I can take what we want—if we choose—if it is our wish. It is our wish at the moment to be content with what we hold."

"So," I said. "That leaves only you, King Gunderic, who are a king of a people without a land. It is you alone then who wishes to serve Rome?"

He said, with a smile, "In the past it was said that Rome turned kings into slaves. Perhaps that was true. I do not know. But then Rome was strong." He smiled again. "She is not strong now, and I have no wish to be a slave. But I am willing to take service in the army of your empire if, in return, you grant to my people a third of the soil of Gaul for them to farm and to call their own." He smiled a third time. "I understand that you need men who can work your farms and you need men who will serve as soldiers of the Emperor. All this my people will do."

Quintus said slowly, "You were with King Radagaisus in Italia. In his army were many peoples who, when they were beaten and Radagaisus was dead, moved north out of Rome's way. A third died at the hands of Stilicho. Do you mean to tell my general here that only the Asding Vandals are in need of new lands?" Quintus held up a letter. "It is all here in a letter to us from the Emperor's General."

The Aleman stroked his beard. "It is as my brother says."

I said, "He had forty thousand men when he crossed the mountains. I am to find homes for two-thirds of those. Is that correct?"

"Yes."

"And if I refuse."

Gunderic hunched his shoulders. "You cannot refuse what we ask."

"It is not you who asks," I said. "I can refuse anything."

The Aleman said politely, "You have a great army, no doubt."

I said quietly, "I would not advise you to find out."

"I have," he said. "We have many friends on your bank. You have only a small force. You could not stand out against one of our peoples even." He paused. Gunderic glanced at him, and said quickly, "It would be wiser to make terms as Stilicho did." He added harshly, "Stilicho is a Vandal. He has wisdom in this matter."

"And I am a Roman." I stood up and Quintus stood up with me. "You, who are a wise man with much experience, will know by now that spies so often tell their masters only what they wish to hear, especially when they receive silver from both sides." I saw his mouth tighten as I spoke. "Besides, you forget, I came from Britannia," I said. "I brought my legion with me but I have more on the way." I smiled. "Nanienus, who beat your father in battle at Argentaria, was my countryman." Rando gave a little hissing breath. One horseman is worth three men on foot," I added gently.

Gunderic said insolently, "That is what my father told me and he fought at Adrianopolis. I forget how many Roman soldiers were killed there. The plain was white with their bones."

"Precisely. My cavalry is anxious to see if they can do the same."

"You have not enough men."

"Try me," I said. "It is your wives and your children who will be sorry. Did I not tell you that the Burgundian King stands on my left side in this matter. And that is the side that matters: the side of loyalty."

The Aleman King rose to his feet. "Remember that we asked to come in peace," he said.

"Share your lands in peace with each other and be content with what you have."

Gunderic glared at me. "If you offered silver as Stilicho did I would not accept it."

"Do not worry," I replied. "That offer was never in my mind."

Gunderic clenched his fist. "When the spring comes—" he said, threateningly.

"Yes, when the spring comes I may decide to hold the right bank of this river instead of the left, as we did in the old days. I await only my other legions. But by that time you may be hungry. I will pray that the winter is a mild one." I turned to the Aleman King. "I hope that your harvest was good so that you may feed your guests with true hospitality. It would be cruel if they were to be a burden to you."

Rando said stiffly, "My friends are my friends."

Quintus laughed, and his sudden laughter startled them. "Of course. Why not? For myself I never let my friends stay too long lest they come to think of my home as their own. Guests are thoughtless people."

As they turned to go I said, "Remember, King of the Alemanni, there is peace so long as the river is between us. But let one of your people set foot on my bank without permission and he will be killed before he has time to dry himself."

They left, discomfited, and we returned to Moguntiacum.

Lucillius, my senior tribune, unlaced his helmet. "I'm glad that's over," he said. "They scared me."

"The question is," said Quintus, "whether they believe our bluff."

"They have to," I said.

Lucillius said, "They were worried at the start when you mentioned the cavalry."

"That was what I intended."

Quintus raised an eyebrow. "I hesitate to criticize but—was it wise to put our dice on the table."

"Why not? If we were strong enough I would be happy to encourage them to do battle, and beat them. But we are not, so I must discourage them from attempting to cross in any way I can."

"But if they know how many men we have—"

"They don't. They suspect we are a small force. Their spies told them as much. Remember, I kept the cavalry this summer always apart in small detachments. They thought us a legion in the old formation. As Lucillius says, they were alarmed at my having a master general of horse."

"Fifteen hundred cavalry," said Quintus softly. "Oh, Mithras."

Lucillius said, "If only the Vandals want to cross—well, surely, there aren't many of them, sir. Wouldn't it be better to come to terms? We could absorb them easily."

"Is that what you think?" I said. "Why did the Aleman King say—and he did not mean to let it slip—that we could not hold out against even one of them? Because the Vandals aren't the only tribe who wish to make the crossing."

Quintus looked at me sharply. "Are you sure?"

"I am certain of it. Radagaisus' men included Ostrogoths and Quadi. They were the advance guard. If their Italian raid had been successful the rest would have followed. But they failed, their retreat home was cut off and they were forced to take refuge in the Aleman country. The Aleman are too strong to be pushed out but not rich enough to feed their unwilling guests forever."

"If the Aleman are so strong why don't they do the pushing?"

"Probably because the Quadi, for one, provide a fine buffer state between them and—" I hesitated. I said slowly, "You heard what Gunderic said. They have the sea to the north as a barrier, and we are the barrier to the west and the south. The barrier in the east is not the desert—it is the Huns."

Lucillius shivered and crossed himself.

Quintus said, "Will they fight each other? That is what you want them to do."

"Yes."

"And if they try to cross now?"

"They won't. They are afraid of my cavalry and they think I have reinforcements coming."

"And just how long will they continue to think that when the west bank is riddled with their spies?"

I said hopefully, "There are other ways of winning battles than by fighting them."

That afternoon I called a council of my cohort commanders. They had all come in from their forts to witness the meeting on the island but, upon my orders and much to their disappointment, had remained in camp. Briefly I told them what had happened. Even more briefly I told them what we must do. I shouted an order and one of the centurions in gilded armor came in and saluted. "They thought this man a general," I said. "And there were nine others dressed alike." There was a roar of laughter. "Now," I said. "They must go on believing that we have the men to serve these generals. It will not be easy but it can be done."

A week later the six ships of the Rhenus fleet made their appearance on the river and I spent a day on board Gallus' flagship, Athena, testing their efficiency. The rowing was competent but not first class. I did not worry about that. It would improve, inevitably, with practice. The archery of the marines was accurate but too slow and the ballistae crew were below standard. The fire tubes were handled efficiently enough, but as weapons they were useless except against other boats at extremely close range. Gallus said he would try to do something to improve this. It was agreed that one ship each should be stationed at Confluentes, Borbetomagus, and Moguntiacum, and the remainder should operate from Bingium, which Gallus would make his headquarters.

Before he moved downstream I said, "I shall hold you responsible for sinking any boat that tries to cross from the east bank."

"Don't worry, sir," he said cheerfully.

"It is you who will do the worrying," I said shortly.

They were famous night fighters and they came with blackened faces and arms on a night when there was no moon because of the heavy skies. Exactly how many there were, I do not know, but I judged a thousand when all the evidence had been collected afterward. They came in two groups from upriver, one trying to land a little above Moguntiacum, the other a little below it, and there were twenty men to each boat. Fortunately for us they were seen by the night patrols I had left on the islands and by a boat of my own that was moored in a concealed position high up the river. This boat let them pass and then followed them down.

Fired on from the warship, fired on from the island, and fired on from the camp they suffered terribly. Many had never met liquid fire before— the fire that cannot be put out—and their screams tortured the sky. Those who tried to land were killed in the shallows, cut down while still wet by Quintus' cavalry. Afterward, the troops on the islands reported that only six boats of wounded and dying men made the journey back to the east shore. The bodies were still floating past Confluentes ten days later.

Just after dawn, while the troops from the camp were clearing up, pushing the dead back into the water, finishing off the wounded with a clean stroke and piling up the weapons for my inspection, I crossed to the east bank with half a cohort. The abandoned bridge-head camp was in a better state than I had imagined. True, the huts had been pulled down and the arched gate had no doors; the wells were choked with rubbish and the roofing had come off the corner towers. But the walls still stood intact and, with a little effort, the place could be made inhabitable again. Beyond it were the remains of the old villas, their walls crumbling gently in the autumn sunlight. Nothing stirred on the plain except the long grass, rustling in the wind. The countryside was deserted and though we pushed inland for four miles we saw no one and were not attacked. Before we turned back I rode north to the hills where Marcomir held watch for me. He was absent when I reached his stockade and an apologetic chief explained that he had gone on a visit to Guntiarus, King of the Burgundians, and was not expected to return before the next moon. I wondered if the absence was a diplomatic one, but there was little point in pursuing the matter at that moment.

On my return the duty centurion came up, a bundle of swords and spears in his arms.

"Would you look at these, sir," he said.

"What is it?" I asked.

"We picked these up on the bank. I thought that you should see them."

The swords were long and with hilts similar to those issued to our cavalry. I took one up, held it, and then swung it once or twice. I rubbed the muddy blade and the steel shone like silver beneath. I felt the edge and then looked at it carefully. It was ice sharp and smooth as a new blade that has never been used. I swung it again while the centurion watched me intently.

"Yes," I said. "I see what you mean."

"They might have been captured in a scrimmage," he said in a flat voice.

"Yes, that is true. Are they all like this?"

He nodded.

I held the sword up by the hilt and looked at the marks on the blade. The word Remi was stamped on it quite clearly.

"A Roman sword, and a new one at that. Spears too?"

The centurion said quickly, "I have told no one except yourself, sir."

"Why not?"

"I did not think that you would want me to."

"Quite right. Give them to Marcus Severus and tell him to speak to me about them."

"How did they get them, sir? I don't understand."

"I do," I said. "No wonder the Alemanni opened up the old silver mine at Aquae Mattiacae." I walked on up to my quarters and there found Quintus and Aquila awaiting me. "It was a try," I said. "They raided us to test our words and see how strong we were. But it was a raid in strength also, in case we proved weak and they were successful enough to establish a bridge head. There were signs," I added grimly, "that ten thousand men at least, I should say, must have been waiting there on the other side in the dark. Bushes were broken, undergrowth trampled down, and footprints by the score, all covering an area the size of a double camp."

Aquila said doubtfully, "Yet we never heard them, sir."

"Then they must move like cats," said Quintus sharply. He was shaken by my news and looked it.

"Never mind," I said. "Who were the dead?"

"Mainly Alemanni and Vandals," said Aquila.

"Who else?"

"A few Marcomanni and some Alans."

"Are you certain?"

"A Frank who knows these people was positive."

I nodded. "Well, it was good practice for our men. But next time it may not be so easy. I expect the Aleman King is now busy killing all his spies. He may believe me now. We shall not be troubled again before the spring."

Nor were we. It was a warm autumn and when the leaves fell my men began to fish the river again and no one watched them from the other bank. In November it rained a great deal and it became very cold, though the only ice that we saw were small floes that had come down from the Upper Rhenus, high above Borbetomagus, and even these were breaking up as they passed us by. In December the Christians began to look forward to their great festival and much time was spent in making preparations for it. They were much cheered to learn—those in the camp garrison who did not know—that it was here at Moguntiacum that the Emperor Constantine, on his way to destroy Maxentius at the Milvian bridge, had the famous vision that converted him to their faith. They laughed a lot and there was considerable drunkenness and the cohort commanders had a busy time soothing the feelings of outraged fathers of young women, while the charge sheets were full with details of men who had overstayed their leave.

One morning a legionary who had stayed out all night staggered into the camp with a knife wound in his chest. At the subsequent inquiry I learned that he had gone to one of the villages—he was drunk at the time—in search of a woman and had been attacked by a night watchman, who caught him climbing the palisade. I punished him with stoppages of pay and put him on fatigue duties for three months. Then I rode out to the village concerned. They were collecting brushwood in a clearing when I arrived, while further down the hill a handful of boys and old men were doing the winter sowing. A hunting party had just returned, singing and laughing, a freshly killed buck swaying from a pole. While I watched, they quartered the animal, cutting the meat into strips which would then be smoked over the hut fires, so many strips per man as the chief directed. On one side of the clearing was a huge mound covered with damp leaves, from under which smoke billowed fretfully.

Their chief wiped the sweat from his face and smiled broadly. "Charcoal," he said, speaking in camp Latin. "We sell it to your soldiers. You have brought us much trade. That is good."

"And trouble," I said.

"Oh, that. He was drunk. Is the man dead?" For the first time he looked at me with an expression of alarm.

"No, a pity he isn't. It would have been a good example to the rest." I leaned forward over my horse's neck. "I am sorry. I do not like my men to molest your women. He is well punished. It will not happen again, I promise you."

He grinned and stroked his beard. "You cannot stop them from trying, but I can stop them from succeeding. Will you come to my hut and drink?"

I had tasted the native beer already. I did not like it. "Thank you, no. Another time." I looked round at the activity. "You are happy here?"

"Of course. That is why we came."

"You are of the Alemanni?"

"Yes. We found the east bank too crowded."

"But surely it is only crowded because everyone insists on living in the same area?" I pointed to the east. "Beyond that river there are vast lands, more than enough for all your people."

He shrugged. "But so much is forest."

"Well, if you cut the forest back then there is more ground on which to sow crops."

He said gravely, "But the forests belong to the gods. One cannot destroy their home lest they destroy ours in turn."

"It is hard work being a farmer, I agree."

He nodded eagerly. "And that is another reason. We are a restless people. It has always been so. Besides, we enjoy fighting, and it is easier to gain what you want by spilling blood instead of sweat."

"And what will happen if more people cross the river?"

His face wrinkled. "Then we should have to fight to hold what we possess. But that is why you are here. They will not come now."

"I hope you are right. Have you heard that the Vandals are looking for a new land?"

He shook his head. "No." He looked alarmed. "I have heard nothing. I have no friends on the other bank. The Vandals, you say." He touched his chin. "That would be bad."

"Why?"

He hesitated. "Why? Because we of the Alemanni fear death, but the Vandals fear nothing. They believe that if they die in battle then they go to a great hall where warriors like themselves are always welcome, and where there is eternal feasting and drinking, and there they live again."

"And do you believe this?" I asked.

His faded eyes smiled a little. "I shall know that when I am dead."

I looked at the ploughed land. "Was the harvest good?"

He shrugged again. "It has been worse; it has been better. The priest prayed for us in the church in the town, but I think"—his voice dropped—"it was better in the days when the Corn King held his court."

"I think so too." I rode back to the camp, comforted. I was glad that someone believed in us and, perhaps, trusted us a little.

Quintus and I, with a dozen others, built a small temple outside the camp, and I, who had passed through all the elements of my mystery, consecrated the altar, and there we celebrated, on the appointed day, our faith. It was a poor temple and compared ill with the old one at Corstopitum—but it was ours. We built it, we cherished it, and we renewed ourselves before the god in whom we believed. I stood there beneath the blue vaulted ceiling, while the light slanted like a lance through the open windows onto the upturned eyes, and the knife moved, and the Bull died. In that perfect moment when everything was clear I could see the way and the pattern and the world of no shadows, and I knew what it was like to be a child in the womb as I knew what it would be like at the moment when I died. I could feel the very skin that covered me age and wrinkle and see the nails grow upon my fingers. I knew then, without doubt or hesitation, that the things that mattered would come right for those of us who had the courage to burn ourselves in the sun.

The Christians, too, celebrated the birth of their mystery with food and wine, and on that day there was amity between us.

It was a happy time. Afterward I would remember the green fir trees, the silver birch and the pines. I would remember the smell of wood smoke from the campfires and the crisp sound of trumpets speaking their orders, remember the rough kindness of the villagers with their fat children and their heavy, smiling women, their dogs and their fleas. Then, even the fox under my tunic seemed a burden I could endure.

In January and February there was more rain and the camp paths turned to mud while the roads between the forts were flooded in many places. The flow of the river was at its minimum during this period, however, and the level dropped considerably. Now was the easiest time to make a crossing and my patrols shivered in the wet as they kept watch upon the far bank. Imperceptibly it became warmer and the hours of daylight lengthened. Fatigue parties were busy cleaning up the huts and clearing the ditches and drains of the mud, sticks, and filth which choked them. Cohorts and squadrons began to leave the camp secretly and by night, only to reappear the next day or the day after, arriving in good marching order with trumpets sounding, while those in the camp cheered heartily as though in greeting of reinforcements. As the ground dried and the sun shone more frequently cavalry sections would ride out with branches dragging in the dirt behind them. Seen from a distance these dust clouds looked as though a regiment and not a dozen men were on the move. Small defensive positions were built along the banks of the river at intervals of a mile and equipped most convincingly with dummy ballistae and firing platforms for nonexistent troops. At the same time we began the real work of erecting a palisade, ten feet high, protected by an outer ditch, along the line of the road between Moguntiacum and Bingium. Work on this was slow, there were so few troops available, and I knew that if we completed it by the middle of summer we should be lucky. The Rhenus fleet kept up a continuous patrolling of the river between Confluentes and Borbetomagus, and I issued strict instructions that no one was to be allowed to cross the river to the east bank who had not passed through a control point, bearing a certificate signed by myself. Anyone attempting to evade interception was to be killed immediately. And all the while, the road from Treverorum was filled with convoys of wagons, moving east and bringing us the supplies and equipment that we so badly needed.

"I want as many bows, arrows, and spears as we can get," I said to Quintus one afternoon, while we were out watching a dummy camp being built three miles to the north of Bingium.

Quintus gestured at the new camp. "Will this deceive them for long, do you think?"

"I hope so. When it's finished I shall have two sections of men put into it from the Bingium garrison. They will be kept busy blowing trumpets at the right times, lighting cooking fires, and patrolling the walls. It will all look quite convincing from a distance."

"The Alemanni have long eyes," he said quietly.

We turned and rode down the road to see how work on the palisade was progressing. Later, I visited the three islands off Moguntiacum where, on each, two centuries were sweating to clear the undergrowth, dig defensive ditches, build fortified towers, and erect platforms from which ballistae could be fired.

"I want this work finished by the end of the month," I said.

"When will they come, sir?" I was asked. That was the question they were all asking me. It was the question I often asked myself.

"I don't know," I said. "But if I was going to make the attempt I should either do it between the end of April and the beginning of June, or in September. The Rhenus reaches flood heights in June and July. No one in his senses would attempt a crossing then, with enemy on the other bank. During those months at least we should be safe enough."

We might be safe but there would be no rest. We had to go on giving an impression of activity and of constant determination. The palisade along the road had to be finished. I needed another dummy camp on the bank beyond the stream, just clear of the point of Harbor Island. In addition there were other plans, less warlike, but in the long run more effective that I hoped to put into operation shortly.

One day I crossed the Rhenus at Bingium with half a cohort and three hundred cavalry to visit Guntiarus. His berg was in a great clearing in the forest, fortified by a palisade and a deep ditch, and there was only one entrance through a pair of massive log gates. The place was not clean. You could smell the stink of humans and animals half a mile away. The dwelling houses were built of timber, with thatched roofs, daub-coated walls, and entrance porches over barred doors. They were arranged in no particular order but each was surrounded by its own barns, stables, and byres, and the cattle rubbed shoulders with men and were not kept apart as on our own farms. The King's Hall was nearly two hundred feet long, an impressive enough place, though very dark and dirty. It was here, surrounded by the warriors of his council, that he received me. He was courteous enough but I could see that he was worried. He sweated like a nervous stallion and it was obvious that he wondered what I might ask of him when the attempt to cross the river was made.

"I am a friend of Rome," he said. It was an expression he repeated at intervals as though to convince himself as much as me.

"That I know," I said. "That is why I take your young men into my service and pay subsidies"—it was the polite word for bribery—"to you so that you may help your people who are poor."

"What can I do for you?"

"I want nothing this time but information."

"I will do my best to help you." He looked relieved.

"Is the King Gunderic still in the land of the Alemanni?"

He hesitated for a moment. "Yes. His people wintered there."

"All of them?" I asked sharply. "Or only those who fought under the shield of Radagaisus?"

"I do not know how many."

"And what of the Quadi and the Asding Vandals whom my general and friend, Stilicho, drove from Italia? Have they gone to their own people?"

"It is as you say. They have joined with their own kind."

He smiled and plucked at his beard. There was a stir among the men about him but though I looked at them hard there was little enough in their faces to tell what they thought. A slim arm that was about to lower a jug of beer onto the table between us shook slightly, so that a few spots spattered the roughly scraped boards. I looked up at the blue eyes of a tall blond girl who stood beside me. Her hair lay in thick plaits upon her breast, about her neck she wore a silver torque, elaborately decorated. I judged her to be the King's eldest daughter. She was certainly a fine-looking girl. She smiled at me, wiped the spots with the sleeve of her gown, said something to her father (it sounded like an apology), and then withdrew.

The King said, "If you have time you must come hunting. I can show you some fine sport."

"I would like that," I said. "It has been a long winter."

Quintus said, "I drink to your health. You have fine sons and beautiful daughters."

"Indeed, yes. Four daughters, but six sons, all old enough to carry their ax, save for this cub here." He dropped his hand onto the shoulders of a small boy who stood at his side. There was a look of great pride in his eyes. "You have sons, too, who will be men now with sons of their own, no doubt."

Quintus glanced at me. "No," he said. "We have no sons."

The King looked troubled. "It is a fine thing to have sons who will bear one's name. But sometimes it is the will of God that it shall not be so."

There was silence. Neither of us spoke. Then he said regretfully, "I am indeed sorry to hear you say that."

I said, "Our camp was attacked last autumn. You heard of the matter, no doubt. There were Alans, Quadi, and Siling Vandals among the dead. None of these belong to the Suevi." By Suevi I meant those tribes whose lands marched with the frontiers of Rome along the Rhenus and the Danubius.

He shrugged his shoulders. "We have peoples of other tribes within our own. It signifies little."

I said, "King Guntiarus, you know and I know that an attempt will be made to cross the river. If those who make the attempt try to march through your lands first, I shall expect you to fight and defend it. If you do, we will aid you. But if the crossing is made outside your frontier, I want you to keep your sword hand empty, unless I ask for your help. You do not want war with the Alemanni and I want them to have no excuse for attacking you. Help me in this matter and I promise that next year's subsidies will be twice the normal size."

"What if they try to take our salt again?" said the King's eldest son in a clear, high voice. "Are we to give it to them as though we were slaves?"

"Neither behave like slaves nor like foolish women who throw cooking pots in a temper. Behave like men. A cool hand is better than a hot one."

The King said hastily, "I understand. I am a friend of Rome. But why are my people on your bank not allowed to cross the river? It is causing much talk and much difficulty."

"Because I do not want offense to be given. If I treat your people differently from the Franks and the Alemanni it will make for difficulties—for both of us." It was a lie, and he knew it was a lie, but there was truth in what I said—a little anyway—and he had to accept it. Thirty years before, the Alemanni had put seventy thousand men into the field against the Emperor Gratian. They were too strong to quarrel with without a reason.

He said, "I am a man of peace. Soon I celebrate the marriage of my eldest daughter to Marcomir of the Franks. It is a good match and will help to bind us all together. There will be a great feast. You and your generals must come and honor my house with your presence. I am, after all, a friend of Rome."

"We shall be happy to come if our duties permit."

He slapped his thigh then. "I promised you one of my daughters," he said with a chuckle. "I had almost forgotten. I remember, I was very drunk at the time."

There was a roar of laughter from the chiefs about the table.

I began to protest. "No, no," he said. "A promise is a promise. The marriage can take place with the other. It will be a fine double wedding and we shall have a great feast. It will bind the alliance strongly between us."

I said quickly, "When my wife died I took an oath not to marry again. I cannot forswear my gods."

He began to look disgruntled. He said, "You should be a Christian like me."

"But I am not and I cannot change now. It would be wrong for your daughter to marry a pagan and one who is old enough to be her father."

He chuckled. "But that is what we need at our age." He turned to Quintus and grinned.

I said hastily, "My friend is also a pagan." I looked desperately at my cavalry commander for inspiration.

Quintus said, "Our senior tribune, Lucillius, is a fine young man, and of good family. It would be a good match and the girl would like him. He is—very active. He is also a Christian."

"Which girl?" I muttered under my breath.

"Excellent. It is agreed." Guntiarus roared his delight and the pact was sealed in wine.

As we undressed that night in the guest house, I said, "And who is going to tell the unsuspecting Lucillius?"

Quintus yawned. "You are," he said. "It is your command."

On our way out of his berg we passed a line of poles upon which the heads of enemies and criminals shriveled in the sun.

"Peace," said Quintus, looking at them curiously. "Only the dead have that."

We rode along the east bank, following a twisting track that rose and fell between the wooded hills and the dark valleys in between. At Marcomir's berg the young chief came out to meet us, riding bareback and carrying a hunting bow in his hand. I congratulated him on his coming marriage to the King's daughter.

"She is a fine girl," he said. "My father would have been pleased."

"When will it take place?"

"After the harvest." He grinned suddenly. "That is a good time for feasting."

I said, "Let us hope that it will be so." I leaned over my horse's neck. "Marcomir, I am sending patrols to hold your side of the river between the Moenus and the foothills. If they are driven in they have orders to light beacons as a warning before they retreat."

"And what do you want me to do?" he asked gravely.

"Nothing, until I tell you. Do not throw one spear, nor fire a single arrow in anger without my word. I will tell you when is the time to strike."

He said, "I understand." He smiled. There was a pause and then he said quietly, "Can you hold them if they attack you with all their war bands?"

"Yes," I said. "I can. They have never met cavalry before."

"But we ride," he protested. He was half angry, half laughing. "We use horses in war. A little anyway."

Quintus said, "Come over the river when you have time. Then watch my cavalry."

In the distance, like a thin smudge of charcoal against the evening sky, I could see the Taunus, the great mountain range that had once marked the extent of our eastern frontier. "That is where I want to go," I said suddenly. "Will you take us?"

We stayed a day in his house and then, with his men guiding us and he riding on my left side, set out along the road that led to the abandoned Limes. I was intensely curious to see them, and so was Quintus. We might never have the chance again. After a time the road, whose surface grew worse with each mile, vanished suddenly and there was nothing ahead but green turf and tangled undergrowth. "They tore it up," said the Frank. He turned to me, his face serious. "You do not know how they hate Rome."

"Why?" I asked.

"There are many reasons: the loss of freedom, the heavy taxes, the injustice of your laws, the cruelty of your military conscription. Even your towns, with their houses and their straight roads, seem like prisons to men who hunt in the forest and whose women cook by an open fire." I glanced at Quintus and shook my head slightly. This was not a time for argument.

The sky clouded over, it grew dark, and the rain began to fall in great splashing drops that soaked the breeches I was wearing and made wet patches on my knees and shoulders. The horses plodded on, squelching through the mud, and we had to duck our heads to avoid being scratched by the branches that barred our way. We saw few people; a hut or two in a clearing, occupied by a sullen farmer and his wife, who watched us suspiciously as we passed, but that was all. The forests were full of game. Twice I saw bears, playing in the watery sunlight with their cubs; once a great boar lumbered across our path, stopped to grunt at us with red eyes, and then trotted off into the scrub. And at night we could hear the wolves, howling in the darkness around the camp. It was then that I remembered Varus and his three legions and was sorry that I had come. All the time we were climbing upward toward a forest ridge that showed itself upon the horizon whenever we came to a clear space between the trees.

On the fourth day we came out of the woods into a great clearing that seemed to extend for miles to the right and left of us. It was as though the blade of a giant sword, red-hot from the furnace, had been placed on the forest and burned a great cut along its length. The clearing was nearly a thousand yards wide in places. In front of us ran a road, half covered now with weeds and dirt. Beyond it, a quarter of a mile distant, stood a square stone watchtower with a smashed roof and a broken balcony. We rode up to it and dismounted, while our squadron spread out and posted sentries in a half circle. Slowly we walked up to the tower through a litter of fallen tiles. In front of it, facing north, half filled in now by the action of wind and rain were the remnants of the great ditch. But the great mound of earth that had been flung up behind it still remained. Not even time could destroy that. On the further side were the fragmentary remains of the palisade. Much of the timber had been pulled out to be used for other purposes, but here and there, a section still stood in its entirety, mute evidence of the slackened power of that empire—my empire—which now fought only on the defensive.

The entrance to the tower was ten feet above the ground, and in the old days the garrison had used a ladder which they then pulled up after them. One of the legionaries made a rough climbing pole out of a loose piece of timber and said, with a grin, "Will that do, sir?" I nodded. I took off my helmet and climbed, entering the gap where the door had once been. Inside was dust and darkness. I found the original ladder that led from one level to the next and mounted it cautiously till I came out onto the balcony at the top. It was raining slightly and there was a cold wind blowing from the north. Scratched on the walls I saw names—the names of men, now dead, and long forgotten; men whose names told me clearly that they had come from Moesia, from Apulia, from Pannonia, and from such far distant provinces as Mauretania and Aegyptus, the southern rim of the empire. Carved with greater care I read the name of the legions from which the men came who had once guarded this section of the frontier. I screwed up my eyes. "Legio IV Macedonica," I said, peering at the faint scratches on the stone.

"What, in the name of the gods, happened to them, I wonder?" said Quintus softly. "I never heard their number in my life."

"Perhaps someone will say the same of us," I said grimly. "They were raised by Caesar and fought with Marcus Antoninus in Macedonia, but deserted to Octavius before Philippi." I peered again. "Here are some more. Leg. XXII Prim. They were here at the death of Nero. But both they and the Fourth were annihilated in one of the Aleman wars of the last century. Now, this looks like Leg. XIV Gemina. They were posted to Moguntiacum by Augustus. Asprenas brought them back to Vetera after the Varian disaster. They came back again, after going into Britannia with Aulius Plautius. They're in Pannonia now."

Quintus scrabbled at the stone work. "Can you read this? It's the Thirtieth, I think. Only the last ten is missing."

"Yes, look at the emblem. They were raised by Domitian and were still here in the time of Hadrian. A detachment fought alongside us in Italia. Do you remember? By the gods, that seems a long time ago."

Marcomir said, "It is a place of ghosts."

"It was not defended to the end," I said. "It was just abandoned."

"That was in the time of Gallienus," said Quintus. "My father told me about it. The cohorts were in forts, seven miles apart, with these posts every half mile in between."

"And now—nothing."

We descended the ladders and walked back to where our horses cropped the grass. I looked at the clearing and at the mound of earth, stretching away into the distance. I said, "Once, you could walk along that under the protection of Roman spears. And if you walked far enough you would travel through eight provinces until you reached Scythia and a great sea."

Quintus said, "I should like to have done that. It would have been a fine thing to walk across the roof of the empire."

We looked at each other and there was the same thought in both our minds.

Marcomir said, "Then, you were the lords of the world. But now...." He did not end the sentence. He did not need to.

At the edge of the clearing I turned to look back but the square tower was almost hidden now by the driving rain. It was as though even the gods had pity enough to weep for our fallen greatness.

A mile from Moguntiacum we reached the furthest of the outposts that I had stationed on the east bank. When I had finished inspecting the men and their weapons I spoke privately to the optio in charge. "What is the matter?" I said. "You look as though you had seen a ghost."

He said, his face tense beneath its leathery tan, "I will show you, General. I have already sent a message across the river."

We walked as he directed. Two hundred yards from the post I could see an object standing above the ground. As we came closer I could see what it was: the decapitated head of a horse, fixed upon a pole. I looked at the dried blood upon the nostrils, the human hand held between the yellowed teeth, and the glazed eyes that crawled with flies. "What does it mean?"

Marcomir said, "It is the common way to insult an enemy in these parts. You may expect trouble from now on. I will warn my people."

Two nights later I was woken by a disturbance and the camp guard commander was at my door, reporting that a small boat had been seen close to the shore, north of the town. The two men in it had been killed with javelins but the guards' efforts to catch the boat had failed. It had drifted downstream in the darkness.

"I do not know what they were trying to do, sir, unless making contact with a spy in the town," he said. I nodded and went back to bed. Long ago I had learned not to worry about small problems that I could not solve. It was as well, for in the morning the puzzle solved itself. I looked at the dead man lying on the bank, close to the point where the guard had intercepted the boat—and I recognized him. "They brought him back to show that they had caught him," I said. "He was a Frank I sent to spy out the camp of Rando some weeks ago. They were not kind of him, were they, Quintus? Pity. Now we shall never know what he learned."

The work of preparation and its problems continued. Complaints from quartermasters about a shortage of boots and rations, queries from armorers concerning warheads for arrows and suitable canisters in which to hold the preparation for liquid fire, difficulties over the stabling of spare horses, requests from cohort commanders whom I visited to advise on tactics to meet this eventuality or that, discussions to simplify our signal system, auxiliaries to be commended for their efficiency, and everyone to be encouraged, everyone to be made to believe that with their aid I could achieve the impossible. The days were never long enough, and though I worked my officers hard and deLegated my authority as much as possible, both Quintus and I began to feel the strain. We woke tired in the mornings and we went to bed at night to sleep as though we were already dead.

Often I had dreams and I stood again on that beach with Julian, knowing every line on that tired, bitter face, creased with the lines of middle age, and hearing again the tired, bitter words that he had spoken. It is I who shiver now.... what happened to my high priest's daughter?... They believed I was a god....

Did he know or did he guess that exile was the punishment that Fullofaudes had intended for him? I often wondered.

CHAPTER XI

Julius Optatus said patiently, "I am sorry to trouble you again, sir, but the supplies for this month are overdue. We are short of fodder for the horses, the remounts we were promised haven't arrived, and General Veronius keeps pressing me to do something."

I looked at the documents in his hand. "What else?"

"There's quite a lot, sir."

"Go on."

"The breastplates for the auxiliaries at Confluentes still haven't arrived; the spear shafts came on that last mule train, but without their heads, and some of the weapons aren't up to standard. The bows from Mantua are too light, and the last consignment of swords are badly balanced; much too heavy in the hilt. Shall I send them back?"

"Can our armorers do anything?"

"They can try, sir, but the master fletcher just got into a rage when I showed him the bows." Optatus grinned. "You know what a temper he has, sir. He snapped the one he was testing and threw it at me."

"I'll write to the Curator," I said. "I'll see what I can do."

I was always writing letters these days: letters to the Governor of Belgica, asking for his support for this or that; letters to the Curator, full of detailed requests and complaints, all of which he answered meticulously but about which little seemed actually to be done; and letters to Chariobaudes, General of the field army in Gaul, asking for the loan of trained centurions and officers whom he always found an excuse not to send. Then there was the difficulty of supplies. These were delivered by the slow wagon post and I relied on this for all foodstuffs, uniforms and arms, timber and stonework. The trouble here was administrative. It was an imperial service which was controlled by warrant. I was allowed only five warrants a year, which was absurd considering the wagon loads of goods I needed. To obtain more warrants I had to write to the Praefectus Praetorio and it took time for the messengers to get to Arelate and back. Even a messenger needed a warrant. Without it he could not change horses at the posting stations. The first time I wrote the Praefectus replied that I had had my quota for the year. It took another messenger and another warrant to persuade him that I needed special consideration. After that he would always send me a batch of five warrants at a time, but never more. I complained about this on numerous occasions but without effect. He was the Emperor's representative and he knew his power. I had met him once, a small, insignificant, shortsighted man, now badly running to fat. He had a dry, pedantic way of speaking, rarely smiled, and was quite without a sense of humor. His only interest outside his work, besides his plain, dull wife, was his curious passion for Greek sculpture, about which he wrote endless dry, dull, and worthless monographs which nobody ever read. He was, and I believed it, honest, incorruptible, and painstaking at his work; but he had no imagination and this flawed what intelligence he possessed. This was the man with whom I had to work to achieve my purpose and, thinking of him sometimes, I could have wept with frustration. He was so typical of the senior administrators who now controlled the destinies of the imperial provinces. Small wonder then that Rome grew downward like a cow's tail.

My principal worry, however, was the shortage of recruits to the auxiliaries. Though I had enough, if need be, to man the signal towers, provide skeleton garrisons for the forts, and to take on those duties that would release my men for the more important task of fighting, I still had hopes that I might raise a field force of reserves from the teeming population in and around Treverorum. I had sent out officers and centurions, in batches, on recruiting drives, but with little success. Between them they had not raised enough men to man a war galley.

"There must be some way of getting them to join," I said in despair.

"We have taken on all the convicts for the fleet," said Quintus. "Now, whenever the magistrates sentence a man they offer him the choice of hard labor in the mines with lashes or hard labor in the legion of General Maximus, with pay."

"What about the slaves?"

"They have all run away or long ago accepted Honorius' offer and gone to Italia."

"If I had time to spare I would go to Arelate and make them help me."

"What help do they give who do not wish to give it," he said in a somber voice. "The Praefectus Praetorio would only smile that thin smile of his, and say that the matter must be referred to another meeting of his wretched council."

"Yes," I said. "I never met a man so terrified of taking responsibility. The only decisions he ever makes are those that affect his own desires. He is quite selfish and quite useless."

At that moment Aquila came in. "A message from Flavius at Treverorum, sir."

I read the letter.

"More trouble," said Quintus, raising his eyebrow.

"Yes. One of his men has deserted him."

"Well, we're best without him then."

I said grimly, "He's taken refuge in one of the churches. Flavius tried to get him out and there was trouble with the priests. They have seen it as an opportunity to denounce us. We tax them to the hilt, steal their goods, demand their food, and then even the men who are meant to defend them desert."

Aquila said, "It could be very awkward, sir."

"It is."

"What will you do?"

"I shall have to go and straighten things out."

"The fuss will die down," said Quintus calmly.

"Will it? Who will take up arms now, when even Roman soldiers are deserting to seek sanctuary in the middle of the city? Flavius is an idiot. He should have let the man get out of the city and then arrested him."

"Well, how was he to know the man would run into a church."

I said irritably, "He just should have known."

I rode to Treverorum, alone but for my escort. I came to Romulus at sundown, just as they were about to close the gates. While the men picketed their horses in the courtyard I sent a message to Flavius. He arrived very late, having come straight from the house of a friend where he had been dining.

He stared at me like a bewildered bear. He was very drunk.

"Sorry, sir. Didn't expect you—sir."

"No," I said. "I can see that. Which church is this man in? What is his name? What is his record? I am going to see him in the morning. I want to know everything about him now."

He stared at me helplessly, swaying on his feet. "Tired," he said.

I rose from my stool, picked up a pitcher and flung the water over him. The shock overbalanced him and he sprawled on the floor, dripping, bruised, and winded.

"Talk," I said. "I'm twice your age and I have just ridden seventy miles in two days. You've made a mess of things and I've got to clear them up. The sooner you start the sooner we shall both get to bed. Wake up."

I had hoped my arrival at sundown might have kept my coming a secret but when I went into the street the next morning there was already a crowd waiting. I did not ride; I walked.

"There may be trouble," said Flavius. "Ride on horseback, sir, and with an escort."

"Then there will be trouble," I said.

"Your sword, sir. You've forgotten to put it on."

I said, "I never forget my sword. I want you and one man to come with me. Leave your weapons in the armory. And keep five paces behind me all the way."

"I—" He broke off and stared in front of him.

"You are a Christian, are you not? I thought you people had a passion to martyr yourselves."

He gulped.

I said unkindly, "I shall be in good company if anything goes wrong. Besides, I don't know the way."

We walked. The crowd pressed about us, fell back to make way for us, and then followed curiously. Men and women, boys and girls, little children even, all had that look I had seen on the faces of the crowd at a circus on the arena, the pale excitement of those who wish to see blood spilled without hurt to themselves. At first they smiled, then they stared, and then, as we approached the church, an ugly muttering broke out. A woman laughed, and a voice cried contemptuously, "What else do you expect of a man who believes in a cattle-thieving God?" There were jeers and insults. Someone threw a stone. It hit me on the mouth and I could feel the blood trickling down my chin. A second struck me above the right eye and the bleeding nearly blinded me. I felt sick with pain but I took no notice. They were scum, like all crowds in all cities. It was my soldier who mattered to me, not them.

The crowd was thickest by the square, on the north side of which stood the church. On the steps were a number of priests, and in the midst of them, the Bishop. Artorius was there, too, standing in the shadow of a pillar, his freedmen about him. Of him I took no notice. It was not him I had come to see. As I approached the Bishop a snarl came from the crowd. The spring sunshine shone upon white vestments and red pillars, upon brown and yellow tunics and upon a scarlet cloak and helmets of bronze and gold. I mounted the steps and came face to face with Mauritius,

Bishop of Treverorum.

"Good morning," I said. "It is a fine day. The Christians among my men send their greetings and pray that you may do them the honor of visiting Moguntiacum so that they may be blessed at your hands."

"What do you want?" he said.

"I wish to enter the church."

"I do not allow unbelievers to enter."

"Can you be sure that I am one? And if I am, is it fitting that another should stay inside it and make it his home?"

"He is a Christian."

"If he is, then you should know that he is a follower of Pelagius, of whom you do not, I believe, approve." I frowned and closed my eye to avoid the blood. "Perhaps 'abominate' is the right word."

He looked startled. "It is not true," he said.

"Oh yes, it is. I know my men even if you do not know yours."

There was a small silence between us but it was not friendly. The crowd was silent now.

He said, "Even if you are speaking the truth, my church is a sanctuary to all who are persecuted. And while he is there no one may touch him."

"Is that the law?" I asked.

He glanced at the Curator. "It is accepted custom," he said. "It has the force of law."

"No one is persecuting him," I said. "He is a soldier. He volunteered, as did all my men from Britannia. He is under oath. He has deserted. I am entitled to arrest him."

"Not in my church."

I said patiently, "I bear no arms. I use no force. I wish merely to talk to one Vibius, a legionary, who has abandoned his duty. Would you not wish to do the same to one who has wandered from his faith?"

He hesitated.

I said, "I will leave my force of strong and brutal men outside; both of them. Do not be alarmed. I shall not destroy your sanctuaries as you have destroyed mine."

He said, "I do not trust you."

"But you do. You trust me so much that you leave me and six thousand men to stand between you and your enemies. You trust me so much that you give me no help of your own free will. Not once since I arrived have you offered assistance of any kind. You ignore me and by doing so you trust me."

He said, "It is not right that a Christian world should be defended by a pagan such as yourself. It is a mockery of our faith, a scandal in the eyes of Our Lord."

"You are quick to pass judgment."

"It is my duty to speak as my conscience dictates."

"And let who will, cast the first stone." I touched my cheek with the tip of my finger.

"You blaspheme."

"Will you stand in my way all day?"

He said, "I shall stand like that rock upon which our church was built. It is you who are in the way, not I."

"My lord Bishop."

"No."

I said in a whisper, "No one has made me so angry as you. If you do not let me in to talk to this breaker of oaths, this deserter of his comrades, this perjurer of his soul, I shall do that for which we may both be sorry."

He smiled. "You do not have authority in this city."

I shook my head to get rid of the dripping blood. I said, "If I want this man I can take him by force and not even you can stop me. The Praefectus Praetorio of Gaul, even, will back me in this matter."

He glanced sideways at the Curator. "You would do that?" he asked.

"If you refuse this request, yes."

He said, "I thought you had come here to defend the state and to uphold its laws."

"I have."

He said, gently, "But you cannot do so. You cannot abolish laws in a state, for without laws there is no state."

I said, impatiently, "You play at words, my lord Bishop."

"And you threaten me."

"I threaten no one. I wish merely to speak to a man who has lost his faith."

"And who will give it back to him?" he asked contemptuously. "You, with your floggings and your executions?"

"Of course not. Only he can recover for himself what he has lost. Shall I tell you about him? His name is Vibius. His father was a poor shopkeeper in a small town called Canovium in the mountains in the west of Britannia. He had two brothers and three sisters. They were always hungry; the town was dying as towns do, and he could not get work. He took to thieving because it was the only way he could live. He would have ended as a convict in the mines, most likely. But when I formed my legion he joined it. It offered him food and shelter and clothes and money, and the promise of a pension at the end. He had security. He sent half his pay home to his family to help keep them alive.

"I turned him into a soldier—a good one—and he gained a self-respect he never had before. He can neither read nor write, but he is clever with his hands and makes leather harness for the horses when he is not fighting. He can build a bridge or make a road, mend a leaking roof or repair a broken wall. You would find him useful in this crumbling city, my lord Bishop. All these things he learned as a soldier."

I paused. I said, "He served with me in Italia. Then we came here. He met a girl in the city; she is the daughter of a man who makes glass ornaments to sell to people of your faith; and he wanted to marry her. The girl's father said no, he was a legionary. He would be here today and gone tomorrow. He was not to be trusted. This made him miserable. He was homesick, too. He had learned that his mother had died. So he deserted. He had some idea of leaving the city, sending for the girl, and taking her home. He is not very clever at thinking. He did not think much about what would happen afterward.

"But what will happen if he does go home? The district he lives in is full of people whose sons have joined my legion. Many of them have since died. Will he be happy with his shame? Will they let him be happy? Will his girl be proud of him when he returns to thieving? Will she grow to despise him as a man who ran away? How much of their time will they spend in a sweat of fear, waiting for the authorities to catch up with them? You are the expert on souls and a man's conscience. Not I."

He said, "Is this true, what you have told me?"

"I may be a pagan, but I am also a soldier. I know my men."

He frowned and his hands played with the cross about his neck.

I said, "We have, both of us, laws to obey. Let me render unto Caesar those things that are Caesar's, and I will let you render unto God those things which are His."

He stood aside and I walked alone into the church.

When I came out again into the bright sunlight the crowd had gone and the square was empty. Only Flavius and my soldier stood there on the steps, at a little distance from the Bishop.

"Well?" he asked.

I blinked. The light, among other things, blinded me. I said harshly, "I spoke to a beggar inside. He told me that Vibius crept up to the great door and listened to our conversation through the crack. When he heard me say—that I would—take him by force if need be, he—he left the door and went to the far side where they sometimes sit and play at dice when no one is about."

The Bishop raised his head sharply.

"He is in your hands now," I said.

I threw the dagger that all legionaries carry on to the steps and held out my hands. They were covered in blood.

I walked down the steps. I said, "Pray for him if you can. He must have been so unhappy, so afraid, so very lonely to do what he did. I, too, have known such despair."

I heard a voice behind me say, "Maximus." Out in the square I turned and looked back up the steps to the silent figure at the top. I said, "He had no faith in either of us."

I turned and walked away from the church. At that moment all that I wanted to do was to be alone.

On the tenth night of May I was woken by a trumpet blowing the alarm. It was a wet night and I shivered on the wall and wrapped my cloak about me as I listened to the swirl of the water and watched the signal beacons flare across the river. On either side of me the troops stood waiting. Faintly through the darkness I heard cries and shouting.

"The outposts are being driven in," I said. "Pray that they make the boats in time."

At dawn, while I was drinking a cup of hot wine, for it was bitterly cold and the rain was still in our faces, we saw movement on the other bank, little parties of men launching the boats that lay concealed there. They were not attacked and I assumed that the enemy were content to let them go.

"Tell the centurion-in-charge to report to me when he gets in," I said to Barbatio. "Tell half the men to stand down and keep watch for any boat bearing a blue cloth on a pole. It will be from Marcomir. He may have news for us, too."

The centurion rubbed a sore on his nose. He was hot, excited, and tired and the steam rose from his wet cloak. He had little to say. All the posts had reported movement in the country to the east and south—this was before the moon rose—all had been attacked a little after midnight. In accordance with their instructions they had fired the beacons and withdrawn half an hour later.

"Were the attacks in strength?"

The centurion said grimly, "If we hadn't left when we did, sir, we should all be dead by now."

"How many casualties?"

"Three dead and four wounded, sir."

I returned to the river. The sun was up and a mass of tribesmen were moving slowly from the woods that surrounded the old villa district to the water's edge. There must have been between five and eight thousand, all told. An excited decurion from a cavalry patrol to the south of the camp rode in to report that the mouth of the Moenus was crowded, for as far back as he could see, with a fleet of small boats. "Filled with armed men, sir."

"Order up the nearest ships of the Rhenus fleet," I said.

"I have done so, sir," came the reply. He was torn between apprehension, lest he had done the wrong thing, and pride in his own initiative.

"Good," I said. "Signal them to attack, but they are to keep out of the narrows. They will be trapped if they go too far in."

My building of the fleet justified itself that morning. The three ships moved rapidly into the mouth and, executing a series of turning movements, opened fire with their ballistae, using both fireballs and iron projectiles. Those of the enemies' boats that tried to close and board had their crews shot to pieces by the archers, while their craft were set on fire. The action lasted a little over an hour and by the end of that time half the enemy boats had retreated to a safe point upstream. The other half had been sunk.

"Signal them to return upriver and anchor," I said at the end. "They may try to concentrate again later."

All that afternoon the Vandal war bands remained close to the bank.

Tents went up, fires were lit, supply wagons could be seen in the distance, while palisades for defense were erected along the riverfront. By the early evening the smoke from a hundred fires hung ominously, a dark blue cloud, above the shadowed plain; and, all the while, the constant thud of axes and the groans of dying trees told us that the woods were being cut back to provide camping space for the mass of people moving in slowly from the direction of the old Limes road. They had come at last: they were determined to stay.

Messages came in from Bingium, from Boudobrigo, from Salisio and from Confluentes to say that all was well and that no enemy threatened the opposite bank. A horseman, riding in from Borbetomagus, however, said that there was an Aleman host encamped opposite the fort but no fighting had taken place.

For a week nothing happened and then a boat pushed off from the other shore one morning, a man bearing a green branch standing in the bows. I met him on the shore. He was a young man with a short beard and he carried no weapons except pride.

"I am Sunno, son of the King, Rando of the Alemanni. I come as a hostage. My father would speak with you in his camp across the river." I withdrew a few paces and said to Marcomir, who stood wrapped in a cloak, the cowl well over his face, "Does he speak the truth?"

"Yes. It is his eldest son. Let me come with you. I understand them. They are akin to my own people."

"Thank you, but no. This is something I will do myself. There is little danger."

"I am a warrior," he said. "It is silly for me to hide behind this."

"I want you alive when the time is ripe, not murdered before it. They cannot be sure of you—yet."

He smiled. "That is true. They have not crossed my land."

"So. They will waste time sending embassies to find out. Time—that is what I need."

Barbatio, less plump now than when I had first met him, said anxiously, "Take care, sir. Rando will keep his word, perhaps, but the Vandals do not even trust their own shadows."

Quintus said, "Let me come then." There was a look of worry upon his face.

I shook my head. "Don't worry, my friend. I will be very careful."

He gripped my forearm. "This is a cold land to live in without your friendship to warm it," he said quietly.

I nodded. "And for me also, without yours."

I stepped into the boat and was rowed across. The level of the water was rising a little each day, and each day the current was becoming stronger. The time of the slack water was past.

We landed amid a crowd of armed men who stared at me curiously but who made no threatening gestures. The Aleman King had his men well in hand. Past the outer lines of palisades, built well back from the river, past the tents, the cooking fires and the stacked spears, we mounted horses and set out along the old road that had led to the Limes. We rode along it for a mile, and on either side it was packed with tents, huts, horses and with men, stretching out as far as the eye could see. Presently we came to an inner camp, protected by a shallow ditch, built to stop horses from straying, and a palisade. Inside was the Aleman King. He had not changed. He was as courteous as before, and as unyielding as an iron blade. With him was Gunderic, still smiling, but the smile was strained now and I wondered how many men he had lost in the fight on the river. The others, grouped round the council table, I did not know.

Rando said, "I have more friends to present to the General of the West: Godigisel, King of the Siling Vandals, Hermeric, King of the Marcomanni, Respendial, King of the Alans, and his cousin, Goar, a notable warrior." A slight figure slipped quietly through the leather curtains of the hut and sat down without a word. Rando smiled warmly. "This is my last brother,

Talien, King of the Quadi; a people of whom you will have heard."

I said slowly, "You do me great honor." They did indeed. Gathered here in this camp, with the exception of Guntiarus, were the war leaders of all the Teutonic tribes between the Rhenus, the Danubius and the steppes of the east. These were the people who, for three hundred years, from the days of Augustus to the days of Valentinian, had waged war, almost without cease, against the empire. There was hardly an Emperor of Rome who had not been forced to fight them, not one Legate along the Limes who in all that time had not reddened his legion's swords with the blood of these people. How many they ruled, I did not know. How many warriors they could put into battle, I did not know. But in the days of our greatness, our confidence, and our prosperity, eighty thousand men had been thought necessary to hold the Rhenus frontier against them. And I, Maximus, self-styled General of the West, had to do my poor best with a single legion.

I added, "I can only hope that the honor I do you will be worthy of a Valentinian and a Julian." I hesitated and then turned to Talien and smiled. "For your sake I should add the name of Marcus Aurelius." He stared at me impassively, without movement of any kind, but I thought his nostrils flared slightly at the thrust.

Rando stroked his beard. "I have no doubt but that you will do that."

I looked at them in turn. Godigisel, King of the Siling Vandals, was short, compact, and with a face like beaten iron. He was a fighter, not a man given to much thinking. Hermeric, King of the Marcomanni, was tall and lean, with the face of a hawk, and, as was customary with his people, wore his hair combed back over the side of his face and knotted. He would be as gentle as a hawk, too, if you fell into his hands. Respendial, King of the Alans, was dark, square-faced, and with bushy eyebrows. He had a deep, harsh voice and reminded me strongly of a bear who might stand on its legs and clap paws one minute or crush you to death the next. His cousin, Goar, was a younger man. He had good teeth still, said little, and reminded me strongly of a man I had once known in another life. Talien, King of the Quadi, was slim and lightly built. He would have made a good charioteer. He had a humorous face, or would have had if he had allowed it to relax. As it was he watched me carefully the whole time like a cat. He was, I judged, the most intelligent of them all, except Rando, and, potentially, the most dangerous.

"Well," I said. "What may I do for you that I have not done already?"

Gunderic said, insolent as ever, "We ask you once again for leave to pass in peace across the Rhenus."

Godigisel said flatly, "We need new lands and are willing to serve in yours."

"As the subjects of my Emperor or as the conquerors of his generals?"

"The one will ensure that you live, the other only that you die."

"Are you all landless then?" I asked. "People without homes? Vagabonds and tramps who must steal from others in order to replace what they could not hold for themselves?"

Hermeric said, "Some of us have seen the Huns, smelled their stinking breath, felt the weight of their swords. They are Barbarians in everything that they do. They are not Christians like us. We are a better people; they are stronger, and all the time they press upon our borders, kill our young men, enslave our women and nibble our lands. This we have endured for years till we can endure it no longer."

"We are farmers," said Goar suddenly. "A farmer needs peace and patience and time in order to make a success of his land. None of this do the Huns give us."

I did not look at him and he did not look at me and we both knew the reason why.

I said, "You are willing to unite against my Emperor, it seems. It would be better to unite against these Huns."

Respendial said, "No one wastes time building a bridge if he can wade through the stream."

I smiled, I who felt so little like smiling. "I will give you nothing but promises. I promise you this, that for everything you try to take without payment, you will pay twice over."

Rando said, "For the last time, I ask that you let my brothers cross in peace. You need people to populate your lands. Gaul and Hispania are great countries. There is plenty of room for all to share their riches. Besides, you need farmers; that I know. I know, too, that you need soldiers. Already, many of our people serve in your armies, yet still you need more and more. We are all good warriors. It would be a fair bargain, and a wise one."

"No."

He said, "If you refuse, then this province of Gaul will learn how to weep and its suffering will be your sin."

"I am not a Christian," I said. "Only a soldier. Which one of you planned that night attack on my camp? The Picts or the Scotti could have done better. Perhaps it was your fledgling sons to whom you entrust command of your warriors? And which of you was so foolish as to imagine he could assemble a fleet of boats in a river mouth in broad daylight, and that I would be so blind as not to see them? Perhaps you are just children, playing at warriors, or perhaps one of you is a traitor who has reasons of his own for not wishing the others to cross. Do not talk of soldiers in my presence."

"Enough," cried Godigisel. He clapped his hand to his sword.

"I am unarmed," I said. "Even you could kill me now. Which one of you has lost the most men? Which one of you wishes to weaken the others?"

Rando said intently, "If what you say is true it is still our business and not yours. We can fight, I promise you."

"Fight then," I said. "Because I will not let you cross that river."

"But you would have a place still, a place of honor if you agreed to our terms."

"I remember. A third of the soil of Gaul. I will give you only enough so that you may be buried with decency."

Gunderic laughed. "Brave words. Tell us, Roman, how far is it to Augusta Treverorum? I hear that they have fine women there."

"Nine days in good weather if you march fast."

"So near."

"Of course. But they will all be days of fighting," I added gently.

Respendial shrugged his shoulders and laughed. "We are wasting our time," he said. "Why talk when we can crush him in a single attack?"

"I agree," said Gunderic, in that lazy voice of his. "He can talk all he wants—later—when he wriggles on the end of our spears."

Hermeric rubbed his long fingers. "Yes, why do we wait? Gaul is no longer a lion to be feared, but a cow waiting to be milked. She is ours if we but stretch out our hand."

Talien said suddenly, "Why do you not trust us?" He had a deep, resonant voice for so small a man. There was a sudden silence and everyone turned to look at him, and then at me, waiting for my answer.

I said, "You promise to serve my Emperor and defend his lands who cannot defend your own, it seems, against the Huns. If you cannot perform the one, why should I suppose that you can perform the other? Why should I suppose you willing to try? You do not live according to our ways and do not wish to do so. We do not live according to yours, and we, too, have no wish to change. Is that a fair answer?"

He said, "Yes, it is fair enough, from your point of view."

I said, "You are all confident in your strength; do not underrate mine."

Rando frowned. "We have in our camp a man of the Marcomanni who has served in your Emperor's bodyguard. He has returned and told us that when Stilicho, the Vandal, faced Alaric it was with the soldiers of the

Germania garrison under his command. You have no army. It is a lie to deceive us."

"If it is, then it is one you can easily disprove. Ask your son when he returns. Perhaps he can give you confidence in the matter."

They looked at me and I looked back with all the confidence and the insolence that I could muster. I said, "I am curious to see how long this vast host can camp by this river and not starve. Soon your camp will be a mud floor and you, having stripped the country bare in your search for food, will be hungry. Your men will become bored, quarrelsome, and difficult to handle. You will have sickness and disease to contend with, and the Burgundians will give you no help. For how long will the Alemanni be content with a king who has brought the locusts to his land? Time can only weaken you; and when the time is ripe I may cross the river and do battle. There, I have told you my plans. I can afford to wait; you cannot."

There was a murmur as though they growled in their throats.

Rando got to his feet. "Come, I will escort you back to the river and there meet my son. There is nothing more to say."

The others sat there at the table, sullen and angry. I smiled, saluted them with a flourish, and turned away.

We rode in silence back the way we had come. During the ride we passed a group of young men, all naked, who were doing acrobatics between swords and upturned spears planted in the ground. A group of older men stood by and watched. The trick was, I supposed, to avoid making a mistake and cutting oneself dangerously. Rando saw me watching. He said, "It is good training for the young. It teaches agility and lack of fear. I, too, could do that once."

I said, "Let them be happy while they can."

When the river was close by he checked his horse and looked at me impassively for a moment. "If you change your mind, then send me a message and I will see that you and your men remain unharmed.

Meanwhile, there is a man who would speak with you. He was once of your kind. He is under my protection and no harm will come to him. You may say what you wish."

I dismounted and walked between the tents, the rude shelters and the huts, till I reached a tree at which he had pointed. Standing beneath it was a man of my own age, wearing the dress of the Alemanni people. He was wrapped in a cloak, and a cowl hid his face. Beside him stood a young woman with two small children clutching at her knees, and on his right side was a young man. The children stared curiously at my armor and whispered to their mother, who watched me with a closed face. The young man had his hand on his dagger and I could see him hating me as I walked toward him, while the tribesmen about me laughed and joked among themselves. The smoke from the cooking fires drifted into the air and a group of horses, picketed in a line, cropped the grass and flicked their tails at the flies. The man in the cloak put his hands up to his head and pushed back the cowl. We looked at each other with curiosity and interest. We had not met now for over fifteen years and time alone should have stilled all emotions. But I felt the blood in my cheeks, the thumping of my heart; and I knew that my hands trembled.

"I told you that we should meet again," he said. A smile flickered behind his eyes.

I said, "I would not have known you but for the lack of hair." I stared at him, trying to see in this creased face the man I had once known. The voice, the movements, and the hands were the same, but the face—the face had changed so much.

"You, too, have altered. You look—" He hesitated. Then he said in a low voice, "You look battered but more distinguished. And you have been a success. I salute you, General of the West." His voice was gentle and mocking, but it was not unkind. I wondered how much he knew but I did not dare to ask.

"And you?" I said.

He spread out his hands in the old gesture. "When we last met I was—I was not happy. I told you I was going to the Saxon people and it was true. I did go. But they were not my friends. They are Barbarians; cruel, savage, treacherous, and lustful. I did not like them, but I had too much pride to say so. Eventually we tired of each other's company. So, I came south and made my home with the Alemanni. Yes, home. I who have no home."

"You are content now?"

"Oh yes, in my quaint foreign fashion. I was friends with the old king and I married his daughter. Rando is my brother. These are my children and my grandchildren. My wife died."

"I am sorry."

"I believe you are."

I said, "What do you want with me now? I have told Rando I will not allow the river to be crossed."

He smiled. "Still the same old Maximus. Fierce, hard, ungenerous, and incorruptible. When I heard tell of the name of the general who barred the river I knew it was you, and I told my brother it would be useless to talk. He did not believe me. He does now."

"And does he expect you to make me change my mind?"

He frowned. "He hopes that I may, for when I heard your name I became angry at things best forgotten, and in my drunken rage I told him something that I, when I was sober, would not have told a living man. He thought I should tell you." He paused. He said dully, "Rando is a good warlord. He knows that if you can defeat the enemy leader, you can defeat his men. Both he and Talien, who heard this thing also, urged me to see you. So, for the sake of the people who adopted me, I—I promised."

"What is it that you will tell me that will make me change my mind?"

He stepped forward, his hand outstretched, palm upward. "This," he said bleakly. On the palm of his hand lay a single gold earring.

I stared at it for a long time and when at length I would have taken it he closed his fist and stepped back. I raised my head and looked at him.

I licked my lips. I said, "That is my—that is mine."

"It is. Catch."

I caught it and turned it over and over in my fingers.

"Look at it carefully. You will see initials scratched on the gold. It was given as a keepsake."

I stared. "How did you get it?"

"Much plunder was taken on the Wall. I was a war chief then, remember."

"Why did you keep it all these years?"

He looked at me and then dropped his eyes. "It had once been your mother's. It was a link between us. And in the times when I did not hate you I would look at it and—and remember." He raised his eyes. "I would remember the happy times."

"And now it is a weapon."

"That is for you to decide."

"I do not believe it."

"If you do not believe me, it is easy for you to find out." He paused delicately. "You are a Roman. You have your honor to think of. It is your honor, after all, for which you have lived all these years."

I said, "I have no honor now."

"Generals who have no honor can afford to treat with their enemies."

I put my hands to my face and I knew then something of the despair that he had known.

He said cruelly, "I have other news. You wrote to Stilicho and asked for troops—you who already have so many. The letter is in our hands. You will have to write again before he can answer. It is a long way from the middle Rhenus to Illyricum where Alaric and the Vandal sit at meat, and play at dice with the empire for their prize. I have news out of your island too. Two men, Marcus and Gratianus, put up for Emperor in turn but were killed by the soldiers. It happened this spring. A third, Constantinus, succeeded. He sits in Londinium, playing at kings. Perhaps he dreams of making a new empire in the west. Is that what you want, who could have been Emperor yourself? You, who have so many men at your command."

"How do you know all this—about—about Constantinus?"

"The Saxons are good tale-tellers and it is easier for them now to walk dry on the Saxon shore. They could not do that in—in our time."

I said, "Please, no."

"Well?"

"We did each other great wrongs. I admit my part. Must we go on tormenting each other until the day we die?"

He said, "I have been dead for thirty years, I who did not kill your father."

"You rose against Rome."

"Twice," he said. "This is the third time. These people need land. They need it as a fish needs water. Who are you with your false Roman pride and contempt to stand in their way?"

"I have my duty."

"To what? To an Emperor who cares only for his chickens? To a Vandal who takes bribes and thinks only of himself? To the people of Gaul who will not lift a finger to help you? To Constantinus who stole half your gold for his own aggrandizement? To your men who follow you only so long as they receive their pay each month? Or is it to the memory of your wife?"

"Be quiet."

"No. Fullofaudes had more mercy than you. But I am not he." I flinched and put my hand to my mouth. "You made a death mask of my dreams," he said harshly. "Why should I spare you yours?" He paused. He said, "You have no honor."

I looked at where he stood. I could hardly see him. I turned and walked to where my horse waited. I mounted it somehow and sat slumped in the saddle. Then I rode to the river with the Aleman King beside me. We did not speak, and he did not look at me once. I felt as though my head would burst. I knew then the black darkness of absolute despair. There was nothing now to look back on with pride, with happiness, or with contentment. There was nothing to look forward to except old age, the unbearable loneliness of my thoughts, the emptiness of death. I had no honor.

I crossed the river, still in silence, and walked alone through the camp to my quarters. And everyone stepped aside as they saw my face. In the headquarters building Quintus stood waiting for me. I told him what had passed at my meeting with the five kings and with Rando. "There is a river, seven hundred and seventy-five yards wide, that alone separates us from total disaster. The Vandals must number over eighty thousand people, including old men, children, and slaves. That gives them roughly twenty-five thousand fighting men."

He whistled and began to fiddle with the bracelet on his wrist. "And the rest?"

"The Marcomanni are as large, if not larger. Once, long ago, they put seventy thousand into the field without difficulty."

"In the days of Varus?"

"Yes. And then there are the Alans and the Quadi. I should say, at a rough guess, that they can put nearly a hundred thousand tribesmen in the field between them. And that still leaves the Alemanni, who have yet to make up their minds, and the Burgundians whom I do not trust."

Quintus went to the table and poured wine into two silver goblets. "We might as well drink our own health. For no one else will." He gave me a mock salute. "We are all gladiators now." He put down his cup. He said, "But will the Alemanni move?"

"Rando is a shrewd man, I do not think he wants his people to cross. He may well think his strength lies in holding what he has. Tribes on the march weaken themselves. They quarrel, they fall out, each man disputing with his neighbor the ownership of newly stolen land. Their loyalty to their kings is not absolute. If a chief loses prestige through defeat in battle, they desert him. In that lies our one hope. I have been in touch, through agents, with Goar of the Alans. If I can persuade him further, he may come over to us and bring half the tribe too. Gunderic lost many men in our attack on their boats. He and Godigisel do not like each other. They are rivals. If I can drive a wedge between them by means of letters …"

"How?"

"It is an old trick to send treasonable letters to one man in the enemy camp and so arrange it that they fall into the hands of another."

He said mildly, "It is not a very honorable way of fighting, but—" He broke off and then said quickly, "What is wrong? Are you ill?"

"No," I said. "I am not ill, only tired."

He said, "Get some rest. You work too hard." He turned to leave the room.

"Quintus," I said.

"Yes."

I held out my hand. "Is this yours?"

He came forward and took what I held out to him.

He looked at it for a long time, turning it over and over in his hand just as I had done. It was as though he could not believe what he held against his flesh. He raised his head at last and looked at me. Then he shut his eyes and opened them again. I had never seen such a look of misery on his face before.

He said steadily, "It is mine. It was given to me."

I stepped back as though I had been struck across the mouth. Then I moved and the blade of Agricola was at his throat, the point just touching the skin.

"Give me one reason why I should not kill you?"

He did not answer. His face was beaded with sweat, his eyes shut tight.

"You took my honor," I said. "You, whom I trusted with my life."

"Kill me," he said. "It is your right."

"You are worth more to me alive than dead." I sheathed my sword with a trembling hand. I said bitterly. "I need my cavalry general too much to be able to afford the luxury of sending him away. Go back to your quarters and laugh, as you have laughed all these years behind my back."

"Maximus."

"Get out," I said. "Leave me alone, at least. I have work to do. It fills the time between one meal and the next."

He left the room. I watched him from the window. He walked with head bowed, his thinning hair blown by the wind. He walked heavily and I realized then how old he was. I had never thought of Quintus as being old.

CHAPTER XII

I rode to Treverorum with an escort of twenty men, taking Flavius and Julius Optatus with me, but I left Quintus in command at Moguntiacum. I think he was glad to be alone, and I—I could not bear to talk to him. It was a hurried journey in the sun. We changed horses at each posting station and never stopped longer than the time it took to drink a mouthful of wine and swallow a bowl of food. It was midday when we saw the white gates of Romulus come into view and, once there, I went straight to my quarters. Listening to the murmur of the crowds in the streets and looking at the thick walls of the fortress in which I stood, it was difficult to believe that the camp on the east bank was a reality and that the danger we had feared all winter was now so close at hand.

I sent for the Curator and, while waiting for his coming, washed my face and hands, tried to comb the dust from my hair, and drank a bowl of white wine. Before I left Moguntiacum I had dictated letters to Honorius, to the Dux Beligicae, to Chariobaudes, and to the Praefectus Praetorio in his palace at Arelate, so far away, so warm and so safe. Now I dispatched them by the imperial post under seals of urgency. My orderly had just returned to report that they had gone off safely when Artorius arrived.

He saluted me politely, but did not smile. He was a man I could not understand. Once I had tried to. Now I no longer cared. "Sit down," I said. "I want a talk with you."

He inclined his head. "I am at your service." He paused and added, "I also have things to say, General."

"You had my letter about the inadequacy of supplies?"

"Yes."

"Well?"

He said, "You have made grave charges of incompetence, laziness, and even"——he hesitated——"of corruption."

"Yes, I have."

"I hope for your sake, General, they can be substantiated."

I raised my head. I said, "It is a matter of indifference to me whether they can be or not. I am not a lawyer, concerned with abstracts like justice and fees; I am a practical man. I want these things corrected. I only want my stores."

He said, "But I shall have to report the matter to both the Governor and the Praefectus Praetorio."

"Go ahead, just so long as you see that things are improved from now on."

He said primly, "They are not my concern. It is all the business of the Governor."

"I made it your responsibility."

"I am responsible to the city council and to the Praefectus, General— not to you."

I blinked. "I know to whom you are responsible—the Emperor; but, as for what, remains something of a mystery."

He was trembling with anger now. He said, "The economic life of the city is my concern, among other things. I must advise you that I have written to the Praefectus to protest against your closing the frontier, and to complain about the manner in which you have burdened this city with the responsibility of feeding and paying for your troops."

"Are you serious?"

"Of course I am serious, General. There have been gross irregularities, particularly in regard to the returns made by your commissariat for supplies for troops who do not exist except on rolls."

I stood up. I said, "Do not judge my legion by the standards of the field army of Gaul."

"You insult the magister equitum. Nevertheless it is true."

"It is a lie. Discuss it with my quartermaster and you will soon find out that you have been misinformed. Better still, come to the Rhenus and count my men for yourself."

"This is no laughing matter, General. There is also the question of the corn tribute. I have had cases reported to me of corn being sold back to civilians at a profit out of your warehouses." He coughed. "Your chief quartermaster, an excellent man, may not be involved, but others are."

"Can you prove this?"

He said stiffly, "Yes, General, I can."

"Then I am sorry. It seems we are both at fault. I will have my military police look into the matter." I looked at him hard but he did not flinch. Suddenly I began to laugh at the absurdity of it all. What did our petty differences matter now? They say that Nero recited *The Fall of Ilium* while Rome burned. I do not know if it is true. Suetonius may have made it up, for he had a nose for scurrilous gossip. Yet he may have been right; he was a good judge of human folly. The frontiers of the Empire crumbled: we quarreled.

He said again, "It is nothing to laugh about."

I walked to the window and looked out at the road to Moguntiacum down which a wagon was creaking slowly, drawn by two teams of oxen. Some children were playing in the dust and a woman was walking arm in arm with a soldier off duty.

"No," I said. "It is no laughing matter." I swung round. "Do you know there are six tribes camped across the river? I have talked to their chiefs. They want a third of the soil of Gaul, and if we do not give it to them they will take it by force, if need be."

He said, "But—it's not true—you are jesting—you must be."

"I rode through their camp. I saw them: warriors with their wives and children, old men and women with all their possessions. They are on a migration. They want this land. A quarter of a million people are sitting on that bank, waiting for the right moment to cross."

He swallowed hard.

I said, "I can only hold them if I have more troops and the supplies I ask for. I have written to the Praefectus Praetorio. I need authority to conscript every able man I can lay hands on."

He said, "If this is true—"

"If!" I walked up to him and he backed away nervously. "They have tried to cross already. I have seen their weapons—good Roman swords, Artorius, sold to them through the greed of good Roman merchants and the corruption of good Roman tribunes. Shall I report that to the Emperor, do you think?"

He licked his lips. I think he thought that I was accusing him. I said, "I am not concerned with the state of the civil administration of which you are so proud to be a member. I want only the things I need, that I may do what I have to do while there is still time. Every day matters, do you understand?"

He said, "The Praefectus is not at Arelate, if you have written to him there."

"Where is he?"

"On his way to see the Emperor at Ravenna."

"When will he be back?"

He shook his head. "I don't know. In two months, perhaps."

"That is too long to wait." I took him by the shoulders and I tried to smile. I said, "You are an imperial official."

"I have no authority in Gaul."

"But you have here. It would do for a start. The Governor of Belgica could raise men, too. The Praefectus would confirm the instructions later. That's the answer. Don't you see?"

His hands began to tremble and he stared at me wide-eyed. He said, "But if I exceed my authority the Praefectus may dismiss me."

"Nonsense."

"No, it is not." He stopped and then said bitterly, "The civic council are already displeased with me over the other matters. One or two even want to get rid of me."

"Ignore them."

"I cannot."

I said brutally, "Have some courage, man. You have come a long way. Are you not now curator of a great city? You are more important than you think. The Emperor will not be displeased at any man who used his initiative to protect the foremost city of Gaul."

He hesitated.

It was then that I made my mistake. I said, "Come, it is not as bad as all that. I am not setting up a private army."

His eyes flickered. He said, in a squeaky voice, "I have no authority."

"Authority was made to be exceeded."

"I cannot."

I smiled. That, too, was a mistake. "Surely?"

"No," he said stubbornly. "Oh, it is easy for you. You are of the equestrian order. You are a soldier—the friend of Stilicho. But I—I am not."

"You have ambitions."

He flushed. "Yes, does that surprise you." He paused, glanced at me doubtfully, and then said, in a low voice, "The Governor of Belgica is due to retire soon. I have some hopes. I cannot help having hopes."

"Then help me," I said. "I spent half a lifetime as Praefectus of a cohort. Yes, I too. Help me and I will use what influence I possess to help you. But if the frontier goes neither of us will have a future. It is as simple as that."

He bit his lip. "You don't understand," he mumbled. "I will inform the Governor. I will write to the Praefectus Praetorio. When I hear from them I will let you know. It is all I can do." He nodded briefly and hurried from the room, his face, shiny with sweat, wearing its usual nervous, obstinate look. His sandals clattered on the stairs and then he was gone, and I was alone in the room again.

I did not learn until much later—and by then it was too late—what it was that frightened him so. And yet, in his own way he was right. I had been born with all the advantages he had spent a lifetime trying to attain. I had all the things he wanted so badly; and I could not really understand his restlessness, his ambition, his lack of assurance, his envy, or his insecurity. He wanted—as we all did—what he had not got. He did not realize that when you reached the crest of the hill, the wind blew colder there than on the slopes.

I sat down on a stool by the window and poured myself some more wine. I felt very tired.

The Vandals tried again. They made a night attack on the islands, hoping to secure them as a bridgehead that would make the final assault on the west bank an easy matter. I had been careful to keep the fact that I held these islands in strength a secret. The centuries on duty there were always relieved at night, the defensive positions were concealed by undergrowth and the garrisons had strict instructions not to show themselves during the daylight hours. Goar sent me a warning, as did Marcomir, who maintained, from the high ground he commanded, a careful watch on the Barbarian camp. Our fleet drove through their boats in the darkness and sliced them in half as you would slice an apple. The liquid fire, projected in special containers (a happy invention of Gallus), destroyed those who remained huddled on the east bank, waiting to embark, while those who reached the islands died, wetly, at the sword's point. It was a complete disaster for them and they lost two thousand of their men in twenty minutes. These were the Marcomanni, and I was glad to think that each king, in turn, was learning to know the bitterness of failure. We lost only a few men, but our most tragic casualty was my senior tribune, whom I had put in charge of the north island to steady the inexperienced centurions who were on duty there. Lucillius was found under a tree, a small hole in his left armpit. He would never marry Guntiarus' daughter now.

After that nothing happened, for the Rhenus was in full flood and we were safe for two months at least. It was then that I sent my soldiers on leave to Treverorum, moved units round from one fort to the next, to give each a change of conditions, turned the cavalry horses out to pasture, and told Julius Optatus to take an inventory of all our stores. His report was not encouraging so I visited Treverorum myself, briefly, and warned the Curator that a levy would have to be imposed in the autumn on corn, sheep, and oxen, and that I should need meat, salted down in vast quantities. "What about the authority?" he said, weakly. "That is your concern," I replied. "Men who fight need food. That is an odd fact to which you must get accustomed, Artorius."

The auxiliaries numbered five thousand now, so that not only could I leave all signal towers to be manned by them, but I could also use them to garrison Treverorum, as well as those forts upon which I knew no real attack would fall. This cheered us all enormously. As I said to Quintus, with a few more volunteers we should be able to turn the whole of the Twentieth into a field army when the time came, which would be something the Vandals had not bargained on.

He said stiffly, "Is it not about time you told me what our plan is to be? What are you going to do when the time comes?"

I was silent.

He misunderstood my silence. He said, "Of course, if I am not in your confidence——"

I said, "You are still my Master of Horse."

"But not your friend."

I said, "While we have the Rhenus fleet they cannot cross."

He looked at me for a moment and then stared at the bare wall of my office. "Let us suppose there is no fleet."

"Very well. This is what I think. They must cross at Moguntiacum. Only here is the country flat enough to bring everyone over. There are so many of them, there can be no secret of their intention when the time comes. They will, however, make small attacks on all the other forts. At any one of those places, if they land a small force they might, with luck, outflank the forts and either move directly on Treverorum—but they don't know how many men we have there—or cut our lines of communication and make nuisance attacks on us from the rear. But when the time comes, however, I shall hold those forts only with auxiliaries and concentrate the legion here."

"All of it?" he said, intently.

"Yes, all of it."

"No reserves?"

"No reserves. That is where I shall fight." I put my finger on the map that lay on the table between us. "My left wing will secure itself to the new camp on the road to Bingium, and my right wing will rest on the north wall of the town. If the fort below us at Moguntiacum is still holding out—and I expect it to—they will have to attack us up a slope, with the river to their backs and an enemy fort firing on them behind their left shoulder. It is a position of great strength. They will have enormous difficulty dislodging us and we shall have the advantage of fighting behind ditches and stakes."

He said slowly, "Yes, I see. It will not be a cavalry action then?"

"Not as you would like it, Quintus. If I had enough men I would fortify the whole length of the bank and destroy them in the water. But I have not. So I shall use your cavalry to break them up when they have failed in their attacks. I must be economical."

"I understand," he said in a flat voice. "And if they succeed?"

"They will only be too strong if we get tired first or run out of missiles. But if that does happen, I shall withdraw the legion to Bingium, cross the

Nava, and hold the further bank, leaving the garrison to defend the fort. It is an easy place to defend."

"And if we still have to retreat?"

I said, "You are very sanguine about this?"

"Yes. I have never contemplated fighting at these odds before. Besides, something always goes wrong."

"Well then, we shall pull straight back, leaving delaying ambushes, and hold the junction where the road splits for Confluentes and Bingium, at the thirtieth milestone. I shall have defensive positions prepared there as well."

"And after that?"

"Oh, after that, if we have any men left we shall try to hold Treverorum." I was silent for a moment. I said, "But if it goes like that there won't be any legion left to worry about."

He stood up, fiddling with the strap of his sword belt, a look of uncertainty upon his face. He glanced at me as though he would say something more, hesitated, and then turned upon his heel. "Thank you," he said politely. "I thought that might be the plan." He went from the room slowly, like an old man, and I returned to my papers.

It was a hot summer and we all sweated as the ditches were dug by night on the slopes behind Moguntiacum, for I had no wish that the enemy should see what we were doing and so guess at the truth of our weak state. The soldiers continued to come and go on leave, and the smoke from the fires on the east bank seemed to multiply each day. But my six ships patrolled the river as before and we were safe.

Sometimes in the afternoons I would ride to the training ground to watch Quintus exercising his men. He had great enthusiasm, great patience, and great understanding. He was tireless in his efforts to perfect the small shock force under his command. The horses' coats glistened in the sunlight and the sweat dripped from the faces of their riders as they tried for the tenth time, perhaps, to carry out some complicated pattern of movement. The troops and squadrons wheeled, broke, and formed shifting patterns of geometrical precision at the snap of a voice or the thin high sound of the trumpet. Finally, as the climax to the afternoon's work, they practiced attacks upon prepared positions and afterward, while the led horses were being circled to cool off slowly, the decurions, squadron commanders, and officers gathered about the tall figure in the burnished armor to hear his comments. He looked hot and tired but he held himself rigidly under control.

I drew closer. I had heard him give this same talk half a hundred times before but I always enjoyed hearing it again.

On horseback, Quintus and the animal were one. I had never seen such a rider, not even among the men of Treverorum, and they had a reputation for their skill in these matters. An officer from the Eastern Empire, who had fought with Stilicho in Italia, had told me that he was a good deal better as a rider than any Hun, and a better horse soldier than any Goth. The officer had met both in his time and I could believe him.

Now he was saying, "You must learn to use your heads and take it slowly. If you know what you are doing, a cavalry charge is the slowest thing in the world. The temptation is always there to hurry when you see them massed to your front—but don't. Never break from an amble until you are within their killing range. Outside that you are safe, so don't waste your horse's energy before it is needed. Don't let your horse run unbalanced; get him collected well before you are in the killing range. Then, when you hear the order, move straight into a canter, but still keep him collected. Don't try to outpace your left and right men; you are not having a race for a jug of wine. Watch them out of the corner of your eye. Keep in line and keep tightly together. And if you are going downhill, remember that those of your men riding big horses will have more difficulty bringing them down than those on the smaller animals. You must watch for that always. This is the most difficult part—when you can see their arrows or spears flickering toward you, and men and horses are going down. Then, you want to get on and be into them. You must resist the temptation. Stay together and wait patiently for that last trumpet. Then, when you hear it—sixty yards from the enemy line—throw your hands forward and break into the gallop. You will hit them with the most tremendous crash and you won't have much time to use your weapons, so you must kill or maim with every stroke. There is no second chance. The man you miss will be behind you before you can strike again and he, then, may well kill a comrade of yours in the second rank. Now, if you hit them properly in a collected line, they will break; they always do. Remember to ride straight through them and out the other side. That is when you break up. Get well clear and then rally on the trumpets and the banner. You must rally quickly, because then you are at your weakest, facing the wrong way and surrounded by the enemy who, even if wounded and in flight, will still try to take advantage of you. So, rally quickly, reform, and charge back while your horses are still warm; and, whatever you do, don't stop to pick up a wounded comrade. If you try that you only endanger your mounted friends and lessen your own chances of getting back. The dismounted must look to themselves." He paused. He said, "It is really quite easy."

"How long does it take, sir?" said a young decurion.

"You can cover two hundred yards in thirty seconds, easily. It will be all over in five minutes. So you really have very little to do. But, your foot soldier has to learn to fight for fifteen minutes at a stretch. That is a long time."

Quintus saw me and saluted, as though I were a stranger.

I said, "You make it all sound so easy."

"The difficult things always do."

"You are a good soldier, Quintus."

He did not smile. He said, "I understand horses, that is all. I am not so good with people."

When August came I received a letter from Honorius. He regretted the inability of his generals to send troops from Italia but, as I knew so well, Stilicho handled these things for him, and besides, he had many problems on his hands. He reposed great confidence in me. He did not think the situation was so serious as I had suggested. There had been such alarms before. If, however, I felt I needed more support he was certain I could rely on the cooperation of Chariobaudes—a most excellent man. It was a relief to know that the Barbarians were no longer massed along the Danubius, for Italia had suffered terribly on the last occasion. He had great hopes that Alaric would prove a powerful ally in the east. The news from Britannia was disturbing. Its army, of course, had always a bad reputation for mutinous behavior. Perhaps, when things were quiet in Gaul again, I would cross to the island with full powers and bring it back in obedience to Rome. He had great confidence in me still and, as a mark of his regard, I was appointed Comes Galliarum, with all the appropriate allowances. Did I know that the climate of Ravenna was excellent for the breeding habits of chickens...?

I told Quintus that he was now officially Master of Horse and that the appointment—it had been a joke between us once—had been ratified by the Emperor. He did not smile. He thanked me stiffly and went to his hut. Once, he would have enjoyed the letter with me. But now—now, we had nothing to say to each other.

I had another letter from Saturninus. Marcus and Gratianus had in fact been killed by Constantinus, who, it was rumored, had his eyes on Gaul and Hispania. But he was frightened to move while I was still holding Gaul in strength. I laughed when I read that sentence. Many people wished that I would return. Constantinus was not liked and they thought the army—"two puny legions, Maximus, my old friend"—should stay to keep the Saxons out. Their raids were getting worse. Constans was the one who kept the troops loyal to his father. He was efficient and well liked. "But dragged in the wake of his father's ambitions, I think. I saw him at Eburacum a week after Gratianus died. I warned him that no good would come of his father's vanity. He laughed at me, bitterly, and said that he knew quite well it would all end in the same way as it ended for your namesake, but that life was short and he might as well get out of it what he could. I feel sorry for him. He would have done so much better to have joined you. Tell Fabianus to write to me. His mother worries a great deal. I am glad that he has turned out a soldier, and is of use to you. I would give much to have a talk of the old days. Perhaps, if the gods are kind, we shall meet again. And give my greetings..."

I read it all and then passed it to Quintus. It all seemed so far away.

The weather held. Each day I prayed for rain and each day the sun shone and the wheat and barley ripened in the fields, while the vines about Treverorum were thick with grapes. The soldiers fished in the river at dawn and dusk, and some of them returned to the old habit of dicing their pay away in the baths while they soaked the sweat and dirt from their tired bodies.

Each day I walked to the river and looked to the east. The Barbarians' camp stretched for two and a half miles along the bank and extended further back than the eye could see. Each day a blue haze covered the plain; it was the smoke from the campfires of six tribes. At dusk the Vandals used to come down to the water's edge to bathe, to wash their clothes, and to dye their hair. One evening a small child fell into the water, the mother screamed, and two of their men tried to reach it with poles, but it was swept out into midstream by a crosscurrent. It was obvious that none of the men on the bank could swim. One, however, more quick-witted than the rest, hurled a wooden shield onto the water. This the child managed to clutch and hang on to. The current took the child across the river, and one of our men on the south island dived into the water on the end of a rope and caught the brat. His comrades pulled him ashore and a boat was sent across to restore the child to its mother. The optio, who took the boat over, said to me afterward. "They wouldn't let us land. They didn't even thank us. Just lined the bank and stared. I was glad to pull away into deep water again, I can tell you."

"What did you expect?" I said. "They are the enemy. If it had been a Roman child they would have let him drown."

In the second week of that hot month we had two days of storm and lightning and torrential rain, and, while the storm was at its worst, a boat slipped across the river to Bingium carrying a drenched messenger from the camp of Marcomir. A cavalry patrol brought him to me in the middle of the night, and I learned that the Vandals were collecting another fleet of ships up the Moenus and that they planned to make their attack on the night of the full moon. Marcomir's information was always accurate so I sent word straightaway to Gallus at Confluentes, and a week later two merchant ships were brought upriver by night, towed by horses, a half century of my fittest men helping them. It was a long, slow haul, for the current was strong and the undertow treacherous, and great care had to be taken to avoid noise, for I did not want the enemy to guess at my plans. Once past Moguntiacum the work became easier though the boat parties had a momentary alarm when fireballs were hurled over the water by the tribesmen guarding the east bank. Nothing came of it, however, and we concluded that a nervous sentry must have taken alarm at the movement of swans, for there were a great many on the river at that time. The merchant ships were weighed down at the stern with rocks and stones. Up forward, they were loaded with timber, wool, and other inflammable material, and the decks sprayed with sulphur.

Two nights before the full moon these ships, manned by a skeleton crew, towed by small boats, and escorted by a warship, were taken into the mouth of the Moenus. Four hundred yards up they were half sunk onto shoals either side of the central channel, and the crews taken off by the two boats. When daylight came it would look as if an ineffectual effort had been made to block the river. The success of our plan depended on the enemy thinking that, because we had apparently failed, there was little point in boarding and examining the two wrecks, whose upper decks cleared the waterline easily. They did not do so or, if they did, made nothing of it. The following night their boats came through the narrow channel, and when all were clear of the sunken ships our fleet moved into the river mouth and attacked them. We fired the two wrecks first and with these blazing behind them the enemy boats were thrown into a panic. Those who tried to turn back found the narrowness of the passage between the burning boats intimidating; the swiftness of the current made navigation upstream difficult, and they were forced onto the shoals and sandbanks, while the armed men on board scrambled wetly ashore. Those who tried to break out of the river were swiftly destroyed by our warships. Only a few boats slipped by to drift silently down the Rhenus, manned by crews of dead men transfixed by arrows, while the survivors moaned a little as they died of their burns.

Gallus was jubilant at his success and I gave a bonus to all who had taken part in the action.

Three nights before his wedding, Marcomir led a night raid on the barbarian camp, with my permission. While a diversionary attack was made on the area where the Aleman King was sleeping (there was always the chance that a valuable hostage might be picked up), Marcomir and fifty men penetrated the cattle park where the herds of oxen, rounded up from the surrounding countryside, were penned. Fire arrows created the stampede that he desired, and four thousand or so maddened, angry beasts broke through the fences and lumbered blindly through the camp. I had told him the famous story about Hannibal, and to a number of the beasts his men had managed to attach lighted torches. In the panic caused by the sound of the stampede the tribesmen, dazed with sleep, ran in all directions. Many were crushed to death, tents were brought down, shelters overturned, and fires started, which raged furiously in a score of places. In their first massed flight the cattle cut a clear swathe of ground, two hundred and fifty yards wide, through half a mile of tents. Thereafter, they broke up into small groups and did not stop until the torches on their horns had flickered out. When dawn came the camp was a shambles and cattle were everywhere. The damage was immense.

When I met him afterward Marcomir was in a good humor. The raid had been a great success, he had suffered few casualties, and four women, including a daughter of Rando's, had been captured, together with a number of weapons and a quantity of silver.

I said, "These successes are only pinpricks on a host of that size. They are good for morale; they do a lot of damage, but they do not really affect the issue. What we need is a real victory."

Marcomir grinned, his mouth full of pork. He wiped his greasy fingers on his tunic and said, "True, but the kings quarreled before our raid over the letters you had sent, accusing Hermeric of treason. He denied it and slew Talien, King of the Quadi, while they sat at meat."

I remembered that quiet, intelligent man. He was quiet forever now. "A pity. Talien should have slain him. I had hoped for better than that."

"It is a beginning. No, there will be no blood feud. Hermeric will pay for his crimes in cattle; the Quadi will feed and the Marcomanni will go hungry and grumble a little, but that is all. It is the custom of these people to settle their affairs so. And yet, it is a beginning." Marcomir paused and then said quietly, "Respendial and Goar quarreled too, each accusing the other."

"Of what?"

"Of all that men do accuse each other when they fall out."

"So?"

"Goar is sick of their stupidity and their greed. He has no faith that they will hold what they seek. Hermeric and Godigisel and Respendial talk incessantly of the lands in Hispania of which others have told them."

"Will he come over to us?"

"Yes."

"Are you sure?"

"He has given his word."

"With how many men and in return for what?"

"Land on the west bank when all this is over, and a post in the imperial service for himself. His father married a Roman girl and admired your people very much. It is young Goar's ambition to be a Roman general—or so he says." Marcomir chuckled.

I smiled. "That should not be difficult. What else?"

"Besides the women, the young and the old, he will bring ten thousand men who will fight on our side."

"Ah."

Quintus said, "Will they let him go?"

"They cannot stop him. He and his followers are on the northeast side of the camp, and if there is fighting they know that you will cross the river and attack them. They are all terrified of your ships. As well as cattle." He chuckled again. "All this my spies have told me. Well, they will leave, pretending to return to their old lands, but, a day's march from the camp, they will wheel round and make for my territory. All will be well."

I looked from Marcomir to Quintus. "That will give us sixteen thousand men on the east bank," I said slowly. He knew what I was thinking. He said, "How would we get the legion across? Even foot soldiers in boats would take time; horses would take longer. Without cavalry it would be too great a risk. We would need a bridge and there is no bridge." He looked at me and said deliberately, "But we could build one, of course."

"No."

Marcomir looked at us in turn. I think he sensed that all was not well between us. He said impatiently, "What is your plan then, if you do not intend to cross or cannot cross? Wait forever till they make the first move?"

I said, "Be patient. For how much longer can they feed themselves in that huge camp? They are nearly a hundred thousand against our thirty. Even with the advantage of surprise our two thousand horsemen would be hardly enough to turn the balance. We should need more than luck to beat them in pitched battle."

Marcomir scratched his beard. "It is the only chance you will have to attack them. Do you rather wish it that they should attack you?"

Quintus said, "Battles are rarely won on the defensive."

"It is a great risk," I said. "Let Goar's men join us first. I want no paper armies, like other generals. Let them weaken themselves further; it will be to our advantage. We have time on our side."

"But—"

"No," I said. "If we lose all, on one throw of the dice, then Gaul is theirs. No more armies will stand in their way."

Quintus said, "What we need is a strong wind in the right direction. Then we might burn their camp. I think that fire is the only thing that will destroy them without risk to ourselves. Fire knows no fear."

I ignored the jibe. "Fire or hunger," I said curtly, and we left the matter as it stood.

Marcomir's wedding took place in the berg of Guntiarus on a hot day, and the whole area was packed with people. It was as though every Burgundian east of the Rhenus was determined to be present at the ceremony. The women wore their finery, and the men their best clothes. The daughter of Rando was there, somewhere, a prisoner in one of the huts, and I told Marcomir she would be better in my hands. I would need her as a bargaining chip—if it ever came to bargaining again. He agreed, readily enough. "She is of no more interest to me now," he said cheerfully. His mind was full of the wedding; it was not a time for interest in slave girls. I was tired and I remembered little of it all afterward except as the memory of a dream I had once been part of.

In the King's hall I found Marcomir with his arm round an elderly man with a battered face, broken and scarred by years of battle. "This is Fredegar," he said. "He was my father's servant and friend, and he taught me to ride and to be a warrior. He has been my sword brother all my life, and I listen to him because he is wise."

Fredegar smiled grimly. "I talk and you listen. That is so." He put his hand on my arm and it was the hardest hand I had ever felt. "I give him advice, oh yes, and he does the opposite. That is how it goes with the young." He had a hoarse voice and I had difficulty, at times, in understanding him. He spoke in looks rather than words and had the cold blue eyes of his people. He was, I noticed, held in great respect by many Burgundians as well as Franks and had been a great fighter in his time. He was a man to like or be afraid of.

The wedding began with a complicated ceremony of present giving and we all sweated in the heat of the Hall while the girl and the man exchanged gifts, and their relatives examined them and argued about them interminably. Fredegar said, "It is our custom, you see. The husband brings a dower: those oxen outside in the pen, and the horses. The number was fixed a long while ago. Now he gives her a bridle made by our best craftsmen—see how beautiful it is—and a shield and a spear. They are his but he gives them to her. And she—watch now—offers him armor, a helmet and breastplate that her father has had made."

"Why?" I asked, puzzled.

"It is a sign." He grunted and pulled at his beard. "It signifies that they share the same work, the same happiness, and the same danger. Listen, Guntiraus speaks the words."

A sudden silence fell and the King spoke to his people across the held hands of the two who were to be married, his own hand on theirs, the other uplifted, as though administering an oath. "Let it be done," he cried. "By our custom and by our sacred way are you joined. Let your fates be the same, in peace as in war. So must you live, and so must you die." There was a roar from the hall and the warriors stamped their feet and clashed their spears against their shields, while the women wailed once, in ritual mourning for the loss of one of their kind. Then food was brought and great barrels of sour beer, and jugs of wine, and the long festival began. And then, Marcomir and the girl—she was very young, very proud, and very serious—were married in the open by a priest who spoke my tongue, and there was a great silence while the words were said. Afterward, there was a second ceremony in the woods, this time to propitiate the gods of the faith they had abandoned, but which, in their hearts, many still revered. Then there was a great feast at which everyone ate too much and drank too much beer, and oaths of friendship were sworn, and the roofed hall, in the center of which a great fire blazed, rang with the noise of laughter and talk. In the cool of the evening, we stood by the stockade gates and watched Marcomir ride off to his land with the girl on the saddle in front of him, a white wreath in her hair, and the men of his bodyguard all about him. Everyone was happy and contented, and it was as though the Alemanni and the Vandals were people of no importance. The girl (it was the one who had spilled my drink that day) smiled, Fredegar nodded briefly, and then they were gone. For a flickering moment or two I remembered my own wedding so many years before, but I quickly dismissed it from my mind. I glanced at Quintus and saw him watching me, curiously. I said nothing and we turned and went back to the Hall, and the silence between us was a wall that we could not cross.

In the morning I said my farewells to Guntiarus, the King. As I mounted my horse, I glanced back for a moment. The prisoner was sitting on a horse between two guards. Her bare feet were roped beneath the horse's belly, and her hands tied behind her back. She was a bedraggled-looking creature, not much improved by a gag of some dirty cloth which concealed the lower part of her face. She stared at me with sullen hatred.

"Is that necessary?" I asked, pointing at the gag. I could see that it had been tied tightly, so that it cut into her flesh.

"Yes, sir. She'll scream her head off, given half the chance. And they may be out looking for her. She's tried to escape twice already."

"Very well. If she tries again I shall hold you responsible."

We rode off and I returned to my forts and my problems. For us there was no rest and little relief.

On the west bank nothing had changed. The soldiers still worked at their duties by day, building the palisade, digging ditches, and improving the defenses of the forts. The armory was filled to overflowing with carefully made arrows and throwing spears, and the armorers grumbled at my insistence that we must have more and more—and still more. Each day the sun blazed in an unclouded sky, and our stock of drinking water had to be rationed, for the waters of the Rhenus were not safe in summer and men, before this, had died of fever after bathing and drinking there. The young cygnets that we had watched in the spring, paddling on the water, had grown large and were a darker color now. Soon they would change altogether and be as white as their parents, who hissed angrily still, each time I threw bread to their inquisitive young. Quintus was fond of roast swan but these we did not take and eat. They had become our mascots and, like the soldiers, we believed that so long as they stayed they would bring us luck. And, all the while, the sentries patrolled the riverbank in groups, stood in pairs upon the towers, leaning upon their spears, or tramped the firing platforms, wrapped in their thick cloaks (it was cold at night) and kept a soldier's watch upon the dark, swirling waters of the Rhenus.

Rando's daughter had been given a hut to herself, with a woman to look after her and a sentry at the door to see that there was no interference.

I sent for her one morning, being curious to see her and perhaps learn something about her people.

She came, escorted by the sentry, and I waved the man out of my office so that we might be alone. She was a tall girl, with fair hair down her back, and she wore a blue, sleeveless gown, cut low across the breasts. It was girdled about the waist and very tight-fitting about the body, as was customary with women of her race. She was very lovely. I shut the door and motioned her to sit down. She refused, with a shake of her head.

"Do you speak Latin?"

"A little. Can you speak Aleman?"

I said, "It is I, my girl, who asks the questions, not you."

"And what will you do if I refuse? Beat me?"

"If I did so myself my motives would be open to misunderstanding."

"So?" She looked puzzled.

"My centurions are experienced enough."

"You would not dare. I am the daughter of a king."

"The last time my people flogged a royal woman, her tribe rose against us. This time the tribe has risen without provocation, so the flogging is overdue. Are you being looked after properly?"

She was startled at the question. "Yes."

"Have you any complaints?"

She laughed, bitterly. "Only the usual one of all prisoners. I want to be free."

"You will be free on the day that your father gives me his assurance that no tribe will try to cross the river."

"He will never do that."

"That will be unlucky for you."

"Why? Do the Romani still eat their prisoners?"

I laughed. "Not these days. Besides, you are too skinny for our tastes."

I knew to what she was referring. Years before, two war leaders of the

Franks, captured in battle, had been given to the wild beasts in the arena, and the story was a familiar one on both banks of the river.

She said in a low voice, "What will you do with me?"

"I could get a good price for you in the slave market at Treverorum." I put my head on one side. "On the other hand, you would fetch more if I sent you south to Rome. They pay twenty solidii nowadays for an unskilled woman." She flushed at the insult. I went on: "There is a demand for white-skinned girls there. And then again, you would fetch a better price still in Mauretania." I paused. "Or I might keep you for myself. I could do with a woman in my house, and I shall need servants when I retire from the army to my villa."

"If you did I would kill you when you were sleeping, and escape."

I smiled. "I believe that you would."

"But you—you would not dare to sell me. We are not at war so I cannot be a slave."

"So you know our law, do you? You are a clever girl. Yet you are wrong. Yours is a race with whom we now have no friendship and no hospitality. If you capture a citizen of ours he is your slave, as you are mine."

She was very white. She said in a whisper, "But there is a treaty, made by your general, Stilicho."

"I agree. But you were taken in an action of war. Marcomir is an ally of ours. So you are still a slave for that reason."

She was silent.

I said, "How many sisters have you?"

"Three."

"Are you the eldest?"

"Yes."

"One will not be missed overmuch."

She began to cry. I stepped forward. "There is no need. No harm will come to you if your father is sensible. I want you to write him a letter. I will have it written for you, and all you will have to do is to sign it."

"He cannot read," she muttered.

"There will be someone in his camp who can. Sign it and I will see that no harm comes to you."

She cried again and swayed forward, sobbing, so that I was forced to hold her. I looked at the roof of the office.

I said, "There is nothing to worry about. Don't cry, my child."

She raised her face. "I will be your slave, if you wish." She pressed her body against me, and her lips parted. She was young enough to be my daughter, but she was very beautiful, and I was still a man. I began to push her gently away. Then her arm moved from her cloak and I felt a terrible pain in my shoulder. I staggered back, shouted, and then half turned and fell across the table. The door burst open and the sentry ran in as she clawed at my face, trying to reach the dagger that was still inside me.

"Get a doctor," I said. I tried to reach the dagger but it hurt too much. The room was full of people now; I was sitting on a stool, blood all over me, and the girl, a great bruise on her face where the sentry had hit her, was standing in a corner, her arms twisted behind her back, the sentry holding her as though he would like to cut her throat.

"You must lie down," said someone.

"Get him to his bed."

"What about that bitch?"

"Kill her," said another voice.

"No," I said faintly. A face loomed above me that I recognized. "Find out how she got the knife—punish them."

"And the girl?" asked Aquila grimly.

I was sick and dizzy with pain. "Flog her," I said.

"It's not enough."

"My orders," I said.

It was a burning hot day and I lay on my stomach and sweated, for the wound was deep and gave great pain. It would be a month before I could use that arm again properly. Out in the sun, the girl, her back lacerated, hung by her wrists from a wooden bar and moaned for water. She was lucky. If it had been a man I would have executed him.

Late that night when I was trying to sleep, Fabianus came and asked how I was.

"I shall live," I said sourly. "She put it in at the wrong angle. Just like a woman—thank the gods."

He said awkwardly, "Could we cut the girl down, sir? She's in a very bad state."

"So am I."

"You said she wasn't to die."

"She won't."

"She might, sir."

I glared at him. "Not that one. She tried to seduce me one moment and murder me the next. Girls like that don't die so easily."

He said quietly, "It was a severe beating. When they salted the wounds afterward, she screamed and screamed."

I tried to sit up. "They all do that," I said. "Did she ask you to speak for her?"

He flushed and shook his head. "No, sir."

"What did she say?"

He hesitated. He said, "She tried to spit at me and then said that she hoped you were dying."

I lay down again. "She'll live," I said. "Haters like that are tenacious of life."

The wound was clean and I made a good recovery. So did the girl, though her hurts took longer to heal. It was a long time before she left her bed, and each day the blue haze of smoke from the campfires on the further bank seemed to grow thicker and more impenetrable.

Word reached me from Marcomir that he was happy, that his wife was a fine woman, and that Goar had done as he promised, had left the barbarian camp and was now in the hills to the north. No other news came from across the river; no boat pushed out from the banks, bearing an invitation to a meeting; no embassy arrived, offering terms or insults. Nothing happened and I began to worry at the silence, at the inactivity. Where would they strike and when? It must be soon. They could not delay much longer, surely. In an excess of irritation, I sent suddenly for Quintus. He came, and I was driven to anger by the sight of his impassive face, his rigid salute, and his carefully controlled politeness when he asked how my arm was getting on.

I said icily, "If you wanted to know that, you could have come to my hut more often when I was laid up. You want some fighting, well you can have it. Get six hundred of your men across the Rhenus with horses into Marcomir's territory, and then report to me. We shall need help from Goar, from Marcomir, and from Gallus. We shall want Fabianus also. You will be in command, and in the unlikely event of the expedition going wrong I shall hold you personally responsible. Is that understood?"

He flushed. I had spoken to him as I would to a young and inexperienced tribune. "Yes," he said. "It is understood." He went out quietly and I was left alone with my bad temper and my thoughts for company. Out in the camp the trumpet blew for the evening meal.

CHAPTER XIII

Ten days later the Rhenus fleet moved into the mouth of the Moenus. It was a little after midnight, and I stood on the poop of Gallus' flagship, listening to the strong beat of the oars. Behind us, following in our wake, came all the merchant ships and small boats that I had been able to muster. On board them was a mixed cohort of heavy and light infantry, under the command of Fabianus. At the same time, Goar and Marcomir, with five thousand men, stiffened by a cohort of my own, together with the cavalry under Quintus, moved across the plateau toward the north side of the enemy camp. Quintus had crossed the river at Boudobrigo and it had taken a long time to get the horses over, for the boats were small and only held six animals at a time. It was growing light now and I could feel the wind on my cheek and see the faint, smudged line of the hills in the distance. "Now," I said, and a fireball hurled into the air. It was the signal for the attack. The boats were jostling past us in the half-light, loaded with men, arms, and equipment, while the catapults of the fleet pitched fireballs and missiles in a steady stream onto the enemy's fortifications. I could hear the grinding of the keels as the boats struck the beach, and then Fabianus was ashore, his men fanning out to right and left of him. He captured the offshore island in one swift, bloody assault, and then poured his men onto the mainland. His attack was sudden and determined, and the surprise complete. Keeping his cohort in a tight, controlled battle formation, he struck straight into the camp before any serious attempt could be made to rally the astonished Marcomanni. Tents were fired, baggage destroyed, wagons broken, and horses killed or stampeded.

On the far side of the camp, Marcomir and Goar led their men in a rush that took them straight through the palisade and the outer defenses.

Supported on each flank by Quintus' cavalry, their attack proved difficult to turn. They had strict orders to disengage and withdraw, the moment the enemy rallied and the impetus of their assault began to waver. I wanted no heroes, no fights to the death, no units cut off and making gallant last stands. I wanted only a limited success, and I achieved it. The camp was in an uproar. There was fire and smoke everywhere, horses neighing, women screaming, children crying, and men shouting in rage and terror. There was no order or discipline among the tribes. War chiefs, struggling to summon their men, were cut down while they shrieked defiance; men, groping for weapons, faced the armed legionaries one minute, only to be driven onto the spears of the cavalry behind the next. Fireballs crashed through the roofs of tents and huts and a thick pall of acrid smoke streamed upward, like a funeral pyre, into the clouded sky. Quintus' cavalry broke loose, formed up as one, and swept like a curved scythe through the heart of the camp. The luck that was with us all that summer held. Rando, King of the Alemanni, trying desperately to rally his men and make contact with his brother chiefs, found himself in the line of the ala's advance. It was Quintus who saw him—Quintus, riding at the head of his men, as though he were that young officer I had known in the old days upon the Wall. Rando snarled and threw his spear. It missed and took a man behind, who fell from his horse with a shriek. He reached for his dagger, saw that he stood alone, and then, too late, turned to run. Quintus laughed, caught him with the curved sword that Stilicho had given him, and the Alemanni, with one blow, found themselves headless.

A trumpet blew the retreat and, with the cavalry covering them, Marcomir's men retreated the way they had come, while Fabianus, surrounded as he should not have been, cut his way out and withdrew back to the boats, as steadily as though he were on parade. The Rhenus fleet kept the enemy in check, but I did not give the order to withdraw until the cohort, in its small boats, was back on the beach at Moguntiacum. Our total losses were under three hundred, and the action lasted for a little under an hour. Three days later Quintus was back in his old tent, very pleased with himself. I was a little envious, for I had done nothing except stand on the deck of a ship and give orders.

"We could have stampeded the whole camp with more men," he said irritably, for a gash on his left knee was giving him a lot of pain.

"Of course. But we hadn't, so why worry? We did all that we set out to do. We proved that the men could fight in battle order; we did an immense amount of damage and we had the very good luck to dishearten the Alemanni. I am quite satisfied and I shall tell them so tomorrow."

"Why tomorrow?"

"It is the day we pay them out of the pockets of the church. It is also their day for vinegar. I think we might give them a ration of wine instead. That should please them."

"You will have trouble with the quartermaster."

"If I do, he will have trouble with me."

He said, "I noticed one thing. There was a lot of sickness in their camp, people on blankets in the open, who did not even try to move out of our way. We rode over them, of course. And the women and children were hollow-cheeked. They are short of food."

"The Alemanni have been sending in food. Will they continue to do so? I wonder."

He said. "It is the end of August now. Two more months and it will be too late for them to make another attempt. They will surely starve if they try to winter there."

"That is what I hope will happen."

"Any news from Fabianus?"

"Not yet."

He whistled tunelessly for a moment or two. Then he said casually, "Will you tell the daughter that her father is dead?"

I stared at him. "I had forgotten her."

"I thought you had."

Fabianus was now on the east bank with fifty men, engaged on liaison work with Marcomir and Goar. I hoped that, in addition to training our new allies, he would find time to take patrols out to spy for information on the movements of the enemy. I had thought to send an embassy, ostensibly to discuss terms. Ambassadors who kept their eyes and ears open often picked up a great deal of information, but now that Rando was dead the temper of the war chiefs was likely to be uncertain. They could be treacherous and cruel, and it was a risk I was not prepared to take. But we heard from him a few days later. The kings had continued to quarrel among themselves, and sections of the tribes, sullen and discontented, had decided to move back to their own lands. Each day small convoys of armed men, ox wagons, and women and children, were breaking away, moving either east or north. Nothing was being done to stop them going.

I sent for Rando's daughter. She should have come to my office, but I was called away unexpectedly and forgot all about her. In the evening I went to my quarters and I was sitting, writing a letter, when there came a knock on the door.

"Come in," I said.

She came in, pushed by the sentry. She was very pale and her hands were tied behind her.

"Sit down," I said. She sat down, and stared listlessly at the floor.

"If you give me your word that you will not try to escape or hurt yourself, I will give you more freedom to move about without a guard." I gestured to her hands. "All this is unnecessary, you know."

"I will never give you my word," she said in a low voice.

I sighed. "Stand up and turn round." She did so, and I picked up a small knife and cut the cord on her wrists. "I will have to trust my men, in that case, to see that you do not escape. Would you like some wine?"

She shook her head.

I looked at her. "I have some unhappy news for you," I said gently.

She raised her face then.

"I am afraid that your father is dead. He was killed in the fight when we raided the camp. He was a brave man."

"It is a lie."

"No. It is not a lie. I have spoken to—to a man who saw him killed."

She did not cry. She said, "My brother, then, is the king now."

"Will he make a good king?"

"What is that to you?"

"A great deal. I would rather not have to fight him, if it can be avoided."

"You should not have killed him," she said colorlessly. "My brother will want revenge."

"Could you persuade him that it is not worthwhile?"

She shook her head. "He is fond of me, but not that fond. I would never wish to persuade him."

I said, "You think you have been ill treated. Had I left you with Marcomir you would have been married off by now to one of his chiefs—if you were lucky, that is. More likely you would just have been a slave in some old man's hut."

"You had me flogged instead," she said angrily. "I would kill you myself, if I could."

"You have tried once already and failed. Don't be so foolish again." I leaned forward. "I have more troops on the way. Two legions from Britannia and two from Hispania, as well as soldiers from Gaul. When they arrive I shall be stronger than ever. Your people on the east bank are short of food; soon they will be starving. Many are already moving back to their old lands. When my troops arrive, I shall cross the river. And when I do so, I shall destroy all those little kings and their princes. You may write that to your brother if you wish. It would be better that he take his people away before they are destroyed utterly."

She caught her lip between her teeth. "Why should I write such a letter? I don't understand."

I said patiently, "If you love your brother and your people, you might wish to save them from an unnecessary war. I would do so, if I were in your place."

She smiled then, and I saw from her smile that I had failed. She said, "When Marcomir took me prisoner, he said to one of his men that I would be worth all the legions that you had not got. He would not have said that, if he had known what you are telling me now." She smiled again. "And yet I do not think that he was lying. It is you who are trying to trick me. I have seen your camp and heard your soldiers talk. I know how many men you have not got. And those you have are forced into your service." She laughed scornfully. "The young men of my people do not have to be branded like animals before they take a spear in their hands." She paused. She said, "I will do nothing to betray my people—nothing."

I said, "You are a clever girl but you are not as clever as you think."

She looked curiously round the room. It was large and very bleak. The plastered walls were white, and bare of decoration of any kind. The floor was of rough wood; the only furniture was a low bed in one corner, the table at which I sat, two stools, and a large chest in which I kept my few clothes. By the bed, there was a native rug that I had bought in Treverorum, and on the table a small oil lamp. That was all.

"This is all you have?" she asked with a puzzled frown.

"Yes."

"But you are a general. I do not understand. Even the chief of a small band among my people has a—richer hut."

I said, "This is how I live. It contains all I need."

She looked at me. "You must be lonely. You have no family."

"But I have—there are six thousand of them."

"I did not mean that."

"Yet it is enough."

She pushed her hair back and said, "May I go now?"

"Of course."

"Please let me go free.'

"Why? There is a man in this camp who was thirty years a slave of your people. He has told me what it was like. They had no pity. Why should I? Talk to him—he works with the farrier—and you will be glad then that you are at least the servant of men who are not Barbarians." I checked and looked at her. I said, slowly, "But I will send a message to your people to let them know that you are—safe."

She said urgently, "It would be better to let me go. If you do not, then you will be sorry. There, I have warned you. I will not do so again."

As she turned and walked from the room, I heard her say in a low voice, "And Marcomir will also be sorry for the shame that he put upon me."

I was startled. I crossed the room and swung her round. "What is that you are saying? Is that true? Did he touch you before I brought you away?"

"Yes," she cried. "He did. And though I hate him for it, he, at least, is a man. He is not like you. You are only a Roman." She wrenched herself free and fled from the room. I did not understand. I went back to the table and sat down. I picked up the map of the area and studied it. Maps were easy to read.

The weather broke at last. The sun and the blue sky vanished and we had days of fine, driving rain that left the fields sodden, and which brought with them a cold wind that made us reach for our cloaks each time that we stepped out of our huts into the open. It was on one of these days that a messenger arrived from Bingium. He had ridden all night and he stood dripping water all over my office while he apologized for the delay due, so he said, to a loose horseshoe. The letter from Fabianus explained his urgency. "Come quickly to the camp of Marcomir," he wrote. "Only you can prevent a great disaster."

I left Quintus in charge, took ten men as an escort under Barbatio, and reached Bingium in a little over two hours. There, a boat was waiting for me and, on the east bank, under guard of a group of Fabianus' men, fresh horses to carry us the remainder of the way. It was still raining when I reached Marcomir's berg; the stockade was full of armed men, and alarm and anger were the signs I recognized on all the faces that I met. Fabianus, his cloak dripping, met me outside the prince's hut. Two dozen horses or more were standing there, fully saddled, and many of the men on guard were Alans as well as Franks.

"Well," I said. "Tell me what is wrong that I must put right."

He said, in a dead voice, "A party of Vandals raided the berg three nights ago. They came secretly and they went secretly."

"If it was not a war party what did they want? To spy?"

"They cut the throats of the few guards, but that was all. They went to the women's side and took the wife of Marcomir from her hut."

I blinked. "Go on."

"They had a two-hour start before the affair was discovered. Marcomir was away at the time visiting a post that had been attacked the previous day."

"That was clever of them."

"Yes. I was in camp. I followed them with two sections and men from the prince's war band. But we never caught them. The trail ran clear, through a litter of murdered sentries and wiped-out patrols."

Fabianus wiped the rain from his face. He said, "She was very popular. It was a good match—a fine marriage. It is an insult to be wiped out only in blood. The whole tribe is arming now."

I said, "He cannot be allowed to go on the war trail. That is what they want. They will destroy him, and then us. And none of it will help his wife."

"I told him all that. He would not listen to me."

"Will he listen to me though?"

"That is why I sent for you, sir."

"Where is he now?"

He jerked his head sideways. "In his hall, holding a council."

"I shall not see him there. Is he armed?"

"Not yet."

"I will talk to him in his hut when he arms. It will be best to see him when he is alone. Now get me a dry cloak and some wine. I am very tired."

I waited under shelter by the stables while men ran past with war harness and gear, and more and more clans poured into the stockade from the outlying districts. It was cold and I was wet through but it was best that no one saw me, so I put my cowl over my head and told my men to do the same.

Fabianus squelched through the mud. "Quick. He has gone. Now is the time."

I nodded and went with him. Outside the hut, with the rain dripping off the porch a light flared suddenly and a bulky figure moved and stood before me. I dropped my hand to my sword and then saw who it was. "Fredegar."

He nodded, his face streaked with wet. "You have come," he grunted. "That is good."

"Have you spoken with him?" I asked.

"Yes. I was at the council meeting. It is all decided."

"And so?"

"Blood has been spilled. It must be repaid."

"I have come to stop him."

"So. You will be lucky. He will not listen to me."

"He is mad."

"Of course." He glanced at me ironically. "Men are always mad where women are concerned. They let their bellies rule their heads."

"But you will go with him?"

"Yes. It does not matter what I think. He is my lord and my prince. Your officers would do the same for you." He smiled with bared teeth.

"Have you no influence? You know what will happen?"

He spat sideways and shook his head so that the raindrops flew from his beard. "Of course. Yet I have ridden too many years at his side not to know that I cannot change the path his horse walks. He goes where he chooses; I follow."

"What about her father? Does he know? Will he help?"

He shrugged. He said, "She is of us now. It is our matter. Besides, you are here; you will aid us."

I glanced at Fabianus and saw him looking at me expectantly. I said, "I am a soldier, not a husband."

"So." He stepped aside. "Go in then and let each do what he must."

I nodded and went in. I pulled back the skins covering the entrance to the inner room and stepped inside. He was standing in the center by his great fur-lined bed, his arms held out, while two young men dressed him in the apparel fitting to a warlord of the Franks. His face was cold, remote, expressionless, like the stone face of a God upon an altar. Only the black marks round his eyes betrayed the reality of his grief.

I said, "I have heard your news. I would share your sorrow if it would help, oh my brother."

He said, "You have come to help us. I am glad. Fabianus will have told you."

"You are going to make war?"

"Yes. I am going to make war."

I said, "It is best to fight when one is cool. Men who are angry make mistakes."

"I am not in the mood for making anything but war."

I sat down upon the bed. I said, slowly, "You made a pact to serve our Emperor, whose general I am. It was agreed between us that no attack should be made without my permission. Do you mean to betray my trust in you?"

He said, "It is not your wife who is in their hands."

I said, "That is understood." I watched his face, saw him adjusting his sword belt with deliberate care, and realized that he was in the grip of a cold rage that nothing could penetrate.

I said, "You realize what you are doing?"

"Yes. I and my people know."

"What is your plan?"

"We shall try to rescue her first, secretly. If that fails, then we shall attack the camp."

"The daughter of Rando is our prisoner. I will be glad to use her as a bargaining chip. That is what I would do in your place."

"But you are not in my place. She is an Aleman and Douna—my wife— is in the hands of Godigisel. The Alemanni and the Vandals will not help each other in this matter."

"If you fight, you will destroy yourself and your people."

He said, "Your men took one prisoner out of their raiding party. He had twisted an ankle and they had left him behind in their haste to escape. You will find what is left of him upon two poles behind this hut. When I have the Vandal King in my hands I shall make him feel that he is dying."

I said, "I am your friend in this matter, as in all other matters. But I must warn you of one thing. Do not ask me to help. If you go out against the Alemanni and the Vandals I cannot support you with even one man from my legion."

He said bitterly, "I have not asked you. But if you were my friend I would not have to ask you."

I said, "If you do this thing, will Goar and his war band help you?"

He hesitated. "Goar has told me that he will help me as a friend would, but that he will obey you."

"In this matter?"

"Yes, in this matter and in all matters." He tightened his belt, slid his sword into its sheath, and moved into the outer room.

I followed, and stepped in front of him. "I had a wife—like your wife. Once, a long while ago, I had to leave her in a town abandoned to an enemy while I retreated away from it with my soldiers. It was not an easy thing to do."

He tried hard to smile. "That is why you became the rulers of the world. I admire your courage. I envy you your sense of duty, but I hate your pride. I am not a Roman, like you."

"You took my Emperor's money. You promised to obey me. March out with your men and you doom not only yourselves but me also."

He said, "I am sorry. You can still march with me."

"Marcomir."

"No," he said. "It is my wife they have taken. For two nights I have dreamed of what Godigisel has done to her. Now I am going to kill him."

I remembered the Vandal, his square iron body, the brutal face and the thick lips, and the hairs on the back of the stubby fingers. I knew what he was thinking.

I stepped aside. "Go," I said. "And in the name of Mithras, do what has to be done." I gave him my salute and watched him go out into the rain at the head of his men. He was a brave man. As a soldier I could not forgive him, but in his circumstances I might, myself, have done the same thing.

I saw the glint of bronze and went across the mud to the stable. "Fabianus," I said. "I have failed. Ride to Goar's berg and tell him what has happened. Ask him to support Marcomir at his discretion. Stay with him and do what you can."

He saluted. He said, "And do we not help?"

"I am a general," I said, "not the captain of a robber band."

On my return I said to Quintus, "There was nothing I could say that would have stopped him. He had that look on his face. I tried, but only because I had to."

He raised that eyebrow of his. He said, "It seems a pity that we cannot help him."

"How? We have already talked of the difficulties and danger of moving the legion across the river. To build a good bridge would take too long, and a good bridge is hard to destroy if things go wrong. I cannot even use the fleet. They have put a boom across the mouth of the Moenus. It would take too long to break it down. In any case, they have strengthened their defenses at just those points we attacked before. As for the east bank, they have pulled their camp back five hundred yards and are out of range of our catapults."

The night raid must have been a failure, because Marcomir was compelled to do battle as he had foreseen. He challenged Godigisel to fight and the Vandal King, under pressure from his allies who wanted no attacks on their part of the camp, was compelled to accept. For a long day the two hosts faced each other and Marcomir, on the advice of Fabianus, waited till an hour before sundown before advancing his men. It had been a hot day, the Vandals were hungry for their evening meal, and it was good tactics to tire them with waiting. Marcomir attacked in strength and, aided by three thousand of Goar's Alans, broke through the enemy center and cut the Vandals to pieces.

Godigisel was taken alive and his men fled back to their camp. Marcomir then made his mistake. He camped where he had fought, eight hundred yards from the enemy, and, all night long, we on the west bank could see the flicker of his fires and hear the sounds of Godigisel dying. Few of us slept, and in the morning when I met Quintus upon the guard walk his face looked as sick as my own. Three hours later Respendial led his men out onto the plain and attacked Marcomir as he was striking camp. Outnumbered, the Franks withdrew in disorder to the hills while small bands, who found themselves cut off, were hunted westward to the banks of the Rhenus and drowned in the shallows. Goar watched the fighting from the scrub and did not allow his men to take part. He had no wish to set one half of his tribe against the other. The Franks were routed utterly.

Late that afternoon an embassy crossed the river and asked to see me. I could guess the purpose of their visit, so I ordered Rando's daughter to be brought to me, and I received them in the courtyard outside my headquarters, surrounded by a guard of honor. Their leader was a wiry man in his fifties, brown-eyed and arrogant in his manner.

"I bring for the general of the Romans a present from Respendial, King of the Alans," he said. He held out a bundle, shook it slightly, and the head of Marcomir fell to the ground and grinned at me with sightless eyes. The girl put her hand to her mouth, but said nothing. Quintus dropped his hand to his sword, and Aquila grunted with rage.

I said, coldly, "I am glad that you kill each other. It saves me the work."

He bared his teeth and said, softly, "When we cross the river we shall do the same to you." His eyes flickered from face to face. "All of you."

The girl said, in a whisper, "I am glad he is dead. Glad, glad, glad."

I heard her. I said, "The day you cross that river I shall crucify the daughter of Rando, a princess of the royal house, upon a stake on the river's edge so that she may see you coming. Tell that to the Alemanni, whose bread you eat like the beggars that you are."

"You would not dare." He was white with rage. "It is against all custom. It is even against your own laws." His sense of outrage and shock was genuine. His people had a high regard for women. They would steal them, make slaves of them, rape them, and force them into marriage, but they did not torture them. That was stupid. It was a waste of a life that might breed and produce new warriors for the tribe.

I said, "There is nothing I would not dare to protect the lands of my Emperor."

He stared at me with unblinking eyes. "I believe you would," he said. He nodded to the men with him and they left abruptly.

I went back to my office and the courtyard was empty but for the girl. She was white-faced and weeping.

Quintus limped after me. He said, coldly, "We should have helped them. Men fight best when there is something to fight for. If Marcomir could destroy the Siling Vandals we could have beaten the Alans. We had the opportunity to destroy them in one pitched battle."

I said, "We had no bridge."

"Only because you would not build one."

"I told Marcomir we could not help him."

"Yes," he said. "You would do that, of course. I can hear you saying it."

"It was my duty."

He said, bitterly, "It always is your duty. Marcomir is dead. Do you ever think of people instead of things?"

I was angry now. I said, "Do you question my command?"

He hesitated. He said, "I question your judgment. There is always a risk in battle. This was our opportunity, and you threw it away." He added in a low voice, "You did not even ask my opinion."

"There was no time. I was on one side of the river and you on the other."

"There would have been if we had had the bridge."

"But we had no bridge."

He breathed heavily. "No," he said. "You are not good at building bridges."

"At least I do not break them down."

He flushed and turned away.

The tribes across the river buried their dead, repaired their camp and nursed their wounded. There was little they could do except wait, and time was on my side and not on theirs.

Fabianus returned to the Franks and tried to put new heart into them, but many deserted, some to join the Alans, others to seek refuge in the shadow of Guntiarus and the Burgundians. Goar at least did not lose his nerve. He quietly annexed the Frankish land on the right bank and made preparations to defend it, but whether against me or against his own kind I could not be certain. I did not trust him as I had trusted Marcomir.

Reports came in that more wagons had been seen moving out and that, imperceptible though it might seem, the camp was thinning slowly, as families and clans moved back to the east in search of better sites in which to pass the winter. Like a swarm of locusts, they had stripped the land bare on which they had lived all summer, and starvation threatened them at last.

Acting on my instructions, a cohort at Bingium moved across the river and, with troops working hard on both sides, the fort commander began to construct a wooden bridge. The river at this point was four hundred yards across, the weight of the moving water and the speed of the current was tremendous, and there was great difficulty in sinking the piles accurately. The water was bringing down a great mass of stone and shingle from higher up, so that the shoals and sandbanks were constantly changing shape and altering their position. Nevertheless the bridge was finished and ready for use eight days after the first tree was felled.

I had it in mind to risk all on a single throw, move the legion across the river at the end of October, and engage all that remained of the enemy in battle, relying on the fact that by that time their courage would be at a low ebb. Quintus urged this course every time we met. We argued the matter with cold hostility. He was confident that the risk would be worthwhile and that the shock of one more defeat would finally extinguish their hopes of forcing a crossing. I was not quite so certain. It was I who bore the final responsibility, not he.

During this time I saw little of our prisoner. She had recovered from her beating and gave no more trouble. Occasionally I saw her at a distance, walking through the camp with a guard behind her, but if she saw me she turned her head and looked the other way. Sometimes, one of the tribunes was with her. It might be young Marius who came from Arelate, or Severus who had joined us after Pollentia. Occasionally it was Didius, one of Quintus' more promising squadron commanders, who had been transferred to us nine months ago from a cavalry unit in Hispania. Usually, however, it was Fabianus, but I did not ask questions. He worked hard, as they all did, and if he found it amusing to spend his spare time in her company that was his affair, not mine.

In the second week of September I received a series of agitated messages from the fort commander at Bingium; Guntiarus was on the far bank, asking permission to cross. He wished to see me on a matter of great urgency. I sent a message back saying that he was to remain on the east bank and that I would come to visit him in his berg as soon as my duties permitted.

When he heard of this Quintus said, bleakly, "He wants more tribute. I can smell his demands a mile away. He is a greedy man. He offered no help to Marcomir. He thinks only of himself."

I said, "He is not alone in that." I pointed to my desk. "I have just received the answers to my other letters."

"What do they say?"

"The Praefectus Praetorio is cautious and diplomatic. I may call on the field army if I need it, but the field army is not to enter Belgica unless and until the Barbarians cross the Rhenus. He is afraid, you see, that I might have ambitions to set myself up in his place. The news from Britannia will not have helped."

"The man is mad."

"Oh yes, but there is some logic in that dull little mind. Germania has always been a breeding ground for usurpers."

"Go on."

"The Dux Belgicae, poor man, has troubles of his own on the coast and cannot spare a man. Him, I believe."

"And our friend, Chariobaudes?"

"He will move his troops as far east as Cabillonum and will help us, subject to the Praefectus' orders."

"How many men has he got?"

I laughed. "That is what is so funny. Oh, he's quite honest about it. He has ten regiments of five hundred men each. All are veterans between the ages of forty-five and fifty. Out of that he can make an effective fighting force of about three thousand."

Quintus said, "They won't be much use. We shall have to rely on ourselves."

"Yes," I said. "But the day may still come when we shall be thankful for even three thousand men."

"How far is it from Treverorum to Cabillonum." He put his finger on the map and traced the route. "Well over a hundred miles."

"Yes."

"It will be of great comfort, when we are in trouble, to know we are so closely supported by the glorious army of Gaul."

I looked up at him. I said, "I have always known that in this affair we should be quite alone. In that there is nothing new."

He said, steadily, "It is only when I think about it that I get frightened. I wake up in the night and sit on the edge of my bed and sweat with fear."

I put out my hand, unthinkingly, but he backed away. He said, "In the day I can pretend. It is easy then. But at night I know the truth, and, sometimes, I cannot face the truth."

Guntiarus said, "It was kind of you to come. My people are poor, as you know, and the harvest has not been a good one."

"A further payment of tribute is not due for another six months," I said, brutally.

"That is understood. Of course, I can always sell food to the Vandals. Their ambassadors are here now. Their people are, I think, starving, and would pay a good price—in silver. But you are my friend and I do not care to help your enemies unless I am forced to."

I said, "You have had all the tribute I can spare. If your harvest was bad, then it was because you are a lazy people and bad farmers. I cannot help you."

"My people are warriors," he said, mildly.

"If you prefer to treat with the men who took your daughter and slew your son-in-law, that is a matter for you," I said, contemptuously. "Make friends of their murderers, but do not come again asking me to give you silver."

"The Vandals are very strong," he said, anxiously. "I am only a man of peace. My people do not wish for war."

"No," said Quintus. "Only for the chance to share the west bank in return for helping these Vandals."

"You would force me to see my people sell them food," he squeaked.

"Those are your words, not mine. But are you certain your men are strong enough to guard your wagons against my cavalry?"

He said, anxiously, "We are friends. We have made a pact. I am in the service of the Emperor. You, yourself, appointed me the Praeses of Germania Inferior." He stumbled over the Latin words awkwardly, but there was an absurd pride in his voice at his remembrance of the meaningless title. It was almost as hollow as my own. "You will not kill an ally."

"No," I said. "I kill only those who oppose me."

We walked out to where our horses stood. His small son, a flaxen-haired child of eleven, was standing by my horse, fingering the harness. I mounted, and then bent down and lifted the boy onto the saddlecloth in front of me. His struggles ceased the moment my knife pricked the soft skin of his throat. There was a growl from the tribesmen around us. My escort of five closed up on me. The King stepped forward and then hesitated. His face had gone white. He was afraid of me, and I was glad. What was a yellow-haired Burgundian to me—I who was Maximus?

"Your son needs a change of air," I said. "I will show him my camp and my soldiers and he will like that. He will be my honored guest and I will look after his health as carefully as my own. You will remember that, Guntiarus, when you think to sell food to the enemies of Rome."

"My son," he cried. "Give me my son."

"When you have avenged your daughter, I will know that you care for your son." I lifted my hand and we trotted through the camp, followed by a great host of men who would have killed me if they had dared. Outside the stockade we dug our heels into our horses and galloped hard for the river. When we reached the shore opposite Bingium I knew we were safe. At Moguntiacum I sent for the girl who was Rando's daughter.

She came and Fabianus was with her.

I said, "Look after the boy. If he goes sick or escapes you will embrace that tree by the river sooner than you think."

She cried out at me then, called me a Roman butcher and a murderer until she ran out of breath. I laughed and she went away in silence, but I knew that the boy would be safe.

On the last night of the month I was awoken a little after dawn by the centurion of the watch, beating upon my door.

"What is it?" I asked, irritably.

"The girl has escaped. We found the sentry outside her hut half an hour ago. He had been stunned."

"Half an hour."

He said, steadily, "I had the camp searched at once. She is nowhere inside. I found a ladder against the south wall by the stables. And this, sir." He held up a woman's sandal.

"Yes, that is hers."

"We had to make sure before we told you, sir."

"She must be found. Take a patrol into the town. She may be hiding there. Search every house, if need be." I flung on my cloak and picked up my sword. "She was locked in?"

"Yes, sir."

"Then she had help." I stared at him and frowned. "One of our men? Is that what you are thinking?"

"It looks like it, sir."

We hurried out. The camp flared with torches and the men were parading outside their huts under the direction of their section commanders. Aquila came up, unshaved, and rubbing his eyes. "Take a roll call," I said. "Find out who is missing."

He saluted and a few minutes later I heard the trumpets sound. Then came a shout from the southeast gate tower. I ran toward it, followed by Fabianus and another tribune. "Up here," shouted a voice. I climbed the steps to the firing platform. The sentry pointed and I saw a boat drifting downstream, a small boat such as fishermen used. It appeared to be empty. Caught in one current and then another, it nosed first one way and then the next. It passed close to the broken bridge, at which the sentry there cried out and flung three javelins in quick succession. Two went into the boat. A third hit the water behind. Then the boat moved outward suddenly, caught in a cross eddy, and passed slowly along the west shore of the south island. The sentry ran back and came panting up to the wall. "There are men on board," he cried. "They are lying on the bottom."

"Use the catapults," I said. "I will give a week's extra pay to all who have a hand in sinking her."

"Shall I sound the alarm?"

"No, you fool. I don't want too much importance attached to it. They know our trumpet calls. The parade call is one thing, the alarm another."

"Number Four and Five ready, sir."

"Fire."

They fired. The boat, guided crudely by a man lying upon the boards, holding an oar over the stern, was moving more rapidly now. It was clear of the island and heading toward the further bank. Fireball after fireball went hissing up into the dawn sky. They landed, with tremendous splashes and great hisses of steam, all round the boat; it was facing the shore now and a difficult target. The seventh shot struck the boat; there came back across the water a hoarse scream and then silence.

"Well, that's that," said the duty optio in a satisfied voice.

Fabianus said, white-faced, "Do you think she was in the boat?"

"I don't know," I said, angrily. "If she was, then she was lucky." He stared at me.

"How many in the boat?" I asked the sentry.

"Three, sir."

"Are you certain?"

"I am positive, sir."

"Let us hope you are right." I smiled at the centurion. "Good work. The sentry and yourself are to be included. Send me the names and I will pass them to the accounts office."

The centurion said, anxiously, "I hope they all drowned, sir."

"Yes, I hope so too. I expect they did."

Two hours later a report came in from the duty centurion on the south island. A man, who appeared to be badly injured, had been seen climbing out of the water onto the east bank. He had then vanished into the scrub. It was impossible to say whether he was likely to die or not. The centurion did not think so, and I was inclined to believe him. He was a man of some experience. He had seen many wounded men in his time. He knew how a man moved when he was dying.

It was day now, too late to go back to sleep. I went to the headquarters building and broke my fast on a biscuit dipped in wine. Aquila came in. He looked tired. He said, "Everyone is accounted for, sir, except the prisoner and— " He hesitated.

"Tell me."

"The tribune Severus, sir."

"Was he on duty yesterday?"

"Yes, sir." He added, awkwardly, "He had no leave of absence from the camp. I have checked that with the camp praefectus."

"I understand." I looked out of the window. I said, "Send the tribune Fabianus to me."

He came. He looked ill, and, as he stood to attention before me, his hands trembled by his sides.

I said, "Who else, besides you, was in the habit of talking to the prisoner?"

He said, miserably, "A number of us used to."

"Anyone in particular? The tribune Severus, for instance?"

There was a long silence and then he said, in a low voice, "Yes, sir."

I rose from my stool and stood over him. "Did you know about this?" He did not say anything. He dropped his eyes to the floor.

"Answer me," I said.

"No, sir. I didn't. But—"

"Go on."

He licked his lips. "A month ago she asked me if I—if I would help her to escape. I refused, of course. I never thought she might try to persuade anyone else.'

"Why didn't you report this?"

"I didn't think—"

"No, you wouldn't. I will deal with you later. You realize this is an offense, punishable by death?"

He swayed on his feet. "Not you, you young fool; the man who helped her."

"But they're dead," he muttered.

"We found the marks where the boat had been drawn up on the mud; there were three sets of foot marks round it, but no tracks leading from the fort to the river. There should have been. It rained yesterday evening and the ground was soft. I think they lost their way; the people who supplied the boat lost their nerve because of the trumpets in the camp and didn't wait. They pushed off and we caught them."

He stared at me in horror.

"Yes," I said. "I think the girl and the tribune are hiding the town."

"What will you do, sir?"

I said, "They had better have died in that boat."

They were found four days later, hidden in a wine cellar, only fifty yards from the east gate. Freedom—of a kind—had been so near, but my sentries they could not pass without discovery. They were brought back under guard; Severus, unshaven, hollow-eyed, desperate, and dirty; the girl, equally bedraggled, but still defiant. They were locked in the guardhouse in separate cells, and I sent for Quintus.

He saluted me formally and I asked him to take a seat. The old ease of manner between us had never returned. There were no jokes and no gossip between us still. We did not talk; we only communicated. Our relationship was so twisted that I did not know how to put it right. I did not know if I even wanted to.

I said, "There must be a trial."

"Yes," he said.

"It is only a formality. The evidence is clear enough. I want you to take charge of it. Find out who the three men in the boat were. I must know that, at all costs."

He raised his eyebrows. "Not at all costs," he said, gently. "But I will do my best."

The trial lasted an hour and when it was over Quintus came to me, a bitter smile on his face. "He talked," he said. "He bribed some Franks living outside the town to help him. They bought the boat from a fisherman."

"You are sure of that?"

"Oh, quite sure. He told me everything, the moment I warned him what would happen if he did not."

"Why did he do it?"

Quintus looked at me. "Do you really want to know?"

"That is why I asked."

"He knows, as we all do, what the odds are against us. He's very young, a little stupid, perhaps, a little too sensitive to make a good Roman soldier." He glanced at me ironically. "The girl worked on him. She is—very pretty. Besides all that, he is an Arian Christian. I did not know that. Did you? His sympathies are a trifle mixed. He thought, too, that your treatment of the girl was barbarous. He is, as I said, a Christian." He paused. He said with a frown, "He thinks that they should be allowed to cross the river, and that it is we who are the Barbarians in keeping them out. He is rather like our good Bishop."

"So he betrayed us."

"Yes. But I do not think he realized he was doing just that."

"What was he going to do when he crossed the river?"

"He had some wild idea, I think, of marrying the girl, obtaining the good wishes of the Alemanni, and acting as a kind of mediator between both sides." He said, sadly, "It would be very funny if it were not so tragic."

"For him, yes."

"And for all of us."

I said, "He joined us in our second year in Italia. Do you remember his father? I promised I would look after the boy."

"Yes, I remember. Do you want to see him?"

I shook my head. "No. There would be no point. If I offered to see him now he would think I was going to pardon him. It would be needless cruelty on both of us."

"He could be banished," he said, in a hopeless kind of voice.

"No."

He sighed. "I did not think you would agree. Tomorrow morning then?"

"Yes, at daybreak. I will see the girl though. Have her sent to me, please. You will arrange everything else."

"Of course."

Rando's daughter, still stinking of the wine cellar and of all the other places in which she had hidden during the past days, was brought to me, in chains. This time the sentry stood inside the room, holding the cord attached to the collar about her neck. She was like a wild animal, trapped but defiant.

I said, "Why didn't you get to the boat? You had time."

She said, hoarsely, "We met a night watchman in the street. He called to us and we ran from him and lost our way in the alleys. We were frightened."

"I thought you were braver than that. You could have bribed him with a coin. That is what most people do. It always works."

"We only thought of that afterwards."

I said, "You made a mistake. You should have kept faith with Fabianus. He would not have betrayed me, but he would not have let you down either."

"Fabianus." Her voice was scornful. "He was too frightened to help me."

"Yet he loves you," I said. "Which is more than Severus does."

"What are you going to do with him? And with me?" she added in a whisper.

"You can watch that tomorrow morning. That will be your punishment. You are responsible, you know. I hope you will remember that when you see him in the morning."

She said in a shaking voice, "One of them got away. I am glad. Now they will know how many men you really have."

"Don't be too pleased, my girl. The sooner they come the sooner you, too, will die."

Thirty minutes after dawn, two cohorts were drawn up in a hollow square on the parade ground. All the centurions and all the officers were present, and the sentries on the walls faced inward. The girl was brought out under escort and tied to a stake driven into the ground. The stake faced a low platform, upon which stood the legion's farrier and a number of military police. The officers wore plumes upon their helmets, and the aquilifer wore a black panther skin and held the Eagle, which was hooded to conceal the shame that we felt. When I came out in my full uniform, which I only wore on special occasions, it was bitterly cold and I could see the lances held upright, quivering as though with fear. It was very cold and very quiet and you could hear the jingle of the bit as Quintus' horse tossed its head.

Then we heard the sound of nailed sandals, and they brought him into the square, walking quickly as a man does who is late for an appointment, and he wore nothing but a tunic and a kilt. His uniform stood in a pile upon the platform, together with his sword and his helmet. It was customary for the sword to be broken, but we were short of such weapons and, at the quartermaster's request, had substituted an old sword with a flawed blade which had been marked for disposal. He mounted the platform, and he looked like a ghost. He kept on wetting his lips with his tongue—or trying to, and his eyes seemed to be bulged with fear. We could all see that he was terrified of dying and he kept on making small whimpering noises, though he did not actually try to speak. The camp praefectus read the punishment and sentence in a high voice that cracked with nervousness. The flawed sword was then broken, ceremonially, across the duty centurion's knees.

The camp praefectus turned to me and I nodded to him to get on with the whole ghastly, stupid, futile ritual. Even Quintus did not guess how I hated it all. The prisoner was asked if he had anything to say. He shook his head, desperately. We could hear his teeth chattering, but this might have been due to the cold as much as to fear. At such a time, it is kinder to give any man the benefit of the doubt. A trumpet sounded, the farrier stepped forward, and the boy was pushed down onto his knees. The trumpet sounded again, and sentence of death by decapitation was performed upon Marcus Severus, former tribune of the legion, for desertion, treason, and cowardice. The girl, soaked with his blood, was left tied to the post, alone with the body of the man whom she had enticed to his death. After an hour, she was cut down and taken back to her hut. The body was buried on the road outside the town; the platform was dismantled, and life in the camp returned to normal. That night, Quintus went out fishing with some of the tribunes and then got horribly drunk, later, in his hut. I went down to the town and attended a cockfight. I won a lot of money. My luck was in, and the day ended better than it had begun.

CHAPTER XIV

As a punishment I sent Fabianus back across the river. He hated it there; he was a man who liked comfortable living. A week later he sent me a signal to say that the movement of wagons out of the enemy camp had stopped. Instead, wagons and families were coming in, and it looked as if those who had left were returning. Of food convoys from the Burgundians, however, there was no sign.

I said to Quintus, "That means the man did not die. They know how many we are; they will stay and wait."

"But they will surely starve if they wait till the spring?"

"Perhaps. These people can smell the weather like an animal. They will wait till midwinter. If the winter is a bad one, the Rhenus will freeze and give them their opportunity. If it does not, they will break camp and head for their own lands."

He said urgently, "What about the bridge? Will you take the legion over now?"

I shook my head. "Not now. They know our strength. Besides, Marcomir is dead and his men scattered. The risk is too great."

He took a deep breath. He said, "We should have made the bridge when he was alive, when it was suggested first."

I held up my hands, palms outward in a gesture of surrender. "Yes," I said. "I missed the opportunity."

"Don't look like that, Maximus."

"Quintus, it is true."

"So. What do we do then?"

I looked at him and, for the first time in weeks, I smiled as I did so. "You and I will go to Treverorum. We could do with a change of scene and I need a rest as much as you. It will be the last chance we shall get this year.

Aquila can command."

On a cool October day, when there was a mist like milk over the river, we left Moguntiacum and set out on the long ride back to the city. It was a road I knew well now. As the miles passed under our horses' feet our spirits rose. The weather held; it was clear and fine. We talked together of the old days on the Northern Wall, of wolves we had hunted, of deer we had killed, and of a boar that we had pursued without success, all through one long wet day. We talked of Saturninus and of his friends who had shared our mystery, and who were now dead. But we never talked of my wife.

The few patches of bracken that I saw were a golden brown and the leaves were brittle on the trees as they changed from green to a brown the color of dark honey. One morning we saw a flight of swans, skimming low in arrowhead formation above the trees toward the Mosella. Sometimes we rode in silence and I would think of Julian in that patchwork camp of strange tongues across the river. What would he do now that Rando was dead? Would he wait to cross with the others or would he turn away and find somewhere else to settle? I did not hate him now and the memory of the past had blurred a little. It was all such a long time ago. He was, after all, still Julian, whom I had once loved as a friend. He was a part of my life, a part of me, and the realization of this made me jerk suddenly at my horse so that he flung up his head. Quintus glanced at me without speaking.

"One half of my life has destroyed the other half," I said aloud, and Quintus flushed and bit his lip. He was too proud to make excuses, too honest to apologize for things he had done, about which he could not be sorry.

At Treverorum we took up our old quarters in Romulus and I could relax inside those massive, cool stone walls, watch the afternoon sun make shifting patterns on the mosaic, listen to the sounds and cries of the city as it went about its business, and make plans for amusing myself in the coming evening. There was, of course, a certain amount of business that I could not neglect. I inspected the cohort on garrison duty, dined with Flavius, watched the training of the city auxiliaries, and made arrangements for improving the defenses of the town. On the surface of the bridge over the Mosella bundles of brushwood were piled against the rails and lashed to the transoms. If necessary, they could be soaked with pitch and fired in a few minutes. I did not expect that an attack, pushed inland, would be made along the northern road but it was well to be prepared. Though, as Quintus said sardonically when I told him what I had done, "If things get as bad as that, who will be left alive to bother about such matters?"

Then I called a meeting of the senators and senior officials, told them what precautions I had taken, and warned them that the next three months would be crucial. I had deliberately selected the great hall of the basilica for this occasion, and though there were thirty of us present, we were dwarfed by the size of the place and our voices echoed strangely in that vast room.

"I am taking over the city," I said. No one moved but I heard Artorius say, "Ah," very softly, and his eyes never left my face the whole time I was speaking. "I have informed the Praefectus Praetorio. The Magister Equitum per Gallias can spare me no troops, because he has none. The Dux Belgicae cannot help either. The Saxons are raiding his coast and he needs all the few men he possesses. The tribune Flavius, as garrison commander, will be my deputy, with full powers. I am issuing an edict to conscript all men of military age, regardless of whether they are exempt by normal laws or not. I would not do this if the situation were not so grave. But it is."

To my relief they accepted this without protest. One or two had already visited Moguntiacum and had seen the camp across the river. But, though they accepted, they could not really grasp the problem.

The Curator said, "Do you wish me to resign?"

"No."

"I am to take my orders from Flavius?"

"Only insofar as they affect the military situation. In all else things will remain the same. I hope that you will be able to work in amity."

He said, coldly, "I shall do my best."

"If they cross the river, can you beat them in battle?" asked the chief magistrate, as though he were questioning a witness in one of his courts.

"Yes," I said. "I can. But I must warn you that to win a battle one needs luck as well as judgment."

"Then we have nothing to fear." He did not understand my caution. He was a lawyer: he understood everything about law, nothing about anything else.

"But if you have, then I will give you good warning," I said. "And, thanks to your help over the past year," I lied, "I pray that all will yet be well."

They grunted their satisfaction, and I was reminded of the pigs I had seen in the forest on my journey there, rooting among the trees for acorns.

Quintus and I went to the baths and listened sleepily to the gossip, while the attendants rubbed us with oil. The price of wine had gone up, the promised corn from Britannia had not arrived, and the merchants who owned the granaries and the senators who owned land were charging high prices for their poor crops. Honorius was blamed bitterly for his edict permitting slaves to join the army; the Praefectus Praetorio had issued an order forbidding citizens without passes from entering Gaul; and a certain actress had scandalized the respectable in the city by the number and rapidity of her lovers, and the priests had been joyously denouncing her from the steps of their churches for the past month. The Bishop, too, was in the news. He had made himself unpopular by granting sanctuary to an escaped slave who had killed his master, and he refused to give him up, despite the pressure of those civil authorities responsible for maintaining order. Conversation everywhere, however, always turned to one topic in the end: the games that Julianus Septimus was providing in the amphitheater and the arena in ten days' time, to celebrate the coming marriage of his eldest son's daughter to a young man from a wealthy family in Remi. The Bishop might not approve (of what did he approve?) but his influence was not strong enough to halt the wishes of the man who had recently, and tactfully, contributed so much to his great cathedral. There would be fights between gladiators brought from Arelate, wild animals from Mauretania, and chariot races between drivers who had competed at Rome. The games were to last five days, and I received an invitation from the Curator to preside over them, much to my surprise. I thanked him and—a happy thought this—told him there would be a tax on all tickets sold, the proceeds to go toward the legion's war chest. If Septimus was prepared to spend so much money—the lions alone were costing one hundred and fifty thousand denarii each—then we were certainly entitled to our share of the profits.

Quintus spent a lot of time down by the docks with Gallus and Flavius. I thought at first it was a new ship they were interested in, but I went down there myself one morning and found them busy with the blacksmith and a model oar, the blade of which was tipped with iron along its edges.

Quintus said, "If the water begins to freeze it might be just possible to break the ice with oars, but they would need to be strengthened."

"What about the boat? That would need protection also."

"We have thought of that, too. What we need is a metal shield on the bow." Flavius grinned. "The General and I have the ideas. Gallus sees if they can be put into practice."

At a banquet one evening Quintus struck up a friendship over the wine with a fat man who bred horses, and whenever he disappeared after that I knew he was over at the fat man's estates, giving them a hand in the breaking-in of the horses.

He was still urging me to make use of our bridge. "I can commandeer fifteen transports," he said. "And we can get more from Confluentes and Borbetomagus."

"You need sixty to carry a legion."

"All right, sixty then. There will be no need to fear our being trapped on the wrong bank if there are boats to take us off, and the bridge is burned." He knew my obsessive fear at having no secure line of retreat.

I said again, "They know just how weak we are."

"They only guess, and you only guess that they guess. You cannot be sure."

"Do you want me to lose Gaul in an afternoon?"

He took my arm. "Upon the Wall you used to spend your evenings studying the campaigns of great soldiers."

"Yes," I said. "Sertorius, Lucullus, and Pompey, though he came to a harsh end."

"Caesar too." He smiled. "You used to tell me that his successes were due to speed and surprise. He exploited the weaknesses of his enemies."

I said, wearily, "I am not Caesar."

"He fought against odds as great."

"The people he fought were not as well armed, nor as well equipped, nor as well led as these. And he was never reduced to only one legion."

"We have my cavalry, which makes us two, if I am any judge of soldiers."

I hesitated.

"If Marcomir had been supported by sufficient horse he could have destroyed Respendial that day." It was true.

"Very well," I said. "I will try it if you wish. But we will do it my way and not yours. I need more cavalry. Get me another thousand and I will fight."

"I shall have to call upon the auxiliary alae then," he said cautiously. "They are not as well trained as I would like."

I laughed. "When they are ready, Quintus, then let me know."

He raised an eyebrow. "I will hold you to that."

We attended the games and I shared the seats of honor with Septimus and his family. Of our previous meeting we did not speak; politeness alone made the occasion endurable. He behaved toward me, throughout, with all the dignity and good manners of a senator who has been advised by his Emperor to open his veins in hot water. And yet, curious as it seemed afterward, once, during the chariot races between the Reds and the Whites, our common enthusiasm for the sport made a bridge between us, and, for a short while, we were almost friends. This, in its way, was remarkable, for friends and families were split in their allegiance to the teams, quite as fiercely as over the Blues and Greens of Constantinopolis. The games were a great success and put the populace in a high good humor. All the seats were sold out; Artorius made a series of lucky bets and won much money; Quintus enjoyed the animal fights and thought them superior to the ones he had seen in Hispania, while the gladiatorial fights were, very properly, fought to the death. I had the rare experience, however, of giving the wooden foil to a gladiator who had gained the crowd's approval, and his face, when I handed it to him, haunted me for days afterward.

Only the Bishop did not share the general festivity. When I met him a day or so later, his face was pinker than usual. He had the look of a man who does not enjoy the martyrdom of unpopularity.

On our last day I went to the baths and had my hair dyed. It was silver all over now and I think the troops knew, to judge by the nickname that they had given me. But I did not care. What were their opinions to me? In the afternoon Quintus went to the deserted Temple of Epona, while I sat in the back room of a merchant's shop and haggled over the price of a flask of perfume for Rando's daughter. Afterward I rode in search of my friend. I tied my horse beside his and then sat down upon a block of fallen stone. The sun shone strongly upon the red and gray of the buildings, and the entrance to the temple was shadowed in darkness. No one came here now and I had the whole square to myself. The sky was very blue, I remember, and the trees stood silent, their once dark leaves already turned a rich brown. Once it had seemed as though they would live forever; now they were dying after so short a life, and would soon crumble into dust. A lizard ran across the paving and concealed itself in the tufts of grass that thrust themselves upward between the cracks, its small body heaving, as though it found the heat too much at that time of the year. I unpinned my cloak and shut my eyes, and felt the sun upon my face. I thought, for a moment or two, of the bustle in the offices of the basilica, and of the legion in its earth and timber forts, and of all the work that awaited me when I returned. Suddenly, I felt very old and very tired. I thought of the villa at Arelate and of the pool in which I had swum as a boy. I thought of the plans we had made, my wife and I. There had been that winter when it was very cold and we had spent the evenings planning a new and proper home in the forest of Anderida. She had sat by the fire, spinning, while I drew the outlines of the new house with a stick of charcoal upon the back of a duty list. We had argued about the size of the rooms and how many we should need. Quintus had joined us, one night, and we had laughed and joked over the wine. That was the night she had washed her hair, and she sat by the fire, drying it and listening to our talk. There had to be a special room for him, I insisted, so that he would come to visit us often; and Quintus had agreed, and they had looked at each other and smiled.

I opened my eyes and stared up at the sky. There were so many questions that I had wanted to ask, so many that I had never dared to ask. I never would ask them now. I shut them from my mind. They were the bad things, about which I could do nothing. It was better, I thought, to remember the happy times instead. Perhaps, when all this was over, we would buy a villa still, and farm it, and Quintus would breed horses, and I would write that military history that had been in my mind all these years. And in the evenings we would sit before the fire and drink wine and remind ourselves of the old days. So I sat there, blinking in the sun, and I was just an old man, dreaming foolish dreams.

When I looked up again, Quintus was standing over me. He saw the flask at my side, and laughed. "It is not for yourself, I hope. I remember your remarks, once, about perfumed tribunes. You kicked the fellow out."

"I did," I said, amiably. We walked in the sunlight to where our horses stood, and I turned to ask him something, and then stopped. He looked back at me in silence, his face quite calm and wonderfully relaxed except for the eyes. He had that look that I remembered seeing once before, when he had been made a present of a fine foal. Perhaps Aelia had known it also. But now, he had been to the temple.

"Yes," he said. "It was good. Oh, Maximus, when I die I like to think that the Goddess will grant my wish, especially if I die in battle in a good charge."

"What is your wish?" I asked.

"There is another." He looked at me steadily. "But this one is more simple: that I may be allowed to drive the golden horses of the sun." And after that he was silent.

Back at Romulus we made our offering before the small altar that we had made to do honor to our God; we made the ritual sacrifice, we offered up the accustomed prayers, and I felt the burden of my fatherhood upon me. All the while a sentry kept watch outside to see that we were not disturbed. After it was over we sat, still in silence, and watched the sun dip behind the hills.

It was getting dark now and the shadows were running back into the room. I struck a flint and lit the tiny lamp that stood on the wine table. Over the yellow, flickering flame we looked at each other. I said, "There is still hope, you know."

"Yes," he said. "I know that." But he had the look of a man who did not care anymore.

I heard the sentry stamp his feet outside the door. There was a murmur of voices, and then the door opened and the Bishop came in.

"You leave tomorrow," he said. "I came to say goodbye." We talked for a while in a polite and stilted manner, and all the time he kept on looking at the brand on my forehead, which always showed when my hair had been cut.

WALLACE BREEM

He said, suddenly, "You have no priests."

I raised my head. "No," I said, "not in your sense of the word. Yet some of us are granted the privilege of acting as guides upon the way. We mediate on behalf of our brothers."

His intellectual curiosity overcame his natural repugnance to discuss a matter of which he disapproved. "Tell me," he said, "why it is that your temples are made below the ground and why your beliefs are kept so secret?"

I looked at Quintus and then at the Bishop. I said, "We believe that power is lost through idle talk. We draw strength from our worship as a community, as you do, and yet—" I hesitated. I said, "The best prayers are made in silence." He nodded. "I understand," he said. He put his cup down on the table and talked of other things then.

"It has been a hard year," said Quintus, in reply to some remark.

"It will be harder yet," said the Bishop calmly, his big hand folded across his lap, the cross upon his throat glinting in the light.

"What do you mean?"

"The berries on the bushes have been taken already, and each night at dusk you can see the geese flying inland from the north." He smiled. "A colony of field mice live just outside the wall at the back of my house, on the north side. You can see their holes, a dozen of them quite clearly. Now they are blocked up and they have made fresh holes on the other side of the wall. They know, too. All the farmers say the same thing. It is going to be a hard and bitter winter."

"How bitter?" I said sharply.

"I do not know, my son, but there will be snow and ice." He looked from us to the altar in the niche in the wall. "Are you afraid of death?" he asked gently. "If you followed my faith there would be no need."

"I am a soldier," I said. "Death is something I have given and it is something that I must receive. I am only afraid of dying, not of being dead."

He was silent for a while. Then he rose to his feet. At the door he paused. He said steadily, "It is easier to be blinded by the sun than by the darkness of the night."

I said, "The sun has died but it will renew itself in the morning."

"You are very sure."

I smiled. "Yes. That is why we have something in common, all three of us."

He did not take up the challenge. Instead he said, "Am I right in understanding that you intend to do battle with the Vandals?"

I nodded, surprised. "How do you know that? I have told no one. Unless Quintus——" I turned to look at him but he shook his head.

The Bishop said, "It was in your face when you came to the basilica yesterday morning. Before that you had the look of a man trying to make up his mind. Yesterday you looked peaceful. The decision had been made. There is only one thing that worries a general—the decision to engage the enemy; the when, the how, and the where."

I said, "You know a lot about soldiers."

He smiled. "Why not? Did you know that one of my predecessors in office was once a centurion in a legion at Moguntiacum? We live in the world more than you think."

I was silent. Quintus said roughly, "Yes, we are going to fight. We have waited long enough for help that has never come."

I glanced at him sharply. The Bishop said, "It is a fine thing that you are such good friends." He regarded us keenly. He said, "I am glad that this city has two such men as you to protect it. I did not always think so. This city and this province have great need of men like yourselves, men who have confidence and authority and right judgment, men who are sure, men who know themselves."

I shut my eyes suddenly. I said, "You are very kind." I thought of Julian, and of my wife. I thought of the girl in the camp at Moguntiacum and of the times I had wiped the blood off my sword after a battle or a fight. I said, "But you are so very wrong. Do not have too much confidence in us, my lord Bishop."

He said, "Do not misunderstand me. As I said, I have been in the world. I can tell a good sword from a bad one. And I know just how a sword is made. If you ever need me I shall be here. You need never feel alone."

I stared out over the window ledges, saw the helmets of my soldiers in the courtyard below, smelled the smell of food cooking in the kitchens, and heard a girl laugh as she strolled through the arcade behind my back, holding hands with a young man, no doubt. In the distance a skein of geese passed silently across the face of the rising moon.

With the auxiliaries manning all the forts from Confluentes to Borbetomagus, the cohorts marched out by night, carrying full equipment, twenty days' rations, and the hopes and fears of their commanders. To muffle undue noise the cooking pots, spades, and entrenching tools had been wrapped in rags and the only sound was the quiet jingling of a horse's bit and the steady tramp of nailed sandals. The men had been forbidden to sing, as they normally did, but they marched cheerfully and in good spirits at the thought of the coming battle. After an hour, riding at the rear of the column, I could smell again the familiar smell of horses, sweat, and leather and began to feel more cheerful.

Eight days later the legion crossed the river, again by night, and before dawn marched ten miles into the heart of the territory, formerly Marcomir's, now held by Goar. We camped near his berg while the men rested during the hours of daylight and troops of cavalry rode forward to make contact with Goar's scouts, who were guarding the foothills north of the plain where the enemy lay. That night we marched again and the second dawn found us drawn up for battle, six hundred yards from the enemy camp. The center, under the command of Fabianus, consisted of the three heavy cohorts, with their ballistae and carroballistae, grouped in the gaps between the massed units. Guarding their flanks were two light cohorts, extended slightly forward at an angle to suggest that they were the wings of my formation. Slightly to the rear of these wings, but outflanking them, and hidden on the one hand by a copse and on the other by thick scrub, were two alae of horse, their men dismounted for additional concealment. As a reserve, under my own hand, I had a third ala, the third cohort of light infantry, and my bodyguard. To left and right of the legion were Goar's Alans, mixed with a stiffening of auxiliaries. Behind us, as an additional reserve, were Marcomir's Franks—what was left of them. Each cohort was divided into ten sixty-man waves and the men sat upon the ground and rested while scouts rode up and down the line, checking that all was as it should be.

For an hour nothing happened. The enemy lined the palisade and watched us, but they would not move. To goad them into action I moved the artillery forward, protected by a screen of light troops, and began to bombard the camp. This had the desired effect and after half an hour a great body of men, the Alans of Respendial, moved out in bands under their leaders and came toward us. I signaled the artillery to withdraw and it did so, the men panting and sweating as they strained to pull the ballistae back into the safety of their own ranks. Seeing this the enemy, who had been moving forward steadily, broke into a run. When they were two hundred yards away the front rank of the cohorts moved out at the double and threw their javelins from a range of fifty feet. One flight of javelins was followed by another and another as each row hurled its weapons in turn. The javelin shower tore great gaps in the enemy and checked their rush for a moment. Then there was the most appalling crash of steel upon steel, of iron upon iron, all mixed up with the cries of men shouting, as the two sides closed in hand to hand fighting. The tribesmen hacked and swung with their longer swords, their axes, and their spears, but the legionaries, their shields close to their bodies, contented themselves with quick underhand thrusts of their short swords, aiming always for the stomach or the chest, never for the head or the shoulders. "Three inches in the right place," I used to say to them, "and he is a dead or a dying man. But give him six inches in the wrong place, and he will kill you before you have time to give the second blow." The close fighting went on for ten or twelve minutes, and then a second wave of the cohorts moved forward to take the place of their now rapidly tiring comrades. Our line held; the Alans could not break it and they fell back a little to recover their breath while, in their turn, others took their place. They tried twice more but still failed to break the center. So many were the enemy that they could not all get into the fighting line at once; so those in the rear spread out and began to assault my two wings, whose archers did terrible damage. When the whole line was engaged and I could see that they had no true reserves left I ordered the trumpeter to sound, and the auxiliaries and Alans under Goar swept round and took the enemy in both flanks. The shock was too much for them. The enemy wavered, tried to hold their ground, wavered again, and then broke in flight back toward their camp. The trumpet sounded again and the auxiliary ala broke from the scrub where Quintus had them concealed and struck diagonally at the retreating enemy. In four minutes it was all over. Less than a third of the Alans got back to the safety of the palisades.

In the lull that followed I held a conference with my staff; the wounded were taken to the rear where the wagons stood waiting, and the ranks reformed themselves. Groups of our soldiers went out to recover all the weapons that lay within three hundred yards of our position, and to kill the enemy wounded who lay upon the ground. The men were allowed to fall out, section by section, to eat and drink; the various units regrouped and the gaps in the ranks closed up. Archers ran up with bundles of fresh arrows, while centurions cried out for more spears and javelins.

A little before midday the enemy began to mass again along the edge of their shattered palisade but, as before, they made no move to come out. To encourage them I had the advance sounded and moved my whole battle line forward three hundred yards. Then I pushed out a line of archers and when they were within range ordered them to open fire. "Watch the wind," I cried, for I could see the arrows fading to the left as they dropped toward the palisade. The ballistae opened fire and the sky was filled with fireballs. Soon the whole length of the palisade, for half a mile, was covered with points of flame and a pall of smoke hung over the camp as the scrub caught fire. Had the wind been in the right direction we could have smoked them out, but it was blowing gently from the southwest. After half an hour they could stand it no longer, and I could see the sun flicker on the points of swords and spears as, suddenly, a great mass of men moved out of the smoke toward us at a fast walk. Their line extended from the river to well past our left flank and must have been twenty deep at least. In front, with their standards beside them, were the war chiefs of the tribes, and as they came closer I could recognize Respendial, Hermeric, Gunderic, and Sunno, who had succeeded Rando as King of the Alemanni. There must have been twenty-five thousand men on the move and I knew that we could not hold them once they closed the fight; they would destroy us by sheer weight of numbers.

To Fabianus I said quickly, "When the artillery cease fire they are to withdraw immediately back to our last camp. Call up the mules now." The ships of our tiny fleet were firing steadily in their efforts to break up the advance, but though they did great damage the enemy still came on at the same steady pace. The skirmishing archers were falling back now, each man being covered in turn by the next until, out of range, they took to their heels and ran for the right and left of our center. My left flank swung round slightly to face the overlap of the enemy right, and then, fifty yards from our motionless front ranks, the Barbarians rushed us. I gave the order to fire and the ranks hurled their javelins while the archers flicked arrow after arrow into the mass before them. The enemy front suddenly became a line of huddled dead that mounted, in another moment, into a rising wall of bodies. As the lines crashed together the trumpet sounded twice and Quintus, at the head of his cavalry, fell upon their right flank with two thousand horse. Had we had more men we could have made of it another Adrianopolis. Trapped between the cavalry and the river they would have been hemmed in, forced to fight and die upon their feet until the collapse of the next warrior enabled each man in turn to fall where he stood. But we had not enough men and our success could be only limited. The shock of the cavalry charge broke up the impetus of their attack. They fell back and, in falling back, were forced to turn to face their new enemy. Ridden round by our horsemen, they closed up and fought back stubbornly. Quintus kept his cavalry under an iron control and the discipline he had installed into his commanders showed its worth. Squadrons charged, withdrew, reformed, and charged again in hard tight formations so that it was difficult for the enemy to surround and pull individual riders down. For ninety minutes we held them and it was they who fought on the defensive, retreating slowly in a gigantic curve toward the river, pressed inward the whole time by our cavalry, whom they could not contain.

From where I sat upon my horse I could see the whole terrible scene quite clearly. I called up Marcomir's Franks to support the center, sent my light cohort out to the left to steady the hard-pressed wing, and then rode up and down the line shouting encouragement. For a few brief moments I thought we might do it, and win. I threw in my bodyguard in a desperate effort to drive a wedge through their center; the charge smashed home and then ground to a halt, checked by the sheer weight of numbers. The air was thick with dust, and the screams of horses, the cries of the wounded, and the yells of the living made the giving of orders almost impossible. Very slowly the enemy began to give ground, but they did not break and their retreat was stubbornly ordered, as they withdrew sullenly toward their camp.

I sounded the advance, but my men were too exhausted to obey me. They stood exactly where they had been when the enemy disengaged, in groups and lines, leaning upon their swords, the wounded sinking to the ground, all too tired to follow up their partial success. The horses were blown and stood with bowed heads, sweating profusely, their riders slumped in the saddle, or toppling sideways as their aching muscles relaxed and the pain of their wounds became too much for them. They were quite unfit for another charge. A handful of skirmishers harassed the retreating enemy with bows and javelins, but that was all. A trumpeter blew the retreat and, with my bodyguard holding the field, the cohorts withdrew slowly toward the escarpment and the safety of their camp. The battle had been a draw.

Later that day the Barbarians came out from their camp for small parties to collect their dead and wounded, and that night we saw the flames crackle and smelled the smoke of the funeral pyres as they cremated their dead.

The following morning I sent the wounded on ahead, in wagons, toward the safety of the bridge and Bingium. While the men rested, we checked our losses, sent patrols back to the battlefield to collect all the weapons and armor they could, and reformed units.

Aquila said, "The casualties are heavy, sir."

"How many?" I asked.

"Four hundred dead and eight hundred wounded, I should say."

"How many cavalry?"

"One hundred dead, two hundred and sixty wounded, and four hundred and thirty horses."

Quintus listened in silence. He looked angry, tired, and beaten.

"We shall have to bring the legion up to strength by drafts from the auxiliaries," I said grimly. "Well, we did all we could. They won't try to cross the river now, which is what we were afraid of."

"No, sir." He added as an afterthought, "They will wait for winter."

Quintus said, "Are you angry that I persuaded you into this action?"

I shook my head. "Only a little. It will have done the men good. They were beginning to get bored with waiting. Now, at least, they know what they are up against."

Aquila said, "We nearly did it, sir. With only a few more men we could have beaten them."

I said gently, "And now we have less than before."

Quintus did not look at me. He said, and his voice was somber, "We, none of us, have any illusions now."

The following morning we broke camp and I stood on a hilltop with Goar and watched the legion limp down the track that led to Bingium.

He said cheerfully, "It was a great battle. Your men fought like wolves."

"And yours also."

"Oh, we—we always fight well. We enjoy it. But we are not soldiers. I see now why you conquered the world. It is the discipline that does it. I—I should like to have been a Roman soldier. Do not laugh at me. It was my father's wish. And mine also."

"I do not laugh," I said. "You will be a general yet when I am dead."

The daughter of Rando had watched the battle from the hill above Moguntiacum and her face, when we rode in, was scornful. "I prayed that you would lose," she said. "And my prayers were answered."

"I did not expect to win, only to weaken them a little with losses. In that I succeeded."

Her teeth snapped. "You are clever at twisting words. I hate you."

"Of course." I smiled. "Why not? You are the enemy too."

We made up our losses by drafting men from the auxiliaries, and I wrote hurriedly to Flavius and told him to send me his conscripted recruits and all the horses he could lay hands on. I gave small awards in silver to those who had distinguished themselves in the fighting, executed two men convicted of cowardice, and promoted three centurions to replace those of my tribunes who had been killed. The badly wounded I sent back to Treverorum, and there was much hard work, repairing ballistae and armor, sharpening swords that had got blunted and damaged, and replenishing our stocks of missiles.

November came, and the winds blew from the north, and we had much rain, and sometimes on the river, in the morning and at night, there was a gray mist so that we could not see from one bank to the other, and the gulls came inland from the sea in vast numbers and perched on the camp walls, or screamed about our heads till they sounded like men dying. And in the dawn the land would be covered with a white frost and, as I rode across the fields, I would see that the pug marks of the cattle were covered with a film of brittle ice.

One afternoon a boat put out from the further bank, bearing a green branch, and I went down to the river to see what it was they wanted this time. The young man who stepped ashore was Rando's eldest son, Sunno. He looked thin and tired and there were purple marks, all puffy, on his neck and upper arms that showed he had been in the recent battle.

"So, you are the king now?" I asked him.

"Yes, I am the king in my father's place."

"What can I do for you that I would not do for your father?"

"I have come to ask for the return of my sister."

"She is not for sale."

He flinched at the implication that she was now a slave.

"What bargain then would you accept for her return?"

"The dispersal of all the men in your camp."

"They will only disperse this side of the river."

I said, "The day that you land on this shore you will look upon your sister, dying."

"So I was told. You mean it then?"

"What is Rando's daughter to me? I am Maximus."

He bared his teeth. "For that some men would call you—butcher." He smiled with an effort. "But I come in peace. May I see my sister?"

"No. But you have my assurance that she is alive and well."

He said, passionately, "You are a man who cares nothing for the feelings of others."

I said, "So men have told me. I care. But my people are not your people."

He hesitated. "Will you tell my sister I came? Will you give her this?" He held out a small silver brooch, such as girls like to wear. Judging from the workmanship it had come originally from the east. "I will do that," I said.

He nodded. "Thank you." He turned to go back to the boat. I took a step forward, unthinking. He swung round toward me: his hand flashed into his belt with the speed of a striking cat. With the knife upheld to throw he stopped and stood motionless as I pricked him beneath the chin with the point of my sword.

I said, "I wondered why you came. A man who loves his sister would have come weeks ago. I wondered, too, why you gave the brooch into my sword hand. Did you think to catch me with such an old trick? I learned that one from the Picts on the Northern Wall when you were—nothing." I pricked him and his back arched and his chin went up as he tried to avoid the point. Blood showed on the blade.

He licked his dry lips. He did not speak.

I said, "I could kill you for that. It would be my right. But—butcher as I am—I will not. Your father would not have been so foolish. Go back to your people, boy, and take your shame and your treachery with you. So long as you remain king I have no need to fear. Who would worry about such a people, led by such a king?" I pushed with the blade and he overbalanced and fell back into the water. I bent down and picked up the brooch, lying between my feet. He swam, splashing frantically, toward the boat, and the men hauled him in, all dripping. They were trying hard not to laugh.

Aquila said, "You should have killed him."

"Perhaps. This tale will be all round their camp by nightfall. They may do it for me. It will save a lot of trouble."

I wrote to Stilicho again, a long letter, in which I told him all that had happened, and sent it off by the government post, but I do not know if he ever received it, for I had no reply.

The colors of autumn had gone and the trees stood bare and black, stripped of their leaves which, at first, rustled underfoot and then, eventually, rotted into the wet ground. The ploughed fields lay bare for the winter sowing and the cultivated strips around the villages were nothing but brown lumps of damp earth, waiting silently for the renewal of life in the distant spring. Sheep and cattle had been driven down from the hills, the older beasts slaughtered and the meat dried and salted down and put into barrels to last out the winter. On the farms and by the villages the peasants were burning back the scrub and digging out the roots and stumps of trees that remained, in an effort to clear more land for cultivation next year. Soon the winter wheat would be sown, and the pigeons that crowded the beech trees behind the town, and which had grown fat in the early autumn, would be hunted down to provide fresh meat for the pot.

Julius Optatus and his staff had been busy buying sheepskins off the farmers to make into winter coats for the officers, and a supply of new cloaks and breeches had arrived from Treverorum. Planks of wood were laid down along the camp paths to provide a firm walk above the mud; fatigue parties went out each dawn to collect firewood which they brought back at dusk, loaded onto a string of patient ponies. Cracks in the huts, where the wood had warped in the summer sun, were sealed up, and curtains of dried skins hung inside the doors of the sleeping quarters to give added warmth. To save unnecessary work I ordered that two days' rations of corn and oil should be issued at a time; while wine or vinegar, pork or veal should be issued alternatively to provide a change of diet. In addition, stocks of salted meat and hard biscuits were built up in the camp by the road, and at Bingium also. If the worst happened, and we were compelled to withdraw, I wanted to make certain that the troops would find sufficient supplies along my proposed line of retreat. Quintus brought the cavalry horses into the stables in the old camp and, like the quartermaster with his food, established depots of spare horses at Bingium, and at the signal posts along the road.

"We cannot level the odds any more than we have done," I said bluntly. "But we can make sure that no one lacks a horse or a spear at the right moment."

"We have done everything I can think of," he said. "Even down to spare bridles and reins. Oh, Maximus, we should have had more cavalry." He was thinking still, I knew, of the battle on the east bank.

"We have been into all that before, a hundred times," I said calmly. "Look at the trouble we had raising the cavalry in the first instance. And look at the trouble, too, you had keeping your men mounted in Italia. It was always the same. There were never enough horses to go round. Besides, it has been a garrison job on this river. As it is we have had over two thousand horses eating their heads off for the last year."

"I know," he said. "It is always the same; not enough horses, not enough men, not enough money to buy them or pay for them." He paused, and in the silence I could hear the wind booming down the valley, as it had done every day for the past week.

"Let us hope," he said, "that it does not shift to the east."

On the advice of Gallus I dispersed the fleet. Four galleys were kept upstream of Moguntiacum, and one each at Bingium and Confluentes. I did not believe that, however desperate they might be, the tribes would try to cross the river by boat or on rafts, but I would leave nothing to chance except the weather. That alone I could not control.

In the middle of the month I received a visit from Goar. He came in, splashing raindrops from his cloak, his red beard dripping onto my polished table. I gave him hot wine and asked for his news. He drank the wine before answering, wiped his hand across the edge of his cloak, and said grimly, "King Guntiarus has betrayed you. He is sending them food. He has been told—or believes—that his son is dead. Perhaps he does not believe—I do not know—but he is doing it all the same."

"How long has this been going on?"

"I do not know—ten days or a fortnight. Perhaps longer." He paused. He looked at me. He said, "Is the boy dead?"

"No. You can see him if you wish."

Quintus said, "He is well looked after. He speaks Latin better than his father now. Maximus, he has called your bluff."

"I do not make threats I do not carry out."

Goar said, "There is little point in killing the boy now. Give him to me instead."

"Why?"

"Guntiarus does not hate the Romans as he hates the Alans. If he knows I have the boy, he may stop sending food. He will certainly stop attacking my men."

"So?" I raised my head at that.

"Oh, yes. We have been fighting skirmishes the past week."

Quintus said, "Let me take a cavalry force across the river and destroy his salt springs. He won't like that."

"Do that," I said. "And if you meet Guntiarus on the way, bring me back his head."

"There is one more thing." Goar looked at me intently. "Can you trust your commander at Bingium?"

"Why, yes." I was surprised. "Why not? He is an auxiliary, of course, not a regular. But he is efficient and faithful. He has given excellent service this past year." I glanced from him to Quintus. "Yes, I would trust him. Why not?"

Goar said, "What do you know of him?"

I thought: Scudilio—a dark-haired, narrow-faced, slightly built man in his middle thirties. He was good looking, attractive to women, and he laughed a lot. A bit nervous in manner, sometimes, but keen and energetic and a fine horseman. His family, so he had told me, had been settled on the east bank for forty years. He was of mixed blood, part Gaul, part Frank, but that was a long time ago. He had joined us some six months after our arrival and had received swift promotion. He was a leader of men, and I trusted him.

I told Goar all this. He nodded and then said quietly, "Would it surprise you to know that he is of the Alemanni?"

"Is that true?"

"Oh, yes."

"Who in this part of the world is not of mixed blood? Look at the people in the town down there."

"He was in Rando's camp two years ago," said Goar relentlessly. "Why did he lie to you if he is honest?"

I said, "I don't know. Perhaps he thought we would not let him join us, and he would, very probably, have been right."

Quintus said, "If he was disloyal he would have had his chance when we took the legion across the river. He commanded at Bingium then. He could have cut the bridge behind us. Is not that so?"

Goar said grudgingly, "That is so."

I said, "What is worrying you?"

He said, "If you have to make a retreat, then you must retreat through Bingium. It is the one place which must be held by a reliable man."

In exasperation I said, "Any man can desert me or turn traitor if he so chooses. This is not the old Rome when every soldier was a known citizen. They join us for many reasons—for money, for security, or simply because they like fighting and they enjoy the life."

He said, "I thought you should know."

"I am grateful to you, of course. It was right that I should know. Quintus, you will be going over the bridge at Bingium. Have a talk with Scudilio. If you have any doubts at all, then replace him."

Goar nodded. "That is just," he said. He looked disconcerted and I wondered if, perhaps, he was annoyed that I did not take his warning more seriously.

In the morning the ala cantered out soon after sunrise, and Goar recrossed the river, taking with him a small boy who wept bitterly. Before he left I asked him a question. "On a matter of trust," I said. "On this thing that we discussed yesterday. If the river freezes, if they try to cross, can I be sure that I may then count on your help?"

He looked at me steadily and did not smile. "Can you win?" he asked.

I stared at him hard. "Yes," I said. "Let there be no doubt about that. With, or without your help I shall beat them. But you have not answered my question."

He smiled slightly. "The King, Respendial, is my cousin, and his people are my people. But I do not believe in kidnapping the young wives of fellow kings. Marcomir and I took the oath to be brothers in blood, before he died." He held up his wrist and I saw the faint scars across it. "Is that the answer you want?"

I gripped his arm with my hand. "Yes. It is all the answer that I want."

CHAPTER XV

It grew steadily colder, and each day I walked down to the river edge and looked at the swirling currents, the drifting logs, the pattern of color that shifted with the light on the great mass of water that moved endlessly past. Somewhere in the high, snowcapped mountains to my right, so far away that I could not see them, this river crossed a great lake on the start of its long journey to the Saxon Sea. Here, it was just over seven hundred and fifty yards across from bank to bank, but it was nine hundred yards wide at the mouth so that at times and places it seemed like an inland sea.

I did not like water really. I was no seaman as Gallus was, whose father had been a river pilot on the Danubius, but the Rhenus was my friend and I loved it in all its moods, as I had once loved the worn gray stones of that Northern Wall where I had passed my youth. It was a defense, this river, against the unknown, and it marked the limit of my Roman world. Beyond it lay only chaos.

The water was very cold and the level had dropped considerably. A great tree trunk that had been ripped out of a collapsing bank, perhaps as high as Borbetomagus, came floating by as I stood there, and on it, whimpering and wet but still alive, huddled a small animal that looked like a cat. Cats had been sacred to the peoples of Aegyptus, I remembered, and I had a sudden absurd desire that it should be saved. Perhaps if I propitiated enough gods they would help me in my turn when I needed assistance. I sent a horseman cantering downriver and later heard that a boat, sent out from Bingium, had rescued the cat and that it was living in the commandant's office. It was recovering on warm milk, and Scudilio had been heard to remark, with a smile, that he thought the General was becoming senile. The soldiers in the fort, however, called the cat Maximus, and I was pleased.

Then the Bishop arrived, a black figure on a black horse, with an escort of my cavalry and a retinue of churchmen who looked blue with cold. If saintliness was next to coldness, then they would have been close to heaven at that moment. To my surprise the Curator was with him and, when he got off his horse, he walked stiffly like a man unaccustomed to taking exercise.

I offered them what hospitality I could and asked the Bishop bluntly why he had come. He smiled for a moment. "I have brought a gift of oysters for you and your friend. I remember your saying that army food was monotonous."

"You have not come all the way just for that."

He smiled. "It will be a bad winter, as I told you. Many of your men are Christians and I feel it right that I should come here to bless them and to pray. You do not object, I trust?"

"Barbatio, order a detail to prepare huts. No, I do not object."

He looked at me steadily. He said, "It is very lonely to be the man in charge, to whom all else must turn for help, advice, and instruction. You can confide in no one. It is a great strain." He paused, waiting for me to speak.

I said, "I am waiting for the wind to change. If it does, if it shifts to the east, it will snow, and if it snows then that river will freeze and they will cross the water on a bridge of ice. When that happens I and my men will all die."

He looked shocked. "You spoke more confidently to the city elders when you last visited Treverorum."

"Yes. I did not wish to alarm them."

"Why tell me now?"

"You knew before. Besides, I do not tell lies; not to priests of any faith. I know—here." I touched my chest.

He put his hands to the cross at his breast. "It is not too late, my son..."

I said, "No. I will not betray my Emperor, nor my General, nor my men.

I will not betray the people of Augusta Treverorum. When then should I abandon my god?"

He was silent. He was too clever, too wise, perhaps, to say, "it is not the same thing." To him, no; to me, yes.

He said at length, "You will let us know what happens if you can. We shall be anxious for news."

"I will do my best."

"You have a young girl here, a hostage of some kind. May I see her?"

"Yes, if you wish. One of my men will show you where her hut is."

He stayed two days, and then a third, and during that time Artorius walked around the camp, looking at everything with curious eyes and chatting genially with my younger officers.

One evening I found him standing on the riverbank looking across the dark water while a swan paddled hopefully few feet away, waiting for food. I went up to him and said, "I hope you approve of the way the tax money has been spent?"

He said stiffly, "I have my duty to do, just as you have. But at least I try not to be so unpleasant in its execution."

I was stung by his remark. "Soldiering is not a soft trade," I said. "You must forgive us if its practitioners are a trifle brutal now and again. It is because we are brutal that you can afford to be gentle."

He said calmly, "Do you imagine that one gets taxes out of people by being gentle?"

"What do you mean?"

"I mean this." He swung round and put his finger to my chest. "You think you are so important because you carry a sword and you have soldiers to back up your every order. It is easy for you. For us it is not so easy. We have to persuade."

"You have taken your time persuading then."

"Everything you asked for has been given."

"Grudgingly," I said.

"You have impoverished the entire city."

"Oh, come, it is not as bad as that."

He said, in a bitter voice, "Treverorum was prosperous till you came with your insatiable demands. I was proud to be its curator. Now everything is ruined. It is taxes, always taxes. And now they do not want me anymore. Look at Moguntiacum, a handful of flea-ridden huts. It was a fine city once. No one will work for a living; everyone begs for assistance. They are scum."

"Is not some of the trouble due to the fact that nowadays people cannot change their occupations without being penalized?"

"That is not my concern. Half the taxes I collect are sent to the central government. But they should be used here, not to pay for idle mouths in Rome."

"Then why do it?"

"Like your officers I obey orders."

"And make a good living out of your own estates, no doubt."

"Why not? I bought them. At least I keep my slaves. They are well fed and well cared for. I don't beat them into running away."

"You are fortunate to have the choice," I said coldly. "I never owned more than two body servants in my entire life."

He ignored my remark. He said suddenly, "Your defenses look very strong. Will you be able to hold them if they attack you?"

I said, "I am not a prophet, only a soldier. But if I have doubts then I will send for your help. That, I am sure, will make all the difference."

On the fourth day the Bishop left, and I walked out of the camp gates to see him go. It was bitterly cold and the sky was a purple-black from horizon to horizon. Wrapped in our cloaks and hooded to the eyes we were still cold, yet I shivered from fear as much as from anything else.

"The wind has turned," he said. "Have you noticed?"

"Yes, it is blowing from the east."

"It brings a cold message for all of us, my son."

The Curator said politely, "Whatever help you need, then send for it."

I said, "You are too kind. You should have made that offer months ago."

At that moment a snowflake fell onto the sleeve of my cloak, and I stared at it and took a quick breath. "It is death," I said slowly. It had come at last and there was no escape.

The Bishop smiled and raised his hand. "Farewell," he said. "May you live in God."

"Farewell," I said. "May Mithras protect us all."

I watched the cavalcade ride up the road till the palisade hid it from sight. Then I turned and mounted my horse, held by a waiting orderly, and rode back to my quarters. It was snowing hard now. It went on snowing all day, and it snowed all night.

For three days it snowed, and my men were kept busy clearing the dry snow from the paths and the sentry walks, and sweeping the falls that came from the roofs of the huts and blocked the doorways each morning.

On the fourth morning the wind dropped, the sky cleared, and a pale sun gleamed weakly between the feathery clouds. I put on my cloak and walked down to the river with Quintus. The bank was lined with soldiers watching the water. It was icy cold to the touch, but the water looked clear and there was no suggestion yet that it might freeze over. There were tribesmen on the far bank who had come out of camp and who stood in groups watching the water, like us. They waved in friendly fashion and our men waved back. Quintus said, "We shall get warning if it begins to harden. The commandant at Borbetomagus will send a message. They will notice it first."

I said, "I know that. What I am worried about is if it continues to snow and the roads become blocked."

That night the wind set up again. It had backed to the northeast now and in the night I awoke to hear it howling through the camp like the spirits of the unquiet dead. Just before dawn it began to snow and this time it fell heavily, blanketing the camp and blotting out our view of the river. I ordered double sentries to be posted, sent out cavalry patrols to break up the loose snow on the roads, and had every man hard at work with iron-tipped spades, clearing the tracks and ditches. Messages came in from all the forts to say that the snow was thick on the roads, that some tracks were impassable but that the river was unaffected.

"What about the fleet?" asked Quintus.

"Well, what about it? It won't be any use to us if this weather continues."

"Do you want the ships to go back to Treverorum or to lie up at Confluentes?"

"Does it matter where they lie up?"

He said patiently, "We might need them in the spring."

I looked at him and after a minute his eyes dropped to the map on the table before him.

"It's really a question of where we can best use the men. We could do with their catapults."

I said, "How much use would they be at breaking up the ice if it comes?"

He grinned. "Those experiments we were carrying out in the early autumn, you remember them."

"Yes."

"If it does not freeze too badly they would be of enormous help in breaking up the ice, but that sort of ice wouldn't be thick enough to carry much weight anyway. If it freezes very hard, however, we shall probably lose the ships. They'll get icebound."

"It would be worth it."

"Shall I arrange it then, along those lines?"

"Yes, you know my mind in these matters as well as your own."

I rode out on a tour of inspection, first to Bingium, where I had a long talk with the legionary commandant and another with Scudilio, who would succeed him when I withdrew the cohort.

"Why did you lie?" I said.

"Your general has already asked me that question."

"It is I who am asking it now."

He said, "I did not think you would let me join you if you knew I came from the Alemanni. That is all."

I looked at him.

He said nervously, "I have tried to be a good soldier. But if you would prefer it I will take the money that is owing to me and go. It would be better to leave than to stay and not be trusted."

I said, "Keep your command. When the day comes that I do not trust you I will tell you so myself."

From Bingium I went on to Boudobrigo, Salisio, and Confluentes. The snow was dry still, powdered on the surface but loose underneath, so that marching was difficult and we traveled at half speed, but using twice the effort. I was nagged with worry because the defensive ditches around the camps were half full of snow that had drifted in with the wind. If we had sleet and the snow became wet it would solidify and provide a firm base on which to make a crossing. The ditches would then be rendered useless.

From Confluentes I rode back down the road to Treverorum, and passed a night at the signal tower by the junction where the roads forked. Here the auxiliaries were digging out the ditches that straddled the road, throwing the snow up into banks to provide extra protection. It was here that, if need be, I would make my last stand, and I spent half a day surveying the ground with care. It all looked different now. The branches of the trees were loaded with snow; hillocks, rough ground, and tracks had all been blotted out, erased by a dazzle of smooth white in every direction as far as one could see. Only on the road and round the signal tower was the ground stamped hard, slippery and dangerous to walk upon. Beneath the surface of the snow the earth felt like rock. I was impressed by the care that the unit took of its responsibilities. Agilio, the post commander, was only a boy, blond haired, slow thinking but reliable. His post was kept absolutely clean and tidy, the men's weapons were in excellent condition and they knew how to use them with efficiency. They obeyed his instructions promptly and each man had a ready grasp of his duties. In the afternoon the signal fires flared and smoke rose into the clear sky. I watched the dark balls rise at irregular intervals and then Agilio came up. "You are wanted back at Moguntiacum immediately, sir."

"Thank you." I leaned down from my horse and looked at his eager face. "Keep the ditches clear and pray that when you see me again it is not at the head of an army."

He flashed a smile and saluted. I rode back hard, my escort behind me, spent the night at Bingium, and reached my headquarters a little after dawn. I had been in the saddle for too long and I was exhausted.

Quintus gave a sigh of relief when he saw me. "Don't go away again," he said. "Next time you might not be able to get back."

"What is it?"

"I want you to look at the river. You know more about these things than I do."

Again we stood on the bank in our scarlet cloaks, legionaries about us, tribesmen on the opposite shore, each side looking at the other curiously. "You can see better from the broken bridge," he said. "Come on."

We stood on the bridge and I watched the swirling water, rippling coldly beneath my feet. The water still looked clean, but every now and again a patch of water seemed to take on a dark, oily look as though grease were floating on the surface like scum. Quintus began to shiver. "It is cold," he said. He looked at my face and said quickly, "What is it, Maximus?"

I said, "I don't know. I am going to stay here and watch. Send a man out with food and some hot wine. I am cold too."

A soldier brought a charcoal brazier and I warmed my hands and drank the wine and watched the water. The tribesmen were watching it intently too and it was obvious that they were excited and pleased. The patches of oily sludge increased so that the river seemed to darken slowly even as one watched it. A messenger came to say that Goar had crossed the river and was awaiting me in the camp; a second messenger came to report that the centurion on island duty had recognized the enemy war chiefs on the far bank. Hermeric, Gunderic, Respendial, and Sunno were there, like me, waiting also. Presently Quintus, who could not stand the cold, came back. "Well?" he asked. He sounded as a gladiator sounds when he asks the order of the fights in which he is to take part.

I said carefully, "This, Quintus, is what a river looks like when it begins to freeze."

We walked back to the camp and there, in her red dress and black fur-lined cloak, waiting for us outside the gate, stood Rando's daughter, a smile upon her face. Beside her was Fabianus. "Are you happy?" she mocked. "I am. This is what my people have waited for all this time: ice and snow."

I said, "You really hate us, don't you? What have we done to harm you and your kind?"

"You made me a prisoner," she said bitterly. "A prisoner and a slave. Is that not enough?"

I looked from her to Fabianus and the look on his face startled me.

"It is enough," I said and passed on, leaving her standing in the snow, looking across the river to where her own people lay.

In camp I called a council of my officers and faced them across my table, Quintus sitting at my right hand and Goar at my left.

"Now listen carefully," I said. "How long the river will take to freeze, I do not know. But freeze it will unless the weather changes. When the time comes I shall call in all regular cohorts from the outlying forts, leaving them in the hands of the auxiliaries. If these forts are attacked in strength, their commanders will hold them as long as possible, then fire their camps and withdraw on the thirtieth milestone as best they can. The legion will concentrate here, and it will fight here. The galleys have been ordered to patrol the river in an effort to keep the main channel clear, and island commanders are to use ballistae to break up the ice as long as possible."

"What about the Bingium bridge, sir?"

"Scudilio will burn it the moment his outpost on the further bank is driven in. Signal post sections are to move on their nearest forts the moment a general attack takes place on their area. General Veronius has their disposition details arranged. The road to Bingium, however, is to be kept manned and open. Is that clear?"

Goar dug his nails into the palms of his hands and then slowly relaxed them. I noticed the movement but I said nothing. There was something wrong, but he would tell me in his own time.

He said, "What do you want me to do?"

"Attack them in the flank the moment they start to cross. Go for the baggage and the supplies. Without food and fuel they will die in the cold. If we cannot stop them, then cross the river yourself, wherever you are, and join up with me between Bingium and Moguntiacum."

He hesitated. He said, "It is better that you know everything."

"Well?"

"The Burgundians wish to cross to the west bank, too, and the main force of the Alemanni intend to cross at Borbetomagus."

"How do you know?"

"I have friends still in all camps. Besides, Sunno is afraid for his sister."

"Will they move with the Vandals?"

"Perhaps. Probably later. The Vandals are the most restless. They talk of seeking a land that is hot and where the sun is always shining. The Alemanni wish only for control of the west bank."

Quintus said, "That makes the odds heavy indeed."

I said, "I have written to the Praefectus Praetorio at Arelate. He has promised to send troops." Quintus raised his eyebrows at this, but I outstared him. "How many?" asked Fabianus excitedly.

"Will they come in time, sir?" asked Aquila bluntly.

Goar dropped his eyes. "Then Stilicho has kept his promise."

I said gently, "Rome does not forget her generals." I looked at Quintus, but he was looking at Goar, now staring blankly at the wall. I said, "There is something on your mind? What is it?"

Goar said, "Because of the Alemanni and the Burgundians, I cannot cross the river. I cannot abandon my people. But I will fight on the east bank for as long as I can. That I promise you."

Fabianus said nervously, "You said, sir, you would kill Rando's daughter if the Alemanni crossed. Will you still do so?"

I stared at him. I said, "I give the orders; you obey them."

I turned round. "Aquila." He nodded and went to the door and shouted. There was a pause and the aquilifer entered, carrying the Eagle. It was of bronze, clean and shining, and worn smooth with much polishing; now it had been freshly gilded and it glowed in the lamplight. I said, "A soldier can commit only two sins: desertion and cowardice. Those I have never tolerated, nor will I now. Anyone who wishes to be released from his oath must ask to be released now or not at all." I smiled as no one moved. I said, "I am not an Emperor, nor shall ever be one. I am content to command the Twentieth. I make no promises; I tell no lies." I held up my hand. "But, before the Eagle, there is only death or victory. In this matter we are at one with the gladiators in the arena, and I am glad that it shall be so."

They saluted the Eagle and they saluted me. And then they left. I poured myself a cup of wine and put it carefully on the table before me. Then I sat down heavily upon a stool and put my head in my hands. I felt very old and very tired.

That night it snowed again.

WALLACE BREEM

It was December now and each morning the birds gathered about the cook-houses, hoping for scraps of food. The wolves howled in the forest at night and the foxes, desperate with hunger, broke through the village palisades in their search for prey. The blue smoke from the enemy camp hung thick and heavy in the cold air and the black sludge on the dark, moving water turned to thin delicate circles of ice. The galleys moved slowly up and down the main channel and the sentries shivered in their watchtowers and cleared the ballistae of snow each morning. Many men went sick; some with sores, others with fever, and those who remained on duty looked thin and pinched with the effort of fighting the intense cold. Others tried to fish, hoping to eke out their diet with fresh food, but few caught anything. Fabianus, who knew about these things, told them that it was a waste of time. "It is no good," he said. "In such conditions the fish only bury themselves in the mud."

The circles of ice began to join together and formed what we called black ice. Floes from higher up came floating down, some to break through the black ice and be carried on to Bingium, others to remain, jammed against the banks or caught and held by the thinner ice. Each day at set times we fired missiles from the ballistae into the water. At the beginning this was successful. The sixty-pound balls of iron broke the ice with ease so that it was carried away by the moving current, but each day there seemed to be more ice on the move than there had been the day before, and it grew more and more difficult. The galleys smashed at the ice with their oars and the water level, which should have been dropping, remained constant. Each day the sun rose, a pale disc in a gray sky, and the rooks, black and hard of eye, sat on the walls, cawing dismally, and watched us at our work. In the evenings now, wolves could be seen. They moved about the edges of the clearings, sometimes snarling and fighting among themselves, but more often simply just standing and waiting as though they knew that we must come to them in the end. They were like the Vandals and they got on our nerves with their terrible, controlled patience. And at night the moon rose to light a land that was white and dead and silent, save for the hooting of the owls that lived on the islands and which were better sentries than the iron-helmeted legionaries who stood there, numb and still, staring with strained eyes across the water and quivering gently with the cold. The ice floes changed color in the shifting light; sometimes they were blue, sometimes green, and sometimes black. Only at the end did they stay white. Each morning the galleys found it more difficult to weigh anchor and cut their way out into the stream. The bows would press against the ice and a thin black line, or a series of lines perhaps, would streak out suddenly, like ropes laid across the frozen water, and there would be a great booming noise as the ice cracked and then a harsh grinding that went on and on as the smashed floes jostled against each other and the galleys forced them apart.

Quintus said, "It will not be much longer now."

"No, not much longer. We have been a long time waiting."

The ice began to thicken along the banks and the ice field spread outward until there was only a narrow stream, a hundred yards wide, down the center, through which the water coiled and writhed like a gigantic snake. The ice was thin still and, as Gallus said, would break up under pressure, but each night it froze again and the work of the day was undone in a few hours.

One afternoon five men tried to cross the river from the east bank. Why they tried we never knew. Perhaps they were ordered to test the ice; perhaps they were desperate or out of their minds through fatigue and starvation; the last most likely. We watched them, five tiny dots in the distance, who, as they came closer, slowly turned into men, scrambling across the hummocks and slipping on the ridged snow. When they reached the center channel they paused and cast about for a way across. One tried to jump onto a floe but it tipped and he lost his balance and fell into the water. Even at that distance we could hear his thin, despairing cry. Then two ballistae from the camp opened fire. The iron balls crashed with sickening accuracy to right and left of the remaining men. The ice boomed and split and the men disappeared into the water. A moment later we saw their heads on the surface as they clawed frantically at the jagged edges of the floes. Then the floes turned slowly in the current, rubbing against each other as though in friendship, and after a while there was nothing to be seen but the black water and the moving ice.

Then the signal beacons flared and plummets of smoke drifted upward, and the signalers were busy with messages from the outlying forts, and an elderly cavalryman with a sun-blacked nose brought a message from Goar that Gunderic would speak with me. "Why go?" said Quintus. "Talking is only a waste of time."

"So is this," I said, pointing at the draughts board where he had my pieces nicely penned up like sheep under the care of an overattentive dog. "Why not? I, at least, have time to waste."

He looked at me with half a smile. "It is your company I value. Time is running out."

"Very well. Let us finish the game anyway."

I went with Fabianus for company. We crossed the bridge at Bingium and cantered slowly up the riverbank till we met Goar, who was quite alone. He led us up into the hills, past our fighting camp, and then through the snow-filled woods to the slopes overlooking the enemy position. It was a world of white up here now, a silent mysterious world of sparkling snow and naked trees. There was no wind and the sun gleamed like a gold coin in a gray sky. A white-winged falcon with a brown flecked body stood on the dead carcass of a goat and tore at the frozen flesh with furious energy. It was so hungry that it scarcely looked up as we passed it by. It was terribly cold and I shivered as I watched the steam from my breath mingle with my horse's in the thin air. Overhead, a skein of swans flew south, and I knew that they came before the threat of a blizzard that lay in the darkened sky to the northeast.

Two horsemen were waiting for us in the distance, close by a stunted, solitary tree. They were two black figures against an infinity of white. As we came closer I saw that the Vandal King was accompanied by Julian. We circled each other for a moment but this was not a time for dismounting. It was warmer to sit one's horse. I did not fear an ambush. What would have been the point? They did not fear me. Why should I kill the Vandal by treachery? What was Gunderic to me? It was his people I feared, not him.

He rested his hands on the saddle and I did the same. Drops of snow sparkled on his thick eyebrows and on his matted beard. He looked gaunt and hollow cheeked, like a famished fox. If his people had gone hungry he, at least, had shared their hunger.

He said, "You are a clever man. You tricked us over your numbers."

I said, "You made it necessary. But still, we gave you a good fight on the east bank."

He said, "For a year now you have held us with trickery, with lies, and with deceit." He glanced at Goar and frowned. "You caused such dissension among us that we quarreled among ourselves. It was well done. And yet—" He paused. "We are still here on the east bank and the river is freezing fast. Soon it will be time for us to cross."

"That I know. What is your problem?"

"In spite of all that has happened, we would still prefer to cross in peace. You are a soldier and we respect you as a good warrior."

"Before you have finished you will think me a great one."

"That may be." He frowned and then rubbed his nose.

"So. Do you speak in this matter for your brother kings?"

"I do."

"Well?"

He said harshly, "We are willing to serve under Rome and take the oath to your Emperor. But we must have land." He held his hands out wide as he spoke. His hands were very large.

"I cannot give it to you."

"That is understood. But I make a new offer."

"Yes."

"We are all equal, each king ruling his own people. Not one of us can be high king over all, else there would be jealousy, mistrust, hatred, and war. But you whom we respect we would trust. Allow us to cross in peace, take Gaul, and we will raise you on a shield, as is our custom, crown you with a torque of gold, and proclaim you Emperor. And we will swear to serve you, if you, in your turn, will swear to serve us."

"On which side of the river will you perform this thing?"

"We will crown you in our camp to show the measure of our trust."

"Do you believe that I will accept?"

He said slowly, "Because you are what you are, we make this offer. If you do not believe me, then talk to this man here. He stands high with the Aleman people and I believe he once knew you well in another life. I will wait." He turned his horse in a flurry of snow and rode off a score of paces to the tree behind him. I signaled Fabianus and Goar to join him.

Julian pushed back his cloak and smiled ironically. "Well?" he said. "It is a great honor."

"Do you think that I will accept?"

He ignored my question. He said, "You once offered me your villa at Arelate. Do you remember? Does it still stand? Did you ever go back to it?"

I nodded. "It stands. I never went back to it."

"A pity. It would have been better to die there in the sun than in this bleak and terrible place." A wolf howled in the distance and the wind whipped at our faces.

I said, "What makes you think that I shall die?"

He said sadly, "If you die it will be because you are—Maximus. For no other reason."

"That is true of every man."

"Perhaps." He leaned forward and patted his horse on the neck. "It is a good offer. You have only a single legion. Which one, I wonder?"

"The Twentieth."

He flinched. "The gods still make jests then about our small affairs."

"There is no man but myself who served with them in our time."

"You love that legion, don't you?"

"Yes."

"Refuse this offer and it would be better that you had sent them to the mines as condemned criminals. They would at least be still alive."

"I know that."

We stared at each other. There was a curious expression on his face that I could not understand. I said, "Surely, you knew before this the number of my legion."

"No." His reply was emphatic.

I shivered. It was very cold.

"Why do you refuse?" he asked calmly.

"My Empire has had more usurping Emperors than I can count. Most were murdered; all weakened the empire they thought to strengthen. I shall not add to their number, not in this way."

"The Empire is dying, Maximus. It is weaker than when you were a boy playing on those sandy beaches of Southern Gaul."

I bit my lip at the memory. I said, "It has recovered before. How many times has the barbarian broken through the frontier and each time men said that Rome was finished? But each time we drove them back and Rome still stands. Rome is. Nothing can alter that. It is her destiny."

He said, "Perhaps. But perhaps not in the way you think."

"What do you mean?"

He shrugged. "I do not know. But we live in a time of great change. Few things last forever. I should know that."

The wind blew harder now and the surface snow whirled, like dust, about our horses' legs.

I looked at him. I said, "You are very thin, Julian."

"It is only the cold and the lack of food." He spoke as a man who was used to these things.

I said, "I will offer you something now: an amnesty to you and to your family. Bring them across the river at Bingium and I will give you money to go where you will, to settle where you please. Take it for the sake of old times."

He said, "Can you strike a rock and bring forth water? I want nothing from you. You gave me enough: the years in the arena, the stigma and the shame. For that I still bear the brand on my ankle to show I was once a slave." He flung up his head. "Well, I accept it. It was the price I had to pay for what I had done. I understand that now." He stared down blindly at the snow. He said in a low voice, "You took the life of my high priest's daughter and you cannot give it back. From you I want nothing. You cannot throw me a coin and make right what has been wrong. I shall do very well for myself without your aid."

I said hoarsely, "I understand. I, too, cannot accept your offer. Tell Gunderic that if I were to do so, I would not be the man he wants for his Emperor."

He said, "If you had been that kind of man the offer would not have been made."

I said, "Did you ever find what you wanted? That purpose that would not break in your hand."

He looked at me then and I was shocked at the pain in his eyes. He said, "I want nothing except to live in peace. When my children and my grandchildren smile at me, then I am warm inside. But even that must be paid for it seems." He paused and when he spoke again I could hardly hear him. He said in a whisper, "Before we went out into the arena we used to offer our prayers at the Shrine of Vengeance which stood between the changing room and the exit tunnel. Down that tunnel you could see the white light that was the arena, and hear the voices of the sentries and the ugly roar of the crowd. But in the tunnel it was dark and peaceful. The rough stone of the walls and the cool marble of the altar were wonderful to touch when you stood there, shivering with fear and excitement. I used to pray for so many things, but I never thought my prayers would be answered." He raised his head for a moment. "Oh, gods, why must they be answered now, after all these years, and in this way?" He sat slumped in the saddle with eyes averted and his shoulders shook.

I said, "Be happy if you can. Live in the present, Julian. It is easier than the past." I held out my hand. "I shall not meet you again. But I shall remember the happy times, I promise you—with pleasure and not with pain."

He turned to me and gave me the parody of a smile. He said, "Goodbye, Maximus, my friend. It is because of people like you that Rome has lasted so long. We shall win the battle but you will not be defeated."

I waited for Fabianus to rejoin me. On the edge of the slopes the two distant horses paused for a moment and one of their riders raised his hand in salutation. I held up my own in reply. It began to snow again and the wind drove into our backs as we made for the river. It was so cold that I could not help shivering, but inside I felt warm. In a curious way I felt almost happy.

The wind increased in strength that night and doors banged and shutters rattled as the cold blew mercilessly through the camp. The channel narrowed, inch by inch, and the snow settled on the ice and piled itself into great ragged hummocks. I ordered the ships to move downstream before they were trapped, and they had difficulty in moving, so that I was forced to use tow lines, and the men heaved and strained on the bank to pull the galleys clear and get them past the safety of the south island. One galley remained, which had a damaged hull below the waterline, and the crew worked all night to make it right again. The delay was fatal, however, and though we got the ship out into midstream, having moved her thirty yards in two hours, she stuck again and the snow fell and we had to abandon her. I gave orders that the moment the weather eased, the crew were to bring off all her stores and useful supplies. They wanted to stay on board but I would not let them. They were safer on shore.

That night the cold became worse and we could hear the ice groaning on the river, as the wind whipped at the surface and the remaining loose floes smashed into each other. Some, driven by the pressure of the ice upstream, were forced out of the water to freeze themselves onto the ice in front. For three days the blizzard raged, the sky was black with clouds from north to south, and the snow fell and smothered everything where it lay. It was impossible to go out, visibility was less than a spear's throw in the camp, and at night nothing could be seen but a whirling mass of black and white. The sentries huddled round the braziers on their towers and turned their backs to the wind. An army could have approached the camp then and the sentries would neither have seen nor heard them. Faintly through the moaning wind you could hear, if you had good ears, the ceaseless crack and crash of the grinding ice. All night long I heard the floes shudder and roar as the wind drove them one into another, and they froze in a series of high-ridged barriers, like a field that is ploughed all ways at once. Two sentries died at their posts during that time, and later, on the road outside the camp, we found a horse and rider, both still erect, who had been caught in the worst of the storm and smothered to death in a drift of snow. The rider had come from Borbetomagus, but what message he carried I never knew. On the fifth day the blizzard blew itself out and the wind shifted to the northeast again, and the sky was clear, except for a few broken clouds overhead and a dark mass away to the east that would not reach us unless the wind changed again.

The river was silent now and the absolute quiet was frightening. I walked down to what I imagined must be the bank of the Rhenus. It had disappeared altogether beneath a desolate wasteland of jagged, lumpy, broken fragments of ice and snow, distorted by the current, whipped by the winds into fantastic shapes of sculptured silence. There was no water to be seen at all. To the right, the broken hull of the abandoned galley stuck out upward at a sharp angle. I walked on over the uneven surface and could not tell whether I stood on land or on ice. Nothing creaked beneath my weight. It must have been inches thick. I shaded my eyes against the hard dazzle and could see men in the distance, tiny black figures against an aching blaze of light. I did not know whether they stood upon the shore or upon the ice. Nothing separated us now, but a short walk that any man might take on a winter's day. I turned and walked back to where my officers stood waiting for me, in a silent group on the high ground before the camp. It was then that my hands began to shake with fear.

"Fabianus, signal the fort commanders to move in with their men, the auxiliaries to take over. Tell the town council that the city is to be evacuated; everyone is to leave by midday tomorrow.

"Quintus, get your cavalry out to break up the snow on the road and on the main paths to the camp.

"Aquila, get those firing platforms cleared of snow. Send reliefs to the islands and issue them with five days' rations.

"Barbatio, all houses within three hundred yards of the camp walls are to be evacuated and then destroyed. See to it now.

"One more thing, Fabianus. Tell the commander at Bingium to burn the bridge before he leaves. Get that message off at once. Scudilio is a good man but he'll have enough to worry about without that on his mind.

"Quartermaster, issue all spare javelins and arrows. They will be no use to us in the storehouse now. Give out three days' rations and tell the section commanders to grind their corn now."

Trumpets blew, orders were shouted, and the troops began to move about their business.

A centurion came up. "Sir, there is a man crossing the river. He's alone. What shall we do?"

"Let me see," I said. I went to the river wall and Quintus came with me. The tribesmen were still on the bank, a faint patch of dark against the snow, like a smear of dirt upon a toga. Coming across the broken ice was a man. As he came closer we could see that he was running gently, his sword in his right hand and a spear in his left.

"Is he mad?" said Quintus in amazement.

"A spy perhaps, sir," said a legionary, standing by with a bow held loosely before him.

I shook my head. "My spies don't come in like that. He's not on an embassy either, not with those weapons out."

The duty centurion said quietly, "Perhaps he is mad."

He came closer and closer. We could see that he was a man of middle age, his beard was streaked with gray, and his face was contorted, but whether with hate or merely with the effort of running I could not tell. There was something strange and terrible about this man's approach. He came on steadily as though nothing would stop him. He was shouting in a loud voice, but at first we could not hear what he said.

Quintus said, "He is mad."

"Shall I fire, sir."

"No. Wait for my orders."

The man wore the dress of the Siling Vandals and he was bareheaded. When he was two hundred yards away I put my hands to my mouth and shouted to him: "Stop where you are or we shall shoot. Put your weapons down and declare yourself." He took no notice. He was crying in a loud, high voice: "Butchers... murderers... my wife... my wife... children ... butchers... starved... butchers... Barbarians..." Fifty yards away he stopped, his chest heaving. "Butchers," he cried. He straightened up and hurled the spear with tremendous force. It passed between two legionaries and buried itself on the parade ground at the feet of a startled soldier carrying a sack of grain. Then he ran forward again, his sword outstretched in his hand. I nodded swiftly to the centurion, who cried, "Fast... stand... loose." Three arrows took him in the chest as he ran hard for the gate. He stopped dead. His body went backward six feet with the force of the arrows, twisting as it did so, and then, arching slightly, lay crumpled sideways upon the snow.

The soldiers lowered their bows and we all looked at each other in silence. No one knew what to say. It was bizarre and horrible, even for us who were professional soldiers. He had been a man out of his mind, as Quintus said.

"Collect his weapons," I said. "Leave the body where it is. The wolves will deal with that." I turned away and walked to the ladder. It was then that I made up my mind.

Quintus, following, said tersely, "Rando's daughter?"

"Well?"

"Don't do it. There's no point now."

I did not answer him and I left him standing by the number four armory, staring after me in bewilderment.

As I went through the camp I saw the signal fires flare as the tar and pitch caught light, and a stray dog yelped suddenly as it cowered against a wall and a troop of horses clattered by. Inside the adjutant's office the clerks were burning all unnecessary documents while the rolls that were to be kept were being loaded into a wagon under the direction of an auxiliary. Fatigue parties went from hut to hut with incendiaries, so that each building might be fired without difficulty when the time came, while others fixed prepared sections of palisading at strategic crossings in the camp, so that if the outer wall fell the Barbarians would still have to fight their way through, building by building. Here, an archer was busy flighting his arrows; there, a legionary was fitting javelins into racks along the firing platform; and the north and south gates were being shored up with great beams of timber. They would withstand even a battering ram when the time came. I spent the morning inside my office, answering questions and giving orders, while messengers came and went with a stream of information. A little before midday Quintus lounged in, his face wet with sweat.

"The girl," he said. "You never answered my question."

I had a headache and I was deathly worried. I looked up at him. He too looked tired, and a muscle twitched at the corner of his mouth. He was always like that before the fighting—over-tensed, wrought up and inclined to be irritable.

"Why the interest?" I said. "Do you want her for yourself?"

He began to look angry, flushed a dull red, started to say something, checked, turned, and went out, slamming the door behind him. I grinned and went on with my work. Another messenger came in with news from Goar. Guntiarus had learned that his son was in the Alan's hands and had promptly discontinued his supply trains to the enemy camp. "I do not trust him, however," wrote Goar. "For the moment he is frightened. It will not last. If he moves against us I shall send him his son in small pieces. I have men on watch constantly, and will let you know the moment the enemy begins to break camp. Can you..." I read on to the end and then ate a meal of pork and beans, washed down with some wine that not even the quartermaster would have drunk.

In the afternoon I picked up my stick and went out into the camp. I knocked on the door of her hut and a faint voice answered. I went in. She was standing by the table, her hands resting on its edge, and she was very pale. She trembled violently when she saw me; she reminded me of a sick dog. The shutters in the walls were still closed and the room smelled oddly. I threw them open. I said harshly, "The river has frozen over."

She nodded, raised her head, and looked at me with dilated eyes. "I thought so when—when I heard the trumpets."

I glanced round the room, saw the crumpled bed, the dried vomit on the floor, and the empty water jug on the soiled table. Of food there was no sign. "Do you always live in such a mess?" I said.

She locked her hands together and did not answer me. She just stared. She was too frightened to speak.

I went toward her and she backed away with a whimper. "Have you been here alone since the blizzard started?"

She nodded again. "Yes."

"In the dark?"

"I had a light at first. Then the oil ran out. The door was locked as usual. No one came. It was—very cold."

I turned to the door. "Sentry. Get me the duty centurion. Now." She had moved behind the table as though she needed it for support. I went up to her. She shrank back. "Is it time?" she whispered.

"Yes," I said. "Time for you to go."

"I am ready," she said in a voice that I could hardly hear. "I am not afraid. No—that's a lie. I am. Will it hurt terribly? I tried not to think about it. I asked the farrier. I asked him after—we were caught. I thought it would be easier if I knew—exactly. He gave me some. These are what will be used, aren't they?" She opened her hands and I saw three great triangular-shaped nails lying across her palm.

They were indeed what we used.

"My poor child," I said. I held her in my arms and she began to cry. Five days in the dark, in that hut, thinking about what. I had threatened, trying to summon up the courage to face the horror, the pain, the unendurable.

"I am sending you to the Bishop of Treverorum. He will look after you. If you remained here you would not be safe, not even from your own people. I have seen how men behave after a battle. Afterward, whatever happens, you may go back if you wish."

"Fabianus," she whispered.

I said, "You must be brave. There are young men of your own people. Perhaps you had one. I don't know."

She tried to smile. "You did not ask me."

No, I had not asked her. I remembered what Julian had once said. I never had asked people. I never had cared.

"Fabianus must stay with me. He is a soldier."

"I love him." She began to cry. "I tried to hate him—he is the enemy—but I can't. I love him."

"You must tell him so. It will help him. We—soldiers always fight better when we know that someone loves us," I said harshly. I patted her on the shoulder. "I will send him to you."

She raised her head. "I thought—"

"I know what you thought." I paused. I said, "I did kill a woman once. It is something I have not been able to forget."

"Why—?"

"You are so like the daughter I always wanted but never had."

I found Fabianus in my office and told him what he had to do. "You may escort her as far as Bingium and that is all. We have not much time."

"How long, sir?"

"I don't know. It will take them as long to get ready as it takes us. Today is the Christian festival. Three days, perhaps. Goar will light a beacon the moment they move. He has prepared three fires on the escarpment slopes in the shape of a triangle. When they are lit we shall know that the time has come. Now get a move on. I have a lot to do."

Later, Gallus came to me, no longer grinning and cheerful, but still as calm and as levelheaded as ever. "I am a sailor without a fleet," he said. "What are the orders for my seamen, sir?"

"They can return to Treverorum if they wish."

"They would rather stay and fight, I think," he said, coolly.

"Very well, let those stay who wish to do so. Form them into a unit under your own command. Get hold of Julius Optatus and have them issued with arms and equipment. Then move them into the old camp. I will keep them as a reserve. They will be paid at legionary rates from now on."

Walking through the camp I saw the ex-slave, Fredbal, stacking swords outside the armory. He had put on weight in the months that he had been with us, and looked fit and healthy, but a centurion had told me that he lived inside himself, was unsociable and rarely spoke, though he was a good worker with his hands. I called out to him and he came up to me and stood rigidly to attention. He could never forget that he had once been a soldier.

I said, "We shall soon be in great danger. If you wish—and I advise it—you may be taken off the strength. I will see that you are given the money that is due to you, and you can go with the others to Treverorum. The Alemanni are too close for comfort."

He said, in that cracked voice of his, "If the General wishes, I will go. But I would rather stay. I am not too old to use a sword, and I have debts to settle with them across the river." He spat as he spoke.

I nodded. "Do as you please." I smiled. "I will help you to settle those debts if I can."

That night I called a conference of my senior officers and we discussed the strategy and the tactics of the coming battle. I wanted to be sure that everyone knew exactly what was expected of him. At the end Aquila said with a grin, "What about the pay chest, sir, and all the other funds?"

There was laughter at this.

I said, "I am not paying the men now, Chief Centurion, if that is what you mean. They will have enough to carry without being loaded down with silver as well. Don't worry. I am sending it all back to Treverorum. We have a number of men who are sick or injured and who will be no use to us here. They will go as an escort. I shall have it put in the safekeeping of the Bishop. I think I can trust him that far. Satisfied?"

He nodded. "Yes, sir."

This year there was no feasting, no celebration, no jollity, no prayers of thanksgiving, only a long line of wagons and people trudging through the snow in a seemingly endless line on their way to Belgica and safety. That night, Quintus and I, and four others, went out of the town, past the old camp, and up the hill to the wooden temple, and there we performed our mystery. I was comforted to think that the long night of our lives would soon be over and that we, all of us, had the courage and the fortitude to face the change. We would move from one circle to the next, and the change would not be for the worst. I had been told that: I knew. So I worshiped the God in whom I was consumed with a quiet heart. Afterward, as we left in the darkness, and the lights of the camp shone below us, Quintus put his hand on my shoulder. It was a rare gesture. In all the years that I had known him we had never touched, save upon a meeting or a departure.

He said, "You forgave me, Maximus, but I cannot forgive myself. That is why I would have made you Emperor if I could."

I said, "I understand." I smiled. I said, "I wonder if Stilicho will remember us. I wrote to Saturninus last night. I sent him your wishes."

We returned to the camp and we waited, but the waiting was not for long. On the thirty-first day of December, in the year of their Lord, four hundred and six, by the Christian calendar, the peoples of Germania, the Alans, the Quadi, the Marcomanni, the Siling, and the Asding Vandals, led by their five kings, broke camp and crossed the ice at Moguntiacum.

CHAPTER XVI

There was a full moon that night and the sky was clear so that the sentries could see the snow across the river. A little before four o'clock three points of light flickered upon the hill slopes behind Aquae Mattiacae. A single trumpet sounded in the frosted air and the legion awoke instantly at the call to arms. There was no fuss, no unnecessary noise, and no disorder. Quietly they dressed and quietly they armed. By sections, the garrison moved to their stations on the walls. Spears in hand they waited, straining into the half light to watch for movement on the ground before them. Details of troops moved off quietly into the abandoned town while the cavalry rode out through the gates to their positions along the line of the road. At five o'clock a light flared away to our left, and then another and another. Signal fires glowed to the right and signalers came running across the hard-packed snow to report their messages.

Confluentes had been attacked in strength, Borbetomagus had been attacked, there was movement on the ice opposite Boudobrigo and Salisio, and the abandoned outpost on the bridgehead at Bingium had been occupied by armed men. The island garrisons reported tribesmen mustering on the opposite bank and moving in the woods behind, from where the sounds of fighting could be heard.

I looked around me. The walls were lined with men I knew, their faces tensed, all sweating a little under the weight of their armor; the ballistae crews stood ready, buckets of heated oil smoked unpleasantly on the gatehouse tower, and the archers were taking their bowstrings from their tunics and stretching their bows. In front of us we could see the ice and the snow of the frozen river, but little else. There was a white mist on the plain where the enemy were encamped and it hid all from our sight.

More messages came in. Confluentes had been outflanked by a

detachment of horse but the main attack had been beaten off, though not without difficulty. The enemy dead had been identified as Burgundians. Boudobrigo was being attacked in strength, and Salisio was surrounded. The enemy here, too, were Burgundians. Bingium was under fire but the auxiliary ala had cut the enemy to pieces on the flats across the Nava. Borbetomagus was in difficulties. The Alemanni were across the ice and the town was slowly being invested. Three attempts to break in had been repulsed and the ballistae were destroying all frontal assaults. Two signal towers had been surrounded south of Moguntiacum, but the tribesmen could not get across the ditches and had moved off to try their luck elsewhere.

"These are diversions," I said. "Clumsy attempts to draw off our troops. The main crossing will still take place here."

Quintus said savagely, "I would like to put three inches of steel through Guntiarus, the treacherous swine."

Fabianus said, "What are the orders, sir?"

"Hold this fort till I signal you to retire. Then fight your way out and make for the camp on the road. If you can't hold the town walls, then pull your men back on this fort and burn the city. Leave them nothing that they can use, neither food nor fuel nor shelter."

"I understand, sir."

"Did you get that garrison established on the broken bridge?"

"Yes, sir, Barbatio is there with fifty men and two ballistae. They will have a job getting at him unless they try to burn him out from underneath."

"Good. Quintus, it is time for you to go. I will join you shortly. If I don't, then you command."

He saluted and left and I watched his escort follow him out of the gates.

"How did they get so far north with Goar's men on the watch?"

"I don't know," I said. "Perhaps Goar has played us false. Perhaps they are only Burgundians opposite Bingium. Perhaps he couldn't help it. I just don't know."

An hour later the sky paled a little and the whiteness of the snow merged with the gray of the horizon. Trees and woods came slowly into focus and the hills to the north seemed to stand up suddenly, like ghosts newly risen from the dead. Behind me, in the fort, the last wagons were rumbling out of the gate, loaded with equipment and stores that Fabianus would not need, and trudging alongside the mules I recognized Fredbal, wearing armor now, a short sword buckled at his side. A signal glowed from the old camp behind the town where Marius commanded, to show that all was in order, while patrols tramped through the empty town, making a last check to see that everyone had left.

A centurion touched me on the arm. "They are coming," he said quietly. The mist had lifted at last, the sun was rising in the east, and we could see.

I looked. The plain, that desolate waste of dead ground between their camp and the foothills, was alive with men, as an anthill is alive with ants. I had never seen such a host before. There were so many that they darkened the ground and the snow was blotted out. One column was making its way steadily across the plain at an angle so that it would reach the river opposite the lower island. Two more columns were moving directly for the upper island, and a fourth column was heading straight toward the broken bridge. Each column was spread over a front of at least four hundred yards, while behind, in the distance, could be seen wagons, mules, ponies, and still more people. It was not an army on the move: it was an entire nation.

Fabianus said, "We shall never stop them."

"Don't be a fool," I said. "They are weak with starvation, and desperate too. We can stop them if we fight hard enough. They've never fought a legion before."

It was an incredible sight. I knew now why the Huns—so it was said—struck such terror into the hearts of their foes. It was the sheer, massive weight of the numbers, the appalling sight of that remorseless advance, as though the whole world had gathered together in one place, and by the simple act of walking forward, threatened to overwhelm it. The columns came on steadily and without haste. It seemed as though nothing would be able to stop them. On the river's edge they paused for a fraction of time and then came out slowly onto the ice, onto the surface of that infernal river that had for so long been our friend and which had now betrayed us. The going was difficult for them, men slipped and stumbled and fell, scrambling awkwardly from one frozen patch to the next, and, by straining my eyes, I could see the banners they carried in their advance, long poles to which were fixed the bleached and grinning skulls of their enemies—our own dead, no doubt, from the fight on the east bank.

They were a third of the way across now and the columns facing the islands were flattening out, like the heads of mushrooms, very close to the banks where my legionaries crouched in concealment.

I raised my sword above my head and then dropped it. A ballista fired and its flaming ball was the signal for which my men waited.

The garrisons on the islands opened fire. Balls of glowing flame arched through the air and crashed, one after one, into the massed ranks of the enemy. The arrow hail flew and men dropped with choking grunts, or cowered, screaming, their hands over their heads as the unquenchable fire hit them. The bolts from the carroballistae hammered gaps in the line and men died at the rate of one every three seconds. Our men had the range to a yard and they fired not only at those directly advancing, but at those behind them and at those upon the banks in their rear. It was impossible to miss. It appeared to be equally impossible to check their advance. For every man that died another filled his place, and if the front ranks checked or tried to take cover, they were pressed upon by the weight of men from behind.

For over five hundred days we had halted their march, checked their ambitions, forced them into hunger, made them watch their wives starve and their children die. Every death in that camp of every man, of every woman, and of every child, no matter what the cause might have been, was blamed on us. We were the enemy and they would destroy us out of fear and out of hatred and out of revenge. They were a Christian people, and it must be so, though only a pagan, perhaps, could understand.

The south island, closer to the east bank than the others, was quickly surrounded and the worst of the early fighting took place there. It was completely protected by a high palisade and wooden towers, from which our archers shot them down while they beat at the wooden defenses with their axes. They reached for it over the piled bodies of their dead, and I knew it would not be long before we were overrun. They had ladders and poles and ballistae of their own, crude affairs, but effective enough, and I could see that these were already in action, from the fireballs that came from the east bank. The northern island was under fire now, and the column advancing on the bridge had been checked by Barbatio and his ballistae. They tried to spread out and encircle him but the firepower of the defenders was too great, and the tribesmen wavered and then broke back to the protection of their own bank.

By midday the garrison of the south island were in difficulties. They were completely surrounded; our fireballs were neutralized by the snow and ice, and all our efforts to dislodge them proved a failure. I nodded to a waiting man and a trumpet sounded, and the garrison, who had not lost a man, fired the positions they had held so well and turned and cut their way out and retreated grimly, in testudo formation, back across the ice to the harbor area. Had it been summer, or even a normal winter, the island would have been a furnace, a wall of fire they could not penetrate, but the snow again neutralized the effects of the fire, and though some damage was caused, it was not great. When the flames had died down the tribesmen crowded onto the island and used our broken defenses for cover while our ballistae from the camp fired on them without pause.

"Shorten the range," I said. "The ice is hummocked badly on this side. It will slow them up considerably."

"We shall never stop them," said a soldier, panic in his voice.

"Pull yourself together," I said. "These are only men, not gods."

The lower island was in difficulties now and the enemy's losses were enormous.

"Fire," shouted Fabianus, and the arrow hail flew from the walls at the column climbing the ice ridges once more toward the broken bridge. Even when they reached the bank they would have an outer palisade, a triple row of sunken stakes with iron-hard points, between them and the ditches. They would have to climb their own dead to reach the fort at all. I did not think that their ration of courage would last that long.

All afternoon the fighting continued. The enemy were held in check in their efforts to take both the harbor and lower islands. They had failed to storm the positions and crouched behind their own dead, flicking arrows at our men whenever they showed themselves, and waited for their chiefs to make a decision. Their wagons lined the east bank now and groups of horsemen were plunging down the slope onto the ice, while there was a constant movement to and fro, of men carrying arms and bundles of arrows. By now, however, Barbatio was in difficulties. He had been half encircled by the enemy, and the Vandals were moving across the river to his right, keeping out of range and probing the defensive power of the town walls. It would not be long before they outflanked the town altogether.

Out of the corner of my eye I saw the movement of horsemen upon the ice. I touched Fabianus upon the arm. "Good luck. May fortune smile on us all. I will see you later." I ran down the steps, mounted my horse, and cantered out of the camp and up the smooth slope toward the road and the ditches where my legion now stood at arms. They cheered me as they saw me coming, and I joined Quintus on the ridge where the cavalry stood in lines, dismounted and shivering a little in the cold. "They cannot keep this up," I said. "Oh for six legions, Quintus. Give me six legions and I would save Gaul in an afternoon."

It was beginning to get dark now; even so I could see that the garrisons of the two remaining islands were in difficulties. Fires were burning at several points within the defenses, and the enemy, aided by makeshift wooden shields, had closed in on the palisades on the east and were hurling rocks and missiles at them, while others were battering at the timber with a handheld ram.

An hour later darkness fell, and all night long we could see a procession of torches crossing the river as the tribesmen moved backward and forward with supplies of food, fuel, and weapons. All night they kept up their attacks and I could see the fireballs hurtling outward from the bridge where Barbatio made his stand, and hear the cries of the legionaries in the fort below me as they manned the walls, hour after hour, in the freezing cold. When dawn came I received a signal to say that the tribesmen had enfiladed the town on the south side, had been repulsed in their attacks on the old camp, but were pressing heavily against the walls of Moguntiacum. A signal from Fabianus informed me that a party of men had crept under the bridge in the night and were trying to get a fire going. Barbatio had made a sortie to dislodge them, but without success. It would not be long before he was forced to retreat.

All day they fought. Fabianus' fort was too strong for them, so they concentrated their attacks on the islands and upon the town. By the afternoon it became apparent that the islands could hold out no longer. A message from Didius, in command of the harbor area, asked for instructions and begged for permission to withdraw. I agreed. A trumpet blew the retreat and the garrisons there broke out and backed across the ice to the harbor, where an ala of auxiliary cavalry was waiting to cover them. The tribesmen massed along the edge of the river, awaiting the signal to move forward, while the horde that had captured the south island the previous day moved against the south wall of the town and fort. Foiled in their efforts to break through the palisade and the stakes, they prowled along the walls and established themselves in the ruined theater, seeking a weak point at which to attack, while others entered the harbor area and engaged in hand to hand fighting with the rear guard of Didius.

Presently, a great mass of horsemen moved from behind the harbor island and came up toward the bank. They were caught in a crossfire projected by both my own ballistae and those of Fabianus and, before they had moved a hundred yards, had lost a third of their men. Those who still remained mounted rode on to the bank and then turned right, intending, no doubt, to head downriver. They checked at the sight of the auxiliary camp and then made toward it at an easy canter.

"They think it is a dummy still, which it was," I said to Quintus. "Now watch."

Quintus said calmly, "Someone is going to get a big surprise."

A cavalry ala came riding out of the camp fast, in three squadrons. The squadrons closed up smoothly and rode toward the enemy. At the very last moment they moved effortlessly into the charge and we could hear the crash of arms as the two groups met. Our men rode straight through them, turned, and rode back. The Vandals broke and fled, and those that managed to reach the ice were killed by the archers in Moguntiacum fort.

"Well," said Quintus. "How does it seem to you?"

I looked toward the east. The entire width of the river was covered with their dead and their dying, and the ravens circled ceaselessly above, waiting to keep them company.

"I would have been happier if the islands had held. We still have them contained between us, the auxiliaries and Fabianus. They won't be able to break the two camps, and to get at us they must come up the slope."

In the distance, across the river, we could hear shouting and see great columns of fire and smoke streaming up into the sky behind the masses patiently waiting on the bank.

"That must be Goar," I said. "Why didn't he attack before?"

Quintus said, "He's going for the baggage wagons."

Messages continued to come in. The commander at Borbetomagus had made a counterattack with his cavalry and had destroyed the Alemanni in his rear; the enemy before Salisio and Boudobrigo had fallen back across the ice, but were still massed on the far bank; Bingium was still under attack and the native village there had been burned to the ground.

We went on waiting, and then at last the enemy moved. The mass of men who had overrun the lower islands split into two. One half turned right and rolled toward the camp of the auxiliaries; the other half, the greater, moved toward the slopes where we stood.

"Now," I said, and the artillery opened fire. "Quintus, take the horse behind the camp and send two alae down to the help of those wretched auxiliaries. Wait with the rest of your men till I give the signal. Then hit them right-handed. Keep a tight control and don't let any one override."

He smiled savagely. "Trust Maharbal," he said.

They came up the snow toward us in big wedges under their chiefs, and broke themselves against our thrown spears, our javelins, and our arrows. They struggled on, but they could not close because of the ditches. Forced to stand there, helpless, they shouted obscenely till we shot them down, while those who tried to force the barriers lay broken in the snow, a hideous bundle of rag and bone. Quintus waited patiently. The alae, sent to help the auxiliaries, ran into a snowdrift and found the going difficult. By the time they had floundered out of it and regrouped they were too late to catch the head of the column, which had spread out and was trying to envelop the fort on three sides. They charged the tail of the column, however, and cut it in half, working outward so that the two sections could not rejoin. I signaled to Quintus and he led a thousand men out and struck the enemy in the flank, just at the moment when they were beginning to tire. The snow was soft on top but firm underneath, and the enemy crumpled under the weight of his attack. I gave the order to advance and my cohorts moved out and descended the slope, shoulder to shoulder, their stabbing swords held low and their shields up. We had all the advantage; my men were fresh compared with theirs, and the ground was in our favor. The tribesmen fell back, fighting desperately, and then turned and broke and ran for the river. On the ground by the water they regrouped, aided by more men who had crossed the ice, but though Quintus charged them twice more, his horses were blown, and the enemy held stubbornly to the settlement area by the harbor. We withdrew slowly back to our positions and I ordered the troops to fall out, by sections, to rest and to eat.

When night fell an hour later there must have been thirty thousand men contained in the snow between the area of my four forts. The Vandals set up a rough shield wall to protect themselves and made shelters out of slats of timber and spare cloaks. There were wagons on the ice now, and campfires sprang up everywhere, on the islands where, so I believe, their chiefs camped, upon the ground by the river, and upon the ice itself. As the moon rose I held a conference in my leather tent.

"If we can hold them between these forts we shall win. All their food supplies are on the east bank and they will die of cold with no proper encampment."

"Can we trust the auxiliaries, sir? There are only two thousand of them." Marius sounded worried.

I said, "Fabianus is holding Moguntiacum with five hundred. Still—we can stiffen them with a couple of centuries if you like. Get Gallus out of the old fort to take over command. That will steady them. See to it, Aquila. Get them moved down while it is still dark. Now, what news from the other forts?"

A cohort commander said tiredly, "All is well, sir. The attacks all failed in the end. Even the Alemanni fell back across the river at Borbetomagus."

A signaler came in. "There's a man outside, sir, who says he has come from the east bank."

"Send him in. What other news is there?"

Aquila said, "Scudilio at Bingium led a counterattack across the river and has fortified the bridgehead. Barbatio is still in command of the bridge but has lost half his men and is short of missiles. Marius has sent half his men to give support to the auxiliaries in the town and has cleared the ground outside the north wall. I think——"

At that moment a man came in. I recognized him as one of Goar's bodyguard. He grinned and said cheerfully, "It is good fighting."

"Yes," I said. "Very good. Why didn't you stop the attacks on Bingium and Confluentes?"

"The Franks attacked us. That is why we were late in helping you. But they have lost much food from their wagons and dare not send any more men across the river for fear of us."

"Is Goar well?"

"He is fine. I am to say that he sent the King, Guntiarus, a special present."

"What?"

"The head of his son." He grinned again. "Now he will know for certain that the boy is dead." His teeth flashed in a smile. "He should be happy at being proved such a fine prophet."

Quintus frowned, and one of the officers, who was married, put his hands to his eyes.

I said, "His treachery was well rewarded then."

Quintus said, "Who lit the fires on the first morning?"

The man hesitated. "We did," he said. "It was as you wished."

Quintus stared at him. "There was fighting then on the east bank while it was still dark. Was it your people?"

The man said sullenly, "I know nothing about that. Perhaps the Vandals quarreled among themselves."

"Perhaps."

A decurion entered, shaking the snow from his helmet. "The patrol you sent out, sir, made contact with the auxiliaries. They report that all is well in camp, but there is a lot of movement on the east bank."

I looked at the map. "If they are moving downstream it means they must intend to cross at the big island just above Bingium. From there they can move on Bingium itself or cut the road behind us."

Quintus said, "We could move those auxiliaries up to block the crossing."

"No. I need them all to hold that camp." I turned to the Alan. "There is work for your people in this thing."

Quintus said, "But, surely—"

"Wait a moment. Where are Goar's men now? Are there any blocking the track down the east bank?"

The Alan nodded. "Surely. He has men everywhere."

"Not quite," said Quintus dryly.

"Then how are the enemy getting along it?" I asked.

The man seemed put out. He said, "I do not know. Perhaps they have broken through."

"Perhaps. Aquila, order up one cohort, with wagons to form a laager, and send them down to the point opposite the lower island, to cover a possible crossing there. And get two centuries to these points along the Bingium road, here and here, to back them. They must move out in fifteen minutes."

Aquila said, "The men are tired out, sir."

"It is better to be tired than dead. Quintus, get some mounted infantry across the river to link up with Goar and hold the track between the river and the hills."

"How many?"

"Two hundred should be enough. If they get into trouble they are to recross and join us. I don't want them wiped out for no purpose at all."

"I'll send Didius. He has a good head."

I looked at the map again, and fingered the east bank route up which I had led the legion only two months previously. "Goar should have held that road." To his bodyguard, I said, "Tell your prince that this is where I want his men, not up in the hills."

A trumpet blew the alarm and an optio thrust his head round the tent flap. "They are moving up the slope again, sir."

"In strength?"

He said, in a scared voice, "It looks as though the whole lot are coming."

"Why can't they be civilized," grumbled Quintus. "All decent soldiers fight in daylight."

I watched the men forming up in their battle ranks, and a signaler from the camp behind ran up, breathing hard. "They are moving on the auxiliary fort as well, sir."

Night fighting was always their specialty and this was proved through the long hours that followed. They attacked Moguntiacum too, and all night long we could see the fireballs from the ballistae arching outward into the snow so that the camp below seemed to be a gigantic fire that spluttered furiously and would not be put out. When the fourth attack had failed, I mounted my horse and cantered along the road to the old camp from which Marius was just about to launch a counterattack. Here, an attempt was being made to encircle the town, but the snow lay thick on the slopes, and there were many drifts, and it provided a natural barrier that we could not have improved upon. The majority of his garrison was now inside the town and only a handful of men were left to protect the camp and the aqueduct. After a quick consultation with Marius' second-in-command, who told me that the tribune had the situation well in hand, I returned to my command. The fighting continued until well past dawn, and when daylight came the ditches were choked with the Vandal dead, so that I began to wish that I had dug them deeper. The men stood down, the wounded were taken to the rear, and the cooks prepared food over the spluttering fires. Fresh bundles of javelins were fetched from the wagons and the armorers were busy, sharpening swords and spears and repairing damaged armor. I went to my tent and lay down on a blanket, wrapped in my cloak.

An hour later they attacked again.

Late the next afternoon a messenger came from Goar. He had crawled across the ice, playing dead, from one pile of bodies to the next. He told me the Alans had suffered fearful losses but had temporarily checked the advance of the column on the east bank. They were grateful for the help I had sent them.

Quintus said wearily, "We are holding them, but that is all. They are too many for us. We cannot beat them without fresh troops."

I said, "I agree. If they had let us rest last night I would have attacked at dawn, and I think we could have pushed them back across the ice. But our men can only fight for so long without rest; they can keep the pressure up by sending in fresh men all the time."

He said, "Why not re-site the ballistae so as to enfilade them?"

I blew on my cold hands. "Yes, they don't like being caught on the flanks; I noticed that. We'll try it then and see if it works."

That night I altered my dispositions, moved the main body of my men onto the flanks, and left the center only lightly held. I was determined to try a counterattack if I could. They came against us for the hundredth time and died horribly between the stakes and the ditches. I waited till I judged that the great mass were pressing in upon the center where the arrow-fire from the palisade was weaker than formerly—and then struck. The cohorts on the wings, flanked by all the horse I could muster, moved out and swept round to take them on the flanks. We moved in the old formation, shoulder to shoulder, a wave of men throwing javelins and then working in with their swords, to be followed by a succession of waves, as each rank tired and fell back to rest. The snow was packed hard by now, frozen lightly on top and slippery in patches where the dead had left their mark. Everything was in our favor, if we could only keep the pressure up long enough. Their line began to bend and writhe as they tried to contain us, and then it wavered as I threw in the last of my reserves. The noise was deafening and the shouting turned to cries of alarm and rage as they broke and fled. Our trumpets sounded and the cavalry, from the two camps below us, burst from the hurriedly opened gates and rode through the Vandal camp, scattering tents and fires and tossing lighted torches onto the wagons that had come up during the day. It was a more successful repeat of our battle on the east bank and, as before, we came within a dicer's throw of victory. They were broken and confused and in a panic, and the panic was spreading swiftly as it always did. We herded them back onto the ice, and they withdrew to form a ragged line between the islands. Had we had more men we could have followed them further and swept them back onto the east bank, and once there I do not think they would have tried to cross again. But our men were exhausted and their impetus was gone by the time they reached the riverbank. They had driven the enemy off but they could do no more, and so the fighting ended without my having achieved the success I dreamed of. I put more men into Moguntiacum, sent a further stiffening of auxiliaries into the camp by the river, told Marius to refortify the harbor area, and cleared the enemy from their positions around the broken bridge where Barbatio, bearded and deathly tired, still held out. Then I withdrew the cavalry back to the road.

At least our success gave us some much needed rest. They did not attack again for seven hours and during that time my men slept for the first time since the old year died.

Quintus said, "How much longer can they keep it up? Their losses are tremendous. How much longer can we keep it up? We are still only just holding them."

"We must hold them," I said. There was nothing else for me to say.

Just before midday they moved off the ice, pushed my patrols off the bank, and assaulted the harbor settlement, coming in upon it fast from three sides in their great wedge-shaped formations, like migrating birds driven before a gale. Marius refused to surrender or retreat. The settlement went up in fire and smoke and the legionaries died upon the walls and in the ditch. They fought in the smoke filled streets and in the doorways of burning homes. They fought with broken swords and blunted spears, with stones and bricks and with their bare hands, until all were overwhelmed. By late afternoon the Barbarians had retaken all the ground from which we had driven them with such difficulty; and then, once more, they began to move up the slope.

For three days and three nights more they kept up a series of attacks, one after one, always using fresh men and never giving us time to rest or recover. We had too little sleep, it was iron cold, and the wind blew from the east the whole time. Huddled in a blanket I would doze, shivering inside my tent until the trumpets blew the next alarm, and then I would stagger out, tired, aching, and sick, to stand at my post beside the Eagle and direct the fighting once more. After the second day Quintus dismounted his cavalry and they joined ranks with the cohorts. He had used too many of his spare horses and all the animals were blown and needed rest. The loose snow on the slopes slowed his charges and tired both man and beast, so that he could achieve only a limited success each time that he took the offensive. On the fourth night it began to snow and the blizzard blinded us so that we could barely see. The bow strings of the archers got wet and two of the ballistae broke because the damp had rotted the cords. Soldiers who were careless, and many were through tiredness, forgot to dry their swords and awoke after sleeping to find the blades heavily rusted. But many died in their sleep from cold and exhaustion, and these, I think, were the happy ones. It snowed steadily for eight hours during that last day and then the wind got up and a blizzard howled across the plain and they attacked us once more with the ferocity born of despair. They could not reach us across the ditches, but their axes could and men who had been holding shields all day grew tired, till they could hold them no longer, and then had no need to. During that time much happened that I cannot remember. There was no night and there was no day, only a long gray twilight when sleeping and waking were one. I remember a figure on a horse cantering across the snow from the river and riding into our camp, and learning without surprise that it was Marius, who had been wounded and left for dead, who had stolen a horse and escaped. And I remember Quintus holding the wounded boy in his arms and saying, with great pride in his voice, "I told you my cavalry were hard to kill." I remember messages coming in from the fort commanders, and they were always messages that were full of hope and courage, never of despair. Scudilio had led a counterattack across the ice and broken the enemy, but had failed to link up with any of Goar's Alans; Borbetomagus was still holding out, and though Sunno had offered the commander terms, he refused to surrender; Barbatio, the bridge set on fire beneath him, had withdrawn into the town, only ten of his original garrison surviving; Boudobrigo and Salisio had pushed patrols out into the surrounding countryside, and, though all was quiet, were keeping their men under arms, for the heights across the river were held in strength by the Burgundians of Guntiarus. Only from Gallus in the auxiliary camp did I detect a note of strain. He sent me a short note when the blizzard was at its height, scrawled laboriously on a wax tablet. "We are just holding them, but the attacks are coming from the rear now as well as from across the ice. The auxiliaries are splendid and the seamen fight well. It feels strange fighting on land again. We are all very tired."

On the morning of the seventh day, when the wind had dropped a little, the Chief Centurion came up to me where I was talking to a group of wounded men. He was unshaven and his eyes were rimmed with black. He said in a low voice, "We have been trying to signal the auxiliary camp, sir, but there is no reply."

"Keep trying," I said.

He shook his head. "They have been overrun, sir."

I walked with him out to the northeast corner of the camp and shaded my eyes. As far as I could judge, the camp still stood but it was half concealed now by a thick pall of black smoke. The ground all round it was dark with men, the living and the dead, but they were not ours. We walked back through a litter of tents, horses, stores, and men, to my headquarters. I did not know what to say.

Aquila said, "They are all round Moguntiacum too, sir. They've got a big camp to the south of the town. They must have made a fresh crossing higher up, during the night."

I looked at the map while Quintus played with his sword belt and Aquila chewed at a dry biscuit. "My first meal today," he said, apologetically. My armor bearer squatted in a corner, rubbing the straps of my breastplate with a greasy rag, and the oil lamp flickered in the cold air. I looked at the map again. The word that the camp had fallen must have spread, for the cohort commanders, Marius among them, came into my tent without waiting to be ordered.

They stood there silently, patiently waiting to be told what to do, waiting for me to deliver a stream of miraculous orders that would set all to right. They had great faith.

I studied the map. The enemy were south of Moguntiacum and the road to Divodurum and Treverorum was open to them. It was not a good road. It would be bad for wagons, for old men and young children, but it would serve for war bands on horses, and they had horses, I knew, for they had used them against us. They were to the north of our position as well, and though the riverbank was thickly wooded and it would take time, yet they would get through and could cut the road to Bingium behind us. They might already have done so. There had been no news from Didius on the east bank at all, and no news from Goar for five days, yet his men were experienced at slipping through the enemy lines.

The tent door was thrust open and one of Quintus' troopers stood to attention before me. "The centuries you stationed along the Bingium road are being attacked, sir. The Marcomanni crossed the river last night."

"How many?"

"About five thousand, sir."

I blinked. "Is there any news from Goar and his Alans? What about the cavalry I sent across the river?"

"I don't know anything about the Alans, sir, but the last news we had of the cavalry under the tribune, Didius, was that they were holding their ground."

"When was that?"

"Two days ago, sir."

"When you left, was there any movement on the road to the northwest?"

"No, sir, but the last patrol sent out came in three hours ago."

"And you left, when?"

"An hour ago, sir. I would have been here sooner, but my horse went lame on the ice."

Quintus raised his head. "You had better do something about him then."

"Yes, sir." He saluted and went out.

I turned back to the map. Goar had been unable to hold them. I was not surprised. We had barely been able to hold them ourselves. Probably, by this time, the cavalry units on the far bank had been annihilated as those centuries would be, too, if I didn't send them help. The others stood quite still, with expressionless faces, waiting for me to speak. I stared up at them and I tried to smile. They were waiting patiently for me to produce a miracle, and I could not do so. If I pulled back half the legion to control the road I might still hold them here, for a while, but I should have extended my lines too far and they would be bound to break through in the end. They had so many more men, and they could build up an attack at any point they chose. The answer lay in one simple statement: we had failed to contain them.

I knew then that we were beaten. Now I never would visit Rome; I never would see the theater of Pompey, the great statue of Trajan, and the arch of Constantine upon which my father had scratched his name when a small boy. I never would see that city which I had loved all my life. Perhaps, like all my hopes, it too was only a dream.

I said, "Order Fabianus to abandon Moguntiacum as arranged, but tell him to make contact with Borbetomagus first and let them know. When the message has been passed, the garrisons of the signal towers are to fall back on their nearest point of safety. Prepare to strike camp here and be ready to move upon my orders. Quintus, send an ala now to help those two wretched centuries. When we march, the wagons are to be in the middle with all the stores and wounded. We shall withdraw on Bingium and hold the line of the Nava there. Inform Bingium of this and tell Confluentes, Salisio and Boudobrigo to withdraw on the thirtieth milestone. Order the garrison at Treverorum to meet them there and await further instructions; and tell Flavius, too, to warn the Bishop and the Council."

"It will cause a panic in the city," said Quintus.

"Of course. This is a retreat, not a strategic withdrawal. Now don't worry." I tried to force a smile and look cheerful. "Everything will still be all right if we keep our heads. You and I, Quintus, have fought on the defensive before."

I motioned Aquila to remain as the others went out. Quintus gave me a long look as he departed. I knew what he was thinking.

"When we pull out I shall leave a small force to hold the palisades here, men with horses. I don't want the enemy to know we have withdrawn until the last possible moment. Do you understand?"

He nodded. He said, "They'll guess, from the lack of numbers."

"Not if we use our heads. There is an old trick, used once by Spartacus, that might help."

At first he looked shocked and tried to protest. I said, "Aquila, I am not a Christian. Yet these things should not matter to you, though they are of great importance to those of my faith. Do you not believe that the soul is more important than the body?"

He bit his lip hard and then saluted me. "I will see that your orders are carried out," he said carefully.

A few minutes later Quintus came back. "Maximus, I'm worried about water, especially for the horses. If the ice is as thick on the Nava as it is here—"

"We can't carry it with us—very little anyway." I rubbed my eyes. "Use your judgment, Quintus. Do whatever seems best."

He nodded. "Of course. But I thought you had better know."

I said, "Yes. Cavalry are so mobile that everyone forgets their damned horses need ten gallons of water a day on full work as well as thirty pounds of food."

"What about the aqueduct?"

"Fabianus has instructions to poison the water tanks in the town. Get it broken, not in one place only, but in as many as possible."

He said, "I dreamed of Rando's daughter last night. Funny, wasn't it? And when I woke I kept on thinking of those children across the river. I would like to have had children of my own—once. But not now."

I said harshly, "Gallus is dead."

"He was a soldier; that's different."

"I shall leave them nothing but the bare earth. Do you understand?"

"I understand."

The signal beacons shone red, and the black smoke drifted upward, like feathers blown on the wind. A thin column of smoke answered from Moguntiacum, and I waited with my staff on the right-hand flank of our position. In front of me were the stakes and the ditches, the bodies sprawled out under a thin sheet of snow, while the ravens circled overhead and cawed pitilessly. Below us the tribes were forming up for another attack on the town. They crouched behind the hummocked snow, behind burned-out carts and hastily made fences, and behind the carefully piled bodies of their own dead. To my rear the legion began to pull out; wagons were harnessed and the wounded and the stores packed inside them; the carroballistae were hitched to the mule teams, and the men dismantled their tents and fell in by sections. Two squadrons of cavalry alone remained, spread out in a thin line along the length of the palisade, and between them, propped against the timber, staring out with blind eyes through the firing slits, their helmets on their heads and javelins in their nerveless hands, stood the frozen bodies of our dead, keeping their last watch upon the enemy below.

A cohort commander came running toward me, his long sword flapping at his side. "Everything is ready, sir. General Veronius has gone on ahead. We await your orders."

"Tell the head of the column to march. When they contact our advance guard they will take their orders from the General. I will join you with the rear guard as soon as I can. I am only waiting for the tribune, Fabianus."

He saluted and went back to his men. In a little while I heard the rumble of wagon wheels and the steady tramping of the cohorts as they marched out of earshot.

I waited. The water dripped through the hourglass in my orderly's hand until it was all gone. Then he turned it over and it started again. . . . I must have dozed for a while for I found myself yawning and shivering with cold. I turned to speak to him, and then I saw fire, great tongues of flame leaping up from the camp, both from the sides and the center. Fireballs hurtled outward into the surrounding town and the huddled rows of wooden shacks caught fire, one by one, as columns of black smoke, thick and oily, spread outward and hid the flames from our sight. The shrieks and yells of the Barbarians came to us, even at that distance, and then out of the smoke I saw what appeared to be a gigantic tortoise, ponderously breaking a way through the surging mass of men outside the gates. The tortoise seemed to flicker with bright pinpoints of light, and I knew that it was Fabianus and his men, using the testudo formation, and that the lights came from the sun's reflection on the metal strips upon their shields. At the same time the old camp to our right went up in flames with a great whoof of sound, and there was a sudden wind upon our faces as we felt the blast of the explosion. The tortoise had charged clear, and then it disintegrated, as though at command, and the men who composed it took to their heels and ran toward us across the wet snow. Men were pouring out of the old camp too, legionaries, auxiliaries, and seamen, their retreat covered by a handful of horsemen. I sent a troop of horse down the slope to cover the escape of Fabianus and his men, and all the while Moguntiacum blazed with fire until the fort and the town were consumed, and the Barbarians were left with nothing but a handful of acres of charred wood and blackened stone as the prize of their conquest.

War bands of the Vandals and the Quadi came up the slope after the retreating legionaries, but the two ballistae left in our lines opened fire and dispersed them in a few moments.

Fabianus came up to me, the sweat dripping from his blackened face. His hair was singed, he had lost his helmet, and his eyebrows were burned off. "We got out," he said, and then grinned.

I smiled. "You got out."

"It went up like a furnace, sir. With enough men, though, I could have held that fort forever."

"What are your casualties?"

"I left two hundred dead in the camp. They were all chest or face wounds."

I said, "It was well held, but they have broken through further down the river. We're falling back on Bingium. I've got your horses here. Get your men mounted and go on ahead. I stay with the rear guard."

He said, "I had one message from Borbetomagus. They thanked us for the news of our withdrawal. Sunno is dead, and the Alemanni disorganized. They thought they could hold out for three days more. Then, if their commander could not get terms, he would break out and withdraw upon Vindonissa. He wished us luck."

I said, "It is he who will need the luck."

He hesitated. Then he turned away. Over his shoulder he said, "Barbatio is dead. He was killed by an arrow early this morning." He strode off to the waiting horses and I noticed that he was limping slightly.

The wagons were coming across the river now in a steady flow, and the tribesmen were massing again upon the edge of the smoking ruin that was Moguntiacum. I mounted my horse and sent my bodyguard riding through the camp in pairs, lighted torches in their hands, setting fire to each building in turn. The tribesmen, seeing the fires, came up the slopes in a rush. Abandoning the camp and the field defenses to the enemy who, in seven days of ceaseless fighting, had been unable to take them by direct assault, we rode off as the first of their war bands reached the ridge. The fire and the smoke concealed our retreat effectively enough, and I thought that by the time they had reorganized themselves for a pursuit we should, with luck, have a lead of between three to five hours.

It was seventeen miles to Bingium but the road was ice hard, slippery, and cut into ridges by the wheeled traffic of the refugees who had left Moguntiacum the week before. Many of our men were wounded, all of us were on short rations, and none of us had eaten a hot meal for twenty-four hours. The legion ahead, I thought, would march slowly, and so kept my horse at a gentle amble, though I dropped pickets every half mile to keep watch for signs of a pursuit. It was very cold, and only the thought of the hot meal and the proper bed that I should find awaiting me in Bingium kept me awake upon my horse. Behind me I left the dead, who were my friends, unburied in the snow.

CHAPTER XVII

It was snowing again by the time we reached the milestone where I had ordered the two centuries to hold the track running up from the river. There, by a huddle of burned-out huts that had once been a village, I found Quintus, standing with his feet apart, resting upon his naked sword. I looked at the smashed palisade, at the burned-out signal tower, at the bodies in armor, and at the limp figures, hanging from trees to which they had been skewered while still alive. A man whom I could not recognize sat upon a fallen tree trunk, wearing a cloak and a hood. From his attitude it seemed as though he held his head in his hands. All about me I could hear movement, as though men stood in the darkness of the wood, waiting quietly, but shifting from one foot to the other to avoid the numbing cold that was upon us all.

Quintus raised his head but he did not smile. He said to the tribune with me, "Tell the men to go on. They must not talk or make any noise. They will be directed where to go."

I slid from my horse and looked about me, and I could see little groups of legionaries, drawn swords in hand, watchful and somehow menacing, posted in a wide circle about us. I felt the hairs prickle on the nape of my neck.

"What is it, Quintus?" I said.

He did not move. He said, in a tired voice, "That is for you to judge. When I reached here with the advance guard, the two centuries were still fighting, after a fashion. One half had been wiped out, and the other driven back across the road. The way was barred by about two thousand of the Marcomanni. There were others too, Franks and Alans." He paused and then said very carefully, "It was difficult, you understand, to know who was fighting whom. The rest of the Marcomanni were still down by the river, looting the native town there. That went up in flames at dawn, so a wounded soldier told me. The Marcomanni have been crossing the river all day. There must be nearer ten thousand than five by now. The woods are thick with them. I drove my lot off in one charge and they broke and fled, but I think they will come back." He stopped and then spoke again, his voice quite without expression. "Then I met Goar with a handful of his men. He told me the rest."

"Goar!"

"Yes, he is here with us now."

The man, sitting upon the log, stood up and put back his hood. I could recognize him now—Goar with a sword in his hand, and a cut across his face, and a look in his face that I had never seen before.

"You crossed the river after all," I said. "What has happened, man? Tell me?"

Goar said, "We failed to hold them on the east bank. We were forced back into the hills. I made a detour and circled round, intending to cross at Bingium and come up the west bank to your aid. On the shore opposite Bingium, two days ago, we caught a man. He was an auxiliary from the fort there. He was a Frank. He had messages from the commander, for Guntiarus." He paused, and I could see that he was sweating. He said, "We hurt him until he talked. Then I crossed by night and lay up in the woods, waiting for you to come. I have only a few men with me." He hesitated. He said, slowly, "We did our best. I gave you—my word."

Quintus said, "It would seem that Scudilio has betrayed Bingium to the Barbarians. To test them, and—and prove Goar right, I sent a patrol of three men to the town with orders to return. That was three hours ago and they have not come back."

"They might have been ambushed and killed, or even delayed."

"No, Maximus."

I was silent. He was right. I knew that none of these things had happened to these men on their journey to Bingium. They had been ambushed and killed inside the camp, not out of it.

"Where is the legion now?"

He said, in a low voice, "In a valley, about a mile down the road, just off a track to the left. I told Aquila to halt there and await your orders."

I looked at them in turn. I said, "They have all the stores that we need: food, arms, water, everything."

"I know," said Quintus. "Everything."

"When did they betray us?"

"I do not know." He spoke in a curious voice, and I knew, from the way he looked at me, that something was still wrong.

"Is that all?"

"It would seem to be enough, but it is not, in fact, quite all."

"Go on."

"We have a prisoner here, a Frank, who tells a curious story. Centurion!"

An elderly man was dragged before me, his hands tied behind his back. He had gray hair and a gray beard, and I recognized him. It was Fredegar, the sword brother of Marcomir, whom I had not seen since the night I made that hurried, hopeless journey in the rain to avert a catastrophe, and failed.

I said, "What do you do here?"

He said, hoarsely, "You did not bother about us when our Prince died and we were defeated. You never asked what happened to us and to our people."

"What did happen, old man? You forget that Marcomir broke faith with me."

"You let that man take our lands." He nodded to Goar, who stared at him contemptuously. "He was your ally then. We did not matter."

"Come to the point, old man, or I will lead you to it myself, and it will be sharper than you think."

He said, "The Alans took our land, our bergs, and our young women. Yet, despite the fact that you no longer thought us of any moment, we stayed loyal. Marcomir would have wished it so. When the fighting began, we tried to help. The Alans did not want us. But when things began to go badly we crossed the river to join you and found the Marcomanni attacking your Limes. We fought them, and then your men came up. This one"—he pointed with his chin at Quintus— "took us for the enemy and fought back. When I had been captured I told him what I knew, but he would not believe me because this man had spoken to him first."

"What would you say again that my friend did not believe?"

"That the Vandals tried to bribe the commandant at Bingium, and failed, then when the fighting started the Alans held off. It was we who attacked the Vandals in the dawn of that first morning, for you had told Marcomir you wanted the wagons destroyed. Only later in the day, when it seemed that you were holding them, did the Alans at last make war on your side." He spat. "They are a people who are loyal only to the strong. Later, when things did not go well with you, they retreated to the hills and let the Marcomanni cross the river, and they murdered the cavalry you sent to the east bank, while pretending to be their friends. I, myself, saw their messenger carry the head of Didius to the Vandal kings." He paused, and then said, in an even louder voice, "They crossed the ice at Bingium and made for the camp, pretending one thing but doing another, and when the commandant let them in they took the camp by storm and destroyed your garrison. All that happened today. All this would I say, still, even were you to burn me on a fire."

Goar said quietly, "It is, of course, a lie. Bingium was betrayed by a man who had Aleman blood." He turned to me in exasperation. "Did I not warn you of the risk you took? I do not blame you for it. It is only traitors and idiots who make fools of clever men. But that is no consolation to the clever men."

"Thank you," I said.

He gave me a strained smile. He said, "I, too, made mistakes. Your cavalry were a great help. But there were too many Vandals. We could not hold them, any more than you could. And you are trained soldiers. We are not."

I turned to Fredegar. "Goar of the Alans was a brother in blood to your dead prince. That is a strong oath that he took. It is dangerous to meddle with the gods. Would he break it, do you think? Would you?"

"He is a liar," said the Frank bitterly.

I said coldly, "I cannot busy myself with your feuds. They are not my concern."

"What is then? Ask him why he crossed the river when he told you that he would not be able to do so."

Goar said angrily, "I crossed to let the General know what I had done. My men are still on the other bank. But we have fought together and I owed him much. So I came to see him and to wish him well."

"He is a liar," said a voice out of the darkness.

We all turned. Straining my eyes, I could see a shadow against a tree and then the shadow became a man, dark against the white snow. He walked slowly toward us, like an old man, hunched and feeble, until we could see his face. It was Scudilio, the auxiliary commandant at Bingium. He was wearing his uniform, and his helmet was on his head. He held his right shoulder in his left hand and I could see blood upon the hand. His face was a ghastly color and I could hear his breath rasp in and out, as it does when a man is in great pain. No one moved or spoke. He came forward until he was almost face-to-face with Goar. The Alan did not move. "Traitor," he spat.

Scudilio stood there, swaying on his feet. He said in a whisper, "If I am, then tell me whose arrow is in my back."

He turned and fell sideways to the ground. The shaft of a great arrow protruded from his shoulder blade, and it quivered slightly as the wounded man fought for breath.

Quintus stepped forward, knelt down, and touched the arrow. Then he looked up at me and said softly, "This is an arrow such as the Alans make. Look at the feathers, and this colored cock feather here that they use as a guide for notching."

Goar said, "When they betrayed Bingium they must have left the camp and met some of my men."

Scudilio groaned. I bent down beside him. He said in a whisper, "We were surrounded by Burgundians. Then they withdrew. Later, some recrossed the ice. Then the Alans came. They shouted to us that the Marcomanni were crossing the river higher up and that they would reinforce us in return for food and weapons. I was a fool. I let them in. But Goar was with them and I knew you trusted him. Inside the camp they attacked us. There were too many of them. We fought back. We tried to escape. I fired the camp. Some of us broke out. Then we blundered into the Marcomanni. I gave my men a meeting point and told them to run and hide, and find it later, in the dark. We split up. I was wounded and lost. I made for the road. That is all I know."

Fredegar said, "He speaks the truth, that one. The Alans had spears on which were the heads of those men you sent across the ice." He looked at me and smiled. "You do not know your friends."

"What Roman ever does," I said bitterly. "How many men have you?"

The Frank said, "I brought two thousand over the river. Some are dead. Some are prisoners in your laager down the road. The others are scattered. But they will come back."

"How many, Scudilio?"

He gasped with pain. He whispered, "I do not know. Perhaps three hundred."

I said sharply, "Get that wound attended to, one of you."

I turned back to Goar, who was standing alone, very straight and still, his face gray in the moonlight, the sword naked in his hand. It was very cold, but I could see the beads of sweat slipping down his face as he stood and waited.

I said, harshly, "This was planned. Who planned it?"

Quintus said, impatiently, "Does it matter now?"

I stared at Goar. "Oh, yes," I said. "It matters. Guntiarus is not that clever. Respendial would never come to terms with those who had betrayed him, even though they were his brothers, and Gunderic has too sharp a tongue. Talien was a clever man, but he is dead." I paused. I said, "It needed someone else, someone who knew me and who knew how I might think and plan my campaign, someone who had done this kind of thing before. ..."

Scudilio muttered, "I was approached and offered bribes, but I refused."

"You should have told me."

"I did not like to. You trusted me so little. I knew that, when you gave the orders to the tribune to burn the bridge, and not me. I was afraid."

I said to Goar, "He got at you, didn't he? After Marcomir was dead, he worked upon you. You were loyal to me so long as you thought I might end by being the victor, but after the battle on the east bank you were not so sure. You thought I might lose, and you were afraid for yourself. So you began to change sides, and promised to betray me when the time was right. Oh, you chose it well. It was brilliantly done; you took the boy and returned him to his father to secure your rear, and you fought a little to make everything right. You might even have stayed on my side if I had stopped them crossing the river. But how could I, when you let the Marcomanni through, and murdered my wretched men? They were only fools because they trusted you upon my orders."

I turned my back on him and mounted my horse. Quintus looked at me questioningly. I said, "Get mounted. We must get on. We have wasted too much time already on a matter of little importance."

Goar said hoarsely, "What will you do with me?"

"If you were a man I would let Scudilio have the privilege of killing you. But you are not a man—you are nothing. Put down that sword before you cut yourself with it."

He saw Quintus mounted, watching him intently. He dropped the sword into the snow. I looked about me and then caught Quintus' eye. We had everything that we needed. Our thoughts were the same.

I said, "You are a Christian, I believe."

He tried hard to swallow. He licked his lips and I saw his red beard quiver but not with cold. "Yes, I am," he muttered. "What is it to you?"

I said, "Then I will give you an end fitting for a proper Christian." I turned my head. "Centurion, crucify this man."

The moon was rising now and we moved on in silence, our horses plodding one behind the other, their riders sitting slumped in the saddle. I closed my eyes in a stupid attempt to shut out the full horror of what I now knew. For the man I had left behind me in the darkness I felt nothing. I thought only of the final treachery, of the destruction of Bingium, and of Scudilio, whom I had not trusted enough.

I said, "But we parted friends. Why, Julian? Why?"

We rode on to where the legion rested in the snow. They were used to the cold now. They did not shiver: they slept. The cohort commanders got to their feet and gathered round my horse. I told them what had happened.

"We cannot storm Bingium—or what is left of it—with the Marcomanni in our rear. If we wait till tomorrow they will have closed the road and their men will be lining the Nava. Our only chance is to outmarch them—now. We shall skirt the Bingium hills and move upriver. There is a ford some way up and a track that will bring us back on to the road to Treverorum. One of Scudilio's men will guide us."

I coughed. "Quintus, I want a detachment of five reliable men to ride on to Treverorum and see that all the available weapons and stores are brought out to the thirtieth milestone without delay. In addition, I want two squadrons to go with them to patrol the road in the direction of Bingium. If contact is made with the enemy they must send word back at once. I want to know what signal towers are still held for us. Those in opposition must be taken or burned—whichever is the easier. Arrange for more cavalry to forage for food. The men are to go on half rations as from tonight." Aquila nodded. "Someone find Fredbal, the farrier. I want a word with him. Now get moving."

He came, in a few moments, and stood before me, his head down, his hands clutching at his sword. The marching had tired him and he looked ill and old. Perhaps I looked the same to him.

I said, "This is not your fight. You paid your debts long ago. I want you out of this. I need a man to go with the messengers to Treverorum and carry a letter I have written." I was writing, as I spoke, clumsily upon a tablet. "Give this to the Bishop. It is instructions about the safety of the legion's treasure chest. He will know what to do. And this"—I handed him a second tablet—"is for the Curator. He must tell the army of Gaul to hurry, or they will be too late."

He said, "Why trust me and not your men?" He spoke as to an equal.

I said gently, "There are thirty reasons and they are all years. You are a good hater."

He nodded. "I would rather stay and kill a Vandal." He spoke with a fierce regret.

"That I know. You will still have the chance, believe me."

He stuffed the tablets inside his tunic. "I'll go," he muttered. "You can trust me."

I shook my head. "It is your hatred I trust. Now go and join the others."

He gave me the parody of a salute and shambled off into the darkness.

We marched in silence, so that there was no noise but the jingling of a horse's bit, and the steady crunch of nailed sandals upon the hard snow. The moon was well up now, so that it was not difficult to see the way. I prayed that both the Alans inside Bingium and the Marcomanni outside it would believe that we had camped for the night, somewhere between the two of them, and would not have patrols out, keeping watch. Presently, we came under the shadow of the wedge-shaped hills, on the other side of which lay the ruined camp on which I had staked all our hopes. Here, the road ran straight toward the Nava and the fort, and here, too, the track that we must follow, curved left toward the ford of which Scudilio had spoken, before we put him with the other wounded on the wagon. At this junction the column came to a slow, unsteady halt, and a horseman cantered back to say that the advance guard had run into a night patrol of Marcomanni, that a sharp fight was going on, but that the General had the matter in hand.

The men stood off the side of the road and I sat, relaxed upon my horse, waiting. I called out softly to a decurion of cavalry, "Find out how the commander, Scudilio, does, and send me that Frankish man we took prisoner." He saluted and rode off down the line.

After half an hour the column moved on again and I rode over bloodstained snow, saw bodies lying in a ditch, and two of our men with arrows in their chest. A few minutes later a beacon glimmered on the hills to our right, and I knew then that we had been seen by watchers on the cliffs, and that the alarm would soon be given. We quickened our pace and dropped down a steep slope between tall pine trees, bowed with snow, and could hear the patter of water somewhere to our front. The wagons were in difficulties and men had to be detailed to help them over the bad ground. They held our tents, our cooking gear, our palisade stakes, our entrenching tools, fodder for the horses, our medical supplies, our wounded, and our spare arms. They were essential to our continuing life as a legion, and without them we should be doomed. Each man carried his weapons and rations for five days; that was all the food we had, and some of it would have to be shared with the men who had come out of Bingium and who had been able to bring nothing with them, save their weapons. There were others to feed as well: Franks, who were loyal to Fredegar the remainder of the garrison at Moguntiacum and the sections from the signal posts, who joined us as we passed them by. How many all these made, I did not know. I left matters like that to my quartermaster. He would tell me soon enough.

Our pace was slower now because of the bad going. The men sweated, even in the cold, and they walked hunched up against the drifting snowflakes. Sometime before midnight there was another halt, and in the silence I could hear the screams of horses, the clash of swords, and the sound of men shouting. This time our halt was much longer, and a messenger rode back down the line to tell me that the cavalry had had to dismount because of the steepness of the bank on the far side of the Nava, and that a cohort was in action against a group of tribesmen.

"Are they many?"

"The General thinks about eight hundred. They are armed with bows and axes, and are well placed."

"Do you need me?"

The trooper grinned. "No, sir. I was told that the Legate was not to be troubled. The ala commander has the matter in hand."

"Which ala?"

"The Fourth."

"Ah! Marius. Very good."

It was two hours, however, before the enemy position was taken and a cohort had to be called in to assist.

The Nava was wide but shallow, which was fortunate, for the ice did not hold, and we had to wade clumsily through the bitter water that rose to our waists and numbed us with the cold. Then we had a two-and-a-half-mile climb up a steep and twisting track that barely showed through the thickening fall of snow. It was hard work, walking in wet boots on a surface that made one slip back every time a step was taken. The horses had to be led also, and the wagons pushed and pulled by hand, ten men to a wagon. And all the time we were conscious of empty stomachs and tired eyes, and the wind cut through our cloaks, so that we were wet outside with the snow and wet through with our sweat. But no one dropped out or complained.

Once at the top of the climb the going became easier and we walked through a pine forest that protected us a little from the eternal beat of the wind. We had had no sleep now for twenty-two hours and we stumbled on mechanically. The agony of marching was to be preferred to that which the enemy would offer if we fell alive into his hands. Two miles further on we dropped down a shallow slope and walked along the shoulder of a high ridge that banked a narrow, twisting stream. There was no track that one could see and the men marched in pairs, so that each might help the other while the wagons were pushed and pulled between one tree and the next. Then we left the stream and struck a track that was deeply rutted beneath the loose surface snow. It was dawn now, and we could see each other's faces, dark of eye, unshaven, and deathly tired. Two hours later, walking as though in our sleep, with blistered feet, cramped muscles, and shoulders rubbed raw by the friction of our armor, we reached the road that led to Treverorum. To my front was a smooth, round pillar, nearly as tall as myself, and with a cap of snow upon it. It was one of the milestones set up by the Emperor Hadrianus, and the lettering upon it, I remember, was so worn that it was hardly legible. After I had seen it for the first time, I had complained to the officials at Treverorum but they had simply shrugged their shoulders, and nothing had been done. To the right of the stone, a cavalry picket slept beneath the tethered heads of their horses, and a tired sentry rocked on his feet, leaning upon his spear before the embers of a wood fire.

I kicked the squadron commander awake, and he yawned in my face, apologetically. "The signal posts between here and Bingium, sir, are in their hands. I burned the first four and we killed their men as they jumped to safety. At the fifth the enemy were guarding the road in strength, so we retired. The first three posts back up the road, however, are still loyal."

Quintus said, "Can we hold the road here?" He looked at the high bank with the thick woods that stretched upward to the skyline. "It's a strong position to defend."

"Perhaps. I'm too tired to think. The men are dead on their feet, too. They had better camp here, off the road. Put the wagons across the pass in front of the tower. A pity we had to burn it."

The squadron commander choked back a laugh. "We couldn't force our own ditches, sir."

"Yes, they were well sited. Put a guard inside the place anyway and tell off a party to repair the palisade."

We slept for four hours and when we awoke it was to a black sky and falling snow. The nearest enemy had been three miles away when we slept, and the main force six miles further on at Bingium, where only the Alans, if they were not too drunk on the garrison's wine, would have been in a fit state to march at dawn. Had they done so, we should have been attacked by now. Yet it was more probable, I thought, that they would remain there and leave matters in the hands of the Marcomanni. The Alans were leaderless now, and they had their own lands to look to. The Marcomanni under Hermeric were our nearest foe. So far they had proved to be clumsy and slow and stupid. Gunderic, I was sure, would never have let me get so far. The Vandal host was another matter. They needed food desperately and there was little enough in the surrounding countryside, with its pitiful handful of villages and its wasted land. They would march for Bingium, where they knew there was food, but not enough. There would be quarrels between the chiefs, and fights between their men. It would all give us a little time.

"We have about three hours, possibly five, Quintus. In that time we must fell trees, build palisades, and dig ditches. We have no ballistae worth speaking about." I looked at the road. It looped and coiled, like the

Mosella, between high hills whose steep slopes were covered with trees. "All they have to do to outflank us is to climb through the woods. This road looks easy to defend, but it isn't. And I can't make any effective use of cavalry here."

A bearded man, who had been drawing lines in the snow with a stick, said quietly, "Is it wise to go on fighting like a soldier?"

It was Fredegar.

I said, equally quietly, "It is the only way I know how to fight. We held them for seven days at Moguntiacum because I was a soldier."

He said, "I understand."

"How many of your people are with us now?"

He said calmly, "I have not been able to count them all. I am waiting, still, for more to come in. About three thousand."

The man I had spoken to the night before came up and saluted. He said, "The commandant, Scudilio, will be all right, so the doctor says. The arrow has been removed, but without too much loss of blood. He is trying to get up, but the orderlies are holding him down on the wagon."

"Keep him there. He can walk when he is fit and not before. Aquila, how many of his men are with us?"

"Two hundred and forty, sir."

"Does that include the wounded?"

"It is all those who can fight."

Fredegar said, "Let me hold the pass for you. Leave me two centuries of your men. Give me some auxiliaries also. I will hold this position for two days while you withdraw and set up further ambushes at each signal post down the road. Leave me one troop of horse, also, to act as messengers and to fight as a rear guard. In this way we will slow them down and give time for your ballistae to arrive."

I hesitated. He put his head on one side and smiled. "I am not a young man, but I am a good fighter."

"Right. We will do as you suggest."

At that moment the sentry shouted, and we saw a horseman coming down the road from Treverorum at a canter. Quintus shaded his eyes and swore softly. At first I thought the animal was riderless, but as it came nearer I saw that its rider was lying along the beast's neck. The horse trotted up, blowing froth, and then stood still before us with heaving flanks and lowered head. Its rider slipped sideways out of the saddle and fell to the ground before anyone could catch him. He was one of the five men I had sent on to Treverorum the night before.

He was still alive but there was blood on his neck and on his left thigh. They looked like spear wounds. He was bleeding badly and his face had no color in it. I bent down and took him in my arms.

He said in a whisper, "We got six miles up the road to that big bend. There we met the survivors from the garrison at Boudobrigo." He choked. "Water, please." A soldier ran to fetch some. He swallowed a little. "The fort fell two days ago. They were hunted across the hills." He spat blood, choked again, and was silent. Presently he opened his eyes. He said, "Burgundians on the road to Treverorum. They caught us. Two got away. We covered them. The others died. I escaped." He stared up at me, his eyes frightened. He was only a boy. He said, "Guntiarus has his war host out. Thousands of them." The blood was coming very slowly now from the wound in his thigh, in spite of the efforts of the medical orderly who knelt beside me. The wounded man looked faintly puzzled. He said in a whisper, "I didn't know it was so easy." I looked at the orderly, who shook his head. Presently the blood stopped coming altogether and I laid him down upon the snow.

Quintus said quietly, "I could not have ridden two hundred yards with a wound like that."

Fredegar said calmly, "Let my plan stay. It is still the only one. But keep your cavalry. You will need them all. Leave me only a few horses."

"As you wish."

Quintus said, "Well, I had better get on and clear the Burgundians off the road."

"Yes."

The trumpet blew, and I said to Fredegar, "Join us when you can."

He stroked his beard. He said, "If I cannot join you, then I shall be with Marcomir. Either way I shall be content."

I gripped him by the arm, and then swung myself onto my horse.

He looked up at me and smiled grimly. "I have much to avenge."

The Franks were spreading out on the slopes above the road; trees were being felled, and the palisade round the tower was being straightened up, as I rode off at the head of my legion. Ahead of us, Quintus and his cavalry were fading from sight into a blur of falling snow. I wrapped my cloak about me and chewed a dry biscuit. I was sick with fatigue and with worry.

We marched, and, at intervals of two miles, a double century would fall out to prepare defenses and lay an ambush. Three hours later we reached the scene of the fighting. The Burgundians had blocked the road with fallen trees, had roasted the garrison of the signal post to death, and were spread out along the slopes, on either side of the road. Quintus had failed to break through, had taken his horses well to the rear, and was feeling the enemy position with his scouts. The main body of his troopers were off the road and out of sight. It was then the middle of the afternoon and behind us, in the distance, echoing between the hills, we could hear a distant murmur that was the sound of Fredegar and his men engaged in battle.

By nightfall we had failed to dislodge the Burgundians, and it was then, while we were sitting, exhausted, round a small fire, that a messenger rode in to say that Fredegar was in difficulties.

"Our people cannot hold them," he said, in his vile Latin. "They are fighting all the five tribes at once, and soon they will be surrounded. We have used the last of our arrows." He put his hand on my arm. "My chief does not ask this, but I do. He is an old man and was a great warrior once. Can you not help him? He is prepared to die, not for your Emperor, but for you, and to keep faith with Marcomir."

I rubbed my eyes. "Quintus, we've got to get behind these Burgundians. Try to get a cohort round to the left, if it takes all night. Send fifty horsemen across country to make for the road in their rear. Send men with loud voices who can blow trumpets. They are to pretend to be reinforcements. Brushwood tied to the saddles will kick up the snow. It's dry enough."

He said, "That trick won't work twice."

"It will. We never played it on them. Get those men moving now. And send another detachment down to help Fredegar. Give them trumpets too. Make the Vandals think the Burgundians have been beaten and that we've sent help."

I turned to the Frank. "Tell your chief to ask for a truce. They will grant it. They have lost enough men already. Fredegar can say what he likes, but while he is saying it, the bulk of his men are to retire down the road upon us. In this way he will escape."

"But it is not honorable."

I shot out my hand and seized him by the shoulder. "I am not fighting for honor," I said. "I am fighting for the life of this province, and I will employ any means to protect it. Go now and do as I say."

"What will the Vandals think?" he muttered dismally.

"What do I care what they think? What are the Marcomanni and the Vandals to me? My honor lies in my hands, not in theirs."

The deception worked. It was an old trick, though I had never tried it before. Gunderic and Hermeric at first refused to parley, but Respendial, whose pride had been hurt by the defection of his cousin, insisted on a truce. If he could win another tribe to his side it would restore his self-esteem and his position in the eyes of the others. The meeting took place at daybreak and, while Fredegar talked, his men began to slip away from their positions, keeping to the woods and not descending to the road until they were well out of sight. Difficulties arose over terms and Fredegar said—it was of course a lie—that we were camped a little way down the road, that it was necessary to reassure me that he could hold his position, and that to make victory certain, the Vandals should pass through his lines that evening. They could then make a night attack and take us unawares. In return for this the Franks, under his leadership, were to be allowed to return to the Rhenus and hold land on both banks, between Bingium and Moguntiacum. It was now time for the morning meal, so both parties withdrew to eat in their own camps and consider the terms. All this Fredegar told me when he rejoined us.

"How long did it take them to discover they had been tricked?"

"I do not know," he said cheerfully. "We kept a sharp watch but we never saw them following us. How goes it with you?"

"Our trick worked, too. The Burgundians have retreated north into the hills."

"So!" he said. "And what do we do now?"

"We march," I said. "Nothing stands between us and Treverorum except fatigue. That is the most difficult enemy of all that we have to conquer."

The retreat went on. We were out of the worst of the hills but, all the time, we were climbing upward to a highland plain that exposed us to the worst of the weather. The wind had fallen, however, there was no more snow, and the sun shone and warmed our spirits. At intervals I would drop a mixed group of soldiers and Franks to make an ambush and, in every instance, my orders were the same. "Hold the position until they look to be overwhelming you. Then burn the signal tower, if there is one, and retire behind the next ambush and march on the rear guard. Keep your casualties as light as possible. Don't try to be brave. There will be time for that later."

We marched slowly and in self-imposed silence. There was only the everlasting rumble of the wheels of the ox carts, the monotonous clanging of the cooking pots that hung beneath them, the tired shuffling of feet, and the occasional whimper of a wounded man, tried beyond the point of human endurance. The men held their spears reversed over their shoulders, the blades wrapped in cloth to keep them dry, and the centurions strode stolidly behind their men, swearing softly if a soldier showed signs of falling out. Once, a man parched with thirst picked up a handful of snow and raised it to his mouth. I struck him across the back with my stick. "Lick the frozen snow, you idiot, and you may blister your tongue. Be patient. Wait until the next halt."

The cavalry led their horses. Every hour we stopped for ten minutes, and the section commanders would pass round a flask of vinegar, so that each man might swallow a mouthful, while the mules were offloaded and their backs examined for gall marks. At midday I went back to the wagon train and spoke to Scudilio. He had a better color in his face now, and pleaded with me to let him march with his men. "No," I said. "You will need all your strength at the thirtieth milestone."

He said, "I let you down. All your plans in retreat depended upon the holding of Bingium."

I shook my head. "We might not have been able to hold it in any event. Don't think about it. Remember, I trusted him also. Up to the very last, I trusted him. If there is blame, then let us share it equally. It does not matter now."

"I should march with my men," he said. "I know what you think of the auxiliaries. I wanted, so much, to prove you wrong."

"There is nothing now to prove."

That afternoon, because of the icy conditions, we made only six miles, even though I took the precaution of continuing the march an hour after sundown, in order to keep our lead on the enemy. The next morning we set out a little after sunrise, as was our custom, and I had cavalry patrols range the countryside, looking for farms, huts, or villages where they might pick up food, for the men were suffering acutely from being on half rations in the intense cold. They were more cheerful now, however, and began to sing those tuneless marching songs that all soldiers sing. They were all the same, usually obscene, about girls or a girl, had innumerable verses, and seemed to go on forever. But I had not heard them sing since that last time when we had marched out of Treverorum, in what seemed to be another life. Then, we had been a legion. We were a legion still, and I was much cheered by the thought.

Two hours later, a messenger rode up from the rear guard.

"There is the noise of fighting behind us. We are short of two ambush parties, sir."

"They must have caught up at last. Tell your commander to hold his ground till he has collected the two groups. I want no one left behind. Do you understand?"

He was back again, an hour later. "Their horsemen are in sight," he said breathlessly. "We picked up one patrol, but the other, so they think, was wiped out."

I nodded. "Your commander knows what to do."

By the middle of the afternoon we could see their horsemen coming down the road. They were a great distance away, but they were clearly silhouetted against the white dazzle of the snow. They closed up slowly, for there were not many of them, and then attacked the rear guard. Their charges were wild and undisciplined, and were beaten off easily enough. Later, more and more horsemen joined them, and they got bolder, and followed us closely, making quick, fierce attacks whenever the opportunity occurred. Quintus kept a screen of cavalry either side of the column, for there were heavy drifts on the road, and the marching was slow and painful. Soon our men got so used to watching cavalry fights take place out of bow-shot range that, presently, they took no notice. Occasionally, an enemy horseman would break through and canter up in a flurry of snow, and make a clumsy sweep at a helmeted figure trudging alongside a cart. The legionary might go down, unprotesting, too tired to defend himself, and the Vandal ride off, brandishing his sword in triumph. Sometimes, however, a bowman would hastily string his bow and loose an arrow, so that the man would continue his journey back to his waiting comrades, dying over the neck of his horse.

On the third day, after they caught us, we marched ten miles, and now there were horsemen all about us, in groups ranging from a dozen to twenty or thirty, but of the columns of their infantry there was no sign. That night their cavalry camped within two miles of us, and we were attacked, when the moon rose, by men both on horse and on foot. The enemy were a mixture of Vandals, Quadi, and Marcomanni, and their efforts were, as Quintus remarked contemptuously, halfhearted in the extreme. A second attack, just after daybreak, was ended by a high wind and a sharp fall of snow which created a small blizzard, and both sides were compelled to cease fighting because of these conditions. That night I broke camp as soon as it was dark, despite the fact that the men had been on the march for nine hours. Again we made a forced march through fresh snow, the cavalry breaking the trail ahead of us in slow and coldly painful fashion. The pickets that we had left to keep the fires alight caught up with us late the next day and reported that the enemy had not sent out patrols to the camp until well past daylight, and did not realize they had been tricked until the pickets rode off. We marched again all day, the men singing their tuneless songs, Fredegar limping beside the aquilifer, and Quintus bringing up the rear of the column and looking, as usual, a part of his horse.

In the late afternoon the sky cleared and I could see the sun, a circle of molten gold, just above the tops of the trees that thickened the horizon to our front. We dropped into a hollow, passed an abandoned straggle of huts, and then began to climb up a long slope, and either side of the road the snow lay thick and undisturbed, as far as a man on a horse could see. The legionaries began to quicken their pace, and the cavalry, as though at command, mounted their horses. A stir of expectation ran through the column, and faces began to peer through the slits in the wagon covers. There, ahead of us, between a gap in the trees, black against the sky, stood the framework of a signal tower, and the smoke from it streamed upward into the cold air, as a message of welcome against our coming. We knew then that we had reached our destination—the thirtieth milestone out of Augusta Treverorum.

It was now the thirteenth day of January. For seven days we had held Moguntiacum against the hatred and envy and greed of five tribes. Then, we had retreated for six days through the hills in the most appalling conditions of ice and snow, fighting a rear-guard action of savage skirmishes over a distance of seventy-odd miles. Yet not one man had fallen out who had not previously been injured by the swords or axes of the Barbarians. It was still a legion that I commanded. As I went forward to greet the post commander, while my tired men began to bivouac behind the ditches we had prepared all those months before, a raven flew above my head and cawed dismally. I shivered. I knew, in my heart, that the legion had made its last march.

CHAPTER XVIII

Inside the palisade I met Agilio, no longer the carefree boy I had last seen a short while ago; his face was strained and he looked anxious the whole time.

"Is everything in order?" I asked.

He nodded dumbly, his eyes wide as he watched my tired men file past toward the site of their camp in the rear. He had not believed me when I had warned him of what might happen; he had not visualized the possibility of defeat.

"Is Flavius here?"

"Yes, sir. He has been here several days."

"Have you seen anything of the garrisons from the other fonts—Salisio, Boudobrigo, Confluentes?"

He shook his head.

"I signaled them to withdraw days ago," I said. "They must have been destroyed by now. We saw nothing of them upon the road."

Flavius was inside the tower, and Quintus and Fredegar joined me there. We sat down on the narrow benches in the living quarters and drank the wine Agilio offered us, in silence. We were so tired and so cold that nothing seemed to matter except sleep. Even death would have been welcomed as a friend at that moment. At length I roused myself with an effort. "What supplies have you got?"

Flavius said grimly, "All I could lay my hands on. Many were evacuating the city when I left. I had to kill in order to take what I wanted. I have thirty wagons, loaded with biscuits, salt meat, corn and vinegar, as well as a little wine. Also arrowheads and shafts, ballistae bolts and spears. Enough food, that is, for five thousand men for two days on full rations."

I said, "We have Fredegar's Franks to feed, as well as the signal post people we picked up on the way. How many did you bring?"

"The two centuries you left me, and four hundred others."

"Any horses?"

"Sixty. That was all I could muster. I had to use mules for the wagons."

"Artillery?"

"Four ballistae and six carroballistae."

"Very well." I nodded my dismissal.

Flavius stood his ground. "There is just one thing, sir. I saw the Bishop before I left. He told me he had written to the Praefectus at Arelate, begging for help."

"So did I, but I had no reply."

"But I have a letter from the Magister Equitum per Gallias."

"Give it to me." I read Chariobaudes' letter carefully, while the others waited. "I would help you if I could and as I promised. But I learn that the Alemanni are across the Rhenus in strength and have captured two other cities, as well as Borbetomagus. This means that the road to Divodurum lies open before them. It must be obvious, therefore, that my first duty is to protect this city, else they would have an open pathway into the heart of Gaul. The Praefectus Praetorio has confirmed this decision. Do not think too harshly of me, therefore. I am confident that all will yet be well with you. Treverorum is a strong city to defend and these people are not good at siege warfare." I read it through to the end and then flung it at Quintus. "So much for the help he promised us. The praefectus can escape by boat, of course. He risks nothing; he forgets nothing, save his duty."

Quintus said carefully, "From Chariobaudes' point of view he is quite correct."

"Of course. Only he doesn't realize that the Alemanni have no intention of marching inland. He will keep his men there, and nothing will happen."

Quintus looked at the others in turn. "You will keep silent about this message. Is that understood?" They nodded. To me he said, "There is still some good advice in the letter." He paused. He said, "If we pull the legion back to Treverorum we could hold it against them easily. If we stay here we risk being destroyed."

"Fetch Aquila."

He came, shaking the snow from his shoulders as he entered.

"It is snowing again," he said.

"Aquila, can the men march another thirty miles back to the city?"

He hesitated.

"If we march at dawn? Can they?"

He shook his head. "I do not think so," he said slowly.

Flavius said, "There is a lot of heavy snow on the road between here and the city. I had difficulty in getting through with the wagons."

Aquila said, "The men must have some rest, sir."

"It is only thirty miles," said Quintus. He paused, as an orderly entered and lit the lamp. He leaned back and stretched himself. He said, "They won't give us long even if we do stay here."

Fredegar said, "They are tired, as we are, and just as hungry. Yet behind these ditches we are safe until they attack us." He gazed at me ironically.

The post commander said anxiously, "I kept the ditches cleared as you ordered, sir, though it was not easy."

I smiled at him. "Nothing has been easy for any of us."

Quintus said, "They must have Treverorum. If we hold it, then they cannot have it. Without food they will die."

Aquila said, "I understand that, sir." He glanced at me. He said, "They know you intended to fight here. They are full of confidence. This they will lose if they are asked to march again. As for myself—" He hesitated.

"Yes?"

"They are marching faster than we. In spite of our start their cavalry has already caught up."

The door swung open and Marius burst in. He said, "One of my patrols has just come in. The main Vandal column has just reached that village in the valley."

"Are they camping?"

"Yes, sir, but they have cavalry out in the snow, about four hundred yards from the palisade."

I looked at Quintus. He smiled and shrugged his shoulders.

"That settles it," I said. "Put out double sentries; get those enemy patrols driven away and establish pickets of our own, five hundred yards from the camp. They must have fires ready so that they can signal at a moment's notice. Now, let us get some sleep.

But there was little rest for any of us. Units had to be reorganized to allow for casualties, food distributed, and time allowed for the repair of broken equipment and damaged boots. The armorers had to get fires going; spearheads had to be fitted onto new shafts, bow cords renewed, and arrows flighted. The ditches, partially filled, in spite of Agilio's efforts, with the loose snow of the night, had to be cleared, and the artillery sited on hurriedly built platforms. The wagons were emptied of their supplies and drawn up in arranged positions on the flanks, so as to make a barricade against attack by infiltration, and the palisade had to be strengthened with timber and brushwood.

The camp was its usual square, twelve hundred yards on either side, surrounded by a timber palisade and an earthwork, built the previous year. The two corners facing the enemy were strengthened by the addition of wagons, as well as platforms on which were mounted two carroballistae. Fifty yards in front of the gate was the signal tower, surrounded by a circle of triple ditches and a palisade. In front of this, stretching to left and right, was a four-foot palisade, earthed and well dug-in, behind which the legion would fight when on the defensive. Protecting this there was the usual line of triple ditches, their bottoms spiked with sharpened branches. In addition, however, I had had dug in front of this a wide zigzag ditch. It was fifteen feet wide and ten feet deep, with narrow gaps at the ends nearest to our position. An enemy approaching would be forced by the closing up of this ditch to concentrate his attack at single points where the gaps occurred. We, however, could concentrate our fire on these gaps and so destroy him as he tried to come through. In this way I hoped to reduce the effectiveness of the enemy's vast superiority of numbers. Squadrons of cavalry and archers would protect our flanks, and I had no doubt but that we could hold our ground, so long as we had sufficient men and missiles to last out.

All morning the men worked, while Quintus and I rode carefully over the ground upon which we would fight. Facing east, from the signal tower, the ground was level for about two hundred yards. It then sloped gently to the trees in the distance. On the right of the road the ground sloped away to a great wood of firs that guarded our flank. On the left the ground dipped for, perhaps, half a mile, and then climbed a long gentle slope to the horizon. The plain was thinly covered, here and there, by clumps of bushes. A little to the right of the Bingium road there was a small copse in which I intended to put a century to lie in ambush. The snow was packed hard underneath the surface, and there appeared to be few drifts. Quintus seemed satisfied and, at length, we returned to camp.

At midday, while I was eating a bowl of hot porridge, we saw their horsemen in the distance. They came up to within a hundred yards of our furthest pickets. They circled the ground slowly but did not attack us. Presently they rode off, and in the afternoon the men who were not on duty washed themselves, and then sat outside their tents. The wind had dropped, the sun shone fitfully, and the soldiers laughed as they rolled the dice and gambled away the pay that so many of them would never receive. They looked less tired after their long sleep; they smiled, made jokes, told each other bawdy stories, and some of them sang.

Just before dusk one of the sentries reported men on the Confluentes road. I climbed the tower, and I could see them, a dark, straggling column, moving slowly toward us. The Vandals could see them too, and their horsemen spread out and rode toward them. Quintus hastily mounted three squadrons and led them out to intercept the Vandals. An hour later, with bloody cavalry skirmishes going on behind them, the column reached the safety of the palisade. It consisted of three hundred men, wounded, hungry, and exhausted, all that was left of the garrison at Confluentes and the crews of the signal posts along their line of march. Of the garrisons from Boudobrigo and Salisio there was no news, and I knew now that they would not come. They had been destroyed in the hills by the Burgundians, led by their King, Guntiarus, who had once been proud to call himself an ally of Rome.

I went to the signal tower. There, I washed and shaved carefully. My beard was quite white and I was glad to see it go. I was drying myself with a towel when Quintus came in.

He said, "What do you intend to do, Maximus? If you will take my advice it would be best to hold our position here. Let them break themselves on the palisade, as they did at Moguntiacum. On the defensive we shall lose fewer men, and they will starve and grow weak out in the snow."

I said, "We have supplies for only a few days. There will be no more help out of Treverorum now. What do we do when we are out of food and missiles? Beg for mercy?"

He was silent.

I said, "By rights, we should be in winter quarters; all campaigning over for the season." I smiled bitterly. "But this is not a civilized war; it is a fight to the death."

"You have a legion still," he said quietly. "Are we to throw all away on a gamble then?"

I threw the towel on the bed. "Oh, Quintus, it has all been a gamble. What Stilicho proposed that night was only a gamble. I have known that all along."

"Well then?"

"We might hold them, as you say, on the palisade. If the men were fresh I could be certain of it. But, in any case, you never win a battle by fighting on the defensive."

He looked at me steadily. He said, "You are going out to fight them on the plain, in pitched battle." It was a statement, not a question.

"Yes. I doubt very much if we can beat them. But whatever we do is a gamble. We should never survive a retreat to Treverorum now. All generals, at the very last, must be gamblers at heart. I shall stake all on a last throw."

He gave a long sigh. "In a way I am glad," he said. "It is better to try, and fail, than not to try at all."

"Oh, I am going to try all right."

In the evening we walked through the camp, and I chatted to the men as I went, and inspected the defenses carefully.

"Well?" said Quintus when I had finished. "What do you think?"

I said, "Even if they beat us, it will cost them more than they realize. We shall not have failed altogether."

In the darkness we stood on the platform of the signal tower and watched the lights of their fires; little sparks, winking across the snow. Later, there was a single clash of arms when one of their patrols met one of ours by mistake. Both withdrew at once and there were no casualties. I went to bed early that night, and I slept well and I dreamed no dreams.

At dawn the legion marched out of camp, leaving only its wounded behind. The men paraded in their ranks, century by century, cohort by cohort, their backs to the palisade, while I inspected them. The light shone upon their scarlet standards, upon the polished armor of the officers, and upon the white cloaks of the cavalry. Then, one of their number, who claimed to have been a priest in his time, blessed them. I sat my horse, with Quintus on my right hand and Fabianus on my left, and I spoke to them. It would be for the last time; I knew that. I had no illusions.

"You'll be glad to know that we have stopped running away. What generals call a strategic withdrawal, and you a long bloody march, is now over." There was a murmur at this and some laughter. I went on: "The tribune Flavius, has told me that in a few days we shall have help. The army of Gaul is marching to our aid. Like you, I think they have left it a bit late, but that's better than not coming at all. Your old general, Stilicho, has kept his promise. I knew he would not let us down." They cheered loudly at this.

I said, "You have held them already for fourteen days, and you can hold them for four or five days more. They, too, are tired, hungry, and cold, and they have no supplies such as we have received from our gallant civilian friends at Treverorum." They laughed.

I paused. I said, "Now, we are going out to do battle. I am not fighting behind ditches this time. We are going to beat them, as we beat the enemy before at Pollentia. One hard fight is all I ask, and then it will be over." I paused again.

I said, in a loud voice, "You wanted once to elect me to the purple, and I refused. Win this battle for me, now, and I will not refuse if you do so again. I promised you gold when this campaign was over, and I shall keep my promise, if you will keep yours to me." I turned and pointed at the Eagle, borne by the aquilifer at my back. The worn, polished bronze of that fierce head and outspread wings had been a silent witness to speeches like this before. Below, on the placard, were stamped the letters that had been carried into every corner of the empire—S.P.Q.R.

"A good many weak-headed people think that the Empire is dying," I said. "That is what the Alemanni of Sunno, the Quadi, the Marcomanni of Hermeric, the Alans of Respendial, and the Vandals of Gunderic think." At my signal, the aquilifer held the Eagle high, so that the early-morning sun glinted on the polished metal. "Prove to me now, in the name of the senate and the people of Rome, and of the Eagle of the Twentieth, that they are wrong."

Normally, they cheered at the end of a speech, but now they remained silent, and I was startled and worried. I coughed to clear my throat. For a moment or two I had almost believed what I had said to them. Their silence began to frighten me.

To my surprise, Quintus moved his horse forward, so that he was sideways onto the front rank. He drew his sword, that lovely curved sword that Stilicho had given him, and raised it in the air. "I give you a new Emperor," he cried. "I give you an Emperor of Gaul—and of Britannia, too, if the fates are kind. I give you a new Emperor of the West. I give you—Maximus!"

They cried my name then, three times, and began to pound their shields with their spears. And, as the roar of "Maximus!" filled my ears, I raised my hand in acknowledgment, and it was hard for me to see.

The legion deployed quickly onto the frozen ground in front of the ditches. My center was composed of a mixture of heavy and light cohorts, drawn up three deep, so as to give the maximum width to our front. There was one carroballista to each century, run slightly forward so as to have a good field of fire. Then, on each flank, there was a wing of archers, their lines slanted forward at an angle. Behind the center, spread out two deep, were the auxiliaries under the command of Scudilio, and mixed in with them, to make the line seem more solid, were the auxiliary horse, arranged three deep, by troops and not by squadrons. On the left wing, beyond the archers and slightly to their rear, were Fredegar's Franks, who had strict instructions to prevent the enemy from turning the flank. Beyond the right wing of archers, and flung well forward, were the seamen and signal post auxiliaries, a weak band, strengthened by a handful of legionaries and commanded by Marius. He was to turn the enemy's flank when the opportunity arose. Far out from the battle line, to left and right, were the regular cavalry, spread out in the shape of crescent moons. The left was under the command of Quintus, the right was led by Fabianus. In the copse that lay between Marius and Fabianus, I had concealed a small party under the leadership of Flavius. It was composed of all the men he had brought from Treverorum. They were fresh and determined, and he was a good soldier. I placed great reliance on his judgment to act at the right time. My headquarters I established behind the center of the third row of the fighting line. Agilio and Aquila were with me, and my bodyguard were deployed behind, dismounted and awaiting my orders. Julius Optatus was in charge of the camp and of the tiny reserves I had left there to defend it. He was responsible for bringing up spare horses and missiles, as required, and for the removal and care of the wounded.

The Barbarians, seeing that we intended to fight in the open, came on in six massive columns, made up of their usual wedge-shaped groups, each under its local chief. The Marcomanni were on our left, the Quadi and the Alans on our right, and the great host that made up the two Vandal tribes was in the center. Their cavalry rode ahead of the infantry, a series of ragged lines that broke and wheeled to left and right when they saw where our horsemen were placed. A host of foot followed them at a run. Quintus, who held the left, was engaged first and found himself trying to deal with a mixture of horse and foot, both armed with bows. He broke through the enemy horse without difficulty and then charged the foot. In the thirty seconds it took him to close the two hundred yards that separated them, the enemy loosed four flights of arrows and unhorsed half his front rank. Unable to break through the enemy spears he disengaged, and withdrew his squadrons in good order. The remainder of the Marcomanni suffered fearful losses, trying to close with the archers on the wing, and a section, in desperation, tried to outflank them. Fredegar, shouting, swung his men round and fell upon them, and a grim hand-to-hand struggle followed.

On the right, Fabianus had charged the enemy in the flank, but the Quadi, instead of standing their ground and waiting to be slaughtered, opened ranks, stepped aside, and flung their spears and axes at our men as they rode past. This, however, proved a mistake, for the auxiliaries under Scudilio, who had already checked the enemy horse with their arrows, charged them on foot before they had time to regroup, and swept them back toward Fabianus' cavalry, who easily rode them down. The Quadi fell back in confusion and Scudilio slowly began to turn their flank.

In the center the Vandals came at a run in a dense mass. The bolts of the carroballistae ripped great gaps in their ranks, but did not stop them. The fighting ranks stepped forward and flung their javelins, one after one; nine arrow flights went home; but they still came on over the bodies of their dead and there was a tremendous shock and clash of arms as the two lines of infantry met. Our line bent for a moment and then held. For over half an hour a fierce struggle went on, with neither side giving way, and then Quintus fell on their right flank with seven hundred horse. A minute later, Fabianus attacked the left, just as Scudilio's men were beginning to tire, and the Vandal wings crumpled as men began to throw away their weapons and run. I signaled my bodyguard to mount, and then led them round to the right, intending to reinforce Fabianus. At this moment, the Franks under Fredegar broke under the weight of the Marcomanni, who had been strengthened by reserves pouring from their camp. The Marcomanni began to close in upon the rear of Quintus' wing, which was now almost at a standstill in the midst of a vast, struggling mass of screaming, shouting men. The din was appalling. I shouted; my trumpeter saw my mouth move and blew the two blasts that meant "change direction." I wheeled round and crossed the rear of our center just as the Marcomanni, mingling with the Vandals, were beginning to fall upon it. My men heard us coming and fell back quickly as we poured through the gap in our line and charged home. It was a tight, controlled, compact charge, and the enemy broke and gave way before us. At my order, the trumpet sounded again, and the front line disengaged and fell back, reforming as it did so. The enemy, glad of a breathing space, did the same. They also had had enough for the moment.

I said to Quintus, "Don't charge home into a mass that size. It's like trying to drive your fist through a barrel of glue. Ride round them and cut them down on the perimeter."

He wiped the sweat from his eyes. "I'm sorry. I thought it was worth a try." He hammered the pommel of his sword angrily. "With only two more alae I could have broken them into pieces."

I said patiently, "If we go on like this, it is we who will break into pieces."

There was a long lull in the fighting, while the wounded went to the rear, and the men's wounds stiffened in the cold. I issued a ration of biscuit and vinegar to all ranks, and two hours later we tried again. I pulled Fredegar's Franks back into line with the left wing of the archers, split my reserves into two halves and pushed them out toward the wings, and then ordered the whole line to move forward until contact was established with the cavalry. In this way we gained about four hundred yards of ground, while the enemy watched us from a distance and made no move. Then I ran the carroballistae forward and they opened fire at two hundred yards, supported by a screen of bowmen who had instructions to fire into the air, so as to drop their arrows into the enemy center. As the nine-inch bolts tore through men's stomachs, and smashed ribs and backbones at a single blow, the Vandals fell back sullenly. I ordered the advance, and the cohorts' first waves moved out at a trot. The two lines met, wavered, and again held. The enemy cavalry waited on the flanks, watching our horse, while we goaded them with arrow fire from the wings. I sounded the trumpet, and Fredegar and Scudilio moved out to take the enemy on the flanks. More men were pouring out of their camp now and forming up on the rear of their center. The carroballistae on my wings now opened fire and an enemy horseman went down at every shot. Angered into action they moved outward to where my cavalry stood waiting patiently for my order. I waited till they were well clear of their main body, and then ordered the trumpet to be sounded. Our cavalry charged, and within three minutes it was all over. Half the Vandals were unhorsed and dead, the other half were in flight back to the camp. With no horse to oppose them, the two alae, led by Quintus and Fabianus, fell upon the enemy's flanks and began to ride round the Vandals, working their way in, closer and closer to the center. Slowly my front line began to move forward again. Still more men came streaming across the plain to help the enemy host. They were principally bowmen, and, from their position at the rear, they began to fire inward, regardless of whether they struck our horse, or their own foot. Our men, who had fought all day in grim silence, now began to shout, as though they sensed that victory was within their grasp.

"Now," I said to Aquila, and the two reserves on the flanks moved into action. At the same time, Flavius broke from the copse and led his men straight through Scudilio's and into the weakening left flank of the Quadi, who began to give ground rapidly. I blew the "Advance" and ordered my bodyguard to mount. "They'll break," I cried to Agilio excitedly. "Any moment now and they will break."

At that moment there came a sudden wailing cry, which even I could hear above the shouting and the dreadful, familiar clatter of iron upon iron. Our cavalry checked—it was an appalling sight—and began to break backward, as though overtaken by panic and fear. This feeling spread to the infantry and they hesitated, and then began to give ground. Through a gap in a flurry of horsemen, I saw a figure in a red cloak, lying across its horse's neck, and being cantered back under escort. I tried desperately to rally the infantry, but they were giving way now steadily, each rank retiring, in turn, through the next. "Come on," I shouted to Agilio. We cantered through our own men—I heard our foot shout, "Ware horse"—and saw their startled faces drop away from me. Then we were moving at a fast gallop into the midst of a horde of yelling, excited Vandals. The weight of our charge, its very unexpectedness, carried us through and out the other side, leaving a swathe of dying and broken bodies behind us. We turned quickly, in the midst of their startled archers at the rear, cutting down every man we could reach, and then reformed and charged back. There is nothing quite so demoralizing as being attacked from the rear. To this the Vandals and their allies were no exception. They broke away from us, their advance crumbled uncertainly into isolated fragments of ragged, exhausted, and defiant men, so that, when we had ridden clear, and the cohorts had reformed, they turned and withdrew slowly toward their camp, collecting their wounded as they did so. A few minutes later I gave the signal to retreat, and the tired centuries plodded back across the blooded snow to the safety of the ditches, the palisade, and the camp.

I gave my horse to my orderly and walked to the signal tower. Every man I passed gave me a salute or a grin, or a greeting of some kind, and every man seemed to be wounded. I felt exhausted and sick. We had so nearly succeeded; we had so nearly failed.

A voice shouted my name, and Fabianus rode his horse toward me, picking his way carefully between the crowds of men making for their tents. "They are coming," he cried. "The reinforcements are on the way."

I shook my head. "You must be mad."

He said, excitedly, "No. There is a column of infantry a good half mile down the Treverorum road."

I walked out with him, and I could feel the excitement spread around me, as the word was passed from one tired and wounded man to another. Marius joined me, wiping his sword on a piece of rag. Aquila came up, limping from a cut across the thigh. Scudilio was there, too, and Fredegar was with him, his terrible battle ax resting across his shoulders.

The dark column, heads bent against the driving lash of the wind, moved toward us at a slow pace. At their head was a man on horseback. Two cohort commanders walked slowly to join us, one of them half carried by the other. The wounded man was Flavius, his left arm wrapped in dirty bandages. We stood there, smiling stupidly, and waiting. We could be sure of victory now. I was so relieved I felt almost happy. "Mithras," I said aloud. "My prayers have been answered." I turned my head and saw Flavius watching me, a startled and disbelieving look upon his white face. He said, "It—it cannot be the—I can see the rear of the column from here."

I said cheerfully, "It is the advance guard then. That is good enough for me. Let us go and greet them. They have come in good time."

We met their leader on the road behind the camp, and he dismounted, in advance, when he saw us coming.

"Artorius," I said.

The Curator of Treverorum flushed at my tone, and then drew himself up and saluted awkwardly. He wore a leather tunic, leather breeches, and a leather helmet. Strapped to his waist was a long sword. His eyes flickered from face to face, and then he looked at me steadily. "I have come to put my sword at your service," he said. He spoke rather fast, like a man who has been practicing what to say. He spoke defiantly, too, as though he thought I might laugh at him. His men had come to a ragged halt behind. They were similarly equipped; not one man wore armor, but each had either a spear or a sword.

"What of the Army of Gaul?" I said harshly.

"It—it is on its way."

"I don't believe it. Chariobaudes wrote—"

"He changed his orders," said Artorius quickly. His eyes flickered and then he stared defiantly, for a moment, at the wounded Flavius. "They are marching to Treverorum, to our—to your aid."

"You have come on ahead?" I was too tired to cope with the problem of Chariobaudes and his shifting mind.

"Yes." He looked, with frightened curiosity, around him. He was used to the bustle of a forum, not the squalid muddle of a battlefield. "I know I am breaking the law. I have no authority to bear arms, since I am only a civilian. I don't know what the Praefectus Praetorio will say." He paused, and I remained silent. "I wish to help," he added in a low voice.

"How many men have you?"

"Only two thousand. Some are gladiators and slaves, to whom I have given their freedom. I had no real authority to do that either, I suppose."

I was silent with disappointment. He tugged at his helmet and then held it, awkwardly, in the crook of his arm, as he had seen my officers do. "I spoke to the Bishop. I felt I must do something."

"Of course." I turned away. Two thousand men out of a city of eighty thousand.... I felt too sick to speak. He came after me, stumbling over the slippery ground. He said, "You haven't accepted my..." His voice trailed away. He cleared his throat, nervously. He said, "We want to help. I—" He broke off, as he tried to avoid a wounded man. "Don't send us back. We can be of some use, surely. Besides, the men could not go back now. They are tired out."

I said, "Yes, and I and my men are tired, too. We are soldiers."

He flinched at my voice. He said desperately, "I know I am only the Curator; but I thought—"

I turned my back on him. I went to the signal tower, leaving the column still standing upon the road, and my officers silent behind me. I would have struck him had he spoken again.

I stumbled through the door. I sat down on my bedding roll and put my head in my hands. We had been so near to victory. Even if Chariobaudes did come in time, he had too few men to be of real help. We should be beaten just the same. The wind rattled the door. It was very cold, and I began to shiver. I knew what it was like now to be a defeated general.

Fabianus came in. He said, "I would like to speak to you, sir."

"Yes," I said.

"That was ungenerous," he said.

"Ungenerous! I?" I stood up, and he backed away. "He has had two years, and in two years he has done little except at the point of a sword. Now he comes whining with offers of help. What help will that ragged crew of comics be, do you imagine? Help. When it's too late. Too late, do you hear."

Fabianus said, "It is you who are ungenerous. He has come to help, and you, sir, turn your back on him."

"It is what he deserves."

He said, doggedly, "I don't agree, sir."

"Why?"

He did not answer at first. He stood there, his hands clenched at his sides, just looking at me, tired and resentful. It was how his father had looked when I told him that the sentry who slept at his post must be executed.

"Why?" I said again.

"Because—because he has come out here to die with the rest of us, and that makes him my friend, if not yours."

I got to my feet and went toward him. He did not move. "How dare you speak to me like that. Don't presume too far upon my friendship with your father."

It was then that he lost control over himself. He said, angrily, "If I dare, it is because you taught me how to speak to an Emperor when he is in the wrong."

He turned and went out. I called after him but he did not come back.

Quintus was brought to the signal tower an hour later. He had suffered an arrow wound in the neck, and had lost blood. He lay on his bed, gray-faced with shock, his hands, raw with the cold, lying limply upon the blankets that covered him.

He opened his eyes. He said, "I am sorry. I ruined the day. My men lost heart, the idiots." He beat feebly upon the blankets.

"No," I said. "It would have happened anyway. They are too strong for us, and we are too exhausted. Fresh troops might have done it, I agree. But our men—" I broke off and sat on the stool beside him. What else was there to say?

"Will you try again tomorrow?"

I shook my head. "Our losses were tremendous. So were theirs, but they can afford them. We can't risk losing another man. Flavius fought well. He timed that charge brilliantly."

He groaned. "I know. How many did we lose?"

"Aquila is making a count now."

"Well, if we hold on, this relief army may come in time."

"Yes, of course." I trimmed the wick of the oil lamp and poured water into a bowl and began to wash myself.

He said, "Fabianus did well, too." He paused and stared at the ceiling. "Agilio told me that Artorius has brought men from the city."

"Yes."

"He has told me what you said."

I dried my face on a towel and looked on my bed for a clean tunic. I had just one left. I put it on. Then I poured out two cups of wine. Still he did not look at me. He said, gently, "It is not politic for Emperors to turn their backs on those who offer them support."

I said bitterly, "My horse is more dependable. And braver, too."

"Do you really think so? He could have been on his way to Arelate and safety by now, with the rest of them. It doesn't matter about the past. It takes courage, Maximus, to sit alone in a panic-stricken city and decide that the right thing to do is to collect a few men with rusty swords, and go out to help a man who despises you." He looked at me then. "I should know that. It takes even more courage to admit that you are wrong."

I did not answer him and he turned his face to the wall.

Presently he said, in a tired voice, "What is the plan far tomorrow?"

"Hold the ditches and the palisade. I shall use the cavalry only for counterattacks and to relieve pressure, if things get difficult."

"Maximus?"

"Yes."

"Do you wish now you had refused Stilicho's request?"

I was silent.

"Do you?"

"I am not afraid, Quintus, if that is what you mean." I looked up, and saw him watching me with unhappy eyes. I smiled. I said, "You know, I was happy on the Wall. Yes, I mean that. I have never felt at home here in Germania."

He said, "If I hadn't ridden to Eburacum that day—only Saturninus knew why I went. I owed so much."

"I understand."

He said, "I wish I could believe that."

"Get some sleep. We shall need all we can get from now on."

Later, I went the rounds of the camp. I inspected the sentries, cheered the wounded with stupid jokes, and talked with my cohort commanders. On my return, I saw a man being sick in the snow. I went across to him, thinking it was a wounded soldier who had been given too much broth. He straightened up when he heard me coming, and turned awkwardly away. I saw then that it was Artorius. He was bareheaded, and he had his hands to his mouth. I recognized the look on his face only too well, so I called after him.

"No," I said. "Just a moment."

He stopped and turned round, hopelessly. He tried to stand to attention, and I knew what it must be like to be the wild beast in the arena when it has cornered its human victim. It would have looked just like Artorius then.

"Something disagreed with me," he mumbled, and then added a hasty, "sir," as though I might hit him for omitting it.

"Are you very afraid?" I said.

He nodded, his knuckles to his mouth. I could see his face quiver.

"So am I," I said. "I am too afraid to be sick anymore."

He stared at me incredulously, as though I were laughing at him. "But you are a soldier," he said.

"Oh, yes, but it doesn't stop you being afraid. We all are: it is the waiting beforehand. It's not so bad when the battle line is drawn up, and you watch for the signal to advance. You can smell your own sweat and the sweat of the men beside you. You hug to yourself the feeling that they are there, guarding your left and your right. You bolster yourself up with little jokes out of a dry mouth, and they answer you, and you pretend it's a game, like all the training exercises that have gone before. You pretend the worst that can happen is a dressing-down from the Legate and an extra fatigue from an irate centurion. Then the advance is sounded and the line moves forward. Inevitably, you spread out to avoid rough ground or a clump of bushes, and your companions are no longer within touching distance. You see the enemy hurl their javelins, and men scream and go down. You don't worry about being hit; that's the funny part of it. You have the soldier's illusion of invulnerability. It is always the other man who will be wounded or killed—never yourself. And the more this happens—even though it is to your friends—the stronger the feeling. If you didn't have it, you could never advance at all."

I paused. His face had lost, for the moment anyway, that frightened look. He was absorbed in what I was saying.

I said, "But then, as you get closer to the waiting enemy, comes a terrible sense of isolation. The man on your left, five yards away, might as well be five thousand. It grows and grows, this feeling of loneliness, until you are sure that you must be the only man advancing in the whole of your army. Then, you are afraid, and you want to turn and run. Only a curious sense of pride keeps you going. And then the enemy strikes at you with his spear or his sword, and discipline and training take over, and from that moment on you don't have time to worry about fear or loneliness anymore. You just fight, and you go on fighting until it is all over."

He said, "You make it sound so easy."

"When it comes to the point, it is."

He lowered his head. "I thought I had the courage," he said. "It seemed to be so easy in my room in the basilica. They were all leaving, and I was ashamed. I knew then that we had let you down, and that somewhere out here you were all risking your lives, just for us. I thought—I thought I must do something too even though it was so late. I didn't know I was such a coward." He tried hard to raise a smile. "It is humiliating," he said. "You must despise people like me."

I said, "I was not generous earlier on. I am sorry. Will you forgive me?" I held out my hand and gripped him by the arm. "I know you are not a fighting man," I said. "That is not so very important. But you have come to help us. That is important."

He wiped his mouth. He said, "Will it be long? It's the waiting that is so hard."

"Two hours at the most, Artorius. If you can endure that two hours, you will never be frightened again."

CHAPTER XIX

They came against us in the early dawn, and only the startled cawing of the rooks, disturbed at their horrible feast, gave warning of their approach. They were more cautious now, determined to wear us down, as a wolf pack wears down a stag that it is hunting. Flights of arrows, a quick charge, a flight of axes, a retreat, silence, and a flight of arrows again. They circled the defenses, probing for the weak spots. A sudden rush on the flanks that could only be broken by a charge of horse, a rush through the center that even the carroballistae could barely check. Hour after hour they kept it up, and hour after hour my men stood at the palisades until they fell or were relieved. By midday Marius was dead, killed leading a desperate counterattack against the enemy's barricades, and Agilio had been badly wounded in the chest. In the afternoon it began to snow and they attacked again, gray, ghastly figures looming out of the swirling storm, to throw death with their two hands, or to receive it—it was all one to them. The ditches were choked with their dead and their wounded, and still they came, an endless stream of men, who breathed hatred and envy of all that we stood for. Fire arrows came sizzling out of the darkening sky, to start pools of flame that spluttered along the palisade, burst into roars of white fire when they landed on a wagon, or set a horse screaming with agony when it was hit. There was no respite, no rest of any kind. The hard, relentless pressure was maintained all day, all evening, and all night, so that men who were trying to sleep could not do so, because of the sounds of the dying, the exultant cries of the enemy, and the smell of fire upon the snow.

At midnight I held a war council in the signal tower.

"We are out of arrows, nearly," I said. Julius Optatus nodded, grimly. "The last issue has just been made—thirty to a man. We have issued the last javelins—fifteen to a man. The ballistae are short of missiles, and the carroballistae have about thirty bolts each. When those are gone we shall have only our bare hands."

No one spoke. They stood round me in a half circle, gaunt and unsmiling, but they were with me, and I was glad.

"Fabianus, get the wagons hitched up and put the wounded aboard. Those who can walk must drive the wagons or go with them. They are to make for Treverorum and seek shelter where they can find it. I suggest they make for the Temple district. They will be safer there than in houses where there are men and women, food and valuables. Get them out before daylight."

Quintus, his arm in a sling, said, "What do you want us to do, Maximus? We will do whatever you ask."

"In a moment," I said. I turned to Fredegar, who had a bloody bandage about his head. In his thick furs, and with his gray beard, he looked like some fierce and indomitable bear. "This is not your fight," I said. "Not any longer. I suggest you withdraw your men. Make terms, if you wish, or go into the hills."

He said, "Are you asking me to go? Or is it an order?"

I touched his shoulder. "It is neither a request nor an order. It is just a suggestion."

He said, "I served Marcomir's father and, from the day the boy threw his first spear, I stood always on his left side. I should have stood there on the day he died, but the fates willed it otherwise." He reached for the wine jug and gulped down a great draught. Spots of wine hung on his beard like blood. "I will tell my men what you said, but I do not think they will hear me. As for myself—" He paused. He said, "I stay."

I looked at Quintus, who shrugged his shoulder. I turned to Aquila. "Are you sorry now that you did not kill me that day in Treverorum and elect another Emperor?"

He flashed a smile. He said, "Afterward I was ashamed."

I said, "I can only repeat what I said before at Moguntiacum. If any man wishes to go, then let him go now—quickly."

Aquila touched the standard with his big hands. "I carried this many times through many years when it had the right to be ashamed of the soldiers who called it theirs. Now I am not ashamed. I have no wish to be a Vandal slave."

The door rattled in the wind, and I was reminded of the night when Stilicho came to my tent with an officer, or an order—what it was I could not remember; I was too tired. It did not matter anyway. It had all led to this—this narrow circle of existence: a dozen exhausted men, gathered in a wooden hut on a winter's night, and planning quite calmly how best they might end their lives.

Aquila said, "We have a thousand men under arms on foot."

"Eight hundred horse," said Quintus.

"Four hundred of my people," said Fredegar proudly.

"And I have fifteen hundred of the city," said Artorius.

Scudilio coughed onto the back of his hand, and I saw that there was blood on his mouth. "Five hundred auxiliaries, all told," he spluttered.

I turned to Artorius. "Your men fought well today. You have a right to be proud of them."

He fingered a cut above his left eye, and smiled. He had the look of a man who was at peace with himself. He said, "There is something I forgot. The Bishop sent a message. He has sent the girl away into safety."

"Was there anything else?"

"Yes," he said. "Tell Maximus I shall see him again. That was the message."

"In heaven, no doubt. Did the girl have any messages for us?"

"I gave it to him," said Artorius, dryly.

I looked at Fabianus. He was smiling. I did not ask what the message was.

"We are almost a legion still," I said. Quintus gave me a long, steady look. He remembered, I think, as I did too, that day I landed in Gaul, and he met me at the camp, and we had been so absurdly proud and so happy at the greatness of our command.

"What about the Eagle?" asked Fabianus.

"It will not fall into their hands," I said. "That I promise you."

Aquila said anxiously, "You are sure?"

"I swear it upon the sword of Agricola."

They went out then and I was alone with Quintus.

I said, "We were both wrong. I would never have thought our casualties could have been so heavy, or that our supplies would have been used up so quickly. I would never have thought the Barbarians could have fought the way they did these last two days."

"Nor I," he said. "But you know, Maximus, they have their women and their children in their camp behind them. That makes a great difference. And they do not mind dying either; our men do. That makes a difference also."

The wind had dropped and, in the ghastly, gray light of the dawn, we lined the palisades with the last of our men. The bodies of horses were dragged into the gaps where the fencing had been smashed or burned, and the dead bodies of our men were pulled clear and laid in rows inside the tents they had last occupied when alive. All the spare weapons that could be found had been collected and stuck into the ground by our feet, for ease of use. Under Aquila's direction, small parties hurriedly crossed the ditch into the killing area to pick up whatever weapons and missiles they could find; on the flanks the cavalry were saddling up their horses, while Quintus walked along the line, checking the girths; and in the camp behind us the cooks were lighting fires and preparing the morning meal. Huddled against a carroballista I saw a man I recognized.

"Fredbal," I said. "What the devil are you doing here?"

He looked up at me defiantly. "I come back," he said. "I saw your message delivered. I done what you told me."

"But——"

"They killed my woman and my children. Thirty years ago, that was. So I come back."

There was nothing to say. I touched him on the shoulder and smiled, and then turned away. Agilio, who was at my side, said suddenly, "I did not know you believed in devils, my Emperor."

I laughed. "It is through living too long with Christians I expect. I find myself talking as they do."

"My lord Bishop will make another convert yet."

"I doubt that very much."

We walked back toward the signal tower. I rubbed my cold hands together, and had a sudden absurd wish that my cloak could have been clean instead of dirty. A voice cried suddenly out of the half dark, and a figure approached and I heard the words, "Truce... truce... we want a truce... we would speak with you."

"Hold your fire," I cried.

Quintus cantered up. "Steady, it may be a trap."

The man came up to the outer ditch. "King Gunderic would speak with your General. Let him come out alone to the ditch and talk. I, his brother, will be a hostage for our good faith."

"Don't go, sir," said Agilio. "It is a trick."

"Has he a brother?"

"Three," said Fredegar. "The youngest is a wolf cub called Gaiseric. But this is the eldest by his voice."

"Don't go, my lord."

"Why not?" I said. "It will give us time to breathe for five minutes."

A gap was made in the palisade and a plank run out across the first ditch. Gunderic's men came forward and threw a plank over the outer ditch, and then stood back.

Quintus said, in exasperation, "If you must go, then take my shield.

But be careful."

"Watch the flanks," I said to Aquila. "Kill the first man who moves."

I put the shield on my right side, under my red cloak, and went forward, my sword in my left hand. Before me, Gunderic stepped out onto the bridge, and we met alone on the hard, frozen surface between the outer ditches, that forty feet we called the killing area, and over which so many Vandals had run and died. The ditches were three-quarters filled with dead, and there were dead, too, on this ground, over which we had to pick our way carefully to avoid stumbling. We met in the center, Gunderic and I. He looked more gaunt than ever. There was a rag tied round his right arm and a long cut above his eyes, which looked to be swollen and bloodshot. He had the angry, famished look of a beast of prey that has missed its kill, and I was suddenly afraid. I could smell the danger in our meeting through the sweat of my own fear.

He said, "You refused our offer. I shall not make it again."

"I did not expect you to do so." He was a tall man, but he had to look up to me as I spoke, and this he did not like. "But I will make you an offer." I spoke through my teeth. "Give me the wife of Marcomir living, and I will let you return across the Rhenus unharmed."

"She is dead."

"In the Roman fashion?"

"Yes." He spoke coldly.

"Ah!"

"Unharmed you say?" He glared at me, and said in a blaze of hatred, "Unharmed. You poisoned the wells—butcher. My wife and my children died, and I watched them and could do nothing."

I said, "I warned you of what would happen."

He looked at me coldly, "You are a great fighter," he said softly. "When I am old, I shall be able to boast of how I destroyed Maximus, a Roman general, who barred my way into new lands."

"Will you also tell them how few men it was who barred your way, and for how long?"

"Of course. That is what makes the story that my people will sing." He spoke coolly now, but with respect, and I was surprised. I knew so little, really, about these people.

"Will you also say how you were aided by the Marcomanni, the Quadi, and the Alans?"

His teeth snapped. "We have done the hard fighting," he said. "Their share has been small."

He lifted his head and looked at the sky. "The moon sets," he said. "In a little while you will be destroyed with all your men, and your bleached bones will litter the snow. A good end for warriors, but a waste of life. Unbar the way, and you may take your men where you will. I have enough wives who weep in my camp. I do not want more."

I said, "Once, on a summer afternoon, I met six kings. Are they still all living, Gunderic of the Vandals? I told you when last we met, that you would walk in blood to Treverorum. You must walk in my blood, too, before you get there."

"Why?"

I smiled. "If all men bar your way, as we do, then how strong will you be when you at last reach those lands of which you dream? I think you will be so weak that, in the end, you will be destroyed in your turn. You will be remembered only as a people who could kill. For yourselves, or for other people, you will make nothing that will last."

He snarled softly in his throat, like a dog. He said, "You are wrong. You bar my way as an enemy, but the day will come, when you are dead, that I and my people shall be the servants of Rome, calling ourselves its citizens. Does not that seem strange?"

"Perhaps. I do not know. I shall not then care. But why should you need Rome, if you hate her so much?"

He said, as though to a child, "There has always been a Rome. It is a great empire, it is needed, but it needs us also."

He stroked his beard then, and his eyes flickered sideways. He said, "Rome has been wasted on you. I would not wish—"

"I do not think, King Gunderic—"

At that moment the archer fired. I felt an agonizing pain as the arrow drove through my cloak and shield, and into my shoulder. I went sideways with the shock, and felt two more arrows drive home into the shield as I stumbled and tried, desperately, to regain my balance.

"Quintus!"

Gunderic stepped back and to his left. Like a striking cat, his hand dropped to his sword. It came out with a dreadful rasping sound, a blur of light and steel, and I saw it glint high in the air as he raised it for the killing stroke.

I moved one step forward, the sword of Agricola pointing toward his right side, my arm slightly bent as I did so. His sword came down at arm's length as I straightened my elbow, and then fell from his hand across the rim of my shield onto my shoulder. For a moment we stood there, quite still, facing each other.

"You should have been a Vandal," he said, in a tired voice.

"Three inches is enough, even for a king," I said.

He buckled at the knees and I caught him as he fell.

The archer, who had lain in ambush along the edge of the ditch, was dead with six fire arrows in him. I backed across the plank, holding the dead king before me, while the Vandals roared, and arrows flickered to and fro, and a clamor of arms sounded on both sides. Across the inner ditch I withdrew behind the shields of a dozen men who had come out to help me, and was dragged to safety while a bowman fired at the plank on the outer ditch until it burst into flames.

"Are you all right, sir?"

"Yes," I muttered.

"It was a trick. I warned you."

"Yes." I bit my lip. "But a good one."

"What about the hostage, his brother?"

I looked at him through my pain, standing between his guards, a sword at his throat. I sank to the ground and, while an orderly attended to my damaged shoulder, which was bleeding badly now, said curiously, "How did you expect to escape?"

He said, "You killed my brother."

"He tried to jump the palisade," said Aquila.

"Well?"

"It was a risk. I lost."

"You did, indeed. You are the first Vandal to enter my camp alive."

"Kill him," snarled Fredegar.

"Send him back with his brother," I said.

"Kill him," said Fredegar again.

"Crucify him," said Agilio angrily.

"Be quiet, my friends. Do what I tell you, Quintus."

He started to protest, looked at my face, and then nodded. "Of course," he said.

Supported by my orderly, I walked to the palisade. "Peoples of the East, listen to me." I cupped my hands to my mouth. "Listen to me, I say." Slowly the noise died down and the firing ceased. "Peoples of the East: I break no truce, I keep faith with my own people and with yours. Go back the way you came, or your women will weep blood for their unborn sons. I will not give you the city of Treverorum, or another yard of land. This land is mine." I paused, and then cried, more loudly still: "I am Maximus. I give you only death and the body of your King. I give you—Gunderic."

"Fire," said a voice. The long arm of the ballista swung up, and there came a long, thin scream, as the two brothers, the one living and the other dead, returned to the earth and to their own kind.

For an hour there was a lull, while they watched us from behind the rough defenses they had built within flight range of our arrows. They used movable shields of rough wood, the piled bodies of horses, and sacks of straw, mixed with hard earth or snow. The sun rose, and the cold winds blew again, and they came out of the flying snow like snarling wolves, and attacked us with the same ruthless courage, the same hungry despair, the same cold hatred that they had shown before. Time and again, Quintus and Fabianus led their cavalry out. Swinging right or left handed, they would close up, steady their line, move smoothly into a canter, while Quintus shouted "Steady, steady," at the top of his voice. Then the gallop over the last two hundred yards, the charge smashed home, the swords red with blood, and men shouting; the breakup of the formation, when it was every man for himself, and you had to watch for the man with the knife under your horse's belly, as well as the man with the ax who tried to take off your thigh; the hasty rally, while horses and men were still warm but not yet blown; and then the charge back, every yard taking you nearer and nearer to safety. Safety was the cold wind, and the sweat on your face, and your horse blowing at the ground. Safety was the silence from Barbarian voices, the swinging sword, the flying ax, and the smell of blood that was everywhere.

All day we fought, the men retiring in little groups back to the camp, to squat, exhausted on the ground and eat a hot mess of crumbled biscuit, chopped up veal, and beans, with trembling fingers, and swallow wine with mouths dry with fear.

In his second charge, Quintus lost, in two minutes, three tribunes, four decurions, fifty-seven men, and thirty-nine horses. And with each charge that followed, our losses grew heavier and heavier. The cavalry, backed by Fredegar's Franks, held the wings, and the cohorts and the auxiliaries held the center. We tried to save arrows and missiles as much as possible, and volunteers would rush out during a lull to snatch the arrows from the dead, as well as the spears that littered the ground beyond the palisade, like timber in a builder's yard. They were the only weapons that broke up the terrible rushes of maddened, angry men, who stormed the ditches, now choked and full, climbing the bodies of their own dead, as they had done at Moguntiacum, to reach us behind our thin fence. And at the end of each fresh assault, I would ride along the crooked rank of dark-faced men, black with dirt and sweat, who leaned, panting, upon their swords or their spears, and do my best to encourage them with a smile and a jest. But each time I did so the lines of men in Roman helmets grew thinner, until there were few reserves left, except those who were wounded.

My right shoulder was stiff and painful from the arrow wound, and I could only lift the arm with difficulty. My left shoulder was damaged, too, but I knew that when the time came I should have to use my sword left-handed. I was of little use as a fighting man now. I walked back along the palisade, and stumbled over a bundle of fur huddled in the snow. I turned it over, mechanically, and looked at the blind, still face. It was Fredbal. He had had his wish, and he was happy now. He was not alone anymore.

Outside the signal tower I found Agilio, sitting exhausted upon the steps. He was so tired he did not even look up as I passed him. I climbed the ladder—it was the tenth time that day—and went out onto the platform. I turned and looked back toward the west, in the hope of seeing signs that the relief forces from Gaul were on their way. But nothing moved in that vast and desolate waste of snow. It was empty of human beings and of hope. I descended the ladder and sat down on a bench, my sword unbuckled, and took the bowl of food that my orderly offered me. Quintus came in then, rubbing the snow from off his shoulders. He looked exhausted, and the stubble of his beard was white, like my own. We did not speak until we had eaten and drunk. He said, tiredly, "Flavius is dead. He went with me on my last charge. When we got back to camp he was still on his horse, with four arrows in him. He was always a good rider."

I nodded. I felt very tired. I said, "I wanted so much to see Rome. My father once told me how he had stood in the Curia, the senate house down in the Forum, watching the senators offering incense to the figure of Victory before they went to their meeting. It stood on a pedestal at the end of the chamber, opposite the entrance, but it has gone now, like all the best things in our world. I wanted to see that, too."

He said, "Oh, Maximus," and touched my arm.

They came again and the fighting was as before. During a pause in the battle, while they prepared for yet another assault with ladders and planks, I walked down to the southern end of our defenses to where Artorius stood, surrounded by his handful of battered gladiators and freed slaves. He held his sword as though it belonged to him now, and he grinned and saluted me as I came up.

"Artorius."

"Sir."

I took him by the shoulder and spoke quietly, "Where are those reinforcements that you promised us? Where is the Army of Gaul? The advance guard should have been here by now. Tell me."

He said simply, "I don't know."

I held him close. I said, "It was a lie, wasn't it? It was a lie to keep up morale? All lies?"

"Yes," he said. He stuck his sword into the ground and rubbed his hands. They were covered with chilblains and he had difficulty in moving his fingers. He said, "We asked for help, and when the message came that there would be no help, we thought it best to pretend that everything would be all right. It is an old merchant's trick, of course." He spoke quietly and with confidence. Whatever else he was—he was not frightened anymore.

I said, "You did right. You should have been on my staff."

A trooper came up, dragging his right foot upon the ground. He said, "General Veronius sent me. If you do not need your horse, sir, could I have it? We are short of mounts."

I nodded. "Take it. I do not need a horse now."

He saluted his thanks, swung himself awkwardly into the saddle, and disappeared in a flurry of snow.

I called out then, for Aquila. "Tell my bodyguard to join General Veronius. He has need of all the horsemen he can get."

He looked shocked. "But, sir—"

I clapped him on the back. "You and I, Aquila, will walk out of this world on our feet. It is just as easy."

And then, during another lull when the sun, low behind us, was in their eyes, came the moment that I had dreaded all day.

Aquila came up to me and said, "We are nearly out of missiles. What do we do when they attack us again?"

Fredegar, gulping wine, rinsed his mouth and spat. "None of my archers has arrows left. What do I do next when they come round on the flanks?"

I walked down the line, pausing to ask each man a question. No one smiled now. They held out their hands and showed me their weapons, and that was all. Fabianus said, "The ballistae are now useless, like my horse." He began to make patterns in the snow with the point of his sword. He knew, as I did, that he would never see the daughter of Rando again, but he did not speak of it. His life's span was now little more than the length of his sword, but he was worth more to me dead than to her living, though I did not tell him so.

I said nothing, but shut my eyes to avoid the sight of his young face.

Quintus walked up to me, limping heavily, his horse following with lowered head. He had changed horses four times this day, and the present beast was a bay with a white star on his forehead.

He said, bleakly, "I can mount four hundred men. That is all. What are the orders, O my General?"

I opened my eyes. The sun was just above the hills and the short day would soon be ended. "Where is Julius Optatus? Hurry."

"Sir." He came up to me, still the same stocky, cheerful man, slow in the uptake but careful in his accounts, whom I had first met, so long ago, in Segontium in the west. I owed him so much for his efforts to keep us supplied with everything that we needed, but I did not tell him so. He would only have been embarrassed. I said, "What have we left?"

He held out his hands. "Nothing, sir. I have issued every last weapon and missile in the camp." His deep voice cracked for a moment. "I am a quartermaster without any stores. Friend Aquila at least still has some men." He was almost crying with rage and frustration.

"Never mind. Bring everyone up from the camp who can walk, and put them into the firing line. Yourself included."

"Couldn't we hold the camp, sir?"

I shook my head. "Not enough men. Did you send out all the walking wounded?"

"Yes, sir. All who can't fight, but who can walk, have been going out all day." He grinned savagely. He said, "You can see their bodies marking the road to Treverorum."

I turned away and looked up at the signal tower. That, at least, was still standing; one thing that I had built was still standing, but not for long. Everything that I had built was crumbling to pieces in the wet snow.

I raised my arm. Agilio, Scudilio, and the other commanders moved toward me, expectantly. In the distance I could see Artorius coming at a painful run, his right arm, wrapped in a rag, held close to his side. They stood around me in a half circle. Perhaps they were hoping for a miracle; I do not know; but their faces were quiet and relaxed as I spoke to them. They knew and were prepared.

I said, "There are no orders now. We stand here until we die."

The wind blew the top off the ground snow, and I heard a faint sound and saw a flight of swans, skimming above the trees on their way to the

Mosella, which we should not see again.

Quintus spoke to my orderly. "Fetch a bowl of wine and bring it to the left flank. Quickly now." He took his helmet from his arm and set it carefully upon his head. As he buckled the straps under his chin I noticed that his hands were quite steady. He said, "Give me all your men, Fabianus. They are massing again. When they come close I shall ride out at the head of my ala and try to break them up a little."

Fabianus said, "No, it is not worth it."

Quintus smiled. "You are so very wrong," he said. "It has all been worth it. Do not ever think otherwise." He looked round us in turn, giving each man a smile and a nod. When he turned to me, I said, "I will come with you." Fabianus moved forward, but Aquila held him by the arm.

I walked with Quintus to the left flank and watched him give his orders. His men mounted and formed up. They looked very calm and determined. They were very young, most of them only boys.

"Well?"

He turned and we tried to smile. "I did my best to be Maharbal," he said.

"I know. And I to be Hannibal."

He gripped my arm and I his, and then he mounted his horse. He took the standard with its red banner and its silver Eagle, that Stilicho had given him, and settled it comfortably in his shield hand. "This time, I carry it," he said. "It is my right."

I nodded. The orderly came up and I took the cups of wine. I handed one to Quintus, and we looked at each other, and then we drank.

He said hoarsely, "It was better to do this than grow fat and rot upon the Wall."

"I have always thought so."

"Maximus."

"Yes."

"I never laughed."

"I know," I said. "Go now, my dear friend, in the name of Mithras, and may the fates be kind."

"And to you, also, my General. In the name of Mithras." He threw the wine cup onto the snow, and then saluted and rode off.

I returned to my post. The plain was dark with the great hordes of moving men. They stretched out to the woods on either side, and I knew that nothing would stop them. The aquilifer fetched the Eagle, and a wounded man brought a brazier glowing white-hot with our fire, and stood it by the signal tower.

"When they reach the palisade, take the Eagle from its standard and do what has to be done," I said.

"Upon my life," he replied.

Artorius came up to me, his face working. He was shivering like a dog. He said, and his voice was curiously calm, "This is the end for all of us."

I nodded.

He said, "I wanted so much for my family. Not this." He gestured with a shaking hand.

I said, "You are a brave man, Artorius. I have known men less frightened who would have run from the field long since."

He said, "You make it all sound so easy."

"It is very easy. I promise you that."

He nodded and stumbled away, back to his waiting men.

They came nearer and nearer, and then a trumpet sounded, and Quintus Veronius, former commander of the Ala Petriana, and now Master of Horse in the Province of Upper Germany, raised his sword high, so that the blade glinted in the dying sun, and led his cavalry out across the snow on their last charge.

The charge went home: the mass broke up, and the horsemen disappeared into a tumultuous sea of men. I saw the bright helmets vanish, one by one; watched rigidly as the standard dipped suddenly, as though the Eagle dived in flight; had a glimpse of a red cloak thrown high by a triumphant foe; and then the Vandals were across the ditch and smashing at the palisade with their axes. They swept round on the flanks, riderless horses with bloodstained saddles among them, and Fredegar's Franks fell back, dying at every step. A loose bay with a white star fled past, snorting with terror, as we closed up in a tight circle about the signal tower Fabianus and Aquila on my left and right, while Artorius and Scudilio stood a little beyond. I called out then: "I am dying in good company," and they turned, smiled, and lifted their sword hilts in salute. As the enemy checked and fell back before the thrust of our swords, I heard, above the screams of the wounded, and the hard yells of the Vandals, a deep voice that shouted, "Hail and farewell."

I turned. I saw the Eagle of the Twentieth, bright, fierce, and once immortal, standing upon the fire. As I watched, it turned red and then black, and soon ceased to be anything but a lump of dripping, melted bronze.

They stormed the ditches and the ringed palisade. Fire arrows set the wooden tower blazing above our heads, and I could hear the wounded in the camp scream, as the Barbarians fired the wagons and the tents, and butchered with their swords everything that moved. They closed in again and came at us, snarling like foxes, a mass of colored shields and whirling swords. I thrust and parried and thrust again, until I was fighting behind a litter of their own dead; but still they came, and the circle grew smaller and smaller. Artorius, sobbing with rage and fighting like a madman, dropped with three swords in his chest, and Aquila, dying, killed four men with quick thrusts before he fell on the point of a boar spear. Fredegar, decapitating two men with one stroke of his great ax, was struck in the face by a fire arrow. He staggered backward, flung up his arms, cried, "Marcomir!" and disappeared under the feet of an enemy horseman.

Scudilio said, across the body of my Chief Centurion, "I always wanted to be a Roman citizen. It is too late now."

I said, "You have been a friend, which is better still."

I smiled grimly, saw Fabianus lying in a huddle at my feet, and felt a searing pain in my right arm. I thrust desperately, and felt the sword go home as the bearded faces snarled about me. I heard a voice say, "Remember me to the gods," and, as I fell, it was Scudilio who dropped across my back with blood pouring from the javelins in his chest and neck.

It was the sixteenth day of January in the year one thousand one hundred and sixty, after the foundation of Rome, when the Twentieth Legion, the last to carry the Eagle, died at the thirtieth milestone, upon the road to Augusta Treverorum.

The last cohorts lay in their triple ranks behind the palisade, and they were as quiet as if they had been on parade. But they would salute no general as their Emperor now, they would draw no gold for their pay, and they would hear no trumpets. They were beyond all hope and all fear, and they were colder than any snow.

EAGLE IN THE SNOW

EPILOGUE

Maximus stirred the ashes of the dead fire with a stick. It was light now, and the shadows were drawing back from the broken walls of the shattered camp where the listeners crouched in silence.

He said, "There is little more to tell. I remember a tent and a wagon, and voices that spoke a tongue I did not understand. I remember a voice that cried, once, in Latin, 'He is mine. Give him to me.' I remember the walls of a tent flapping in the wind, and a great pain in my wrist and hand. I remember warmth and hot drinks, and times of sickness and fever. I remember little else.

"When I began to recover I was in a house, and the Bishop was in the room. He had a livid scar on his cheek, and his hair was now quite white. He told me that two months after the city had been sacked, a man in the dress of the Alemanni brought me to him in a cart, secretly and by night. Before he left, the man spoke to the Bishop. He said, 'If he lives, which I doubt, tell him it was for the sake of the happy times.' That was all.

"I stayed there a long time. I was very ill, very weak, and very tired. Also, the hand that I had lost hurt me a great deal. The city was like all sacked cities, a place unclean and full of horror. The Bishop was kind, and I stayed on, for I had nowhere else to go. I had no purpose. I had nothing. What else was there for me to do?

"The Barbarians devastated Gaul, and the provinces never recovered. They burned and sacked city after city, and made for the south, for that land of sun which was barred to them by high mountains that they could not cross.

"That summer when I was stronger, we had news that Constantinus had crossed to Gaul. He came to Treverorum, and I watched him ride through the streets with his men—the sweepings of the old Sixth and Second—on his way to the south. His son, Constans, was at his side. He had not changed. He rode with a swagger and his chin up, and I remembered there had been a time when he had offered his sword to another man. His father, plump and smiling, made promises, and the people shouted for him. But one man cried out, 'You should have come before and helped Maximus who is dead.' I shrank back against the wall when I heard that name, and pulled my hood about my face. Maximus had been a general, Dux Moguntiacensis, and Legate of the Twentieth. What was Maximus to me, who did not even own the cloak upon my back?

"I watched the young Constans ride out in the summer sun to his great adventure. And I wished him luck. He would need all the favors that the gods could bestow, and even then he would still end as Maximus had ended.

"In the late autumn I borrowed a horse and I rode out through the great gate that ghosts had once named Romulus, and down the road to Moguntiacum—that road to nowhere. I stopped at the thirtieth milestone, where the road forked right and left, and looked at the ruins of my past. The bleached bones of my dead lay where they had fallen, but there was no message for me there, in that long grass among the broken spears, the rusted sword hilts, and the smashed helms. I saw crows perched on a fragment of splintered paling, while a field mouse ran up and down the scorched pole of a burned-out wagon. I poked at an overturned brazier, but it had been used as a nest and was full of dried grass. It meant nothing to me now. The ditches had been carelessly filled in, and the raw earth was covered with green weeds. A light wind ruffled the long grass, but that was all.

"No voices spoke; no one cried out and reproached me for what I had done, nor for what I had failed to do. I looked at the sun, warm and friendly in a blue sky, and I prayed that Quintus' dream had come true, and that he now drove the horses he had so long desired.

"They say that if you listen long enough, and have the gift, you may hear the sounds of the past, which never die. I do not know if that is so, but as

I left that desolate and ghastly place, it seemed to me that I heard the faint sound of voices that cried, 'Maximus, Maximus,' as though in acclamation. Yet when I looked behind me, I could see nothing but the bowed grass, and hear nothing but the plaintive cry of a kestrel, gliding before the wind.

"I returned to the city, and I was empty with pain. I went up the stairs in Romulus to that room where I had once stood and made plans, and held false dreams of the Purple. I remember that I sat beside the window, and I put my head in my hands, and I wept. And then the Bishop came and touched my shoulder. He did not know what to say.

"I cried out then: 'I do not know what to do? I should have died out there with my men. Oh, Mithras, God of the Sun, why did you not let me die?'

"The Bishop held out his hand, and in it was a sword that I recognized.

"'It is yours.' he said. 'It was left for you by the man who brought you to my house. Do what you wish, Maximus. Stay here; I shall not ask questions. I have neither thanked you nor cursed you for what you did. It is not for me to judge, and I shall not do so.'

"I looked at him in despair, but even I could see that he looked ill. He, too, had suffered through my failure.

"I stayed. What else was there to do?

"He was more sick than I realized and, before the winter came, Mauritius, Bishop of Treverorum was dead, and I was more lonely than ever.

"In the spring, a new Praefectus Praetorio arrived, sent by Honorius to investigate the damage that had been done. It was a difficult time. There was war in the south, Constantinus was maneuvering against the imperial troops, and the land was still full of plundering bands who had deserted the main body of their tribe." Maximus paused. He said, contemptuously, "But the first thing they asked the council for—was chariot races to amuse the people. Nothing had changed, you see.

"Later, I heard that Stilicho had fallen. The intrigues of a court eunuch succeeded where Barbarian soldiers had failed. He could have fought back, but he did not wish for civil war. Unjustly condemned by the Emperor he had served so faithfully, he walked to his execution with free hands.

"Then I grew restless, and I thought, why not? I have nothing to lose? I will go to Rome. I am an old man. No one will harm me. That, at least, is one ambition I can fulfill without hurt to any man. I took a little of the money that the Bishop had left me, and I went, but I was too late. The countryside was filled with wagons and people, fleeing as though before an invading army. I knew the signs so well."

Maximus paused, and laughed quietly. "I stood on the road, a mile away—think of that—only a mile from the Aurelian gate, and I watched Rome burn as Alaric and his Goths sacked the city after their fashion. I watched his hordes straggle up the road with their booty, and I saw a frightened woman upon a horse, her ankles tied beneath its belly, who was their prisoner. It was Galla Placidia, but I did not help her. Honorius would not have cared, and I had no wish to be a slave.

"I turned and made my way back to Gaul, and on my way I met a courier in the imperial service, taking a rescript to the government of my old island. It was a long and hazardous journey, and he had little stomach for the task. He offered me gold to take it for him. I agreed. I carried the letter in the end of my sleeve, pinned over my damaged wrist, for safety, you understand.

"So I came back, and I went to Londinium, and I found a man who called himself Governor of that city. 'Well,' I said. 'You may choose as many Emperors as you please. Honorius has freed you at last. You must look to yourselves now—if you can.' Then I went north and found Saturninus, and I broke his heart with the news of his son. He asked me to stay and, if Fabianus had been alive, I would have done so. But he is dead, and I could not. So—I came back here to Segontium, where it all began."

Maximus stood up. "I have kept you awake when you should have slept. You are safe enough here in your cold mountains."

The chief of his listeners rose and faced him. He was a tall man with cold eyes and a beaked nose. He said, "We do not always sleep. Somewhere we shall find others who are like ourselves. And somewhere there will be a man with a sword, who has a purpose as you had."

"He may be hard to find."

"We shall find him."

"You are quite certain."

"Yes," said the tall man. "Quite certain."

Maximus said, "They have no tombstones. Not one man in Treverorum wept for their passing." He looked at his audience in turn and smiled. "In the name of Mithras, my master, may the gods be kind to you on your journey."

"And you?" asked the tall man.

"I, also, have a journey to make."

"Where do you go?"

"To the gods of the shades."

The tall man nodded. He said, formally, "Then may you live in God."

Maximus bent down and then straightened up, the sword resting in the crook of his arm. He raised his head and turned his eyes upward to the sun. He said, "What is the end of it all? Smoke and ashes, a handful of bones, and a legend. Perhaps not even a legend."

They watched him go through the broken gate, heard his feet, heavy on the flint-strewn path. "He is going to his temple in the woods," said the tall man. "Listen."

There was a long silence, and then a deep voice cried, "Mithras!" and the cry echoed back across the hill. And after that the silence went on forever.

WALLACE BREEM

LIST OF PRINCIPAL CHARACTERS

Those marked with an asterisk are known to history.

Aelia	wife to P. G. Maximus
Agilio	post commander, Thirtieth Milestone.
*Alaric	Prince of the Visigoths
Aquila	Chief Centurion, Twentieth Legion
Artorius	Curator of Augusta Treverorum
Barbatio	Praefectus of auxiliaries at Moguntiacum
*Chariobaudes	Commander in Chief of the Army of Gaul
*Constans	son to Constantinus
*Constantinus	Chief of Staff at Eburacum; later self-styled Emperor
Didius	squadron commander, Twentieth Legion
Fabianus	son to Saturninus
Flavius	garrison commander at Augusta Treverorum
Fredbal	a prisoner of war
Fredegar	sword brother to Marcomir
*Fullofaudes	Commander in Chief of the Army of Britain
Gaius	Second in command of the Tungrian cohort
Gallus	tribune of the Rhenus fleet
*Goar	Prince of the Alans; cousin to Respendial
*Godigisel	King of the Siling Vandals
*Gunderic	King of the Asding Vandals
*Guntiarus	King of the Burgundians
Hermeric	King of the Marcomanni
*Honorius	Emperor of Rome
Julian	cousin to P. G. Maximus
Lucillius	senior tribune, Twentieth Legion
Marcomir	Prince of the Franks
Marius	a tribune of the Twentieth Legion
*Mauritius	Bishop of Augusta Treverorum
*Maximus *(Magnus)*	Chief of Staff to Theodosius in Britain; later self-styled Emperor
Maximus *(Paulinus Gaius)*	a Roman soldier
Optatus *(Julius)*	quartermaster, Twentieth Legion
*Placidia *(Galla)*	sister to Honorius
*Rando	King of the Alemanni
*Respendial	King of the Alans
*Saturninus	Chief Centurion, Tungrian cohort
Scudilio	commander of auxiliaries at Bingium
Septimus *(Julianus)*	retired Curator of Augusta Treverorum
Severus *(Marcus)*	a tribune of the Twentieth Legion
*Stilicho	Military Master of the Western Empire
Sunno	son to Rando; later King of the Alemanni
Talien	King of the Quadi
Veronius *(Quintus)*	a cavalry officer
Vitalius	adjutant of the Tungrian cohort

HISTORICAL EVENTS

353   Martinus, Vicarius of Britain, "killed" by Constantine II.

364   Valentinian I, Emperor of the West.
        Picts, Scots, Attacotti, and Saxons raiding Britain.

367   Picts, Scots, Attacotti, and Saxons, in conspiracy, overwhelm
        the Wall and overrun Britain.
        Fullofaudes, Duke of Britain, and Nectaridus, Count of the
        Saxon Shore, slain.

368   Count Theodosius, sent by Valentinian I, reconquers Britain and restores
        the Wall.

375   death of Valentinian I.
        Valentinian II and Gratian, Emperors of the West.

378   Battle of Adrianople.

379   reign of Theodosius I.

383   Magnus Maximus, military commander, acclaimed Emperor in Britain,
        conquers Spain and Gaul from Gratian, who is killed.

388   Magnus Maximus defeated by Theodosius I, and executed.

395   death of Theodosius I.
        Honorius, aged eleven, Emperor of the West: Stilicho, the Vandal,
        appointed his guardian.

?   Stilicho improves the defenses of Britain and withdraws some troops.

403   Alaric, the Goth, invades Italy.

406   Stilicho defeats Radagaisus, who invades Italy.
        Constantinus proclaimed Emperor in Britain.
        coalition of Marcomanni, Quadi, Asding, and Siling Vandals
        cross the Rhine at Mainz and overrun Gaul.

407   Alemanni sack Worms and annex the right bank of the Rhine.
        Constantinus, with his son Constans, crosses to Gaul with the last remaining
        troops in Britain, and establishes himself at Arles.

408   Stilicho murdered at instigation of Honorius.

410   Rome sacked by Alaric: Honorius bids the Britons look to themselves.

411   Constans and Constantinus killed by Honorius' troops.

PRINCIPAL PLACE NAMES

Adrianopolis	Edirne, Turkey
Aegyptus	Egypt
Aesica	Greatchesters, England
Anderida	Pevensey, England
Apulia	a region of Italy
Arelate	Arles, France
Astures	from second ala of Astures
Augusta treverorum	Trier (Germany)
Belgica	Belgium
Bingium	Bingen (Germany)
Borbetomagus	Worms (Germany)
Borcovicum	Housesteads, England
Boudobrigo	Boppard (Germany)
Bravoniacum	Kirky Thore, England
Britannia	England
Cabillonum	Chalon-sur-Saône, France
Caledonia	Highland Scotland
Calleva	Silchester, England
Colonia	Cologne (Germany)
Concordia	Concordia Sagittaria, Italy
Confluentes	Koblenz (Germany)
Constantinopolis	Istanbul, Turkey
Corinium	Cirencester, England
Corstopitum	Corbridge, England
Dacia	Romania
Danubius	Danube river
Deva	Chester, England
Divodurum	Metz, France
Dubris	Dover, England
Eburacum	York, England
Florentia	Florence, Italy
Gaul	France
Germania	Germany
Germania inferior	lower Germania
Germania superior	upper Germania
Gesoriacum	Boulogne-sur-Mer, France
Graecia	Greece
Hibernia	Ireland
Hispania	Spain
Illyricum	parts of Bosnia, Herzegovina, Serbia, Montenegro, Albania

Isca, Isca Silurium	Caerleon, Wales
Italia	Italy
Larissa	Larissa, Greece
Lemanis	Lympne, England
Londinium	London, England
Macedonia	present-day Macedonia, parts of Greece, and Bulgaria
Maglona	Old Carlisle, England
Mantua	Mantua, Italy
Mauretania	Morocco
Mediolanum	Milan, Italy
Moenus	Main River (Germany)
Moesia	parts of Serbia and Bulgaria
Moguntiacum	Mainz, Germany
Mona	Isle of Anglesey, Wales
Mosella	Mosel River (Germany)
Nava	Nahe River (Germany)
Novaesium	Neuss, Germany
Oriens	parts of northern Egypt, Israel, Lebanon, Syria, Turkey, Georgia, and Bulgaria
Padus	Po River (Italy)
Pannonia	Hungary, north Croatia, and northeast Slovenia
Petriana	Stanwix, England
Philippi	Philippi, Greece
Pollentia	Alcúdia, Spain
Ratae	Leicester, England
Ravenna	Ravenna, Italy
Remi	Rheims, France
Rhenus	Rhine River (Germany)
Rutupiae	Richborough, England
Salisio	Salzig, Germany
Saxon Shore	southeast coast of England
Scythia	region comprising east of the Danube River to China
Segontium	Caernarvon, Wales
Steppes	region of central Russia and Central Asia
Taunus	range of hills and forests east of the Rhine
Ticinium	Pavia, Italy
Vetera	near Xanten, Germany
Vindolanda	Chesterholm, England
Vindonissa	Windisch, Switzerland
Vironconium	Wroxeter, England

GLOSSARY OF TRIBAL PEOPLES

ALANS—a nomadic tribe that dwelled in the area that constitutes present-day Russia to the Danube River

ALEMANNI—a tribe of Germanic people who eventually settled in what is now southwestern Germany

ASDING VANDALS—the southern tribe of Vandals, who lived in what is now southern Poland and Hungary

ATTACOTI—a tribe located in what is now Ireland

BRIGANTES—a tribe located in what is now northern England

BURGUNDIANS—a tribe of Germanic people located in what is now Eastern Germany

FRANKS—a Germanic tribe who were partially integrated into the later Roman Empire

GOTHS—a tribe of German people who lived between the Baltic and Adriatic Seas

HUNS—a nomadic tribe originating in the Far East, possibly from China; led by Attila, wreaked havoc throughout central Europe and the Roman Empire

IBERIANS—peoples from the regions constituting present-day Spain and Portugal

MARCOMANNI—a Germanic people who fought against Emperor Marcus Aurelius, as recorded by the historian Eutropius

MOORS—an Islamic migratory people in North Africa who later invaded and ruled the Iberian Peninsula

OSTROGOTHS—the Eastern Goths that entered the Roman Empire in fourth century A.D.; Ostrogoth ruler Theodoric the Great defeated Odoacer, who deposed the last Western Roman Emperor

PARTHIANS—the people living in the region that constitutes present-day Iran and Iraq

PICTS—a people living in what is now Scotland north of the River Forth

QUADI—a Germanic tribe living in the region now constituting the Czech Republic and Slovakia

SARMATIANS—a tribe from southern Russia

SAXONS—a Germanic tribe from northwest Germany and the eastern Netherlands which invaded England in the Middle Ages

SCOTTI—the generic name given by Romans to raiders from Ireland

SILING VANDALS—a northern tribe of vandals who settled in Poland

SUEVI—a Germanic tribe originating from an area around the Baltic Sea who crossed the Rhine River with the Vandals, Alans, and Alemanii in 406 A.D., settling in Spain

TEUTONS—a tribe from the northeastern and southern parts of Gaul

TREVERI—a Celtic tribe living in the regions now constituting east Belgium, northeast France, and southwest Germany

TUNGRIANS—a tribe living in the western Ardennes in central Europe

VACOMAGI—a Celtic tribe living in Britain

VANDALS—a Germanic tribe who invaded the Roman Empire in the third century A.D. and settled in North Africa

VISIGOTHS—western Goths who famously fought and defeated the Roman Empire at the Battle of Adrianopole in 378 A.D., eventually settling in Spain

GLOSSARY OF TERMS

ADJUTANT—a staff officer, third in command of a legion

ALA(E)—a cavalry regiment, originally 500 to 1,000 men, divided into 16 or 24 squadrons, respectively

AQUILIFER—the officer carrying the Eagle, the sacred insignia of the legion

ARCANI—the Roman intelligence service

ARIAN CHRISTIANITY—a strand of Christianity; many Germanic tribes converted to Aryanism by Ulifas in the second century A.D.

ARMORER—an enlisted man responsible for the upkeep of arms in the camp

AUXILARIES—originally, provincial troops formed into cavalry regiments (alae) or infantry regiments (cohorts) 500 to 1,000 strong; later, troops of the frontier army

BALLISTA(E)—a type of artillery for throwing heavy missiles, varying in size and performance; the smaller ones were often called scorpions or onagers

BASILICA—a building in which judicial, commercial, and governmental activities took place

BRAZIER—a pan for holding burning coals

CARDO MAXIMUS—the major thoroughfare in a Roman city, usually running north to south

CARROBALLISTA—a type of mobile field artillery which fired 9- to 12-inch bolts with iron heads

CENTURION—usually the officer commanding a century; a rank for which there is no modern equivalent

CENTURY—the smallest unit (100 men) of the legion, which originally contained 60 centuries

CIRCUS—a space or building designed for the exhibition of races and athletic competitions performed at public festivals

COHORT—originally, a tactical unit of the legion comprising six centuries; also an auxiliary regiment

COLUMN—a body of troops formed in ranks, one behind the other

COMES (e.g., COMES GALLIARUM)—count; an honorary title often conferred upon senior military and civil officers, in some instances designating special duties

COUNT OF THE SAXON SHORE—(Comes Littoris Saxonici) the general commanding the defenses of the southeast coast of Britain

CURATOR—a civilian official who fulfilled the functions of a mayor

CURIA—the meeting place of the Roman Senate in Rome

CURIAL CLASS—the provincial class from which municipal and local government officers were selected

CURLEW—a long-legged bird with a long, slender, downward-curving bill

DAIS—the high or principal table at the end of a hall where the guests of honor were seated

DECURION—a junior officer in an auxiliary cavalry unit commanding a troop

DENARIUS—a Roman silver coin

DRAUGHTS—checkers

DUX—the commander in chief of a provincial army

ENFILADE—to pierce, scour, or rake with shot in the direction of a line of troops

ESCARPMENT—a steep slope in front of a fortification

EPONA—the Celtic horse goddess

FATIGUE PARTY—a small band of soldiers assigned to obtaining supplies and labor

FIRE TUBES—a priming tube or friction primer to be used with explosives

HYPOCAUST—a hollow space extending under the floor of a chamber, in which the heat from a furnace accumulated for the heating of a house; a room heated from underneath

INFANTRY—foot soldiers

KESTREL—a small falcon

LAAGAR—a defensive encampment encircled by armored vehicles or wagons

LEGATE—the commander of a legion

LEGION—originally, a brigade of troops, 6,000 strong, commanded by a Legate and recruited solely from Roman citizens; in the late empire, the legion was smaller, commanded by a Praefectus, and was part of a frontier army.

LEGIONARY—a soldier in a legion

LIMES—a military frontier

MASTER OF HORSE (Magister Equitum)—a subordinate general commanding all the imperial cavalry; the Magister Equitem per Gallias was the general commanding the Field Army of Gaul

MILE CASTLE—one of the camps established every Roman mile (≈4800 ft), housing a garrison of men that protected the Roman frontier from invaders

MILESTONES—a stone pillar placed on Roman roads at each mile that marked the distance from the pillar to the city of Rome

MILITARY MASTER— (Magister Militum) the general officer commanding all the Imperial troops

MITHRAS—an Eastern god who had a great following among Roman soldiers because of his emphasis on discipline, truth, honor, and courage

OPTIO—an officer junior to a centurion; often his second in command

OSTLER—an individual who takes care of horses

PALISADES—a fence of pickets forming a defense barrier or fortification

POOP—an enclosed structure at the stern of a ship

POSTING STATION—a location used for changing horses and replenishing supplies

PRAEFECTUS—prefect; a general term for civil or military officials holding posts of varying degrees of responsibility

PRAEFECTUS PRAETORIO—a civil official responsible directly to the Emperor for the administration of a group of provinces.

PRAESES—a temporary governor

PRAETOR—a governing appointment only open to senators

PROSCRIBE—to denounce or condemn

PROW—the projecting part of a tent

QUARTER—to traverse an area of ground laterally back and forth while slowly advancing forward

QUARTERMASTER—the officer responsible for the food, clothing, and equipment of the troops

QUAESTOR—a civilian official, often in charge of finance

SESTERIUS—coin used during the time of Commodus

SIGNAL TOWER—an edifice used to watch borders and send warning signals to other stations

SOLIDIUS—a unit of gold currency introduced by Constantine the Great during the first half of the fourth century A.D.

SUBORN—to induce a person to commit an unlawful act

STANDARD—the soldier bearing the flag of the army

TESTUDO—"tortoise" or "tortoise-shell," an interlocked group of shields held over the heads of soldiers attacking a wall; a formation providing protection and allowing movement as a single unit

TRIBUNE—a senior officer of the legion; also an officer of the civil administration

VALLUM—a broad ditch running the length of Hadrian's Wall on the south side, defining the area under control of the military

VICARIUS—the governor under the Praefectus Praetorio immediately responsible for the administration of a group of provinces

VICTORY—the Roman goddess known to the Greeks as Nike

BIBLIOGRAPHY

Baatz, D., and H. Riediger. *Römer und Germanen am Limes.* 1966.

Baume, P. La. *Die Römer am Rhein.* [1964].

Birley, A. *Life in Roman Britain.* 1964.

Bruce, J. C. *Handbook to the Roman Wall;* 12th edn., 1966.

Cambridge Ancient History vol. 12. 1939.

Cambridge Medieval History vol. 1. 1911 and vol. 2. 1913.

Collingwood, R. G., and J. N. L. Myres. *Roman Britain and the English Settlements;* 2nd edn., 1937.

Dill, S. *Roman Society in the Last Century of the Western Empire.* 2nd edn. 1899.

Frere, J. S. *Britannia.* 1967.

Jones, A. H. M. *The Later Roman Empire.* 3 vols. 1964.

Parker, H. M. D. *The Roman Legions.* 1958.

Reusch, W. *Treveris: A Guide through Roman Trier;* 2nd edn., 1964.

Schleiermacher, W. *Der Römische Limes in Deutschland.* 1961.

Starr, C. G. *The Roman Imperial Navy, 31 B.C.–A.D. 324.* 2nd ed., 1960.

Vermaseren, M. J. *Mithras, the Secret God.* 1959.

Webster, G. *The Roman Imperial Army.* 1969.